Julian Ralph

Dixie

Or, Southern Scenes and Sketches

Julian Ralph

Dixie
Or, Southern Scenes and Sketches

ISBN/EAN: 9783337003555

Printed in Europe, USA, Canada, Australia, Japan

Cover: Foto ©Andreas Hilbeck / pixelio.de

More available books at **www.hansebooks.com**

DIXIE

OR

SOUTHERN SCENES AND SKETCHES

BY

JULIAN RALPH

AUTHOR OF "ON CANADA'S FRONTIER" "OUR GREAT WEST"
"CHICAGO AND THE WORLD'S FAIR" ETC.

ILLUSTRATED

NEW YORK

HARPER & BROTHERS PUBLISHERS

1896

Greeting

To that happy society of women and men whose innermost souls have been bared to me all over the world, whose lodges are hospitable homes, whose passwords are terms of buoyant friendship, whose grips are of the tendrils of kindly hearts, and whose aim is to enjoy and to make joyous the fellowship of their comrades, this book of Southern notes is admiringly dedicated.

AUTHOR'S NOTE

THE chapters which make up this volume first appeared in HARPER'S MAGAZINE and HARPER'S WEEKLY as a series of papers upon the development of what may well be called "Our New South" and its resources. The descriptions of scenery and present conditions are my own, but the statements which are of the most value and importance to a student of the material resources of the country are such as were made to me, and then verified by others—by the most shrewd and skilled, and at the same time disinterested, residents of the localities to which they apply. It would have required years of residence and special training for me to gather such information from my own experience.

Perhaps the chapter upon St. Louis will not seem to be as wholly in place here as in the companion to this volume, called *Our Great West*. Truly, St. Louis belongs somewhere between the two sections, or more properly in both, for it is a Western city with a Southern and Southwestern trade. It is treated here because it is impossible to correctly consider the Southern States without a knowledge of its forces and influence, and because these studies, and the main journey for making them, were properly begun at that city—the gate of the old way to the region bordering upon the Mississippi.

The other chapters are intended to describe the vast and prospectively opulent section of our country which has undergone a tragic revolution and is already beginning to attract the population, capital, and energy by means of which it is entering upon a new and exceedingly prosperous career.

CONTENTS

ILLUSTRATIONS

DIXIE

OR

SOUTHERN SCENES AND SKETCHES

I

THE OLD WAY TO DIXIE

It was quite by accident that I heard, while in St. Louis, that I could go all the way down the Mississippi to New Orleans in one of a fleet of packets that differ in no material way from those which figure in a score of *ante bellum* novels like *Uncle Tom's Cabin*, and which illuminate our Northern notions of life in the South when its planters basked in the glory of their feudal importance.

I could see the mighty river during a journey as long as that from New York to Liverpool; could watch the old-fashioned methods of the Simon Pure negro roustabouts at work with the freight; could gossip and swap stories with the same sort of pilots about whom I had read so much; could see many a slumbering Southern town unmodernized by railroads; could float past plantations, and look out upon old-time planters' mansions; and could actually see hard winter at St. Louis merge into soft and beauteous spring at Vicksburg, and become summer with a bound at New Orleans.

More wonderful than all besides, I could cast my lines off from the general world of to-day to float back into a past era, there to loaf away a week of utter rest, undisturbed by a telegraph or telephone, a hotel elevator or a clanging cable-car, surrounded by comfort, fed from a good and generous kitchen, and at liberty to forget the rush and bustle of that raging monster which the French call the *fin de siècle*.

A   1

"And how many do it?" I asked.

"Very few indeed," was the reply; "not as many on the best boat in a season as used to take passage for a single trip. The boats are not advertised; the world has forgotten that they are still running."

The only company that maintains these boats is the old Anchor Line, and there are no departures for New Orleans except on Wednesdays; but this was Saturday, the sailing day for Natchez, only 272 miles from the end of the route, and therefore serving well for so bold an experiment. I packed up at the Southern Hotel, and was on board the *City of Providence*, Captain George Carvell, master, an hour before five o'clock, the advertised sailing hour. The strange, the absolutely charming disregard for nineteenth-century bustle was apparent in the answer to the very first question I asked.

"Does she start sharp at five o'clock?"

"No, not sharp; a little dull, I expect."

The *City of Providence* lay with her landing-planks hoisted up ahead of her like the claws of a giant lobster. She was warped to a wharf-boat that was heaped with barrels, boxes, and bags, and alive with negroes. At a rough guess I should say there were 125 of these black laborers, in every variety of rags, like the beggars who "come to town" in the old nursery rhyme. Already they interested me. Now they would jog along rolling barrels aboard with little spiked sticks, next they appeared each with a bundle of brooms on his shoulder, and in another two minutes the long, zigzagging, shambling line was metamorphosed into a wriggling sinuosity formed of soap-boxes, or an unsteady line of flour-bags, each with ragged legs beneath it, or a procession of baskets or of bundles of laths. As each one picked up an article of freight an overseer told him its destination. The negro repeated this, and kept on repeating

2

ROUSTABOUTS

it in a singsong tone as he shambled along, until one
of the mates on the boat heard him and told him where
to put it down, the study of the mate being to distribute the cargo evenly, and to see that all packages sent
to any given landing were kept together. It seemed
to me that all the foremen and mates were selected for
their conscientious intention to keep their hands in their
trousers pockets under all circumstances, for their harsh
and grating voices, and for their ability to say a great
deal and not have a word of it understood by your humble servant, the writer.

The roustabouts looked all of one hue, from their
shoes to the tops of their heads. Their coffee-colored
necks and faces matched their reddish-brown clothes,
that had been grimed with the dust of everything

3

known to man—which dust also covered their shoes and bare feet, and made both appear the same. When a huddle went off the boat empty-handed they looked like so many big rats. They loaded the *Providence's* lower deck inside and out; they loaded her upper deck where the chairs for the passengers had seemed to be supreme; and then they loaded the roof over that deck and the side spaces until her sides were sunk low down near the river's surface, and she bristled at every point with boxes, bales, agricultural implements, brooms, carriages, bags, and, as the captain remarked, "Heaven only knows what she 'ain't got aboard her." The mates roared, the negroes talked all the time, or sung to rest their mouths, the boat kept settling in the water, and the mountains of freight swelled at every point. It was well said that twenty ordinary freight trains on a railroad would not carry as much freight as was stowed aboard of her, and I did not doubt the man who remarked to me that when such a boat, so laden, discharged her cargo loosely at one place, it often made a pile bigger than the boat itself.

The *City of Providence* was one of a long line of Mississippi boats edging the broad, clean, sloping levee that fronts busy St. Louis. She was by far the largest and handsomest of the packets; but all are of one type, and that is worth describing. They are, so far as I remember, all painted white, and are very broad and low. Each carries two tall black funnels, capped with a bulging ornamental top, and carrying on rods swung between the funnels the trade-mark of the company cut out of sheet-iron—an anchor or an initial letter, a fox or a swan, or whatever. There are three or four stories to these boats: first the open main-deck for freight and for the boilers and engines; then the walled-in saloon-deck, with a row of windows and doors cut alternately close beside one another, and with profuse ornamentation by means of jig-saw work wherever it can be put; and, last of all, the "Texas," or officers' quarters, and the "bureau," or negro passengers' cabin, forming the third story. Most of the large boats have the big square pilot-house on top of the "Texas," but others carry it as part of the third story in front of the "Texas." The pilot-house is always made to look graceful by means of an upper fringe of jig-saw ornament, and usually carries a deer's head or pair of antlers in front of it. We would call it enormous; a great square room with space in it for a stove, chairs, the wheel, the pilots, and, in more than one boat that I saw, a sofa or cushion laid

THE "TEXAS"

5

over the roof of the gangway from below. The sides and back of the house are made principally of sliding window-sashes. The front of the house, through which the pilots see their course, is closable by means of a door hinged into sections, and capable of being partially or fully opened, as the state of the weather permits. The wheel of one of these great packets is very large, and yet light. It is made as if an ordinary Eastern or Northern wheel had been put in place and then its spokes had grown two feet beyond its rim, and had had another rim and handles added. There are many sharp bends in the river, and I afterwards often saw the pilots using both hands and one foot to spin the big circle, until the rudder was "hard over" on whichever side they wanted it.

These Mississippi packets of the first and second class are very large boats, and roominess is the most striking characteristic of every part of them. They look light, frail, and inflammable, and so they are. The upright posts that rise from the deck of such a boat to support the saloon-deck are mere little sticks, and everything above them, except the funnels, is equally slender and thin. These boats are not like ours at any point of their make-up. They would seem to a man from the coast not to be the handiwork of ship-builders; indeed, there has been no apparent effort to imitate the massive beams, the peculiar "knees," the freely distributed "bright-work" of polished brass, the neat, solid joiner-work, or the thousand and one tricks of construction and ornament which distinguish the work of our coast boat-builders. These river boats—and I include all the packets that come upon the Mississippi from its tributaries—are more like the work of carpenters and house-builders. It is as if their model had been slowly developed from that of a barge to that of a house-boat, or

6

ROUSTABOUTS GETTING UNDER WAY

barge with a roof over it ; then as if a house for passengers had been built on top of the first roof, and the
"Texas" and "bureau" had followed on the second
roof. Pictures of the packets scarcely show how unlike our boats these are, the difference being in the
methods of workmanship. Each story is built merely
of sheathing, and in the best boats the doors and fanlights are hung on without frames around them—all
loose and thin, as if they never encountered cold weather
or bad storms. All the boats that I saw are as nearly
alike in all respects as if one man had built them. I
was told that the great packets cost only $70,000 to
$100,000, so that the mere engine in a first-class At-
lantic coast river or sound boat is seen to be of more

value than one of these huge packets, and a prime reason for the difference in construction suggests itself. But these great, comfortable vessels serve their purpose where ours could not be used at all, and are altogether so useful and appropriate, as well as picturesque and attractive to an Eastern man, that there is not room in my mind for aught than praise of them.

It was after six o'clock when the longshore hands were drawn up in line on the wharf-boat and our own crew of forty roustabouts came aboard. To one of these I went and asked how many men were in the long brown line on shore.

"Dam if I know, boss," said the semi-barbarian, with all the politeness he knew, which was none at all, of word or manner. It occurred to me afterwards that since everybody swears at these roustabouts, an occasional oath in return is scarcely the interest on the profanity each one lays up every year.

In a few moments the great island of joiner-work and freight crawled away from the levee and out upon the yellow, rain-pelted river, with long-drawn gasps, as if she were a monster that had been asleep and was slowly and regretfully waking up. How often every one who has read either the records or the romances of our South and West has heard of the noise that a packet sends through the woods and over the swamps to strike terror to the soul of a runaway darky who has never heard the sound, or to apprise waiting passengers afar off that their boat is on its way! It is nothing like the puff! puff! of the ordinary steam motor; it is a deep, hollow, long-drawn, regular breathing—lazy to the last degree, like the grunt of a sleeping pig that is dreaming. It is made by two engines alternately, and as it travels up the long pipes and is shot out upon the air it seems not to come from the chest of a demon, but

8

THE SALOON OF A MISSISSIPPI STEAMBOAT

from the very heels of some cold-blooded, half-torpid, prehistoric loafer of the alligator kind. To the river passenger in his bed courting sleep it is a sound more soothing than the patter of rain on a farm-house roof.

I had been in my state-room, and found it the largest one that I had ever seen on a steamboat. It had a double bed in it, and there was room for another. There was a chair and a marble-topped wash-stand, a carpet, and there were curtains on the glazed door and the long window that formed the top of the outer wall. The supper-bell rang, and I stepped into the saloon, which was a great chamber, all cream-white, touched with gold. The white ribs of the white ceiling were close together over the whole saloon's length of 250 feet, and each rib was upheld by most ornate supports, also white, but hung with gilded pendants. Colored fanlights let in the light by day, and under them other fanlights served to share the brilliant illumination in the saloon with the state-rooms on either side. At the forward end of the saloon were tables spread and set for the male passengers. At the other end sat the captain and the married ladies and girls, and such men as came with them. The chairs were all white, like the walls, the table-cloths, and the aprons of the negro servants, who stood like bronze statues awaiting the orders of the passengers. The supper proved to be well cooked and nicely served. As the fare to New Orleans was about the same as the price of a steerage ticket to Europe, it was pleasant to know that the meals, which were included in the bargain, were going to be as admirable as everything else.

After supper I was asked to go up into the pilot-house, then in charge of Louis Moan and James Parker, both veterans on the river, both good story-tellers, and as kindly and pleasant a pair as ever lightened a journey at a wheel or in a cabin. That night, when a dark pall

10

hung all around the boat, with only here and there a yellow glimmer showing the presence of a house or government light ashore, these were spectral men at a shadowy wheel. In time it was possible to see that the house was half as big as a railroad car, that Captain Carvell was in a chair smoking a pipe, that the gray sheet far below was the river, and that there was an indefinable something near by on one side which the pilots had agreed to regard as the left-hand shore. They said "right" and "left," and spoke of the smoke-stacks as "chimneys." But over and through and around the scene came the periodic gasp — shoo-whoo — from the great smoke-stacks, as gusts of wind on a bleak shore would sound if they blew at regular intervals.

Back in the blaze of light in the cabin I saw that the women had left their tables, and were gathered around a stove at their end of the room, precisely as the men had done at theirs. The groups were 150 feet apart, and showed no more interest in one another than if they had been on separate boats. I observed that at the right hand of the circle of smoking men was the neatly kept bar in a sort of alcove bridged across by a counter. Matching it, on the other side of the boat, was the office of Mr. O. W. Moore, the clerk. To Mr. Moore I offered to pay my fare, but he said there was no hurry, he guessed my money would keep. To the bartender I said that if he had made the effervescent draught which I drank before supper I desired to compliment him. "Thank you, sir," said he; "you are very kind." How pleasant was the discovery that I made on my first visit to the South, that in that part of our Union no matter how humble a white man is he is instinctively polite! Not that I call a bartender on a Mississippi boat a humble personage; he merely recalled the general fact to my mind.

11

The boat stopped at a landing, and it was as if it had died. There was no sound of running about or of yelling; there was simply deathlike stillness. There was a desk and a student-lamp in the great cabin, and, alas for the unities! on the desk lay a pad of telegraph blanks—"the mark of the beast!" But they evidently were only a bit of accidental drift from wide-awake St. Louis, and not intended for the passengers, because the clerk came out of his office, swept them into a drawer, and invited me to join him in a game of tiddledywinks. He added to the calm pleasures of the game by telling of a Kentucky girl eleven feet high, who stood at one end of a very wide table and shot the disks into the cup from both sides of the table without changing her position. I judged from his remarks that she was simply a tall girl who played well at tiddledywinks. No man likes to be beaten at his own game, the tools for which he carries about with him. Even princes of the blood royal show annoyance when it happens.

I slept like a child all night, and mentioned the fact at the breakfast table, where the men all spoke to one another and the clerk addressed each of us by name as if we were in a

12

boarding-house. Every one smiled when I said that the boat's noise did not disturb me.

"Why, we tied up to a tree all night," said the clerk, "and did not move a yard until an hour ago."

At this breakfast we had a very African-looking dish that somehow suggested the voudoo. It appeared like a dish of exaggerated canary seed boiled in tan-bark.

"Dat dere," said my waiter, "is sumping you doan' git in no hotels. It's jambullade. Dey done make it ob rice, tomatoes, and brekfus' bacon or ham; but ef dey put in oysters place ob de ham, it's de fines' in de lan'."

I had not been long enough in the atmosphere of Mississippi travel to avoid worrying about the loss of a whole night while we were tied up to the shore. There had been a fog, I was told, and to proceed would have been dangerous. Yet I was bound for New Orleans for Mardi-gras, and had only time to make it, according to the boat's schedule. But I had not fathomed a tithe of the mysteries of this river travel.

"It's too bad we're so late," I said to Mr. Todd, the steward.

"We ain't late," said he.

"I thought we laid up overnight," I said.

"So we did," said he. "But that ain't goin' to make any difference; we don't run so close to time as all that."

"Don't get excited," said Captain Carvell; "you are going to have the best trip you ever made in your life. And if we keep a-layin' up nights, all you've got to do is to step ashore at Cairo or Memphis or Natchez and take the cars into New Orleans quicker'n a wink. You can stay with us till the last minute before you've got to be in New Orleans, and then the cars 'll take you there all right. I only wish it was April 'stead of Feb-

13

THE PILOT

ruary. Then you leave a right cold climate in the North, and you get along and see flowers all a-blooming and roses a-blushing. Why, sir, I've been making this run thirty-nine years, and I enjoy it yet."

" Come up in the pilot-house," said Mr. Moan. " Bring your pipe and tobacco and your slippers, and leave 'em up there, so's to make yourself at home. You're going to live with us nigh on to a week, you know, and you ought to be friendly."

It was by this tone, caught from each officer to whom I spoke, that I, all too slowly, imbibed the calm and restful spirit of the voyage. Nothing made any difference, or gave cause to borrow trouble—not even hitching up to the river-bank now and then for a night or two.

We had been at Chester for nearly an hour. The clerk went ashore, visiting, and disappeared up the main street. We were to take on 500 barrels of flour, and for a long while these had been jolting and creaking and spurting out little white wisps of powder as the black crew rolled them aboard. The pilot remarked, as he looked down at the scene, that when we came to leave we would not really get away, because we must drop down to a mill half a mile down stream, and then to a warehouse farther along, and then, "if there are any other stops near by, some one will run down with a flag, or a white handkerchief, and call us."

I alone was impatient—the only curse on the happy condition. In the middle of a lifetime of catching trains and riding watch in hand I found that I did not know how to behave or how to school myself for a natural, restful situation such as this. I felt that I belonged in the world, and that this was not it. This was dreamland—an Occidental Arabia. True, we were moved by steam, we lifted the landing-stages by steam, and swung

15

red farm wagons to the hurricane-deck and blew whistles, all by steam; but it was steam hypnotized and put to sleep. Could I not hear it snore through the smokestacks whenever the engineer disturbed it? As we swung away from Chester, Mr. Moan pointed across the river and said:

"That's Claraville over there. It's a tidy place. Been that way since I was a boy. It don't grow, but it holds its own."

I harbored the hope that I would appreciate that remark, and the spirit which engendered it, in five days or so of life on the lazy boat. Even then I could see that it was something to "hold one's own." It was an effort, and perhaps a strain. It is more than we men and women are able to do for any length of time.

We pushed high up a stony bank at a new place. Again the clerk went ashore, and this time the captain followed him. Another wabbling stream of flour-barrels issued from a warehouse and rolled into the boat. I think I began to feel less forced resignation and more at ease. I was drifting into harmony with my surroundings. It was still a little strange that the voices on shore were all using English words. Spanish or Arabic would have consorted better with the hour. As a happy makeshift a negro came out and sat on a barrel and played a jews-harp. He was ragged and slovenly, and was the only black man not at work; but perhaps a man cannot work steadily and do justice to a jews-harp at the same time. He turned his genius upon a lively tune, and the serpentlike stream of barrels began to flow faster under the negroes' hands, as if it were a current of molasses and the music had warmed it. The church bells—for it was Sunday—broke upon the air at a distance; at just the right distance, so that they sounded soft and religious. The sun was out. Only one other thing was needed— tobacco.

When I went to get my pipe, the youngest of the ladies in the saloon was at the piano, and "A Starry Night for a Ramble" was trickling from her fingers' ends. I dropped into a chair to listen, and to think how prone the Southern folk are to insist upon a recognition of caste in every relation of life. First, the captain at the head of all, then the ladies and their male escorts—these were the aristocrats of the boat. The lonely male passengers were the middle class, graciously permitted to sleep on the saloon-deck. Finally, the negro passengers and the petty officers

"I's FIXED FOR LIFE, BOSS, IF DE GOVER'MENT DONE HOLD OUT"

were sent up above, to quarters far from the rest. But the young lady saw me sitting there, and the music stopped. She left the piano stool with a flirt of her skirt; not a violent motion of the whole back of her dress, as if she was really "put out" by my intrusion, but just a faint little snap at the very tail of the eloquent garment. How many languages women have! They have one of the tongue, like ours; one of the silent, mobile lips, as when school-girls talk without being heard; one of the eyes; one of their spirits, that rise into vivacity for those they love or seek to please, and that sink into moodiness or languor near those they don't care for; and finally, this of the skirts.

But that was only a faint whip of the very tail of the skirt, down by the hem. It hinted to me that we were to become acquainted soon. There was plenty of time; I would not hurry it.

I went to my great comfortable room and experimented with the locked door which was opposite the entrance. It opened, and let out upon the outer deck, past all the other state-room doors. That was exquisite. It was like part of a typical Southern home, with the parlor opening out on a veranda over a river I was reminded of the first true Southern house I ever stopped at, in the Blue Ridge Mountains. There were two long arms in front of the main building, and the rooms in these arms had a door and a window at each end. I was enraptured with my good fortune until night came, when I discovered that neither window sported a catch and neither door had a lock. I might as well, I might better, have been put to bed in the fields. All the stories of murder I had heard during the day —and they were plenty—came back, and sat on the edge of the bed with me. I complained in the morning, and the proprietor laughed, and said there was not a lock on a door in the county. They murdered there, but they did not rob. That was a consolation.

The Mississippi proved not so unlike a Northern river as might have been expected. The Hudson is as wide in some places, and I have seen parts of Lake Ontario with just such shores. Fields of grain ran to the edge of the bluff, and here and there were houses and patches

18

of trees. The Illinois side was a long reach of wooded bluff. The water itself was mud. Senator Ingalls is quoted as saying that it was "too thick for a beverage and too thin for food." Everywhere the yellow water, running the same way as the boat, seemed to outstrip our vessel. Everywhere it was dotted with logs, twigs, and little floating islands of the wreckage of the cottonwood thickets of Dakota and Montana, perhaps of the forests at the feet of the Rocky Mountains. That was the main peculiarity of the river—the presence of thousands of tons of débris floating behind, beside, and ahead of the steamboat. Here and there we saw a "government light," a little lantern on a clean white frame-work, suggesting an immaculate chicken-coop. Men who live in nearby houses get ten or fifteen dollars a month—the lights being of two grades — for lighting them every night and putting them out every morning. Mr. Moan told of a negro down below where we were who gets fifteen dollars a month for keeping a difficult light, and who, on being asked how he was getting along, replied that it was money enough for the keep of his wife and himself. " I's fixed for life, boss," he said, " if de gov-er'ment done hold out."

I noted with keen pleasure that neither Pilot Moan nor Pilot Parker blew the whistle as the boat was backed off the mud at a landing. In New York they would surely whistle and shriek "good-bye." In France they would blow all the time. The Mississippi plan is better. There they whistle only when approaching a landing, "to notify the labor."

For miles and miles we floated out in the channel and were alone in the world—we and the distant blue hills, the thin bare forests, and the softly speeding stream. Not a house or a fence or a ploughed acre was in sight. What a country ours is! How much room it offers to

19

future peoples! They are not hurrying—they who have so much more at stake than we on that boat. Why, then, needed we to hurry? When a house or a village hove in sight, it was not always wooden, as in the West. Often the warehouses, the mills, and even the manor - houses were of stone or brick. Some of these places were inac-

A MISSISSIPPI STEAMBOAT CAPTAIN

20

cessible to so big a boat as the *Providence*, but from its decks could be seen little waggle-tailed stern-wheelers puffing and splashing up to them for freight.

At one stop which we did make, Captain Carvell ordered a barge pushed out of the way—"so's we sha'n't make a bunglesome landing," he said. The nearest great landing-stage, a long gang-plank hung by the middle from a sort of derrick, and capable of connecting the boat with a hill or a flat surface, was let down on the bank. The unavoidable flour-barrels came head foremost along a wooden slide this time, and a darky on the boat sang an incessant line, "Somebody told me so," as a warning to the men below that another and another barrel was coming. They are fond of chanting at their work, and they give vent to whatever comes into their heads, and then repeat it thousands of times, perhaps. It is not always a pretty sentence, but every such refrain serves to time their movements. "O Lord God! you know you done wrong," I have heard a negro say with each bag that was handed to him to lift upon a pile. "Been a slave all yo' days; you 'ain't got a penny saved," was another refrain; and still another, chanted incessantly, was: "Who's been here since I's been gone? Big buck nigger with a derby on." They are all "niggers" once you enter the Southern country. Every one calls them so, and they do not often vary the custom among themselves.

These roustabouts are nothing like as forward as the lowest of their race that we see in the North. Presumably they are about what the "field hands" of slavery times were. They are dull-eyed, shambling men, dressed like perambulating rag-bags, with rags at the sleeves, up and down the trousers, at the hems of their coats, and the rims of their caps and hats. A man who makes six changes of his working attire every year by contract

21

with a tailor would be surprised at how long these men keep their clothes. Some wear coats and vests and no shirts; some wear overcoats and shirts and no vests; some have only shirts and trousers — shirts that have lost their buttons, perhaps, and flare wide open to the trousers band, showing a black trunk like oiled ebony. They earn a dollar a day, but have not learned to save it. They are very dissipated, and are given to carrying knives, which the mates take away from the most unruly ones. The scars on many of their bodies show to what use these knives are too often put. "Who's dat talkin' 'bout cuttin' out some one's heart?" I heard one say as he slouched along in the roustabout line. "Ef dar's goin' to be any cuttin', I want to do some." Though they chant at their work, I seldom saw them laugh or heard them sing a song, or knew one of them to dance during the voyage. The work is hard, and they are kept at it, urged constantly by the mates on shore and aboard, as the Southern folks say that negroes and mules always need to be. But the roustabouts' faults are excessively human, after all, and the consequence of a sturdy belief that they need sharper treatment than the rest of us leads to their being urged to do more work than a white man. There were nights on the *Providence* when the landings ran close together, and the poor wretches got little or no sleep. They "tote" all the freight aboard and back to land again on their heads or shoulders, and it is crushing work. Whenever the old barbaric instinct to loaf, or to move by threes at one man's work, would prompt them, one of the mates was sure to spy the weakness and roar at the culprits.

The mates showed no actual unkindness or severity while I was on that boat. But they all — on all the boats — have fearsome voices, such as we credit to pirate chiefs on "low, rakish, black boats" in yellow-clad

22

THE MATE OF A MISSISSIPPI BOAT—"NOW, THEN, NIGGER"

novels. Any one of them would break up an opera troupe. They rasp at the darkies in their business voices, with a "Run up the plank, nigger; now, then, nigger, get wood"—and then they turn and speak to the passengers in their Sunday shore-leave voices, as gently as any men can talk.

Mr. Halloran, an up-river pilot of celebrity who was studying the lower river, told me that he remembered when it was the custom for the mates to hit the lazy negroes on the head with a billet of wood, "and knock them stiff." The other negroes used to laugh (presumably as the sad-faced man laughed when the photographer clapped a pistol to his head and said, "Smile, — you, or I'll shoot you"). When the felled negro came to, the others would say, "Lep up quick an' git to work, nigger; de mate's a-coming." They do not urge the help with cord-wood now—so the mate of the *Providence* told me—because the negroes get out warrants and delay the boat.

I have said that the blacks all call themselves "niggers." The rule has its exceptions. I went ashore at a plantation called " Sunnyside," and saw a cheery old "aunty" standing near a cabin doorway from out of which pickaninnies were tumbling like ants out of an ant-hill.

"How many children have you got, aunty?" I inquired.

"I 'ain't got none yere," she said ; " mine's all out in de fiel'. Dese yer two is my gran'chillen ; de oders I'm takin' car' of fer de ladies ob de neighborhood."

There was a fine barber shop and "wash-room" on the packet, and the barber and I often conversed, with a razor between us. He asked me once how I liked my hair trimmed, and I said I always left that to the barber.

"Dat's c'rect," said he ; "you kin leave it to me safely; and you kin bet I'm more dan apt to do it in de mos' fashionablest manner." Then he turned and called to his assistant, a coal-black boy who was working his way to New Orleans. "Hey, dere! you nigger! Git me a high stool outen de pantry. How you 'spect I's gwine cut de gemmen's ha'r ef I doan' hab no stool?"

I mentioned the fact that the roustabouts were working very hard.

"Dat dey is," said the barber. " We call 'em 'roosters' on de ribber, but rous'about is more correc'. Dey wuk hard night an' day, an' dey git mo' kicks dan dollars. Ef I got rejuced so's I had to do manual labor, I'd go to stealin' 'fo' I'd be a rooster. Certain su' I would, 'cause dey couldn't wuk a man no harder in de penitentshuary ef he got caught dan dey do on dese boats."

At supper on the second night I began to find fault with the custom of separating the ladies and the gentlemen by the length of an enormous saloon. The gulf between the men and women was yet as wide as ever. There they sat at their separate table. Later they

DANCE MUSIC ON A STEAMBOAT

would make a ring around a stove of their own, or retire to an especial saloon called "the nursery," which spans and shuts off the whole back end of the boat— the most attractive part of our Northern steamboats. There were four women and a little baby girl on this boat. The tiny woman, though only four years old, had been to visit me during the afternoon, and had told me her own peculiar version of Cinderella. Poor little tot! She was with a man and woman whom she called papa and mamma, but they made the cruel mistake of telling everybody that she was a little orphan waif, the child of a pauper, and that they had adopted her—the last thing, one would think, that they would noise abroad.

25

I wondered whether her name might not be Cinderella, and that led me to think that I did not know even the name of the youngest of the grown women, who, by-the-way, was only eighteen or nineteen, with jet hair, coal-black laughing eyes, and a smiling mouth set with pearls. She was perfectly formed, and being beautiful, was also amiable, for there can be no true beauty in a woman who is not sunny-hearted. It was she who played the piano for the women—until a man listened. Perhaps another time I may be able to enjoy such a restful break in my life to the uttermost, and not draw comparisons or seek faults to find; yet on this second night I was unable to help recalling the only other trip I had then made on a Southern river. It was on the Ohio. Half the passengers were Kentuckians. As soon as the boat started, a negro roustabout was hired to fiddle in the saloon, and every man sought a partner and fell to waltzing. It was idyllic; it was a snatch of Arcadian life, of Brittany or Switzerland imported to America. A young Kentuckian, who introduced himself to me and then to all the women, kindly introduced them all to one another and then to me. That was better than this Mississippi plan of putting a whole boat's length between the sexes. This suggested a floating synagogue.

We stopped at Cairo on the second morning out, and were pulling away from there while I ate my breakfast. I told Captain Carvell that I was sorry to have missed seeing that important town, but I found that, as before, my regrets were groundless. Nothing is missed and nothing makes any difference on that phenomenal line. "You won't miss Cairo," said the captain; "we are going up a mile to get some pork, and down half a mile to get some flour. We shall be here some hours yet." I ate a leisurely breakfast, saw the town to my heart's content, and was back on the boat an hour before it got away for good. A railroad train whizzed along above the levee like a messenger from the world of worry and unrest, and I looked at it as I have often looked at a leopard caged in a menagerie. It could not get at me, I knew.

The beautiful black-eyed girl had kept in the ladies' end of the saloon, wrapped up in Cinderella, the Chicago man's tiny daughter; but on this day, as I was on the upper deck, I could not help seeing her mount the ladderlike stairs to the pilot-house. It is amazing that four women and half a dozen men should have been together so long and not become acquainted. To be sure, I could have followed the pretty brunette to the pilot-house and been introduced by one of the pilots; but there was no hurry. Besides, at the time, a young commercial traveller from Providence was telling me of his uncertainty whether or not he was in love. The subject of his doubts was a young lady whose portrait he carried in a locket which he kept opening incessantly.

I spent much time every day in the pilot-house. I heard very much about the skill and knowledge the river-pilot's calling required, but I saw even more than I heard. This giant river does not impress those who study it with its greatness so much as with its eccentricities. It runs between banks that are called earth, but act like brown sugar; that cave in and hollow out, and turn into bars and islands, in a way that is almost indescribable. Islands in it which were on one side one year are on the other side another year. Channels which the steamboats followed last month and for years past are now closed. Bars no one ever saw before suddenly lift above the surface. Piloting on the Mississippi is a business no one ever learns. It is a continual subject of study. It is the work of years to understand the

27

THE CHICAGO MAN

general course of the channel, and then the knowledge must be altered with each trip. The best pilot on the river, if he stops ashore a few months, becomes greener than a new hand. The pilots not only report their new experiences for publication in the newspapers, but they make notes of remarkable changes, and drop them into boxes on the route for the guidance of others in the business.

In the lower part of the river, below Tennessee, the whistle of a boat may often be heard between twelve and fifteen hours before the boat reaches the point where the sound came. This is because of the manner in which the river doubles upon itself. A town which may be only four or five miles across one of these loops will hear the boat, but the distance around the bend, and the stops the boat makes, may allow a prospective passenger to do a day's business before he boards the vessel.

Nothing could be more primitive than many of the boat-landings. The vessels simply "run their nozzles agin the shore," as John Hay has sung that they do. Villages, planters' depots or mills, are found on the edge of a rude bank, and the boats run up close as they can and lower the stages. The darkies tumble up and down

28

the bluff, the spectators line its edge. There is no stair-
case, pier, or wharf-boat, sea-wall, or anything. If there
was, it is a question whether it would last out a single
season. I seldom looked long at such a bank that I did
not see a piece of it loosen and crumble and fall into
the rushing, yellow river. Sometimes it was only a ton
that fell in; sometimes it was a good fraction of an
acre. Captain Carvell told me that once he was looking
at as noble and large a tree as he ever saw in his life,
standing inshore and away from the edge of a bluff.
Suddenly the land slipped away from around it, and it
fell and crashed into his steamboat. At many and many
a stopping-place the pilots call to mind where the banks
were when they began piloting, and always they were
far out in the present stream. One pointed out to me
an eddy over the wreck of a steamer that sunk while
warped to the shore. She was now in the middle of
the extraordinary river. Any one may see Island Number Ten, and call to mind its exciting part in the late
war; but it had no part in it, for old Island Number
Ten disappeared years ago, and this is a new one, not
on the site of its predecessor. Yet the true Island
Number Ten bore very ancient, heavy timber, and many
fine plantations. The new one is already timbered with
a dense growth of cane and saplings.

At Fort Pillow we saw the river's most stupendous
ravages of that particular time. The famous bluff, fifty
feet high at least, was sliding down in great slices and
bites and falling into the river. One great mound was
in the water, another had fallen just behind it, and these
had carried the trees that were growing in the earth
flat down in the mixed-up dirt. But beyond these a
huge slice many rods long and many yards thick was
parting from the bluff and leaning over towards the
water, with huge trees still standing on it, and reaching

29

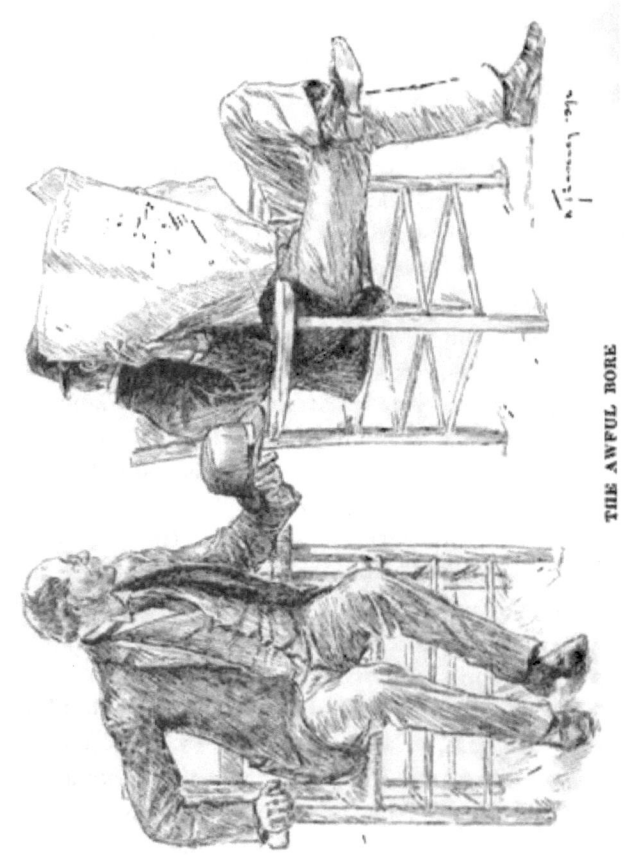

THE AWFUL BORE

their naked roots out on either side like the fingers of drowning men. Below, at what is called Centennial Cut-off, the eccentric river has reversed its original direction. It used to form a letter S, and now it flows down the central curve of the S where it used to flow northward. The two loops are grown with reeds and form a vast amphitheatre, at the sides of which, five miles off, one sees the distant banks covered with big timber.

Still farther down the river, in places where the men of the River Commission had been at work, we saw the banks cut at an angle like a natural beach, and sheathed with riprap. In places the water is said to have got under the sheathing and melted the work away, but there was no disposition among the navigators I was with to criticise the government work, so great has been the continually increasing improvement of the water-way. We saw few of those snags which were once as common as the dollars of a millionaire, but we did see many places where the crews of the snag-boats had been at work. The men chop down the trees so that when the bank caves the trees and their roots will both float off separately. If left to pursue the wicked ways of inanimate things, the trees would be carried out into the stream to sink butt downward, and project their trunks up to pierce the bottom of the first boat that struck one. The government boats have done splendid work at pulling up snags. It is said that their tackle is strong enough for any snag they ever find, and that "they could pull up the bottom of the river, if necessary."

Down on the Mississippi State and Arkansas shores we began to note the consequences of former high stages of water. The water-marks were often half-way up the cabin and warehouse doors, and tales were told of families that take to the second stories of their houses on such occasions, not forgetting to put their poultry and cattle on rafts tied to trees, to keep them until the flood subsides.

It was on the third day that I became acquainted with the beautiful nunlike pianist. I found her in distress among the firkins and brooms and boxes on the upper deck, among which the boat's cat had fled from the too violent endearments of little Cinderella. My hands and those of the pianist met in the dark crannies of the freight piles, and we fell to laughing, and became so well acquainted that soon afterwards she dropped into a chair beside me. In fifteen minutes she had told me her name, age, station, amusements, love affairs, home arrangements, tastes, hopes, and religious belief. The manner of the narrative was even more peculiar than the matter. Her mother, then on board with her, was an Arkansas widow, who kept a hotel to which commercial travellers repaired in great force, and at which—so I judged from what the young woman had imbibed— they paid their way with quite as much slang as cash. As I have seen such girls before in my travels in the Southwest, and have always found them different, in a marked way, from the girls in large towns, I will try to repeat what I jotted down of her observations.

" You're married, ain't you?" She was a pretty girl, as I have said, and she had large, deep black eyes. These she set, as she spoke, so as to give a searching glance that showed her to be expectant of a denial of my happy state, yet confident she was right. " I knew it. Well, the married kind are the worst that come to our hotel. My mother keeps a hotel at ——, you know ; the captain 's told you, I suppose. It's a village ; but I know a few things. The band plays ' Annie Rooney ' where I live, but it ain't up to me, for I know ' Com-

DECK OF A MISSISSIPPI BOAT—"YOU'RE MARRIED, AIN'T YOU?"

rades,' and 'Maggie Murphy's Home,' and the very
latest songs the boys bring to the house. That Providence feller's in love, ain't he? Well, say, I thought
it was either love or dyspepsia that was ailing him. Say,
do you believe in—pshaw! I was going to ask if you
believed in love, but of course you're married, and you've
got to say 'yes.' I always call 'rats' when I hear of

THE MAN FROM PROVIDENCE

anybody being in love. Ain't it dull on this boat? I
never see such men. I believe if a woman knocked 'em
down they wouldn't speak to her. You're the only one
that ain't glued to the bar; you and Admiral Farragut
—that's what I call the captain. He's nice, ain't he? I
think he's too cute. I love old men, I do."

A pause, and a rapt expression of a face turned upon
the river-bank as if in enjoyment of the tame scenery.

"Say! what's the latest slang in New York? The
boys—travellers that stop at our house, you know—'ain't
brought in anything new in a long while. You're from
New York, ain't you? Can't help it, can you? My!
what a jay-bird I'd look like in New York! Well, you
needn't get scared; I ain't a-going. I'm going to stay
where I'm on top. Bob Ingersoll lives in New York,
don't he? He's immense, ain't he? No, I see you ain't
stuck on him. Well, neither am I, and I'm going to tell
you the truth. Everybody my way is crazy to read
everything he writes and says, but I'm going to stick
to my little old Bible till a good deal smarter man than
he is comes along. If I was Ingersoll, and knew for
sure that I was right, I wouldn't stump the country to
try and take away the comfort of every poor old widow
and young girl and decent man; because our belief in
religion is close on to all that most folks has in this
world."

I spoke of my surprise that she should believe in religion and not in love.

"Say!" said she; "I help run a hotel, and I agree with
everybody that comes along—for the price. But I ain't
in a hotel now, and you're married, and I'll give myself
away. I made fun of love, but, gee whiz! I didn't mean
it. I reckon a girl don't fool you talking that way.
I'm in love, right smart in love, too; up to my neck.

"My mother hates him. You see, we used to be well

35

PASSING A SISTER-BOAT

off, and father's people were 'way up, and mother keeps
in with all her old friends.. They're all as poor as we,
but they're prouder'n Lucifer, and mother'd ruther we'd
marry poor quality folks than see us rich and happy if
our husbands were common stock. Well, I want to do
what's right, but what must I go and do but fall in love
with a German. He's a civil engineer, and he was lay-
ing out a railroad and come to our house. You'd think
he was a chump to look at him; but, say! he's just splendid. Ma saw what was going on, and she ordered me
not to write to him. I told him that, and he said for us
to run away. Oh, he's immense, if he is a German. I
let on I was real angry. I told him I was going to
mind my mother, and he shouldn't put such ideas in my
head. I scared him pale; but I liked him all the better:
he was so cut up. But he said 'All right,' and we don't

write—except he writes to my aunt, and I see the letters. We are waiting two years till I'm twenty-one, and I'm telling ma I love him three times a day so as to get her used to it. She's praying for everything to happen to Jake, but, say! it takes more than prayer to kill a German, don't it?"

Our remarkable *tête-à-tête* was interrupted by the announcement of dinner, and we put the length of the cabin between us. I never more than "bade her the time of day," as the Irish say, after that, for it seemed more profitable to divide my time between the pilot-house and the towns ashore. At Columbus, Kentucky, we saw the first true Southern mansion, with its great columns in front and its wide hall through the middle. We began to make many stops in midstream to deliver the mail by a yawl, manned most skilfully by the second mate and several roustabouts. At Slough, Kentucky, we saw cotton-fields and corn-fields opposite one another, and felt that we were truly in the South. At every village the houses were emptied and the levee was crowded. Darkies were in profuse abundance, and forty were idle to every one who worked. Every woman and girl, white and black, had put on some one bright red garment, and the historic yellow girls made no more effort to hide the fact that they were chewing tobacco or snuff than the old negresses did to conceal the pipes that they smoked.

Down and down we went with the current, and no longer noticed the deep snoring of the engine, or thought of the rushing world to the north and east. The table fare remained remarkably good, the nights' rests were unbroken; never did I stop marvelling that the boat was not crowded with the tired men of business, to whom it offered the most perfect relief and rest. The hotel-keeper and her frank and beautiful daughter got off at a picturesque town fronted by great oaks. The daughter waved her hand at the pilot-house and called out, " Ta-ta."

There was mild excitement and much blowing of whistles when we passed our sister-boat the *City of Monroe*—the prize Anchor liner from Natchez.

"Hark!" said the first mate in his society voice. "Stop talking. Listen to her wheels on the water. It's music. It's for all the world like walnuts dropping off a tree. When she made her first big run the roust-abouts got up a song about her: 'Did ye hear what the *Monroe* done ?'"

As the days went by it was apparent that the woods extended along both sides of the turbid river, with only here and there a clearing for a town or farm or house. The population does not cling to the shore; it is too often overflowed. At Pecan Point (pecan is pronounced "pecarn" along the river) we saw the first green grass on February 23d, and the first great plantation. It was, as we have all read, a great clearing, a scattering of negro cabins, and then the big mansion of the planter, surrounded by tidy white houses in numbers sufficient to form a village. Here a darky put a history of his life into a sentence. Being asked how he got along, he said : " Oh, fairly, fairly, sah. Some days dere's chicken all de day, but mo' days dey's only feathers." We saw the first cane-brake in great clumps, and as each cane was clad with leaves from top to bottom, the distant effect was that of thickets of green bushes. We saw many little plantations of a few acres each, usually with a government river light on the bank, and consisting of a couple of acres of corn and as much more of cotton. We learned that in this way thousands of negroes have kept themselves since the war. We saw their log huts, their wagons, and the inevitable mule, for a mule and a

ROUSTABOUTS UNLOADING A MISSISSIPPI BOAT

shot-gun are the first things that are bought, by whites and blacks, in this region.

Memphis proved an unexpectedly lively town, with a main street that was rather Western than Southern. Here the freight from and for the boat was handled in surprisingly quick time, by means of an endless belt railway something like a tread-mill. We left the dancing lights of the city, and moved out into a pall of smoke suspended in fog, and then I saw how well and thoroughly the men in the pilot-house knew the mighty river. After a run of a few miles the captain declared it unsafe to go farther. The electric search-light was thrown in all directions, but only illuminated a small circle closed in by a fog-bank. In absolute, black darkness the pilot and the captain discussed the character of the shores, to hit upon a hard bank with heavy timber to which it would be safe to tie up. They agreed that some unseen island across the stream and lower down would serve best.

"Look out for the bar just above there," said the captain.

"Yes," said the pilot; "I know where she is."

The wheel was spun round, the boat turned into a new course, and presently the search-light was thrown upon the very timber-studded reef they sought—as fine an exhibition of knowledge, experience, and skill as I ever witnessed.

We now had Mississippi on the left and Arkansas on the right, and saw the first commercial monuments of the great industry in cotton-seed and its varied products. This was at Helena, Arkansas, and already, two days after Washington's birthday, the weather had become so hot that the shade was grateful. The negroes warmed to their incessant, laborious work, and the black processions to and from the shore at the frequent land-

40

ings became leaping lines of garrulous toilers. The river becomes very wide, often miles wide, in long reaches, and at one part the boat's officers pointed to where it is eating its way inland, and said that a mile in the interior snags are found sitting up in the earth, far beneath the roots of the present trees, as they did in the old bottom, showing either that the river was once many times wider than now, or that it has shifted to and fro as it continues to do.

To tell in detail what we saw and did during two more days, how we saw green willows and then dogwood and jasmine in bloom, or even how Captain Carvell got out his straw hat at Elmwood, Mississippi, would require a chapter on the subject. We often heard the cry of " Mark twain," which Samuel D. Clemens took as his *nom de plume*, and a line about that may be interesting. The *Providence*, laden down till her deck touched the water, drew a little more than four feet; and though the river has a depth of 80 to 120 feet, there are places where bars made it necessary to take soundings. Whenever this was done a negro on the main-deck heaved the lead, and another on the second deck echoed his calls. These are the cries I heard, and when the reader understands that a fathom, or six feet, is the basis of calculation, he will comprehend the system. These, then, were the cries:

" Five feet." " Six feet." " Nine feet."

" Mark twain " (12 feet).

" A quarter less twain " (10½ feet)—that is to say, a quarter of a fathom less than two fathoms.

" A quarter twain " (13½ feet).

" Mark three " (18 feet).

" A quarter less three." " A quarter three " (19½ feet). " Deep four." " No bottom."

The tows that we saw were too peculiar to miss mention. On this river the loads are "towed before" instead of behind. The principle underlying the custom is that of the wheelbarrow, and is necessitated by the curves in this, the crookedest large river in the world. The barges and flats are fastened solidly ahead of the tug-boat in a great fan-shaped mass, and the steamer backs and pushes and gradually turns the bulk as if it had hold of the handles of a barrow in a crooked lane. We saw a famous boat, the *Wilson*, from Pittsburg, come along behind a low black island. It proved to be a tow

A RAFT OF LOGS

of large, low, uncovered barges, thirty of them, each carrying 1000 tons. She was therefore pushing $105,000 worth of freight, for the coal sells in New Orleans at $3 50 a ton. The work of propelling these tows is so ingenious that the pilots are handsomely paid. They cannot drive their loads; they merely guide them, and a mistake or bad judgment in a bend may cost thousands of dollars through a wreck. The barges are made of merely inch-and-a-half stuff, cost $700 each, and are seldom used twice. They are sold to wreckers.

42

This is in the region where the levees, that are said to have cost $150,000,000, line the river-side through whole States—mere banks of earth such as railways are built on where fillings are required. Some of these are far away from the water, and some are close beside it; some are earthy, some are grassy, and some are heaped up with banks of Cherokee roses that blossom in bouquets of hundreds of yards in length. These are the levees into which the crawfish dig and the water eats, and we read of crevasses that follow and destroy fortunes or submerge counties. But they are mere incidents in the laziest, most alluring and refreshing, journey that one tired man ever enjoyed.

II

NEW ORLEANS, OUR SOUTHERN CAPITAL

" THE biggest little city in the country," is what an
adopted citizen of New Orleans calls that town. With
but little more than a quarter of a million of inhabitants, the Crescent City has most of the features of a
true capital and metropolis. It is among the few towns
in our country that can be compared with New York in
respect of their metropolitan qualifications, but New
Orleans leads all the rest, though in population it is
small beside any of the others. It has an old and exclusive society, whose claims would be acknowledged in
any of our cities. It supports grand opera; its clubs
are fully what the term implies, and not mere empty
club-houses. It has fine theatres and public and church
buildings. The joys of the table, which Chesterfield
ranked first among the dissipations of intellectual men,
are provided not only in many fine restaurants and in
the clubs, but in a multitude of homes. No city has finer
markets. Its commerce is with all the world, and its
population is cosmopolitan, with all which a long contin-
uance of those conditions implies. Like the greater
cities, it has distinct divisions or quarters, which offer
the visiting sight-seer novelty and change. Its "sights"
are the accumulation of nearly two centuries, and of
Spanish, French, and American origin.

It is of value to study the qualities which make the
Southern capital what it is, because it is evident that it

is to become the chief winter resort of those who journey southward to escape the winters in the North. The *mardi gras* carnival is advertising its attractions to such an extent that the last occurrence of this festival found 100,000 strangers there, representing every State and large city in the Union. It is on the southern or winter route to California, it is on the way from the West and Northwest to Florida and the Georgia resorts, and it stands in the path to Texas and Mexico. It is the best of all the American winter resorts, because it has what the others possess (which is to say, warm weather and sunshine), and, in addition, it offers the theatres, shops, restaurants, crowds, clubs, and multiform entertainments of a city of the first class. It is *par excellence* a city of fun, fair women, rich food, and flowers. Its open-air surface-drainage system is about to be replaced by a different one that may not be more wholesome, but will have the advantage of being out of sight. Only one other reform must be instituted, and even that is almost accomplished. The local idea that a hotel which was the best in the country in 1837 would remain first-class forever was an untenable proposition. A new management, fixed rates that do not bound into the realm of extortion when a crowd comes along, and a modern million-dollar establishment would fetch more persons there, keep them longer, and send them away happier than most of the citizens have any idea of. Those other cities that are at the end of a long route of travel, out on the Pacific coast, exemplify the value of first-class hotels in all their histories. The consequence is that in a tiny city called Fairhaven, at the upper end of Puget Sound, there is a better hotel than can be found along the whole coast of the Gulf of Mexico west of Florida. The Pacific coast people have found out that tourists will pass an otherwise important place to stop in one that boasts a fine hotel. We Americans will exchange a Wyoming stage-coach for a log-cabin inn, but we will not leave a Pullman train for a bad hotel if we can help it. It is good to know that a great modern hotel-building is at last under way there, for strangers arriving in New Orleans could not all be expected to know how remarkably fine are the better class of boarding and lodging places, or how charming a mode of living it is to secure good rooms and coffee of a morning, and dine about in the restaurants.

On *mardi gras*, the day before the beginning of Lent, is the time to be in New Orleans, particularly for a stranger, because in the scenes of the carnival is found the key to the character of the people. They are not like the rest of us. Our so-called carnivals, wherever and whenever we have tried to hold them, have been mere commercial ventures, illustrated with advertisements, carried out by hired men, and paid for by self-seeking persons, who had not the backing of any populace. But in New Orleans the carnival displays are wholly designed to amuse and entertain the pleasure-loving, light-hearted, largely Latin people who originally took part in them, but who have surrendered active participation to the leading and wealthy men of the town.

The secret carnival societies are six in number, and are named the Argonauts, Atlanteans, Krewe of Proteus, Mistick Krewe of Comus, Momus, and Rex. Business men, and those who have earned the additional title of "society men," make up the membership of the societies. If any one or two of these coteries fancy themselves of "higher social tone" than the others, the fact would be natural, but the distinction will not be pointed out here. The oldest of the societies is the Comus, which was organized in 1857 to give a night parade and ball. These it has given ever since. In

1879 the Momus Society came into being; in 1880, the Rex Society; in 1881, the Krewe of Proteus; and in 1891, the Atlanteans and Argonauts. The members pay into the treasuries of these organizations a fixed sum per annum, and this, added together and drawn upon by a treasurer, who supervises all the accounts, is used to defray the expense of the whole carnival.

The keeping of this especial festival is a very old custom of Latin and Catholic origin, like the establishment of the city itself. For many years it was entirely popular and promiscuous in the sense that it was unordered and without either head or programme. The Mistick Krewe of Comus brought order and form into the first night parade in 1857, and in 1880 the Rex Society, by taking the lead in the open-air pageantry on the day before *mardi gras*, made it possible and advantageous to do away with the promiscuous masking and merrymaking, attendant upon which had been the throwing of lime and flour, the drunkenness, and the usual disorder which must everywhere characterize a loosely managed festival of the sort. Since then the only spontaneous masking among the people has been by children; there has never been a serious affray; there are no more tipsy persons in the streets than on any other day; and there has seldom been an occasion to make an arrest for a cause traceable to the carnival spirit.

All our cities are distinguished for the orderliness of their holiday crowds, but such absolute self-control as is shown by the people of New Orleans at *mardi gras* is a thing above and beyond what is known anywhere else in the country. To me it was inexplicable. I could understand the patient good-nature of a people trained for an occasion, but in the crowds were 100,000 strangers, many of them of the sort that would naturally be attracted to a festival that was to be followed by a prize-

47

fight between noted pugilists. It must have been that all caught the spirit of the occasion. It is chiefly on Canal Street that the bulk of the holiday crowd assembles when there is a parade, but only ten policemen

ON CANAL STREET

were detailed to keep order during the day parade of Rex in 1892; only seven for the greater night pageant of the Comus Society.

The actual *mardi gras* celebration is only the climax of a series of festivities lasting ten days or more. First is held the Bal des Roses, in the week before the week which precedes the public carnival. This ball is purely a "society affair," like our Patriarchs' Ball in New York.

The week which follows is one of almost daily sensations. First, on Monday, the Argonauts begin the prolonged festival with a tourney and chariot-racing. A ball at night follows. On Tuesday the Atlanteans give their ball. On Thursday Momus gives a ball, with tab-

48

leaux, in costume. On Friday of this gala week is held the Carnival german. The Carnival German Club is composed of twenty-five society men, who give the german by subscription. Only seventy-five couples participate in it.

The carnival proper is celebrated with pageantry and dancing that occupy the afternoons and nights of Monday and " Fat Tuesday." Rex, the king of the carnival, comes to town on Monday afternoon. Who he is a few persons know at the time; who he was is sometimes published, as in 1891, and more often is not. What is called a royal yacht is chosen to bring him from some mysterious realm over which he rules in the Orient, to visit his winter capital in the Crescent City. Last time the royal yacht was the revenue-cutter *Galveston*, but ordinarily the societies hire one of the big river steamboats. The yacht is always accompanied by ten or fifteen other steamers, gayly decorated, crowded with men and women, and appointed with bands of music and all that makes good cheer. It is supposed that the yacht has taken the king aboard at the jetties. The fleet returns, and the royal landing is made upon the levee at the foot of Canal Street, amid a fanfaronade of the whistles of boats, locomotives, and factories, and the firing of guns. The king is met by many city officers and leading citizens, who are called the dukes of the realm, and constitute his royal court. These temporary nobles wear civilian attire, with a badge of gold, and bogus jewels as a decoration. Many persons in carriages accompany them. A procession is formed, and the principal features of the display are a gorgeous litter for the king, a litter carrying the royal keys, and a number of splendid litters in which ride gayly costumed women, representing the favorites of the harem. This the public sees and enjoys.

The king goes to the City Hall accompanied as I have described. The way is lined with tens of thousands of spectators; flags wave from every building; music is playing, the sun is shining; the whole scene, with the gorgeous pageant threading it, is magnificent. At the City Hall, the Duke of Crescent City, who is the Mayor, welcomes Rex, and gives him the keys and the freedom of the city. The king mysteriously disappears after that, presumably to his palace.

That night, the night before *mardi gras*, the Krewe of Proteus holds its parade and ball, and in extent and cost and splendor this is a truly representative pair of undertakings. "A Dream of the Vegetable Kingdom" was what the last Proteus parade was entitled. It consisted of a series of elaborate and splendid floats forming a line many blocks long, and representing whatever is most picturesque, or can be made so, among vegetable growths. The float that struck me as the most peculiar and noteworthy bore a huge watermelon, peopled, as all the devices were, with gayly costumed men and women, and decked with nodding blossoms, waving leaves, dancing tendrils, and the glitter and sheen of metal, lustrous stones, and silk. Butterflies, caterpillars, birds, a great squirrel on the acorn float, snails, and nameless grotesque animal forms were seen upon the vegetables and their leaves, while men dressed as fairies, of both sexes, were grouped picturesquely on every one. These devices were not inartistic or tawdry. They were made by skilled workmen trained for this particular work, and were not only superior to any of the show pieces we see in other pageants elsewhere—they were equal to the best that are exhibited in theatres. They were displayed to the utmost advantage in the glare of the torches and flambeaux carried by the men who led the horses and marched beside the hidden wheels. The figures in Paris-made

CREOLE TYPES

costumes, theatrical paint, and masks were 150 to 200 members of the Krewe—serious and earnest men of affairs during the other days of each year.

On Tuesday, *mardi gras*, Rex really made his appearance, leading a pageant called "the symbolism of colors," just such another display of the blending of strong and soft colors, but a thousand-fold more diffi cult to render satisfactorily by daylight. The twenty enormous floats in line represented boats, castles, towers, arches, kiosks, clouds, and thrones, and one, that I thought the best of all, a great painter's palette, lying against two vases, and having living female figures recumbent here and there to represent such heaps of color as might be looked for on a palette in use. Canal Street, one of the broadest avenues in the world, was newly paved with human forms, and thousands of others were on the reviewing-stands built before the faces of the houses, over the pavements. The sight of such a vast concourse of people was as grand as the chromatic, serpentlike line of floats that wound across and across the street. That night all the people turned out once again and witnessed the parade of the Mistick Krewe of Comus, a Japanesque series of floats called " Nippon, the Land of the Rising Sun." The display was, to say the least, as fine as any of the season.

But the splendid function, one that I never saw excelled in this country, was the ball of the same society, that night, in the old French Opera-house. All the kings and their queens, representing all the carnival societies, were in the opening quadrille, all crowned and robed and with their splendid suites. Looking down upon that brilliant mass of dancers were seven rows of the belles of the city—rows unbroken by the jarring presence of a man. These ladies were all simply attired in white, pink, pale blue, and all the soft faint colors which distinguish the dress of New Orleans women. Here and there a young girl wore upon her head a narrow fillet of gold; but jewels were few and far apart—a striking omission which greatly dignified the gathering and enhanced the beauty of the spectacle. If the reader has seen the beauteous women of Spanish descent and the petite and sweet-faced French creoles of that city, let him fancy these, and the loveliest American belles, forming seven rows in a theatre of grand size—and then let him try his best to picture to himself the wondrous garden of personified flowers that was thus presented.

I have said that "society" controls the opera. This institution, regularly maintained only in New Orleans, of all the cities of our country, is almost self-supporting. It is grand opera, and it is always French, and

IN THE OLD FRENCH QUARTER

given in the old French Opera-house, which reminds New-Yorkers of the "Academy," in Fourteenth Street. The troupe that I saw was a complete one, with a double

53

set of leading voices, with a *corps de ballet*, and a force of *bouffe* artists for the presentation of comic opera, which is given at regular intervals, and always on Sunday nights. Many of the chief performers were from the Grand Opéra of Paris.

The fashionable society of New Orleans is not in any sense a plutocracy. The wealth of those who have it is shared by or hidden from those who have it not. This is because the pride of birth and family, inherent in all our Southerners who have an excuse for it, meets an equal pride of family and name among the poorer creoles. The two combine to create a large exclusive set, among whose members the terrible ravages of the war spread a disaster that is privately understood and publicly ignored. Among the fashionables, the rich and the impoverished meet on a footing which the rich are at such pains to make equal that they are often plain in their entertainments in order that they may not hurt the sensitiveness or strain the resources of the others when it is their turn to open their houses. The men and women of this society maintain among themselves the purest, most wholesome, and honest conditions, unblemished by any hint of scandal, latitude of speech, or debatable behavior.

Again, while " society " here loves pleasure keenly, and, as we have seen, makes a business of some sorts of it, there is, nevertheless, an intellectual wing to it, with a liking for and an inclination to pursue art and literature. Several ladies, led, perhaps, by Mrs. Mollie E. Moore Davis, who has a marvellous gift for gathering bright folks about her in her quaint house in the French quarter, find it a pleasure to entertain and introduce such visitors as have interested them by their work. In the intervals between these gracious ministrations these ladies—with not a blue-stocking, but a host of beauties among them—entertain one another with well-written papers, wise debates, and music and recitations at meetings that only end with the fracture of a circle that has formed around a tempting display of refreshments.

Though a winter resort, New Orleans is pre-eminently a summer town—a city of galleried houses, of gardens, of flowers, and of shops which open wide upon the streets. It is hot there from June to November, and during those months the Americans who can afford to do so exchange it for the mountains and the forests. The

AN OLD COURT IN THE FRENCH QUARTER

wealthy among the creoles are apt to go to France, and there are many who divide the year thus, wintering in New Orleans and summering in Paris. Those who are obliged to stay insist that it is not dreadfully hot, and that there is almost always a breeze. They have no patent on that; we say the same thing in New York and Philadelphia and Boston and St. Louis. But I suspect New Orleans has a very debilitating air in summer. The most unobservant visitor can see one general proof of its heat in its architecture, whether it be of the new or the old, the creole or the American houses. I refer to the ubiquitous balconies—"galleries" they call them there. And for every gallery you see from the streets there is at least one in the back, on the courts and gardens. Thus the creoles, having the warm weather solely in view, are like the Italians at home, who stoop over their charcoal hand-stoves during the few days when it is very chilly, suffering a little time in order to enjoy the greater part of the year. I did not hear how they dress in summer, but when I rode through the Garden District —the new part of the town—my lady friends pointed to the galleries and said : " You should see them in the summer, before the people leave or after they come back. The entire population is out-of-doors in the air, and the galleries are loaded with women in soft colors, mainly white. They have white dresses by the dozen. They go about without their hats, in carriages and the street cars, visiting up and down the streets. In-doors one must spend one's whole time and energy in vibrating a fan." They have mosquitoes there, but they have also electric fans which mosquitoes eschew.

The water supply is from the Mississippi, which has had millions expended upon the improvement of its banks, but not a cent upon its water. It is not offered in the clubs, but they did not hesitate to serve it in the old-fashioned hotels, the burning of one of which has led to the building of the greatly needed modern one.

In the clubs mineral water is freely set about on the dining-tables. This is attractive to the eye, but those who have not already made the discovery will find that effervescent waters are too thin and gaseous to satisfy thirst ; in fact, nothing but honest water will do that. Therefore I drank a great deal of Mississippi water, and followed the local custom of dashing a pitcher of filtered fluid over me after each bath. The residents of the American quarter use it filtered. One of the strangest and most distinctive features of New Orleans is the presence of the collecting-tanks for rain-water in almost ev-

ery door-yard. Rising above the palms, the rose-trellises, and the stately magnolias are these huge, hooped, green cylinders of wood. They suggest enormous water-melons on end and with the tops cut off. The creoles keep the rain-water cool in enormous jars of pottery sitting about in their pretty courts—such jars as Ali Baba had an adventure with, in which oil was once stored, and probably is now, in the Orient. They are from half to two-thirds the size of flour-barrels, symmetrical in shape, and come from the south of France. They are painted with some light fresh color, and prettily ornament the cool, paved, jalousied courts. Nine-tenths of the water used for cooking and drinking is this cistern water, and when the cisterns get low, as they do two or three times a year, there is actual suffering in the poor districts, back from the river. The river water was not filtered when I was there, but large filters were contracted for, and are by this time supplying an abundance of clear water.

I should think that the coolest place in New Orleans in summer must be the Boston Club. It suggests some club-houses that I have seen in the

WINDOW IN OLD FRENCH QUARTER

Cuban cities, but it is little like any other in this country. It is white without and light and open within. An open porch on one side, hidden from the street, serves to cool the entire house in summer, and as a pleasant retreat for card-players and smokers all through the year. There are four notable clubs in New Orleans, and they stand near one another in a row upon Canal Street. The Boston is the oldest and choicest. It was organized in 1845, and was not named in honor of the Athens of America, but after a game at cards which was popular at the time. Another game furnished the Chess Club its title, though that is but a nickname, the full title being "The Chess, Checkers, and Whist Club." The Harmony is the Jewish club, in essence, though it is not sectarian. The most modern house and most youthful club in member-ship and spirit was the Pickwick; but since my visit there this club has vacated its fine quarters, which have become those of a hotel of the same name. The club is temporarily housed in a more modest manner. The Boston Club, always the more exclusive, has taken upon itself the full burden of popularity as well, but it does not offer what the Pickwick did in its glory. There, after the opera or a country ride, or rout of any sort, the most brilliant beauties of the old and the new town were to have been seen in the softened light of electric-ity lunching with their cavaliers, while the usual club routine went on above the ladies restaurant as if there were no women near.

The best place to see the famed belles of New Orleans is in the French Opera-house on a fashionable night at the opera. Then there are scores there—blondes with limpid blue eyes, and complexions of roses and cream; brunettes of the purest types with rounding forms, great black orbs, hair of Japanese black, and skins of softest brown; Spanish creoles with true oval faces, long narrow eyes, the same soft sun-kissed complexions, with proud bearing, and mouths like Cupid's bow. With

THE NEW ORLEANS YACHT CLUB

them are our American girls from all over the country, boasting the eclectic beauty of many blended nationalities. The place is like a great bouquet. They dress almost like Parisians, and that is one great secret of the splendid fame they have won.

To a great extent the creoles even now remain apart from the Americans, in pursuance of the spirit that led their ancestors never to cross Canal Street beyond their own old quarter, and even to riot when the shipping began to collect in front of the American half of the town.

But there is more and more mixing of the races, and marriages between the two grow more and more frequent, so that it is felt that another generation may break down all the false barricades between the peoples. As to the marriages, it is said to require a bold and indomitable man to court a creole, because when he calls upon her he finds the court and the parlor dark, and he waits while the servants light up the place for him. Then the parents come in, European fashion, and sit in the room while he "sparks" the ravisher of his heart. But all agree that when the end is come, and she is his bride, he is going to be envied among men, for there are no better wives or lovelier mothers than those dark-tressed, brown-skinned, graceful, soft-voiced creole women.

It gives a peculiar sensation to hear Cable abused by the creoles—and you never can hear anything but abuse of him. "George W. Cable and Benjamin Butler? Bah! Let them show themselves in New Orleans; that's all." This astonished me, though I had heard I was to expect it. It had seemed to me that they must in their hearts recognize the tenderness with which he deals with many of his heroes and heroines, the grace with which he clothes them, the soft light he turns upon most of them; and to-day I believe that in their hearts they know that he has done for them something of what Longfellow did for the Acadians in "Evangeline." Surely he it was who lifted them to a sentimental and romantic realm, out from their walled-in courts of the French quarter. I still believe that it is only a sense of mistaken self-respect that causes them to fancy that they must assail him, because they showed me many of the places he described, and told me with poorly hidden pride that much, aye, most of what he describes is true. But he was a New Orleans man, and should not have betrayed

AT THE OLD FRENCH OPERA-HOUSE

his neighbors. Some said "he was of the South, yet he writes like an old-time abolitionist." And yet these are not the true reasons for their animosity, not the whole truth. I believe I am right when I say that what really wounds them most deeply is his mocking their broken English. As a writer, I have never been so certain of hurting the feelings of others as when I imitated their dialects, or mistakes in grammar, or awkward efforts to pronounce our words. It angers every race; and the more intelligent the race, the deeper the sting and the anger. I am the more sure this diagnosis of the case in point is correct, because the manner in which he makes his characters talk was always bitterly alluded to, if at all. "He puts negro words into our mouths; he copies the servants' talk, and puts it in the mouths of the la-dies and gentlemen."

The funeral notices tacked upon the telegraph poles and awning posts interest strangers. I have heard Northern men in business in New Orleans speak in praise of this method of publishing the deaths, because, they say, these cards are read when the newspaper funeral notices might not be. I copied one or two, and will reproduce them here, with the names changed, of course:

JEANNE,

Fille de James Coudert et de Adèle Palm.

Les amis et connaissance des familles Coudert, Palm, Rochefort, et Bellecamp sont priés d'assister à ses funérailles, qui auront lieu Same-di, après-midi, à 4 heures.

Le convoi partira de la résidence des parents, No. 2091 rue Plaisant, entre St. Jacque et Couronne.

And here is one in English:

BIRMINGHAM.

DIED,

Wednesday evening, March 2, 1892, at half-past six o'clock, R. I. BIRMINGHAM, aged forty-seven years.

The friends and acquaintances of the Birmingham, Smith, Robinson, and Decatur families are respectfully invited to attend the funeral, which will take place this (Thursday) evening at half-past four o'clock from Trinity Church.

An eccentric gentleman, exercising the inalienable privileges of freedom, makes it his business to read all these placards, and to tear down those that have served their purpose, else no one can say what would become of the poles and posts as they accumulated. Another custom in mortuary matters there is the publication in the *Picayune* and *Times-Democrat* of eulogistic references to the dead by way of notifying the public of the sad occurrence. These obituary cards are quite as peculiar in their own way as the rhyming notices of Baltimore and Philadelphia.

Without turning far from the subject, it may be said that (though I do not in any degree favor the custom which leads our citizens everywhere to insist upon driving visitors to the cemeteries as first among the "sights" of our cities) it is certain that the cemeteries of New Orleans are worth a visit. They are not only unlike any burial-yards known to the rest of the country, they are beautiful as well. The grounds are laid out much as are our own in the North, but the white shell roads and paths enhance the neat and tidy effect such places usu-

READING A DEATH-NOTICE.

ally boast. They are truly "cities of the dead," for the tombs are houses built upon the ground, and provided with cubby-hole or drawerlike compartments, to be sealed with a marble slab as each coffin is put in place. The term "oven tombs" describes them well. I can easily believe that in no other cemeteries is seen such evidence of a great outlay of money, for these mausoleums are built of marble and granite, or, at the worst, of brick stuccoed to look like stone. Some are round-topped, but more are of the form of miniature Grecian temples. They exhibit statues, crowns, crosses, and even most elaborate panelling and carving. These buildings rise white and gray from mounds of green, beside white shell roads, beneath orange-trees laden with golden fruit, magnolias, cedars, and oaks, some of the trees being draped or bearded with pendant moss.

Of course it is understood that the burials are above-ground because of the moisture in the soil. Yet I saw earthy graves in a shabby little cemetery in the city, where also weeping-willows lent a familiar aspect to the scene. This was at the yard of the chapel of St. Roche (pronounced " Roke "), by far the strangest place of worship I have seen—even in Canada or California. Standing up tall and shallow, like a kitchen clock, is a little brick chapel whose front is all but hidden behind ivy. It has kneeling-benches but no pews, and under its altar is a recumbent life-size figure of the Saviour, un-clad as He was lifted from the cross. But it is what is on the altar that is most novel. All about upon its shelves are lozenges of marble shaped like great visiting cards. On them are carved such legends as " Thanks "; " Thanks, J. W."; " Merci "; " Thanks, granted June 30, 1891." Hanging by ribbons on the same altar are wax casts of little baby hands, or hands and fore-arms, or tiny feet. One large pair of hands stands there in a glass

ALONG THE SHELL ROAD

case. All these are offerings of those for whose prayers such members have been rescued from disease or uselessness. A double score of candles burn on the altar, and as many men and women pray before it. The fourteen stations of the cross, seen in all Catholic churches, are here placed out-of-doors in little shelters of openwork wood, upon which vines creep and illuminate their foliage with blossoms. It would be difficult to find in New Orleans anything more picturesque than is seen when hopeful women are passing from one to another of these holy emblems, to kneel at each in prayer.

A very remarkable German was in charge of this sanctuary, and unconsciously relieved the tension upon those who were awed by the funereal and religious character of the premises. He did not mean to be funny, but he was exceedingly so. He went about hammering the virgins and saints on the figured tablets of the stations of the cross, and saying, " You see dot. Dot vos pronze from Munich; chenuwine pronze." He bustled into the chapel, past all the kneeling supplicants, and talked about the things there—even the most sacred ones—like an auctioneer. Those who knew him very well all united in declaring that he was a zealous and dutiful janitor.

" Ach," he exclaimed to me, " I do vish dey vouldn't bury all der time. Efen on Sundays dey bury; all der whole vhile it goes on, und I can't get avay by mineself for a rest. In Chermany, vhere I used to been, ve took Sundays off, und tied from a bell alretty some strings to der big toe of each corpse. Sure, then, if der corpse gets alive und moves, der bell rings—eh? But here it is efery day de same—bury, bury, all der whiles. Vell, it don't matter, pecause vhen I do go avay to haf a gwiet glass of beer I get no beace. Everybody knows me, und everybody points me out und says, ' See! dot's der olt man from St. Roche's.'"

He wondered if he would ever be where people would not point him out and tell one another who he was. Alas! it will not be in heaven, good old soul. Even those whose tongues are silent in the yard you watch will find voices there to tell the others who you are.

I have neither the space nor the inclination to describe the French market, the cathedral, the French quarter, and those other really charming bits of the city which have been the subjects of descriptive articles and letters since our grandfathers' days. I like them none the less, and they remain powerful magnets to draw future battalions of tourists there. These are parts of the thing we call the "foreign air" of the city, and I hope that with the manifest new energy of New

THE QUEER OLD CHURCH OF ST. ROCHE

Orleans they will not be "improved." I suppose it cannot be expected that people will ever understand the full value of the relics of their past. The bric-à-brac we treasure is always what some one else has parted with. Here in New Orleans, as up in Montreal, the people insist upon taking visitors to see the new part of each city, among the modern residences; and the visitors persist in hastening back to the old French quarters, always and every time.

St. Charles Avenue and the Garden District are almost semi-rural, like the best parts of "the Hill" in Brooklyn, or the outlying parts of our finer cities. The large galleried houses stand back in broad gardens, with the most beautiful surroundings of lawn, banana-plants, orange-trees, clouds of roses—especially of Cherokee roses, which bloom in clouds—magnolias, China berries, and hedges of many sorts. Trees of pretty shapes and lordly shade-giving quality stand in ranks along the streets, and the views down the cross-streets are bowery; often they are vistas under meeting branches. There are some rambling old Southern mansions with halls through the centres, some modern stately mansions, and some little boxes of the universal sort that coquet with the tiresome memory of good Queen Anne.

THE CLAIBORNE COTTAGES—A SUMMER RESORT OF NEW ORLEANS IN THE PINY WOODS

Those bashful men whose courage grows weak on the door-steps where they are about to make a call would never, I am sure, get into the average house in the Garden District if they did not know any more about New Orleans customs than I did when I paid my first visit there. They would find before them a door with a handle, and no other protuberance — button, knocker, pull, handle, or anything else. Much to the delight of several very young ladies on an opposite veranda (the thought of how much pleasure I was able to give them will long console me), I fell at last to knocking with my

A BIT OF OLD ARCHITECTURE IN THE FRENCH QUARTER

knuckles, like a mendicant at a window. By-and-by a maid let me in.

"Oh, was that you making that funny noise?" the mistress of the house inquired. "I've been listening to it for a long while, and could not imagine what it could be."

With what pride remained to me I modestly suggested that I could not ring a bell when there was none to ring, as spirits do in table-rappers' closets. I added that I would give five dollars to the local blind asylum if any one could show me a bell anywhere on or around the front door.

"Of course there isn't any," remarked the lady; "in New Orleans we put the bell on the post of the front gate."

How on earth—who could blame—but, as she remarked, that is where they hide the front-door bells in New Orleans.

Certainly a typical Chicago man would throw up his

hands in horror at the lamentable backwardness of the
city, at the absence of most of the newfangled means for
making modern lives automatic and mechanical. We
who seek change in travel, and who are rested where
others rest, love New Orleans all the better for its so-
called faults. The chief beast of burden is the mule, and
they have the finest mules and the sorriest horses im-
aginable. But the noted mule-cars of old, that used to
creak and jolt and rattle and bump through the heart
of town, have at last given place to age-end trolley-cars.

STREET IN THE OLD FRENCH QUARTER, FROM THE HÔTEL ROYAL.

The electric lights are mounted on tall towers of iron lattice-work, just as they were in Detroit the last time I was there, and as if the object of the people was to light the clouds rather than the city. The milk-carts are worth going to see. They are little two-wheelers, like our New York butcher-carts, and each one has in front two gorgeous great cans bound with brass hoops that are as lustrous as jewelry. Women drive many of these carts, but when they are managed by men they dart madly about, and accidents to them are frequent. A lady friend of mine who once failed to receive the day's milk went to the door next day to dismiss the offender. She came back almost in tears, for he appeared to her with his face peeled and one arm in a sling. "Par-r-r-don me," he said; "ze 'ole business h'all tip ovaire on de street."

The hod-carriers tote the bricks on their heads, balancing heavy loads on cushions that fit upon their crowns. The dog-catchers go about snaring vagrant curs with slip-nooses at the end of short sticks. Then they pitch the dogs into strange barrel-like wagons. Such a row as a New Orleans cur sets up when he feels himself jerked up by a hind leg ought to soften the hearts of the stones under their feet. It does bring the women out from the doors and windows of several blocks of houses. Men stand about selling alligators that they keep in baskets and cages, many of the beasts being too young to know that the proper thing for an alligator is to be sluggish and slow. In their ignorance they slap about and climb and snap with their jaws with the activity and malice of so many hornets. Women sell *pralines* and pecan candy, of which we know nothing until we go there, and "oyster loaves" (advertised as "family peace-makers: take one with you

when you go home late") are among the queer edibles
of the place. I desired to taste one for the peace
of my curiosity, but I never found out where I could
take or what I could do with a loaf of bread stuffed
with cooked oys-
ters. Men make
jewelry in the
streets by curl-
ing gold wire
into the forms
of the written
names of wom-
en, and these are
worn as breast-
pins. Such arti-
ficers know more
than wiser men;
for who would
dream that wom-

BAKER'S CART

en would care to display their given names and pet
names to the public in shining letters? But the men
were kept busy as long as I was there, and I saw
a two-hundred-and-twenty-pound woman fasten the
word "Birdie" to the throat of her dress and walk
proudly away.

The law courts are in the ancient Spanish government
building, and, in keeping with that still impressive pile,
the officials barricade the street in front with a chain
drawn across it, to preserve quiet during the proceedings.
The police, who are few in number, for there is no hood-
lum or "gang" element of ruffians in the city, are dressed,
like our New York firemen, in caps and coats with silver
buttons. The lottery being legalized, tickets are openly
displayed in the shop windows, and are sold on the sidewalks by men, women, and children. One store for the

sale of these tickets bears such a legend as this on its sign: "This is lucky Number Eleven. More winning tickets sold here than anywhere else in town."

There was a drawing while I was in the city, and knowing that the lottery company was not to ask for a renewal of its privileges, and that its power and the scenes and customs growing out of it were soon to become mere memories, I availed myself of the opportunity to witness its chief public operation and the historic characters who have been induced by large salaries to figure for it. The drawing took place in a theatre called "the Academy of Music," at eleven o'clock in the morning. The yellow gas-jets battled feebly with the daylight in the lobby into which the people were pressing without let or qualification. The theatre was two-thirds full at last. On the stage, set with a parlor scene, was a knot of men between two wheels. The wheel on the right was a band of silver, with sides of glass and with a door in the metal rim. A bushel of little black gutta-percha envelopes the size of dominoes had been poured into this wheel, and a white boy, blindfolded with a handkerchief, stood at the handle of the crank by which the wheel was turned. He had one arm in the door of the wheel, and with the hand of the other arm was offering a tiny envelope to General Beauregard—the last surviving general who served on either side in our late war. A fine, most gentlemanly-looking man he was, with the features of a French courtier, with snowy hair, a white mustache, a little goatee, and the pinkest skin a baby ever knew. He was faultlessly dressed. Across the stage, beside a very much larger wheel of parti-colored boards, sat Major-General Jubal A. Early — a perfect type of the conventional figure of Father Time; tall, portly, stoop-shouldered, partly bald, and with a long, heavy white beard. He was dressed all in the color of the uniform he distinguished by his valor as a soldier. Alas, for human frailty! These two heroes were said to receive $30,000 apiece each year for their duties performed at the monthly public drawings of the lottery.

By each general stood a blind-folded boy, taking numbers out of the wheels and handing them to the generals. From the big wheel to Major-General Early came the numbers of the tickets; from the little wheel to General Beauregard came the numbers of dollars that formed the prize each ticket had won. By each general stood a crier. Early read out, "Twenty - one thousand one hundred and fifty - two"; and Beauregard, having shelled the gutta-percha case off a billet, read out, "Two hundred dollars." Then the criers took the billets and cried the numbers, "Twenty - one thousand one hundred and fifty - two" from one; "Tew hundred dollars" from the other, who, by-the-way, called out tew hundred dollars at least tew hundred times. But all the prizes were not of that amount. I chanced to hear the capital prize read out.

A NEW ORLEANS
POLICEMAN

"Twenty-eight thousand four hundred and thirty-nine," said Early. "Three hundred thousand dollars," said Beauregard.

The effect was startling; indeed, the startled senses refused to grasp the meaning of the words. The criers repeated the figures. The people in the theatre craned forward, a hundred pencils shot over pads or bits of paper in men's and women's laps. Then a murmur of voices sounded all over the house. The routine on the stage was halted, for the criers took the two bits of paper to some clerks, who sat at tables in the farther part of the stage, to allow them to verify the important figures. Then the routine began anew. The wheels were revolved every few minutes, and the rubber shells rattled around like coffee beans in a roasting-cylinder. The boys took off their bandages, and other boys were blindfolded and put in their places. The criers were relieved by others, and General Beauregard at last grew tired, and went out for half an hour. Among others came two criers who kept their hats on. Think of it! There hats on, covered, in the presence of the God of Chance! It was an offence against the unities; it was making light of the solemn mystery of luck. Every man who drew a blank that month owes those rowdies a kick. I wondered whether such a thing could have happened before the passage of the postal bill which took the cream off the business and the nerve out of the misguided men who had been pressing for a renewal of the lottery charter.

They have a stranger thing than the lottery in New Orleans, and that is the word "lagniappe." "Take that for a lagniappe" (pronounced lanyap), says a storekeeper as he folds a pretty calendar into the bundle of stationery you have purchased. "What are you going to give me for a lagniappe?" a child asks after ordering five cents' worth of candy. A lagniappe means something thrown in, something extra, something more than is paid for; and lagniappes are looked for in New Orleans by servants and children especially. The merchants give something, if it is only a stick of candy or a shining trinket, and he who chooses such things wisely profits in an increased business. It is the thirteen of "a baker's dozen," the "this for good measure," which we are all more or less accustomed to. I read an unlikely story to account for it in one of the New Orleans papers, telling how a grocer kept a long ape that annoyed him by pilfering, and how, when a child came to complain that he had not given good measure to her mother when she had bought butter that day, he threw the ape at the child, saying, "Here, take lagniappe [long ape], and be off with you." I asked many of the more intelligent men of the town, but not one who could give me the derivation of the word, the custom itself being familiar as humanity, though seldom practised so generally in a large city.

VENDER OF LOTTERY TICKETS

The second - hand shops in New Orleans, taken together, equal a great museum. Strangers hang around them like moths near candle-lights, for in the city are many old families that are obliged to part with heirlooms one by one, or that cease to value them, and prefer newer things. Here, then, one may buy whole sets of solid Empire and Directoire furniture and furnishings—clocks, candle-glasses, china, cut glass, andirons, tongs, snuffers, four-post canopied bedsteads, and no one knows what all.

TYPES OF THE DAGO

I find that, in the space of a chapter, there is not room to do justice to half of what is noteworthy in New Orleans. I had hoped to tell of the picturesque Italians, their occupations, their fleet of luggers, and their standing in the community since " the Maffia affair." I meant to describe the charming resorts and the beauties of the piny-woods regions, the Bayou Teche country, and the shores of Lake Pontchartrain. The delicious cooking and notable dishes peculiar to the place were in my mind when I began this chapter, and — though I had meant to confine myself to what others had not dwelt strongly upon—the educational institutions, the promise of a strong art atmosphere, and even the notable athletic, gymnastic, and yachting clubs deserved description. The excellent sport with rod and gun afforded in the neighborhood of the city also interested me; but I must leave the field to others, and turn to a study of the commercial interests of the enterprising city.

Over fifty per cent. of the active business men of the city are from the North and West, and the work of so-called reconstruction is partly in the hands of nature by means of intermarriage and partly left to business in the forming of commercial partnerships. I did not happen to meet a single "hostile" there. I met only one in the course of my entire journey from St. Louis to Florida and home again. I sympathized with that one because she was an aristocratic old lady of nearly eighty years, who had been locked up in a jail for ten days for refusing to salute the soldiers who had seized her mansion for their headquarters. I was told in New Orleans that there are a few unreconstructed men there; but no one heeds them, and they are such only because in no other way than by startling and loud talking would

DAGOS AND THEIR BOATS

they be able to attract attention to themselves. On the contrary, the warmest patriotism prevails, even among the wrecks and ruins of fortunes and of futures which have turned thousands of lives into the next thing to tragedies. Northern men are made welcome there, and so heartily that in one of the leading clubs heretofore sustained by the native leaders of the people two of the three members elected as the executive committee are men from the North.

It must be remembered that, in a great measure, the original business men of the city were Northerners and foreigners, the natives in ante-war days having been land-owners, planters, and clerks. Now, as I say, the Northern men are in the majority in trade. They tell me, what I heard everywhere in the South, that the prosperity of that most attractive section of our land will be permanently assured when cotton is grown only as a surplus crop or by-product. The planter will then be able to sell cotton for two cents a pound, but will be in a position to demand twelve cents.

New Orleans, from a commercial point of view, is new-born, or, at least, she is but newly recovering the relation to our great country of the present time which she bore to the smaller one of *ante-bellum* days. The constant dread of fever retarded her progress, or she might now have been one of the very great cities of the world. Now nearly two decades have passed without a visit from yellow fever, and it has become evident not only that this dread disease is an exotic, but that the city is in other respects a safe and pleasant place of residence.

It has a fresh-water harbor, with a permanent twenty-six foot channel, and solid, unchanging banks for buildings. Its inland waterways lead to the iron region of Pennsylvania, the lead mines of Missouri, and the copper region of Michigan. It is the seaport terminus of

80

several great trunk railway lines, and the supply depot for Texas, the Southwest, Mexico, and Central America. It commands 1500 miles of seaboard, and its merchants assert that the internal waterways behind it, which are navigable or can be made so, reach 18,000 miles.

The building up of populations in Texas and the Southwest, a region that is growing like a bed of weeds, is helping New Orleans as its natural depot of supplies. Mexico, the Central American states, and the country along the Southern Pacific system to California, are but slightly less tributary to it. The inland water system terminating at New Orleans affects a region extending beyond Kansas City. Chicago, St. Paul, St. Louis, and other Western cities now import through New Orleans,

THE OLD AND THE NEW SOUTH

which is thus put in direct competition with New York for the foreign business with our West. The actual traffic on the Mississippi River and its tributaries is relatively small, yet it establishes low freight rates by land and water, and the more the river is improved the cheaper will be the transportation of all bulky and non-perishable freights.

Business in New Orleans is on a very solid and conservative basis. With cotton grown at a loss there have been practically no failures—that is to say, there has been no increase of failures. The main trouble has been that the capital at hand has been insufficient for the development of industries. The capital, surplus, and deposits of the New Orleans banks is about $33,000,000, and this is relied upon for the handling of from two hundred to three hundred millions of dollars' worth of crops every year.

The importation of fruit through New Orleans is a very heavy interest. Only a few years ago the city was behind New York in the volume of its banana imports, and the receipts of other tropical fruits were small, but during the year ending in the spring of 1892 that city led all the rest in the banana business, beating New York by nearly 170,000 bunches. The trade is only ten years old, but now employs several lines of steamers, bringing from three to five cargoes a week. During 1891, in addition to an enormous mass of cocoanuts and other fruits, 3,735,481 bunches of bananas were unladen there. The reasons for this development are obvious. The run from the fruit lands to New Orleans is a short one, and is made in vessels especially fitted for the trade. The climate of the city insures the fruit against cold that would be injurious to it during its transshipment to the cars, and these cars, built especially for the trade and run on express time, quickly distribute it among all the centres of population in the West. The direct importation of fruits from the Mediterranean shores is also growing into a considerable business, which owes its increase to the constantly multiplying number of vessels that come to New Orleans to get wheat, cotton, and other return cargoes. The swift steamers in the Central American fruit trade carry back American products, and this business is seen to be growing under our reciprocity treaties, which thus operate to give New Orleans a share of this trade, that, but for the fruit business, she never would have had.

The transshipment of wheat from cars and Mississippi barges to steamers for abroad is a tremendous industry that had grown up within a year of the time when I was there (March, 1892). It is a consequence of the immense crops, of the inability of the Atlantic coast ports to handle them, and of the fact that a large number of European vessels come to New Orleans, either with cargoes or in ballast, from other ports to which they have taken cargoes. The wheat reaches this port by way of the Illinois Central, Mississippi Valley, and Texas Pacific railroads,

A RELIC OF THE "OLD" SOUTH

and by the Mississippi Barge Company. The Mississippi Valley Railroad Company has an elevator that is small, but handled three millions of bushels of wheat and corn between September, 1891, and April, 1892. Another and larger elevator and a line of transatlantic steamers were contracted for by this company at that time. The Texas Pacific road was, at the same period, building an elevator with 350,000 bushels capacity. The elevator capacity of the port has alone set a limit upon the volume of this business that can be got, and it is evident that the railroads do not mean to stand in their own way in this respect. The exportation of flour had also been very considerable within the year which closed while I was there. This trade is due to our reciprocal tariff arrangements with Cuba and the South and Central American nations. As it is, the city does not yet include a flouring-mill, and that staple comes from Missouri and Kansas, always in bags, to meet the demand of the Latin countries. Flour, agricultural implements, beeves, mules, and horses are now articles of large export to those lands.

The manufacture of fertilizers is an important industry. Pebble phosphates from Florida are manufactured into marketable phosphate, but there are other fertilizer companies using potash, cotton-seed meal, and phosphate to make a product that is used on the cotton and sugar plantations. It is interesting to find that one staple of the South thus depends upon the other, for cotton-seed meal is extensively used to enrich the sugar lands. About 10,000 tons of this one product are taken off the land in one set of places to be put upon it in another. In all, 15,000 tons of fertilizers for the cotton, sugar, and rice plantations are annually made and sold in New Orleans. But at the same time that cotton thus helps sugar, it is in another way benefited, in turn, by sugar. The sugar is put up in sacks and bags made of cotton cloth. A very large business in cotton and burlap sacks has grown out of the sugar-refining in New Orleans. The Western people, among whom this sugar finds its consumers, prefer 100-pound sacks to barrels.

The sacks are easier to handle, since they must be carried on the backs of mules and men; and then, again, the sacks are more useful after the sugar is used than barrels would be.

The refining of sugar is a notable industry in New

CORNER OF BANK BUILDING

Orleans. There are four refineries in and out of the great sugar combination, and all are kept running by night and by day. This product is made of Louisiana and West Indian crude sugar, and is marketed at home and in the West and Northwest. The business is increasing so rapidly as to lead serious men to predict that in time New Orleans will supply the entire country between the Rockies and the Mississippi.

A side industry of the Southern (cotton-seed) Oil Company is the fattening of two and three year old cattle from Texas on cotton-seed hulls and meal. This results in considerable shipments of cattle to Liverpool and to the stock-yards of the West, and is so simple and profitable an industry that, in view of the quantity of such food which is obtainable, it would seem bound to grow. Cotton-seed oil-cake is a large item of the export business. It goes to England, Scotland, and Germany, to be used in the feeding of cattle. New Orleans is the birthplace of the now great cotton-seed oil industry. It has five or six mills, some that are in the trust and some that are independent, and the seed is brought from Texas, Alabama, Mississippi, Arkansas, and the Mississippi Valley.

The cotton-pressing industry is extensive enough to have tempted English capital, which was offered for the control of it while I was there. It is one of the largest businesses and fields for labor in the city. The cotton is brought to town by rail and boat. It is then classed, graded, and stored, and when sold is reclassed, weighed, and compressed for shipment. The proportion of the cost of a bale of cotton which is paid for the New Orleans labor is so large as to amount to the lion's share, I was told.

The unique position of the city as the point of export for the cotton crop is well understood, and I need not enlarge upon the subject. In 1891 there was handled at that port more cotton than was handled there in any year except 1860, the net receipts being 2,270,190 bales, exclusive of receipts from or *via* other seaboard cities.

New Orleans has two large cotton mills, making brown goods, sheetings, shirtings, unbleached and colored goods, and hosiery and other yarns. One mill

runs 45,000 spindles, and the other 16,000. The city
also has a very large brewing interest, maintaining
fourteen large breweries, and supplying not only the
city and surrounding country, but a heavy demand
from Central and South America.

Four large cigar and cigarette factories employ 2500

ALONG THE LEVEE

hands. The tobacco in use is obtained from Cuba, Mexico, and Sumatra, and from Connecticut, Florida, and
Wisconsin. The cigars and cigarettes are sold largely
in Texas and California, but find a strong market in
Chicago, and, to a less extent, in New York and Philadelphia. One house turns out 36,000,000 of cigars a
year, and the total output of all the factories is 54,000,-
000 cigars a year. One hundred and fifty millions of
cigarettes are made there annually. The output of
manufactured tobaccos is small.

No foreign ice now goes to New Orleans. The eight or ten large factories, run with the ammonia process, supply a great section of country around the Louisiana metropolis, going to the cities and small towns far out on the railroads. Mississippi River water, filtered, is that which is used. This making of artificial ice was begun ten or twelve years ago, but has greatly increased in the last half-dozen years. The people there used to pay $14 and $15 a ton for ice, but it is now sold for $5 or $6 a ton.

Another industry that has grown amazingly in the last three to five years is the manufacture of ready-made clothing. The city has an advantage over its competitors in being able to draw upon an extra-intelligent class of workers on these goods—the creoles and the more intelligent and industrious negroes. Many of these, especially the creoles, will not work in factories, but perform the labor at home, and do much better work for less money than can be obtained in the North. New Orleans supplies the South and South-west, and is even beginning to ship clothing to the North.

All the rough rice raised in Louisiana is milled in New Orleans in twelve or fifteen mills. A trust has been organized there, and has taken in most of these establishments. The rice is of a high grade, and is sold all over the country. There is a small but swelling business in the making of boots and shoes. The fisheries employ 2000 men, the oyster business 3000 men, and the catching and canning of shrimps almost 1000 men. There are more than sixty firms handling Spanish moss, which is used in mattresses and upholstering work.

Olive oil is being made in New Orleans from the fruit of an olive orchard in Mississippi, eighty-four miles from the city. This is thought to be the beginning of a future industry of great extent. It is ten years since olives were first planted by the present experimenter, and he has found that the trees will bear all over southern Louisiana, and that frosts which will destroy oranges will not harm this fruit. This gentleman, one of the shrewdest business men in the city, now has 1500 trees, whose fruit he last season pressed into oil. The trees will bear in five years after they are planted. The fruit ripens in August and September, and the crop is thus ready for picking three to five months before olives are gathered in southern Europe. The fresh American oil will have that advantage over the European oil, besides the saving of freight and the customs tax. The American trees are seen to be prolific bearers, and the fruit is of a large size, and of a quality to compete with any in the world. This gentleman says that the soil of the entire Gulf coast from Florida to Texas is suitable for the cultivation of olives.

Louisiana exempts from license and taxation all establishments employing not less than five hands in the manufacture of textile fabrics, leather, shoes, harness, saddlery, hats, flour, machinery, fertilizers, and chemicals, furniture and all articles of wood, marble and stone, soap, stationery, ink and paper, boats, and chocolate.

They say in New Orleans that the mortality among the colored residents is so much greater than among the same proportion of whites that the published death-tables do not fairly represent the character of the city as a place of residence for the last-named race. I cut from the *Picayune* the death-table for the second week in March, 1892, and found that the deaths among the whites numbered 79, or 22.33 per 1000 per annum, while of negroes 66 died, or 49.55 per 1000 per annum. Of the causes, phthisis pulmonalis and pneumonia led the list.

The signal-service records yield this account of the temperature of the seasons:

Season.	Temperature—deg. Fahr.			Normal rainfall —inches.	Per cent. of sunshine.	Mean relative humidity— per cent.
	Normal mean.	Mean maximum.	Mean minimum.			
Winter...	56	63	49	13.09	47	71
Spring...	69	77	62	13.67	53	70
Summer..	81	88	76	17.97	54	73
Autumn..	70	76	62	11.94	58	72

III

ALONG THE BAYOU TECHE

MR. HORACE FLETCHER, of New Orleans, has an irresistible way, which perhaps he caught from the general irresistibleness of all New Orleans, though it is more likely that it was born with him in Massachusetts. At all events, when he said to Mr. Smedley, the artist, and myself that no one could pretend to have seen New Orleans until he had also seen the Teche or Acadian region, he said it in such a way that it was difficult to wait from Saturday until Tuesday for the steamboat — a steamboat, by-the-way, which has its name painted up in its cabin, with a stove-pipe in front of the letter "c," so that its passengers cannot help but read the name "Te — he," and feel sure that they are bound upon a very merry boat, and certain of a jolly time. The *Teche* and her sister boats go into the 'Cajun (Acadian) country in the old way, the way of befo' de wa' and befo' de railroads, taking a journey of hundreds of miles to fetch them where the cars go in less than a hundred; taking days where the cars take hours.

The course is by two loops whose sides are nearly parallel. One is made by going up the Mississippi until the mouth of the Red River is reached, then down the Atchafalaya towards New Orleans again, and then up the Teche away from New Orleans and almost parallel with the route up the Father of Waters. The three lines of waterway are so nearly beside one another that points upon them which are actually close together by wagon road are great distances apart by the boat journey; for instance, one place which is forty-four miles from another as the crow flies is 376 miles from it by the boat route.

"Take your roughening with you," said the captain, "for we do not sell anything to drink on the boat." Mr. Fletcher does nothing by halves, so that along with a little "roughening" he took a case of mineral water, a mule-load of bananas to be fried in crumbs by the darky cooks, and the current copies of *Harper's Weekly* and of *Puck* and *Life*. We had a dismal, cold, rainy day to start with, and no ladies aboard. The men huddled around the stove at the masculine end of the saloon, and smoked and swapped stories. It was a perfect reproduction of a day in a cross-roads tavern, such as every man who follows a gun or a rod and has been storm-stayed in the country has experienced. The red-hot stove, the circle of men, the wind scolding at the windows and thrashing them with rain, the door opening to allow some one to be shot in with a blast of chilling air, like a projectile out of a pneumatic gun, the weary and worn old newspapers, the gradual torpor that the heat produced among the men — nothing was lacking. In the evening, after supper, we heard subdued music working a difficult way through a stateroom door.

Music! It was inspiration! It was precisely what was wanted to atone for the beastly weather and the imprisonment in-doors. I knocked on the state-room door, and found that the musician was the mulatto "Texas-tender," which is to say the man in charge of the rooms of the pilots and petty officers on top of the saloon roof. Would he stop hiding his melody under a bushel and come out and play for us? "Certainly, sah,

"TAKE YOUR ROUGHENING WITH YOU," SAID THE CAPTAIN

if dat wuz what we wished." So he came out, appearing to us with a guitar in one hand and the upper part of his body enmeshed in a strange arrangement of heavy wire that went around each upper arm and across his chest and up to his mouth, where it was solid and black like a gag. He looked as if he was pinioned and gagged and walking out to a gallows to be hanged with a guitar in his hand. Perhaps that was what would happen to him if he played in a centre of civilization, but we were resolved to be tolerant, though critical. He sat in a chair, and lo! the "strange device" of wire proved to be a patent concertina-holder. The gag was the concertina. For an hour he played for us, very much to our satisfaction, though there were features of dear old "Annie Rooney" that we did not recognize, and "Comrades" became a trifle quarrelsome and discordant at times. We asked the captain if there were no negroes in the crew who could sing or dance.

"I don't know," said he. "They are all in the St. Charles now."

"The St. Charles?"

"Oh," said the captain, "you don't understand. That is what we call the place where the roustabouts sleep, on the main-deck under the boilers."

In the morning the light broke upon a wet and depressing scene. The broad yellow river, so glorious in sunlight, was a hurrying sheet of mud enclosed between lines of dripping willows and mounds of wet Cherokee rose-bushes not in bloom. The great reaches of the levees more than ever suggested earth-work fortifications against the forces of Neptune. The sky was dark and cheerless. Of signs of population there would be none for miles, and then we would see scores of negro cabins, and close by the usually white mansion of their white employer. The smoke-stacks of an occasional

"SCENES OF NEGRO CABINS"

sugar-refinery rising above the trees told us that we were in the sugar country, but rice plantations were plentiful. Now and then a vagabond house-boat was seen, nose up on the bank, or drifting down with the current. Usually the after-part of such an ark was covered over by a projection of the roof of the house, and in that shelter we nearly always discovered the shiftless proprietor, fishing or mending his lines or whittling, or, more often than anything else, smoking and letting his mind take a vacation. We heard much that was interesting about these and other Southern craft from the pilots and the captain.

The house-boats, it appears, are a survival of one among many kinds of boats which were very much more numerous upon the great river before the era of steam navigation than steamboats are now. Among the earlier forms of boats were the famous "Kentucky flats," or "broad-horns," and family boats of this pattern were an early modification, of their general plan, which was that of a strong-hulled ark, long and narrow, and covered with a curving roof. I have read that "family boats of this description fitted up for the descent of families to the lower country, were provided with a stove, a comfortable apartment, beds, and arrangements for commodious habitancy, and in them ladies, servants, cattle, sheep, dogs, and poultry, all floating on the same bottom, and on the roof the looms, ploughs, spinning-wheels, and domestic implements of the family, were carried down the river." Fulton's *Clermont*, which proved its usefulness as the first practicable adaptation of steam-power to water travel in 1807, must have been quickly copied on the Mississippi, for in one list of notable passages up that river I have seen a note of a trip by a steamboat in 1814. But long after that the barges, skiffs, horse-boats, broad-horns, and family boats must have remained very numerous. They floated down stream with the current, and were pulled up again by means of wheels worked by horses or cattle, and by the toilsome and slow processes known as warping and bush-whacking. A boat which was warped up the river kept two row-boats ahead of her, carrying hawsers, which were made fast to the trees on the shore, and then pulled in as the bigger vessels were thus hauled along. When the length of one cable had been pulled in, the other boat had fastened the other cable far ahead, and so the vessel "inched" along against the five-mile current of the stream a little more quickly than a house moves when its owner has decided to move it down a country road to a distant cellar he has dug for it. It took a day to go six or eight miles by that method. Smaller boats were propelled against the current by rowing, sailing, or poling them along; and when the water was high and overflowed the banks, they bush-whacked up stream — that is, they pulled the vessels along by hauling on the bushes that brushed the sides of the craft.

At last came the Mississippi steamboats, those queer creations which seem to be made by house-carpenters who have forgotten how to build houses, and yet never knew the ship-joiner's art. They are huge, flat-bottomed, frail houses floated on box-like hulls, but they are as comfortable as the Southern barons demanded that they should be in the glorious days when they revelled like kings. We cannot tell what sort of boats will travel the great river in the surely coming day when it shall be all walled in and kept in its place, but it is no more likely that the railroads will crush out passenger travel on that majestic and interesting river than that they will upon the Thames or the Hudson. Just now there is a spell upon the traffic. The war interrupted

it, and the people of the North and East must redis-
cover the fact that the journey from St. Paul or St.
Louis is one of the greatest delights and wonders of
our continent. However, Mississippi steamboating has
stood still for more than twenty years. The rocket of
its glory burst with the famous *Lee* and *Natchez* race
in 1870. They still talk of that world-famous brush in
the river pilot-houses, and I heard it referred to more
than once during the nine or ten days I spent upon the
river. One of the captains in that test of speed, historic old Captain Leathers, who commanded the *Natchez*,
is still in the service, though he has a son who is a man
beyond the age of thirty, and in command of a boat
unkindly named the *Natchez*, after the famous racer the
old man captained years ago. The talk of record-break-
ings and of quick runs is all of what we in New York
would call long voyages, since these consume the time
of ocean journeys, and our longest steamboat trips are
to Albany and Fall River, and are accomplished in a
night.

The quickest run from New Orleans to Cincinnati,
made by the *R. R. Springer* in 1881, was done in 5
days, 12 hours, and 45 minutes. The fastest time over
the course of 1013 miles from the Crescent City to
Cairo, Illinois, was that made by the *R. E. Lee* in 1870,
in 3 days and 61 minutes, and was therefore run at the
rate of about 14 miles an hour — against the current,
to be sure. The *Lee*, the competitor of the *Natchez*,
reached Natchez, during their memorable race, in 16
hours, 36 minutes, and 47 seconds, making the distance
of 272 miles at the speed of about 16½ miles an hour.
The speed per hour during the whole race of 1278 miles
to St. Louis figures at about 13¼ miles.

The race took place in the summer of 1870. Captain
Leathers with the *Natchez* completed a run to St. Louis

'CAJUNS

in 3 days, 21 hours, and 58 minutes, and Captain Cannon, of the other and rival king-boat on the river, the *R. E. Lee*, at once announced his intention to beat her on the return trip. The *Natchez* returned to New Orleans in due time, and her captain found that the *Lee* was going to refuse all freight and passengers during the race. More than that, the *Lee* had taken out all her light upper work that could be removed, in order to lessen her draught in the water. Captain Leathers of the *Natchez* affected not to need such advantages. He took aboard a small cargo of freight and some passengers, and the two mighty packets were cast loose from the New Orleans levee on June 30, 1870. Away they went, with their huge white bodies throbbing and their trails of jet smoke curling behind them. The *Lee* made no landings for coal. She had engaged a tender to precede her 100 miles up the river to give her a supply of whatever fuel she needed. Farther along, flat-boats with wood and coal awaited her in mid-stream. They were warped to her as she slowed up alongside of them, were emptied as she swept them along, and then were flung off to drift where they might after they had served their purpose. The *Natchez* copied this method after a time.

The race made a wonderful stir. Boats loaded with spectators preceded and tried to accompany the racers from New Orleans, and everywhere along the river it was said to seem as if the interior had been depopulated, so numerous were the persons who crowded the shores to look on. The *Lee* was lucky, and made the trip in 3 days, 18 hours, and 14 minutes, arriving in St. Louis when thirty thousand persons were assembled on the levee and on the house-tops to cheer her. The *Natchez* had met with unusual detentions by fog and groundings. The time of the boats as they reached each principal city on the way was cabled to Europe, and it was estimated that a million of dollars was wagered on the race.

Thus, with talk of the historic and picturesque past, surrounded by what might be called "the local color," we drove the wretched weather out of mind until we reached a watery corner and turned out of the mighty river into the Atchafalaya. This we called the "Chafferlyer," to be in harmony with our acquaintances. It is fed out of the Mississippi where the Red River joins the Father of Waters, and immediately that we entered it a new scene was presented—a view of a narrow stream between groves which grow not merely to the water's edge, but into the water. It does not look like any river that we know in the North; it is rather like water running through woods, as a flood might appear, or a greatly swollen stream. Suddenly what is called the Grand pours into it, but the Grand is merely a wider belt of liquid mud flowing through a wilderness. Next the land begins to rise, higher banks are formed, and with these come views of cottages, freight-houses, ruins of old brick-sugar-mills, fishermen's tents, negro cabins, bits of greensward, banks of rose-bushes, and patches of cultivated farm land. Our first stop was at a honey plantation, where the half-acre lot filled with beehives, novel as the sight proved, was not as peculiar as the honey-planter himself. He is famous up and down the Teche route as a man who so loves to argue that nothing can possibly happen which will not arouse his instinct for debate. He has some little learning, and even in his worn old suit of homespun suggested traces of gentle blood and breeding as he stood on the river-bank flinging long sentences and uncommon words up at our captain on the main-deck, while his daughter, the only other white person for miles around, leaned her

101

spare form against the side of the cabin doorway, and smiled with affectionate pride as she reflected upon the good time her father was having with his vocal organs. Something which had been ordered by him from New Orleans had not come, and he was begging leave to differ with the captain, no matter how the captain sought to account for the delay. I think I remember that the sum of this man's income each year was computed at five hundred dollars, which proved, it seemed, that he was in very comfortable circumstances, could well afford to go to New Orleans twice a year, and was able to support the position of a man of consequence in that region.

Presently we saw our first Acadians—nowhere spoken of in their own country otherwise than as 'Cajuns. The first one on the route keeps a low gin-mill, a resort for bad characters. The next one we saw was a swarthy, stalwart man with a goatee *à la* Napoleon III., who was catching bait with a net. Moss hangs from the cypress and oaks in great and sad profusion in this part of the route. The wilderness is only occasionally broken by a clearing, and after each interruption it seems to snap shut again as if not even man could overcome the force of the rank growth of vegetation, except here and there, and for a mere geographical instant. There was a fuzz of disappointingly small scrub palmettoes on the ground, and wherever there was a cabin or a man there was also a dugout canoe or pirogue. These boats were not such as men have made in almost every known part of the world by merely scooping out the heart of a log and fashioning its ends. They were the lightest and prettiest boats of the kind I ever saw, mere shells or dishes, very skilfully and gracefully modelled, but so shallow as to be likened to nothing so closely as to half a pea-pod. Bait-catching was the business carried on with them.

The men were after shrimp, but very often caught craw-fish, those relentless allies of the Mississippi River which eat into the levees and let the river through behind them. They are a tenth the size of lobsters, and look like lobsters " out of drawing," as the artists would say —that is, they appear disproportioned, with their tails too small for their bodies. They are red and greenish-red, but some are as rosy as one of the old masters is said to have painted lob-sters in the sea after he had become acquainted with them on the dinner-table. They have blue lob-ster eyes and fierce claws.

The mate of a Tide boat.

In time we came to the mouth of a bayou which was closed during the war, but which, were it opened, would take us to Plaque-mine, twenty - five miles across a country around which we had gone 190 miles to get where we were. Farther on we came to the openings into two or three other bayous, and thus gradually were brought to realize that this region of the mouths of the Mississippi is a land that is nine - tenths covered with water. Travellers by the cars do not comprehend the character of Louisiana, or see, with anything like the view of a steamboat passenger, with what profusion the surface of the earth is littered with bayous, branches, canals, ditches, lakes, and swamps. Lake Chico was a notable incident of this second day's progress. It is merely a swelling

of the Atchafalaya or Grand into a sheet of yellow
water thirty miles long and twelve miles wide. It is
picturesquely littered with snags and floating logs and
channel stakes. The narrow entrance to it, where
wooded promontories all but block the way, is much
admired by persons afflicted with the fever for kodaking
everything out-of-doors. The Spanish-moss is so abundant there that if I were a sufferer from the epidemic I
would have been tempted to photograph some of the
trees that carried the greatest burdens of the weed, and
looked as if they had been washing out their worn and
faded winter garments and were hanging them up to
dry. But a far better picture would be one that showed
how we felt our way into the lake, being so uncertain
whether there was sufficient water that we wedded our
steamboat to a great scow with ropes, gave our spouse
the task of carrying a good part of our load of freight,
and sent a mate ahead of us in a small boat to prod the
mud with a pole. Whatever the mate discovered he
discreetly kept to himself; but we, not to be retarded
by his reticence, posted a darky on the upper deck
with a sounding-line to chant in the musical lingo
of the Southern pilots the varying but always very
small distance between our keel and the muddy lake
bottom.

Our first notable stop occurred a little after dusk, at
Pattersonville, where we went ashore for a cake of
shaving-soap, and saw vaguely by the yellow light of a
few scattered kerosene lamps that we were the only
souls adrift in a long wide street, which boasted here and
there a dwelling and here and there a neglected shop.
We asked for the soap in one store, and the clerk treated us to a Southern expression that we had not yet
heard upon its native soil. " I'm sorry, sah," said he,
" but I've done run plumb out of it." We added that

to our notes. We had grown quite used to hearing size and distance expressed with the phrases, "A right smart of a plantation," "a smart distance," or "a right smart hotel"; also to hearing every one say, "Where is he at now?" and "I dun'no' where I left my hat at." When night fell, thick and black, our two powerful electric search-lights were utilized with weird and the-

FELLOW-PASSENGERS

atrical effect to throw great shafts of daylight at which-ever bank we were searching for a landing. Each light cut a well-defined path through the night, and when it picked out a grove of trees or a clutter of negro cabins or a landing, it created a veritable stage-picture. These lamps bothered the pilots so much in steering their way through the water that they were only lighted for view-ing the bank, and for helping the roustabouts to see while loading and unloading the cargo. The pilots so quickly shut off the light when they had nothing to do but to pick out an uncertain course, through water and air that were equally black, that they seemed to me like water-cats that could see very well in their element, but were helpless upon land.

In the morning, after many hours spent in throwing spectacular landings on the blank wall of night, and then carrying freight out to them, and wiping them out of existence by turning off our lights, we awoke to find the Atchafalaya basking in the sun and in quite another country. We had travelled from the swamps and cypress brakes of Louisiana to something like the Thames in England—to a pastoral country watered by a narrow, pretty river of clear water that loafed along between patches of greensward, rows of oaks, white manor-houses, cabins set among roses, magnolias, and jasmines, and with great clearings, and men at work ploughing on either side. White bridges that invariably broke apart as the boat approached them, and that were often set upon pontoons, still further domesticated and civilized the scenery. Every plantation had a bridge for itself, it seemed. It was a little jarring to have a man come aboard with two rattlesnake-skins, each large enough to make into two pairs of Chicago slippers; five inches wide and a yard in length the skins were. We had pointed out to us the Calumet Plantation, which is said to be the most orderly and completely appointed sugar farm in Louisiana. The rows of whitewashed negro cabins were formed of houses better than the 'Cajun houses we had been seeing.

Daniel Thompson is the planter here, and his son, Mr. Wibrey Thompson, came aboard and talked very interestingly of the experiments he and his father are making in the analyses of many sorts of cane, the breeding of the best varieties, the perfecting of refining processes, and the broadcast publication of the results of the work

UP THE BAYOU TECHE

in the laboratories, where as many as three chemists are sometimes at work together. Such men are the representatives of the new type of farmers who are numerous in the West and who are multiplying in the South. They do not farm by prayer, or take land on shares with luck or nature, after the old plan. Chemistry is their handmaiden, and she rules in the place of chance. One whom I knew went to Germany and France to study the beet-sugar industry there before he bought his ranch in Kansas, and he mastered French and German so that he could read all that is known of the industry. Others learn chemistry or employ chemists to analyze everything they deal with. These new-school farmers publish all that they learn; they write reports for the government to publish, and they lecture to farmer audiences in the winter, in which season, by-the-way, they are generally as busy as the old-time luck farmers used to be idle. They keep the most minute accounts of outlay and income, crediting the refuse they burn to the fuel account, the stuff cattle eat to the saving of fodder, offsetting their earnings with their fixed charges, wear and tear of machinery, interest on the principal invested, and, in short, tabulating everything. These are mainly Eastern and Northern men, but the new generation of Southerners is not without representation in the scientific class. We shall find, before we leave the Teche country, that there are great districts wherein every plantation is owned by Northern or Eastern men. The cultivation of semi-tropical fruits has been a failure in Florida because the land there was taken haphazard by men who are trying to farm with Providence and dumb luck for partners. Agriculture there was based on the theory that if an invalid who could not endure Northern winters had money to buy land he could grow oranges in white sand. The new school of scientific, take-nothing-for-granted farming is already taking root there, and will in time make more money out of oranges than dumb luck has sunk in planting them where they did not belong.

Mr. Wibrey Thompson, while he was aboard the *Teche*, said that he was convinced that the future source of sugar will be sorghum. It may not be in his time, he says, nor in five hundred years, but the fact that he has demonstrated that it is the most practicable product and economical cane, and that it yields most readily to the processes of selection, satisfies him that the world will in time turn to it for its sugar supply. Sorghum in the rough yields twelve per cent. of sugar, the same as sugar-cane, but in three years, by choosing the best cane and " breeding it," he raised the yield to twenty and a half per cent. He is certain he can plant it and get fourteen per cent. off-hand from a whole crop, and in a short time can get sixteen per cent. Potentially or technically, sorghum is now in the best position it has ever held yet; actually, it is bankrupt and dead. This year only one concern in the country will make sorghum sugar. The reason for this is that it has always been grown from poor seed. It has not been bred or studied, and people have not known how to rid the juice of its impurities. All this is overcome, and it is seen to be the best producer; but in the mean time the sorghum farmers have lost money, and, worse yet, have lost their faith in the cane.

Farther along, from the boat's deck we saw Acadian men and women gathering Spanish-moss from the trees. Our first sight of this peculiar Louisiana industry was of a 'Cajun man high up in an oak-tree, half hid in a mass of waving gray moss. How he got into it we did not see, but now he was tearing his way out of it, cutting and ripping it, and tossing it down upon the river-bank, where it lay in soft, rounding mounds, as the clouds of the sky might do if they were treated in the same violent way. This moss is sold in New Orleans, where it is so highly prized for stuffing mattresses that they say nothing in the bed line can equal one that is made of a moss mattress and a hair mattress on top of a wire-spring mattress. Such a bed, I was told, would even satisfy the princess in Andersen's tale who was bruised black and blue by the three pease the peasant woman put under the mattresses in order to discover whether she really was a princess. The moss-gatherers of Louisiana heap the soft fibrous stuff upon the ground, pour water upon it, and leave to nature the task of rotting it into a black dry mass.

This moss, which is found as far north as Asbury Park on the Atlantic coast, is a very peculiar growth. It is said not to be a parasite and not to live upon anything it gets from the trees. It is believed in most parts of the South that it rids the atmosphere of malarial poison, and where it grows the people boast that fevers and chills are as rare as in the mountains. The weight of testimony favors this theory, but frankness compels me to add that in Florida the tourist will read in the circular of one hotel that the presence of Spanish-moss "attests the healthfulness of the climate," while at another hotel he will be told that the peculiar merit of that locality lies in the fact that Spanish-moss does not grow there. This moss, so green and littered with pinkish blossoms when in its prime, dies on a dead tree when the bark fails to hold it, and then it becomes the color of cigar ashes. Patient study of a mass of it will, it is said, show no root, beginning, or end to it, and any piece of it which is blown from one live-oak to another may take hold and breed a bedtick filling of it.

We entered the Bayou Teche on a glorious day, and

A SUGAR-CANE PLANTATION

thought it part of a drowsy, dreamy, gentle, semi-tropic scene. It runs through the heart of a broad savanna. Afar off, on either side, we saw the forests of the neglected South that has so long awaited the now approaching multitude from Europe, but the land beside the bayou was every acre cultivated or built upon. We could not have found ourselves amid stranger scenes had we gone to the French part of Canada or to England or France. Often there was an edging of reeds or a grove of oaks that would have resembled an old orchard of the North but for the abundance of the funereal moss that bearded every limb. Then we passed villages with funny little Grecian-looking stores and banks and court-houses, all pillared and with pointed roofs. Then there were splendid planters' homes, white and neat, with rows of Corinthian columns in front and a brigade of whitewashed negro cabins in dependent nearness, as little chickens cluster near the mother-hen. There were pretty white bridges here and there, as ornamental amid the greenery as statues on a lawn. On these the "quality folks" always gathered to see the boat, apart from the colored folks, who huddled upon the shore in barbaric colors, every wench wearing something red, and chewing tobacco or snuff, and all giggling and skylarking like the children that they remain until they die. Two sets of sugar-houses were the great monuments of the industry of the region, the old more or less ruined refineries of *ante-bellum* days, and the unpicturesque but practical factories of to-day.

When the boat stopped, as it did with the frequency of a milk-cart on a busy route, we were taken to a country club, sometimes, and the bar-tender was formally introduced as Mr. Belden or Mr. Labiche, whereupon everybody "passed the time of day" with him, as the Irish put it, before ordering the toddy. In one town there had been a ripple of excitement that had not quieted when we landed there. An insult had been offered to a prominent old citizen, " who was as brave as a lion," by a young man whose courage was not questioned. Seconds were appointed, and they found that the young man had made a mistake and ought to apologize.

" We have reached a stage of civilization where a duel would be impossible," said a citizen who was discussing the affair. Then he added, "This would have been peculiarly distressing, as there are at least ten friends of the old gentleman armed and awaiting the outcome of the deliberations, while the younger man has at least six friends who have their rifles in readiness."

The kind of hospitality that obtained along the bayou was simply astonishing to a Northern man. We were begged to leave the boat and visit the homes of friends of five minutes, to stay a week or till the next boat; in one case, to take a month of fishing and hunting. Often when we tore away from these kindly persons they followed us up with bundles of cigars and bottles of good cheer. To have doubted their sincerity would have been like doubting the cause of daylight, and yet, like that phenomenon, it was almost past comprehension. Ah! but it was also a land of pathos and tragedy. The wounds made by the war may almost be said to bleed yet. The clerk of our boat never made a trip without stopping at the noble plantation that his father owned and lost; the mate on every voyage sees the great acres that his parents were obliged to surrender. Everywhere one journeys in the South such are the sights; every time men talk (I had almost said) that is what one hears. It is not true that the war spirit is alive anywhere except in the talk of politicians, and mainly of those in the North, but it is wonderful that it is not true; it is wonderful how the South has adjusted itself to its altered condition.

Through the broad and golden savanna we zigzagged all day, eating only three meals in the cabin, yet seeming to be forever at it. At close intervals everything aboard ship moved forward with a lurch, and we knew that the vessel had grounded her nose at a landing. Down went the great landing-stage that rides before her like an upraised claw, and that grabs the bank when she stops as a swimmer might hold himself up with one hand. Whenever the claw went out to catch the bank a bunch of ragged negroes scrambled off, and fell into the reeds and bushes, weighted down with the boat's hawser, and stumbling, slipping, and falling 'as they fought their way to the trees or the clear ground. Hallooing, swearing, and crashing they made their way, working, as all negroes do (when they have to), harder than any other laborers in America. The boat made fast, order was resumed, and took the shape of a rolling line of blacks, shouldering bags and packages, and shambling to and from the shore as softly as so many animated bundles of rags naturally would, for they were ragged from their tattered hats down to their gaping, spreading, padlike shoes. The length of stay at each place was computed by the number of "packages" on the clerk's list. Fifty meant no time at all, 200 indicated a chance to stretch one's legs on the bank, and 1000 or 2000 carried the opportunity to go to town and shake hands with the hearty folk in the law-offices, the court-houses, or the clubs. When the last "package"—which might be a broom or a steam-engine— was put ashore, the scramble of the roustabouts was repeated. The line was cast off, the claw began to rise by steam-power, and the darkies rushed down the bank, and hung on to it, and climbed up at the greatest possi-

114

THE CLERK

ble risk of being left, and losing as many dollars or dollars and a half as they were days from the city. No officer of the boat ever considered them at all.

These were incidents of a day's travel along the Bayou Teche. Towards bed-time we stopped at one place where the clerk's list of packages assured us we might go ashore and visit a planter whose house was near the bayou. The place proved a typical old manor-house, and yet what a change had befallen it! Instead of the bustling household of before the war—the queenlike mistress, the young ladies with Parisian finish, the little children, the governess, the ever-numerous guests, the troop of servants, the bird and fox hounds, and the pleasure-loving Southern lord—only one room showed a light. The rest of the house was dark. We went in, and found a log fire blazing cheerily on an open hearth in a bachelor's paradise, bare-floored, with magazines, pipes, cigar-boxes, and newspapers scattered all about, and a general tone of disorder and settled loneliness. The planter said that his wife was in Chicago, where he also spent much of his time.

At daybreak we were awakened to find the boat at the plantation of Messrs. Oxnard and Sprague, new-found New Orleans friends who had invited us to visit them. Although it was but daylight, the great colonnaded and galleried mansion, as fine as a lord's country-seat in England, was the seat of a welcoming bustle. Breakfast was spread in the great dining-room upon a snow-white cloth, before a blazing log fire. Again the proprietors were Northerners and bachelors, and the floors and walls were bare, while literature, guns, and smoking implements made picturesque disorder.

I found next day that the plantations lay side by side up and down the bayou for miles, as farms do along a Jersey pike, or cottages neighbor each other on a village road. Were they all maintained by Northern men and bachelors? The inquiry brought the response that not one of the old Southern planters had managed to keep his acres, and that of the new Northern ones only one in that particular neighborhood had his wife with him. Profitable as sugar-planting is, it can only be carried on after a great primal outlay. A modern, well-equipped, economical sugar-house, with its machinery, costs at least $300,000, independent of the cost of the hundreds and perhaps thousands of acres of land bought at $40 each, at an average. Men who have the means to venture upon such an outlay can afford to live where they will; and, as a rule, their homes are in New Orleans or other cities, and the old manor-houses which came with the acres are considered as mere conveniences or business headquarters.

These are the earnest and the scholarly latter-day planters of whom I have spoken—self-instructed plodders or favored college graduates who have learned that the laboratory of to-day, and the scientific reports and periodicals of the age, are better from a business point of view than the wine-cellars and French novels of the departed era. These new-comers will make Louisiana rich, and America royal over princely nations of Christendom. But to find these people and this new condition actually within the walls of the feudal palaces of slavery days sent a sentimental chill to my very marrow. In Mr. Sprague's great house, over and above all the kindness and hospitality he showered around him, and stronger than the kindliness of his very atmosphere, was the sadness of having the dead, assassinated past so persistently thrust into the mind. He will not mind my using his house to point the tale of the revolution in the South, for he knows that it is a thing apart from the merry time he made for me, and from the friendships

that were engendered by his kindness. He must himself have felt that it was strange to walk about the great
wide halls and through the immense high rooms of the
house, with doors and windows a dozen feet high, and
with fireplaces framed in marble, and to think what
such a mansion was intended for, of the departed state
and pride of which such a house is the emptied cage,
the violated tomb. Between rows of moss-curtained
oaks and great pecans was the avenue where the horses
and carriages brought the gentry to the broad galleries
and broader halls, where they disported an aristocracy
that was not out of place in their days.

If the lower Atchafalaya suggested England, the
Teche country was like Holland, with its extended flat
vistas, far along which the sky met the plough-tracked,
water-riddled land. But on high were the Southern
buzzards, noisome to the sight and to another sense, but
ever-beautiful when on the wing. Apparently no Southern view omits them. I could almost say I never looked
up in the daytime without seeing them soaring, with
the grace of better birds, eternally. The mules, the buzzards, and the negroes broke the Hollandish similitude.
Near the Oxnard-Sprague house was a street of negro
cabins in a double row, from which came the varied
sounds of jews-harps, laughter, and quarrelling. The
cabins were of one sort — the single type all over the
South—one-storied, often one-roomed, and with a rude
brick chimney outside and a gaping fireplace within.
Nearly all the white folks who trudged along the highway were Acadians, all but hallowed by the magic of
Longfellow, and it was strange indeed to hear that we
must not call them 'Cajuns to their faces lest they be
offended, that the term is taken as one of reproach, and
that the negro farm hands taken care of on the white
men's places look down upon these people who have to

"WORKING AS ALL NEGROES DO"

take care of themselves, as the darkies elsewhere look down upon "poor whites." Among the Acadians along the Bayou Teche are very many who are ignorant, untidy, and unambitious, though nearly all are saving of what they get. Some perform odd jobs, as work is offered to them, and some work the land for those planters who have more than they can manage, and who guarantee a certain sum which leaves a margin of profit for the crops they are able to raise. We saw some rather pretty Acadian girls, dark-skinned, and just missing beauty because of the heaviness of their faces, and we asked them where we could find a certain group of Choctaw Indians' houses where we might buy Indian basket-work. They did not understand us at all until I bethought me that Indians were *sauvages* to the French mind. I tried the girls with that word, and they brightened up and led us to the Indian cabins, which were in no wise different, exteriorly, from the near-by homes of the girls themselves.

The last of the Acadians to reach this new home of theirs came only a little more than a century ago; yet they were only a thousand strong then, while now they number forty thousand. Whether any of their "Evangelines" wedded Choctaw bucks I do not know, but a sufficient number of the French Nova-Scotians married Indian squaws to lend the Acadian faces of to-day a strong trace of kinship with the people they call savages. Yet I never, outside of British Columbia, saw Indians so uncouth as were many of the swarthy yet kindly and simple exiles from Grand Pré, who here have found a drowsy, luxuriant, flowery, and sunny land just suited to their natures.

I spent twenty-four hours on the plantation, and every wakeful hour brought a new delight, found sometimes in the great bare house, sometimes in the fields, and sometimes in the near-by village. There was no unfriendliness towards the new-comers that I could see; indeed, in the village there were only a few cottages half buried amid flowers along a bowery perfumed road, a somnolent shop or two, a lazyman's hotel, and two restful-looking churches. To turn from that slow-going, placid settlement, moss-grown like its trees, to the huge pulsating refineries of the invaders was to be reminded of a sudden change in a disordered dream.

Yet just such companions as these two forces are found throughout the region. Thus the new South works side by side with the old one, the one vigorous and promising, the other placid, picturesque, and doomed.

IV

IN SUNNY MISSISSIPPI

WE say we like London because of its historic associations and haunts, and we think of them so often that we come to regard our country as lacking the things which awaken reverent emotion. A mere tomb in an English graveyard, or a lettered slab in the pavement of one of the Inns of Court, sends us back a century or two as we ponder what some poet did and how he lived and what were his surroundings. And yet the sentimental mind may find plenty of this sort of delight here in America—delight that should be extreme to an American. I thought of that in Richmond when I saw the portrait of poor Pocahontas in the Capitol, close to that of Light-horse Harry Lee and to those of some of the famous royal Governors. And I thought of how there was a Virginia known to Shakespeare, as well as a "vexed Bermoothes." And so it was again when I found myself in Charleston, with its museum of ante-Revolutionary buildings, and its French traces that point back to the earliest Protestant settlement within our national borders. In New Orleans, again, a wealth of romantic and picturesque and gayly colored reminders of shifting dynasties and exciting history beats in upon my mind. Finally I came to Mississippi, and at Biloxi stood upon the ground whereon M. d'Iberville planted the flag of his royal master of France in 1699, nearly 200 years ago, but 157 years after De Soto sailed the Father of Waters that fronts that same State. Ah! I can be very happy indeed when I find myself in Carlyle's favorite tobacconist's in Chelsea by the Cheyne Walk, but I can command a more brilliant panorama, and one that moves as directly towards my own proud citizenship, when I pursue the same bent of mind in my own country.

To Biloxi one goes to get sick in order to be happy. That is one of the peculiar charms of the entire Gulf coast of the State of Mississippi. Surely as you go there you will fall ill of the local distemper, and that is one of the main incentives for making the journey. When I was in Chattanooga, not long ago, the cream of the gentry were ill and contented by reason of an enforced command for general vaccination to ward off a threat of small-pox which never materialized. But down at Biloxi and Pass Christian (pronounced chris-*chan*) and Ocean Springs and those other bits of dreamland on the Mississippi coast nobody gets sick in order not to be sicker. No one down there takes the local illness in preference to some other disorder. In that peculiar region every one becomes invalided as badly as possible solely for the love of the malady.

I first heard of it in a barber's shop. A man came along, and the barber hailed him. "When are you going to come and get my hot-water apparatus and mend the leak in it?" he asked. "Can you take it now?"

"No," said the mechanic. "I'll call around very soon. I was going to come and get it a couple of weeks ago; and then, again, I was pretty near coming for it the week before that. I'll get around. Y'ain't in no hurry, are you?"

"Oh, well—er—not a reg'lar hurry," said the barber. "I'd be using the thing every day if it was in order. But I'll get along all right."

123

I was in a holiday resort, and this was certainly a holiday spirit which both men were displaying, and yet it seemed that both were rather too slow even for a holiday couple.

"How does that fellow make a living?" I asked.

"Oh, he's a creole," said the barber. "He don't require much for a living. A cigarette and a glass of water makes a creole breakfast, you know, and down in this country you give any young fellow a dugout and a cast-net and he's able to marry."

After a pause the barber said, proudly, "Oh, we've all got the Biloxi fever."

"What sort of a fever is that?"

"You'll find out when you have been here awhile. How long have you been here?"

"About two hours," said I.

"Well," said the barber, "you'll have it bad to-morrow—that is, it will seem bad at first, though really it gets worse and worse the longer you stay. Why, the natives have it so that there's dozens of girls here who are becoming old maids because it is too much of an effort for their beaux to propose to 'em."

The fever seized me at eleven o'clock of the next forenoon, as with my friend Mr. Fletcher, of New Orleans, I was pursuing the truly Northern custom of "taking a walk." Before half a mile had been traversed a store porch appeared before us and impeded our progress. It is true that it was on one side of the thoroughfare, and the way past it was broad and level. But it was a demon porch—a thing with the soul if not the song of a siren. In the sunlight it seemed to smile on us seductively, and it spread its two side-posts like a welcoming lover's arms, while its clean warm floor appeared to advance and insinuate itself under us, so that, without knowing how or why it was, we found our-

GROTTO AT BILOXI

selves seated there, stricken with the fever and at ease. One must catch the complaint to appreciate it. It is not fatal any more than Nirvana is, and in my practical Occidental way of thinking it is very like Nirvana, and better, because it has the advantage of leaving you on earth, and with the same enjoyment of food and flowers and wine and song that you had before. It is not laziness. None but a dull hind would call it that. It is the very thing that the Europeans who criticise us for our fever of unrest should recommend as a substitute, for it is a fever for rest. A mere doctor would describe it as a malady peculiar to the Gulf coast from Mobile to New Orleans. He would say that it has been observed that large numbers of men and women, by combining in large cities, are able to exercise sufficient will power to ward it off, so that it is prevalent in Mobile and New Orleans only among the colored people. Then he would go on to say that its first symptoms are a stiffening of the motor muscles of the legs, followed by a sense of leaden heaviness in the patient's feet. The patient will be observed to talk rationally, and to sustain an ordinary light conversation, but will on no account move from a chair, except it be to drop into the next one he comes to.

In the absence of chairs the patients are observed to sit upon barrels, boxes, store porches, and door-steps in the public streets, even though, before they were stricken, they were in the habit of applying harsh names, such as "loafers," "trash," and "tramps" to those who did the same thing. They sit upon wharves and upturned boats and tree stumps, upon grassy ledges and fallen logs, and, if they are permanent residents of the infected districts, they build seats all about their open grounds. They put benches about on the grass and piazzas, and even on the road-sides. In many cases they order great pavilions like giant nests built around their trees, and having no energy with which to conjure a new and fit name for these airy perches in which they while away precious time, they call them "shoo-flies," a name utterly without significance in that connection. They will hear the news of the day if any one will tell it or read it to them, but they cannot be prevailed upon to take up a newspaper. Northern men, when at home, who take three morning newspapers, an afternoon paper, and a score of weeklies and magazines, show the same aversion for printed news as those who cannot read at all. An instance is related of a Northern editor coming to Biloxi and falling a prey to this strange disorder. Having a New Orleans paper pressed upon him with the hint that it contained a description of the burning of his newspaper building during the previous night, he pushed the sheet away, saying: "Let her burn. I am here for rest, and don't want business mixed up with it."

The same leading medical journal which records this case — so a mere doctor would continue — also cites an instance of a Northern broker in stocks who arranged to pay extra for his board on condition that the hotel clerk should tell him if Western Union dropped below $81\frac{3}{4}$, but should never, under any other circumstances, mention any serious matter to him during his stay in the hotel.

Thus a professional student of the disease would describe the Biloxi fever, missing the very essence of that which any person affected with the complaint would speak of at the outset. That point is its engaging character, its sensuous, dreamy, delicious, soothing nature. No one who has it would be cured of it on any account, until the time came to make a supreme effort of will and catch the train for the North. A poet might liken it to floating on whipped cream in a rose-leaf. Or, to put it so that the dullest mind can grasp it, the feeling is what you are sure a great good-natured Newfoundland dog enjoys when he lies blinking at the sun after a hearty dinner. To be sure, it may be carried to extremes, just as some persons go to great lengths with the measles and chicken-pox, and in such a case I can easily fancy that a man with a good supply of the fever would neglect his wife and babies, and sit on the head

127

of a barrel in the sun for years, without saying who he
was to any detectives that might be hired to find him
and bring him out of Biloxi.

At all events, we sat down on the store porch in the
fever-stricken town, and just then a fire broke out. It

A SHOO-FLY

was announced by a half-dozen lazy strokes of a bell,
which created a great disturbance. There was no yelling or rushing about or surging of crowds. The disturbance was confined to a dozen volunteer firemen.
They were resting in their homes and shops and offices,
and the alarm was unexpected. Some had to dress, and
others had to hunt up their fire-hats. These were things
that are not done recklessly in Biloxi, but are well and

carefully considered beforehand. It was therefore some little time before the firemen began to appear in the streets and to come calmly—as Matthew Arnold would have had all us Americans do—up to where my friend and I were seated, and then next door to the engine-house. On the way, at nearly every gate, the women halted them to ask where the fire was, and in every case the firemen took time to formulate a well-digested polite answer, to the effect that they were sorry not to be able to say at that time anything of value about the fire. In time they got the handsome old-fashioned hand-engine out into the street, and after a little badinage and a resting-spell they shrewdly paused to discuss the route by which they might most easily reach the general locality indicated by the number rung out by the bell. There being several discordant opinions to weigh, this also consumed a few minutes. Finally, like a well-ordered body, they and the machine got under headway and presently disappeared, leaving us to the full enjoyment of the succeeding quiet, which was only disturbed by a thoughtless question put by one of us to a street boy as to what sort of a tree it was that spread its noble height and width across our horizon. The boy replied that it was a pecan (he said "pecawn"); and had he stopped at that all would have been well, but he launched out upon a perfect clatter of facts about the nuts the tree bore, the number of bushels it yielded, the price they brought, and, in short, a shower of disturbing and unwelcome information.

After a long time the firemen came back in the same leisurely, dignified way as they had departed. We heard a woman ask them if they had saved the building, and we heard a fireman's reply, "No, ma'am: the building had gone when we got there; but we saved the ground."

It is to be hoped that before the fever seizes you the country round about the town will have tempted you to enjoy its many delights. They speak down there of the strange habit the Northern men and women have of taking long walks, a thing the Southern mind staggers at newly at each presentation of the phenomenon. In our far South, if one has not a horse or a sail-boat, and cannot borrow either, there is nothing to do but to stay at home. To be sure, the Northern pedestrians take few walks before they are fever-stricken and leg-stiff-ened and stranded in chairs in the sunshine. But what walks! Along the beach the water flashes before the town, all aglitter in the sunlight, and beyond lie the long green islands of the Gulf, fringed with spreading trees, now dense and now mere green lace-work, with the blue sky and bluer Gulf visible through it. The pedestrians turn away and explore the land only to come back enraptured, telling of the templelike forest of pines that overspreads the land, of the light and shade, of the vivid green feathered against the clear blue, of the white sand underfoot with its soft red car-peting of dead pine-needles, of the stillness and the purity and almost parklike semblance of order every-where within the forest. Alas, that they should soon lose the energy to renew such pleasure, and that it should joy them only in their memories!

The village is picturesque, and but that this one is the oldest of these Gulf resorts (and was a summering-place for New Orleans folk in the long, long ago), what is said of it will answer for all the others. It is made up of little cottages of pretty and uncommon designs that have sprung from French beginnings. Often the second stories project beyond the parlor floors so as to provide a lower porch; and here and there are seen prettily shaped openings in the upper stories so as to make additional galleries. When vines trail up the house fronts and frame these galleries the effect is very pretty. Vegetation is abundant, the trees are of great size, and flowers grow in luxuriance, though it is whispered that there is sufficient chill in the air of winter nights to make it prudent to pull the potted plants indoors in cold spells. The green gardens and chromatic cottages lie prettily beside white sand streets, where there are no sidewalks, but borders of grass instead. Natives point out the trees as chinaberries, willows, cypresses, magnolias, oranges, pecans, peaches, plums, and apples. The people love the castor-bean, because it has a tropical look, I suppose, and thrives so well down there. I have seen fifty-three orange-trees in one garden, checkered with golden fruit and greenery, and have found the oranges as delicious as any I ever ate. The buds come upon the trees before the fruit is plucked. The people in the tiny streets and gardens are extremely democratic. They talk to all who pass their way, and if a stranger like myself refuses to make a free exchange of his business for theirs, they will give up theirs quite as freely, if he will stop and listen.

These are often Western folk, for our Eastern people have not discovered this perpetual summer land, but have allowed men and women from the other end of the Mississippi Valley to steal this march upon them. Therefore we find a small section of the place spoken of as a Michigan settlement, and in addition there are many regular winter visitors from Wisconsin, Iowa, and Illinois. They discovered the Gulf coast about seven years ago, and make it a habit to come either in November or after the holidays, and to stay till warm weather reaches the North. The greater number go to Pass Christian, a rather new place, prettily spread along the beach, and with a large well-managed hotel maintained by Chicago people. Ocean Springs, Bay St. Louis, and Biloxi are the other resorts. Biloxi, the oldest, is the most quaintly typical, slightly Frenchified Southern town of them all. Bathing, fishing, driving, and cottage and hotel life are the diversions.

A great many of these visitors buy cottages and modernize them, renting them for a hundred or a hundred and fifty dollars when they go away in the summer, at which time the New Orleans folk come along.

At Mrs. Drysdale's altogether excellent, old-fashioned, but brand-new hotel in Biloxi I could find no fault with anything, but it is said that the Western visitors cannot abide the high seasoning with chile pepper and garlic which the creole taste demands, or the Southern tendency to fry everything, even the fruit, or the coffee that is made "so strong that it stains the cups," or the singular Gulf-coast custom of breaking fast at nine o'clock in the morning and dining at two o'clock in the afternoon. Cottage life, therefore, has the greater number of votaries in that region. They go there to escape the Northern winters, and are told that the Gulf coast has only two cold spells in each winter—one in November and one in February. When these come they are found to bring a temperature like that of boarding-house tea. Bathing can be indulged in all the year— enjoyed all the year by the men, I should say, and indulged in by the women, for the custom down there is for the women to immerse themselves in little pens under the bath-houses, between lattice-work walls.

Interesting Southern peculiarities are plentiful down there. I never saw a pecan-tree, for instance, that I did not think of the famous "nigger candy" of New Orleans—the irresistible candy of the Crescent City sidewalks. There they take the pecan-nuts, which we eat raw, as if we had no more ingenuity than squirrels, and

132

sprinkling them in great cakes of pure brown sugar, produce a confection to which they give the French name of *praline*, but which is so unlike any other candy in the world as to deserve a new American name of its own. The old "mammies" make the candies in disks big enough to cover the bottom of a silk hat, and even yet keep the trade to themselves and away from the merchants, although the visitors to the gay city buy up

JEFFERSON DAVIS'S MANSION, BEAUVOIR, AT BILOXI

whole trays of them, and even ship them to the North and East. Down here in Mississippi the scuppernong grape finds its farthest Southern foothold, I think; at least, I have not found it farther away. Travellers to Asheville and Florida will remember that it is the wine that is served at that celebrated railway restaurant in North Carolina where the proprietor and the waiters vie with one another in forcing "extras" and second portions of the nicest dishes upon the wayfarers. There can scarcely be such another restaurant as that. "Do have another quail," says the proprietor. "Let me give you more of this scuppernong wine. It is made near here, and is perfectly pure." "Won't you take an orange or two into the cars with you ?" or "Here's a bunch of fresh flowers to give to your ladies." The scuppernong wine has even more of that peculiar "fruity" flavor than the best California wines—a flavor that I am barbarian enough to prefer to the "pucker" of the imported claret. You may have it with your meals in Biloxi. And if you are a drinking man, which Heaven forefend, you may have "toddy" in the style that obtains from Virginia to farthermost Texas, and that has been imported to Arkansas, Missouri, and the Indian Territory.

It was on the banks of the Arkansas River, in Indian Territory, that I made the acquaintance of this method of—as a friend of mine would say—"spoiling good liquor." The famous Indian champion, Colonel Boudinot, introduced me to a planter whose two cabins, side by side and joined by a single roof, formed the most picturesque home that I saw on that splendid river. I was introduced as plain "mister," but that would not do down there.

" *Colonel* Ralph," said the planter, "enjoy this yer boundless panorama of nature. Feast yo' eyes, sah, on the beautiful river." (Then aside : "Wife, set out the mixin's in the back room.") "Colonel Ralph, you are welcome to share with us this grand feast of scenery and nature's ornaments. But, sah, I think my wife has set out something—just a little something—in the house. I dun'no' what it is, sah, but if you find it good, I shall be delighted, sah."

So we went into the back room with this other Colonel Mulberry Sellers, and there on the dining-table stood a bottle, a bowl of sugar, three glasses and spoons, and a glass pitcher full of spring water.

134

" Serve yourself to a toddy, colonel," said my host.

" I'll watch you first," said I; " I don't know what a toddy is."

" Don't know what a toddy is?" said the hospitable man. " Why, sah, that does seem strange to me. Back in gran' ole Virginia, sah, we children were all brought up on it, sah. Every morning my revered father and my sainted mother began the day with a toddy, sah, and as we children appeared, my mother prepared for each one an especially tempered drink of the same, sah, putting—I regret to say—a little more water in mine than the others' because I was the youngest of the children."

As he spoke, he dipped some sugar into his glass, poured in a little water, sufficient to make a syrup when the two ingredients were stirred with a spoon, and then emptied in an Arkansas " stiffener " of whiskey—a jorum, as the English would say. That is the drink of the South, where drinking, without being carried to any excess that I ever witnessed, still remains a genteel accomplishment, as it was held to be by the English, Scotch, and Irish who were the progenitors of nearly all our Southern brothers.

Beauvoir, the seat of the family of Jefferson Davis, is close by Biloxi, and as Mississippi reveres his memory as that of her most distinguished citizen, I rode over to visit the old place. I had thought of Mississippi as the last stronghold of the Southern sectional feeling, and so it may be, but I discovered even less signs of it there than anywhere else in the South. Nowhere did I encounter a greater and a closer mingling of the natives with the new immigrant element, which latter is growing strong there in the development of that new relationship which is springing up between the Western people at the head of the Mississippi Valley and the

Southern people at the foot of it. That is a new growth of trade and friendship which the student of this country's development will soon need to take into account.

But it is a strong fresh memory, that natives and new-comers share alike, of the ex-President of the Confederacy as he journeyed to his upper plantation or to New Orleans or walked through the white streets of Biloxi, a tall, spare, impassive man of great natural dignity, and always clad in a suit of Confederate gray, under a soft military hat, until he was seen for the last time. Although a Kentuckian by birth, his life is bound up with the history of Mississippi. For that State he served as an elector in 1844, voting for Polk and Dallas. He was a planter there, and went from there to Congress in the next year. As Colonel of the First Mississippi Volunteers he fought bravely in the Mexican war, and later he was one of the Senators of his State in the Federal Congress and Secretary of War under President Pierce. After the collapse of the Confederacy he made Beauvoir his most favored retreat and resting-place, and there, until he died, he received letters from the young college students of the South asking his advice as to their future courses in life, and visits alike from Northern and Southern folk, the one to make his acquaintance, the others to tender their sympathy and respect.

The way to Beauvoir lies either along the beach or through the woods; but I chose the forest road, that I might as many times as possible enjoy its wonderful order and neatness and beauty. The trees rise, at short distances apart, above the level clean sand, and there is nowhere a suggestion of impurity either upon the ground or in the clear sweet balsamic air. There is a constant suggestion of something cathedral-like in the regular uniform columns of the forest, the meetings of their limbs overhead, and the closing shallow vistas, as of naves, on every hand. The dwarf palmetto, or Spanish-bayonet, grows in little clumps or singly, as one would distribute it for ornament, and the very tropical long-leaf pines, leaping high in air before they put out a branch, and then spreading their tops like palms, are the chief denizens of these silent depths. Here and there are wet spots, it is true, and then the parklike character of the woods changes to a jungle, but a jungle so thick with gum, bay, magnolia, and other trees that one cannot see the dank water they shut in.

By the wood road the back of Beauvoir is first reached, and is found to be a tract of ten acres, devoted to the cultivation of the scuppernong grape. The vineyard is a scene of disorder and neglect. The rude arbors are rotting and falling upon the vines, and the young persimmon and pecan trees that have been set out there are endangered by the weeds that grow riotously, to exaggerate the suggestion of desolation. The mansion is around a bend of the road, commanding the dark blue Gulf, from behind ample grounds whose fence separates the place but does not hide its beauties from the white beach drive that skirts the water. The greatest storm in many years had torn up the road when I was there, and, worse yet, had played havoc with the splendid trees that beautified the noble estate. There are many giant live-oaks and a few hickories and cedars, but, alas! the ground was littered with the débris of their wreckage, and some were prone upon the earth—one of the dead being a splendid big hickory, which it would have been supposed no wind could maltreat. The gate was tied up, and the house was closed, so that had it been pointed out to me as a haunted house, abandoned by its owners, the scene presented there would have been exactly accounted for.

It has been a noble place, and could be made so again with little trouble and expense. No house that I have seen in the South is more eloquent of the full possibilities of the aristocratic baronial life of the planter before the war. To look upon it even now is to recall a thousand tales and anecdotes of the elegant life, the hospitality, and the comfort of the old régime. The main house is a great, square, low building, with a gallery on three sides, reached by a broad, high flight of steps. A great and beautiful door leads to a wide central hallway, through which one could see, when the house was open, either the blue Gulf and distant islands in front, or the great oaks with their funereal drapery of Spanish-moss in the rear. Two other similar but smaller houses stand, like heralds of the old hospitality, a little forward on either side of the mansion. Both are square, red-roofed, one-story miniatures of the manor-house. Each has its roof reaching out to form a broad porch in front. One is the bachelors' quarters, for guests and relatives

of that unhappy persuasion, and the other is Mr. Davis's
library and retreat. There everything is as he loved to
have it around him when he sat in-doors, and out on
the beach is the ruin and wreck of a seat under some
live-oaks where he used to sit and look upon the broad
water and reflect upon his extraordinary and most
active life. Behind these three buildings is the usual
array of out-buildings, such as every Southern mansion
collected in its shadow—the kitchen, the servants' quarters, the dairy, and the others.

IN THE LIBRARY AT BEAUVOIR

I went into the little library building and saw his
books, his pictures, his easy-chair and table, and—behind
the main room—his tiny bedroom and anteroom, the
bedroom being so small that it could accommodate no
larger bed than the mere cot which is shoved against
139

the window. His books would indicate that he was a religious man with a subordinate interest in history. In a closet he kept a remarkable collection of prayer-books, and in an open case were many volumes of novels, which the care-taker of the place called "trash," and accounted for with the explanation that Mr. Davis maintained a sort of circulating library for the use of his ex-Confederate soldier friends. The pictures that still hang upon the walls struck me as a strange collection. One shows some martyrs, dead, in a gladiatorial amphitheatre; one is of a drowned girl floating beneath a halo in a night-darkened stream; one is a portrait of our Saviour beside several madonnas; and only one is a military picture. Thither came constant visitors, for it was "the thing to do" in Biloxi—far too much so for the privacy and comfort of the family, I suspect; but it is recollected that Mr. Davis delighted in showing his library to all who called after twelve o'clock noon. The main house was seen only by those who had a claim upon his affections. I visited it and found it made up of noble rooms and decorated beautifully with fresco-work. But nearly all the furniture and ornaments and pictures were packed up or covered as if ready for removal. The effect upon my mind was sad and almost tragic, and I hastened from the widespread scene of havoc and of neglect, which even threatens the house itself. I learned enough to know that this does not reflect discredit upon the little family that was bereaved by the Southern leader's death, for the maintenance of the place would entail an expense which, if they were able to meet it, would still be an unwise disposition of their means.

It was with less pleasure that, on returning to Biloxi. I conjured up a picture of the old man threading the village streets, where every man who passed him lifted his hat, where all who had grievances stopped him to get his ready sympathy, and where those who had served him pressed his hand as they met him. It may be fitting, in view of everything that has passed, that Beauvoir should become a ruin, but hardly so soon as this.

I said so to the honest old German who is in charge of the place, and whom I found battling hopelessly with the tons of wreckage left by the last great storm. He shook his head, and it seemed to me that his eyes were moist.

"Were you a Confederate soldier?" I asked.

He turned upon me quickly.

"Of course I was," he said; "else I should not be here."

Every prospect from the shore about Biloxi includes at least one of the long low wooded islands in the glittering Gulf, and every look establishes a telegraphic communication by which the islands seem to say, "Come out to us; we will give you joy." On the mainland, too, the people urge you to accept the invitation. "They are different from the shore, and prettier," they say. Lucky are you if you yield to all these solicitations. They are jewels — emeralds studding the turquoise gulf. They are foreign. You feel, even though you have never been to the Sandwich Islands, that these are like them, and that you are in a new and unfamiliar but beautiful country. The mainland had seemed like a bit of ornament, of lace-work on the edge of our country, but these islands appear to be not of our country at all. They are Polynesian, if they are not Hawaiian. They are all long and narrow, sometimes eighteen miles long and only half a mile wide, and they are said to be crawling in the direction they point to—towards Mexico. It is said that the time was when they were joined to Florida, Alabama, and Mississippi, but the water cut them off, and now it keeps cutting away the landward ends and building out the farther points, so that they seem to be lazily moving to the tropics. I do not vouch for the story, but give it as I got it, because it accords with their foreignness to think of them as lazy, indolent travellers, seeking a climate more congenial than that with which fate first bound them.

Out on those islands the sand is as white as the whitest sugar, the water is as deep a blue as that of the Adriatic, and the sky is like the side of a lighted lantern of pale blue silk. The snow-white sand is continually shifting, changing its surface forms, travelling constantly, as if the progress of the islands was too slow for it. Thus it happens that you see towering white dunes of it which reach a knifelike edge into the water, and then rise gradually higher and higher in a soft white plane until they are forty feet high, and there they end abruptly, so that from behind they appear like towering smooth white walls. They bury the trees, of many sorts that you do not remember to have seen on shore, and their dead trunk ends and black bodies protrude here and there above or in the faces of the devouring white hills.

The water is apt to be as gentle and calm as it is blue, basking eternally in the brilliant sunlight. But when a breeze ruffles it billions of brilliant gems appear as its upturned points sparkle all over it. It is a piscatorial Eden, alive with fish. It is so clear that you may see them at their play and work, fishes of ever so many and ever such queer kinds. Great turtles are among them, and sharks and porpoises and gars, darting or hanging, as if they too had the Biloxi fever, above schools of sheep's-head and pompano, and I know not how many other sorts of creatures. You could not see them better if you were looking through the clear glass walls of a vast aquarium. You undress and plunge in to find the water just as you would order it if you could, a mere trifle cooler than the atmosphere, but ever so buoyant. You float and loll and lie about and dream in it, thanking the Creator that you are the veriest bit amphibious, and fancying yourself completely so.

There is little other animal life than what you bring on most of the islands. On some there are people enough to spoil them, but on others there may be only one shanty or a light-house, or no habitation at all, but grazing cattle here and there.

An unexpected feature of life in some of these little Gulf resorts is due to the number of sea-captains one is apt to meet at the hotels and in the streets. They put the little loafing-places in touch with a great deal more of the world than the railroads introduce there, for these generally jolly mariners come from Norway and Sweden and France and England, and even from more distant

A CORNER IN THE LIBRARY, BEAUVOIR

lands. The fact that you do not see their ships lends a little touch of mystery to their presence; but it is a short-lived mystery if you attack it with the first natural question, for then you learn that their vessels are lying within shelter of the islands off shore, loading with lumber. This lumber they swallow up in prodigious quantities. They do this in such a way as to suggest those people whom Munchausen found on an adjacent planet to this, who used to open a door in their stomachs and pop in food for several days when they were going off on a journey. Just so these lumbermen swallow sections of forests without having them cut up to go into their holds, by opening a door into their stomachs, in the shape of a great hole in each bow, into which the long tree-trunks are slid. We are apt to think of lumber and timber as products peculiar to Maine and Michigan, Minnesota and Washington, but every one of the Southern States is a grand storehouse of valuable timber, and none is greater than Mississippi.

That part of her territory which is covered by forests is just four times the size of Massachusetts—or more than twenty-one millions of acres. The reader wonders how that can be true of the king of the cotton States, since that royal rank implies a vast farming area. It is because Mississippi is larger than Pennsylvania by a thousand square miles, or nine times larger than Massachusetts. Her great agricultural development has been reached by denuding more than half of her surface of forests.

To understand this, and the State, it is necessary to remember that Mississippi is divided into three longitudinal belts: 1, the Delta strip, along the Mississippi River; 2, the hilly belt down the middle of the State; and 3, the so-called "prairies," on the side next to Alabama. The Delta soil is alluvial and very rich, and is

144

very productive, of cotton mainly. The hillock land, that which was until recently considered the very poorest land outside of the swamps, is now the source of great wealth, because here are grown the vegetables and small fruits whose introduction is revolutionizing and enriching the State. It is rich also because it is cultivated in small holdings by white labor and by economical methods. We better understand how such an influence affects a people when we reach the prairie belt, now the poorest part of the State, though its soil is black and vegetation planted there becomes luxuriant. It is farmed in large plantations like the Delta land, but it does not flourish because these are rented out and not kept up by their owners. Like the Irish landlords, they spend their money elsewhere instead of on their land, as the small holder does, in fertilizers, improvements, and repairs.

But while this division of the State is actual, the reader must now imagine all three of these belts covered by a vast virgin pine forest from the middle of the State to the Gulf. To be exact, let me say that this forest extends over nearly the whole area between Alabama on the east and the Illinois Central Railroad in the west, and between the Gulf and a line drawn across the State from the city of Meridian to the railroad I have mentioned. This forest region is about 90 miles wide and 180 miles long, and is in the main as beautiful as a park. Pine, gum, oak, and cottonwood are the trees, though on the Delta side cypress, ash, poplar, hickory, and gum are abundant. For fifty years or more this district has been "lumbered" wherever the logs could be floated down the many streams that all flow to the Gulf of Mexico, and yet it is said that but a tiny fraction of the valuable wood has been cut, and not even yet have the lumbermen been obliged to go to a distance from the streams. There are millions upon millions of feet of long-leaf pine in this region, while in the northern part of the State more than one-third as much short-leaf pine is standing.

In this great Southern district of forest a large amount of Western capital has been invested in lumbering, and of the men engaged in the pursuit fully one-half are from the West and the North. Immense tracts of this woodland are held untouched for the great rise

READING-ROOM IN THE LIBRARY, BEAUVOIR

in their value that must certainly follow the destruction of the timber resources of the Northwest. These Mississippi forest lands were public, government land, and the speculative corporations bought enormous tracts at prices that were sometimes as low as a dollar and a half an acre. This unjust and scandalous absorption by the wealthy of that which should have been held for the people and for the enrichment of the State aroused the indignation of those who watched it, and two or three years ago the people obtained Federal legislation, by which what remains of the land is saved for the possession of actual settlers exclusively. Less than half of it—possibly little more than a third—was thus preserved. That which is being cut is not only shipped to Europe, as I have described, but it also goes in great quantities to the West—to Chicago and intermediate points, and to St. Louis as the distributing-point for the farther West.

Down on the Gulf coast I had shown to me the tidy home and thrifty-looking farm of a man who was said to have walked into that section " with nothing in the world but a shirt, trousers, and boots"—the very sort of man that most of my Southern friends say that they don't want as a type of the new blood they aim for in their efforts towards attracting immigrants. But this man picked up a living somehow, as men of the stuff to emigrate are apt to do, and presently he had saved enough to buy a patch of woodland. Then he turned that into a farm, and has become a comfortable citizen, growing vegetables the year round, and demonstrating that a man with the will can establish himself in the South in the same way in which poor men have built up whole Western States, and with as great individual success, if not greater.

Among the places that I visited in Mississippi was Jackson, and there the condition of the old State House suggested the thought that perhaps the rebellious subjects of old King Cotton are more interested in the present day than in any part of their past. Like Beauvoir, it was a pitiful object of neglect. The old clock face on its front had turned into a great plate of rust, the unlooked-for statues of Bacchus and Venus in the once noble lobby beneath the dome now stand ridiculous in a scene of untidiness and slow decay. The Senate-Cham-

SLEEPING-ROOM IN THE LIBRARY, BEAUVOIR

ber has its roof upheld by rough trusses of raw wood, and the originally fine hall of the Assembly is ornamented with the advertisement of an insurance company, the faded banner of a lodge of Confederate veterans, hung awry on one side of the Speaker's chair, and a cheap portrait that dangles threateningly overhead.

The capital itself is a busy and a prosperous place, stirred by men of modern ideas and interests, who proudly show a visitor their rows of fine residences and two bustling business streets, their promising college, founded by a banker in the town who loves his fellow-men. And these leaders are fully alive to the revolution that is pushing the State into prosperity. The Governor's mansion, so strongly recalling the White House at

Washington, is one of the sights of the town, but to me nothing was so interesting as the continual movement of baled cotton through the streets, and the habit the people have of piling it up beside the Capitol, so that one sees the palace of the threatened king, neglected and in need of general repairing, rising above the mountain of the bales that typifies his throne.

Cotton-mills are not as numerous in the State as in the Carolinas and Georgia, and yet one—that at Wesson—is one of the finest in America. There is a yarn-mill at Water Valley, and there are mills for the making of unbleached cotton at Enterprise, near Meridian, and at Columbus. The Wesson cotton and woollen mills show so triumphantly what can be done in the South, as well as wherever enterprise determines to make success, that I wish to speak of them at length. They were founded in 1871, and have been so phenomenally successful as to give certain goods that bear their name an almost worldwide celebrity and rank—so successful as to increase the value of the stock ten dollars for one that has been invested in them. By the reinvestment of the dividends they have been brought to their present completeness and excellence. By constantly replacing old machinery with that which is newer and better they have been made as modern as if they were equipped yesterday. They manufacture all classes of cotton goods — cotton rope, rag carpet, twines, hosiery, jean, wool jeans, cassimeres, ladies' dress goods, and flannelette. They consist of three large brick buildings, equipped with electric lights, automatic sprinklers, and water-towers. The annual output of manufactured stuffs has been about a million and a half dollars' worth. The operatives number 1500, are natives of the State, and are all white. The commercial depression of 1893 caused a partial closing of the mills in August of that year, but the attitude of the owners towards their work-people is such that no misery followed. Winter fuel and house-rent free were given to all the operatives, and the heads of the families were kept employed in order that there should be money for necessaries for all. It did not surprise me in hearing this to learn further that there has never been a labor union nor a day of what is commonly known as "labor trouble" in Wesson. James S. Richardson, of the noted family of cotton-planters, is president of the mills, and the directors are W. W. Gordon, John Oliver, and R. L. Saunders.

But Mississippi has many good tidings of progress and of approaching liberation from the cruel thraldom of that product in which she once led the South. New farming industries and new uses for the land are forcing themselves upon the public as well as the local attention. The Illinois Central Railroad, with its quick and direct service, is fetching sturdy Western people into the State, and sometimes they are leading, sometimes copying the more ambitious natives in the movement away from the exclusive growing of cotton. In Madison, in the county of that name, the pioneer was Dr. H. E. McKay, the President of the State Horticultural Society. A dozen years ago he began experimenting with strawberries, and with such success that his little town of 100 inhabitants now ships as many as five car-loads of luscious berries daily during a season of from four to six weeks. He has 120 acres planted in strawberries, his brother, Dr. John McKay, has between 80 and 100, and their neighbors manage strawberry patches of from 15 to 80 acres each. It was a brand-new business a dozen years ago, and it had to be learned; but to-day all engaged in it are more than satisfied, and declare it to be far better than cotton-planting. I do not know whether the average Northern reader appreciates the importance

THE POTTERY OF BILOXI

of experiments and examples like this, but to me these steps towards assured wealth for the South—especially since I know how belated they have been, and how slowly they are taken even yet—are most interesting.

The Madison berries are the second to enter the market. The first are grown around Hammond, in Louisiana, where the farmers—in the same piny-woods soil that Mississippi's new trucking region consists of—began by raising early spring produce for the North. To-day they embrace their full opportunity down there in Louisiana, and actually ship produce every day, the year round. I will not print the necessary half-page list of what they grow, but it embraces all garden-truck, many small fruits, and much beside; and soon after cabbages are ready for shipment, in December, the next year's full round of incessant crops begins. But to return to Mississippi, where the same processes will eventually bring fortunes to great communities not yet established, let me add that thousands of fruit-trees have been planted on the strawberry farms, and some are beginning to yield. The people mean to put their eggs in more than one basket. They are going into trucking also.

At Crystal Springs, south of Jackson, on the Illinois Central Railroad, a few of those Western people whom that iron highway is bringing into Mississippi are co-operating with the natives in the raising of truck. Tomatoes, pease, cucumbers, and beans are the chief growths, and the town shipped as many as thirty car-loads of "table" tomatoes in one day of last June. In that month Crystal Springs earned and got $350,000, which came just as the cotton-planters needed money. The manner in which these new agricultural methods bring money into the State at all seasons is one of its advantages that is of more moment than we, who live nearer the financial centres, can easily imagine. Durant and Terry are other towns that are feeling this agricultural revolution.

The entire middle section of the State is becoming a great horse-raising region, and it is said that there are as many horses in Mississippi as in Kentucky. This,

SENATE-CHAMBER AT JACKSON

too, is the best hay section in the South, except the blue-grass region. Large quantities of hay are being shipped to New Orleans and to the Delta planters, who give up their lands to cotton. Bermuda and other grasses grow naturally there, but the lespedeza, or Japan clover, is the best. It mysteriously appeared after the close of the war. It had undoubtedly been brought there by the Northern soldiers. Its seeds blow everywhere, and it has spread marvellously far and fast. On the poorest hill land it grows tall enough to mow and bale. It is preferred to any other hay by the cattle, and it fetches ten dollars a ton. In the western part of the State, in Clay and Chickasaw counties, a large number of Northern people have gone into the horse business. They are mainly raising working stock, such as used to be brought in from Tennessee. The butter and milk dearth is ended in central Mississippi. A number of dairy farms have been established, and the keeping of cows is becoming general. Even on the poorest land and among the poorest farmers pork and beef are being raised to insure meat for the families, whether cotton fetches paying or losing prices.

It is thus that the South is forced to acknowledge that the original Plymouth plan is better than the Jamestown experiment. The Jamestown or Virginia idea was to grow nothing but tobacco, and then use it to buy everything else that was needed to support life. The Plymouth plan was to grow the necessaries of life and sell the surplus, if there was any. To-day, from the Norfolk (Virginia) truck farms to the truck farms of Louisiana, the South is paying tribute to the Yankee notion. She is prosperous wherever that is the case. She is otherwise wherever the Jamestown method still obtains.

To be thoroughly successful the Plymouth method required personal industry, on the part of the small farmer at least. They are finding this out also in Mississippi; but to a Northern man, who believes that "work elevates and ennobles the soul," it sounds very funny to hear the people apologizing for what they are doing. Mere farm-work is considered plebeian and vulgar, but they find "dairying and horticulture more refined." They say that men of education do not like to do with the plough and the stable, but that "you see gentlemen and their sons at work in the orchards and berry-fields, and around Crystal Springs you may see a hundred young ladies of good families at work packing fruit." That is great progress and a great concession for the South. So long as the people work they will thrive, and if they sugar their lives by calling fruit-farming by the name of "horticulture," it does not mat-

GOVERNOR'S MANSION AT JACKSON

ter so long as they acknowledge the truth of Poor Richard's maxim that

"He who by the Soil would Thrive
Must either hold the Plough or Drive."

The rule of the Jamestown plan is broken in Mississippi but not destroyed. The cotton-planters in the bottom lands own between 500 and 1500 or 2000 acres each. They farm out these plantations to the negroes.

Each negro gets a cabin, a mule, a plough, and a little garden-patch free, as the tools with which to work. He is to plant and pick fifteen acres of cotton, and is to receive half of what it brings. The cotton yields between half a bale and a bale per acre, and fetches just now $25 a bale. The negro needs the help of his wife and many children to pick it. At an average return of, say, ten bales of cotton to fifteen acres the negro gets $125 for his year's work. The cotton seed brings seven to ten dollars a ton, so that from the sale of that he gets $35 more. Some planters grow corn for market, and others allow the negroes to plant a good deal of corn to live upon. Unfortunately the rule with the negro is to sell his corn before Christmas at 50 cents a bushel, and buy it back in February at $1 25. The negroes deal with the local merchants, who are mainly Hebrews, on the credit plan. They are made to pay two prices, and the Jews limit them to what it is thought their crops will bring. These merchants add about fifty per cent. for the hazard of poor crops, death, losses by storms, and whatever.

The negro is holding the South back in this as in other respects. The small white farmer can adjust himself to circumstances. He can say that if cotton does not pay at this year's price of five cents a pound, he will raise more meat and corn for home consumption. He can also raise enough to feed what tenants he employs. But the negro affects the larger situation. He is not a landlord. He must rent the land he works, and the average planter needs him as much as the negro needs the land. But when the two meet, and the negro asks, "What are you going to pay me for working your land?" the planter can only reply, "Cotton," because corn won't sell in the first place, and in the second place the negro likes cotton, and understands the hand-

COTTON AND ITS CAPITOL, JACKSON, MISSISSIPPI

ling of it better than anything else that grows in the ground. Furthermore, to understand the situation fully, the reader needs to remember that there are a great many more negroes than whites in Mississippi.

The Illinois Central Railroad has come into a lot of rich land through the purchase of a railway nearer the great river than its main line, and it is bringing down a great many Western farmers, who do not go there for their health or for the sake of the scenery, but to make money. They are largely from Wisconsin, Illinois, and Iowa. They are going into horse-raising, dairying, trucking, fruit-growing, and whatever will pay best, and they will exert a tremendous influence for prosperity down there. But on the hilly land of the interior, where the railroad influence is not at the bottom of the immigration, a great many new-comers are seen to try cotton first. They hear that they can get land for from three dollars to ten dollars an acre, and that they can raise a bale on two acres, with a chance of getting $40 for the bale. It does not work. There is too much cotton. It brings only five or six cents a pound, and it has been observed that under eight cents the planters do not pay their way. Contrary to the Carolina experience, the bankers of Mississippi declare that cotton costs seven and a half cents a pound for the raising. And even then "it takes thirteen months in the year to raise it," as they say down there—meaning, of course, that before one year's crop is picked the planter must be preparing for the next. With land cheaper than dirt usually is, with taxes very low indeed, with a combination of soil and climate fitted for the growth of every product of the temperate zone, and many others besides, it is astonishing that the State does not fill with earnest, industrious bidders for the fortune that will so surely be theirs when they embrace the opportunity

The reader may say that there must be some important hinderance, but I know of none. The white people are law-abiding and hospitable, the climate is healthful, the heat is by no means unendurable or such as need deter

FORT MASSACHUSETTS, SHIP ISLAND, MISSISSIPPI

a Northern man from going there, and, indeed, Northern men have told me that the Northern midsummer heat is far more trying. The only problem is what to do with the negro after the white farmers come in, but that will not affect any white man who goes there to work for himself. The negro will have to learn to work as the white man does, or—but that is his concern.

V

OUR OWN RIVIERA

WE started from New Orleans to enter the Flowery State by its back door. In New Orleans the peach and pear trees were throwing sprays of delicate color across many a view, the street boys were peddling japonicas and garden roses, and in the woods near by the dogwood and the jasmine spangled the fresh greenery with their flowers. On our way to the cars we read a Signal Service bulletin announcing the temperature in New York to be 24°, while in New Orleans it was 70°. And in the evening newspaper was word that a party of well-nurtured hoodlums in a Connecticut college had snowballed an actress on the stage of the theatre in the college town. Such are the possibilities in a country of the magnitude of ours, and they made us glad that we were going even farther south.

The next day spied the train in Florida making its way through a tedious region of sand and pine and swamp and cypress. But the glorious eye of day was blazing upon the cars, so that it turned them into bake-ovens, and when the suffocating passengers opened the Pullman windows, in swept the fine, insinuating, choking dust of Florida in such clouds that I, who had started in black clothing in Louisiana, came into Florida looking like a miller. Indeed, I felt like that particular miller of the Dee about whom nobody acknowledged any concern. As is so often the case, the Pullman contained a passenger who talked to everybody in it, and rendered all other speech vain and unprofitable.

"I'm going to get off at Tallahassee," said he, "in order to drive over to Thomasville, Georgia. Better stop off with me — only pretty country and only unspoiled Southern town in Florida. Fact is, though Tallahassee is the capital of the State, it does not belong in Florida. Got pushed over the line by some convulsion of nature. Stop off, and you will not be sorry. The conductor will give you a stop-over check."

The neighborhood of Tallahassee, when it came into view, riveted our inclination to accept this semi-public advice. Plantations, inviting Southern country houses, dense banks of Cherokee roses in bloom, rolling land, a rich chocolate soil, great trees whose foliage formed clouds of green—these were the objects that took the places of the swamps, and of the monotonous vistas of slender pines struggling in sand. We stopped at Tallahassee, and in the main street of the picturesque and comatose old village we met that which attuned our souls for all that we were to enjoy in Florida—that set our thoughts in the right train. It was the regulation summer maiden of the North that we encountered. There she strode, in white kid shoes, with a white sailor hat on her head, ribboned with white satin. She was dressed otherwise in a blue sailor suit trimmed with white, above which appeared a pert face, all sun-dyed, beneath a mass of short and wavy nut-brown hair. She was so precisely like herself as we all saw her at Narragansett Pier in the previous September that it was almost possible to believe she had been walking on and on southward ever since, pursuing the summer like a songbird, or perhaps had stopped now and then to linger with it at Asheville, Charleston, Savannah, Thomasville, and finally there at Tallahassee. She paused and talked,

with many coquettish little graces, to a young gentleman who met her on the pavement. It required but a
little further play of fancy to imagine that he was urg-
ing her to attend some dance or reception, and that she
was saying, just as she used to say every day last autumn: "I'll go, but I can't dress, you know. One half
of my arms doesn't match the other half, and my face
and my neck are at odds; I'm so shockingly sunburnt,
you know." That vision of the summer maiden was all
that was needed for an introduction to Florida. The
magic of it shattered our touch with the old South. It
stood us face to face with the North a-holidaying, and
that makes the essence of life in what the hotel men delight to call "the American Riviera."

When my companion, Mr. Smedley, and I reached our
rooms in the cheerful hotel in the heart of the town, we
found awaiting us a great shallow dish of japonica, rose,
and violet blossoms. Having seen an even larger tray
of flowers in the office of the house, we inquired whence
they came, and found that they were sent by the ladies
of the town to the ladies of the hotel. This was not
only a pretty custom, and a positive proof that Florida
deserves its name, but it showed that for perhaps the
first time in our lives we were domiciled in a pleasure
resort wherein the people had not been demoralized by
so strong a desire for gain that all kindlier human im-
pulses were crowded out of their lives. This pleasant
belief was strengthened when we went into the town to
shop, and found the prices generally moderate. A horse
and carriage may be had, with a driver, for three dollars
a day, and in a comfortable vehicle we rolled through
the old town, noting, by its own hills and those around
it, that it was in a rich rolling country, and by its heavy
Grecian-looking town houses and its cool embowered
country houses that many relics of the time when it was

162

"SHE PAUSED AND TALKED, WITH MANY COQUETTISH LITTLE GRACES"

the seat of a wealthy aristocracy still remained. Of trees and flowers I never saw more or better in any country town even in England. The oaks, always the handsomest trees in the South, were here magnificent, and around them were mulberries, gum-trees, magnolias, palmettoes, figs, China-berries, pines, and many other sorts of trees. Great balls of mistletoe grew on lofty branches, banks of Cherokee roses blossomed by the road-sides, the door-yards were gay with old-fashioned flowers, and the gardens showed manifold rows of luxuriant peach and pear trees, as well as dried and faded banana-palms. Seeing the graves of the "Princess C. A. Murat," and of her husband, "Colonel Charles Louis Napoleon Achille Murat, son of the King of Naples," in the green and white graveyard, led us to drive out to what is called Prince Murat's house, on the outskirts of the town. It was little to see—a mere one-and-a-half-storied frame house with a sloping roof, exterior chimneys, and a broad porch. And the whole was falling into ruin, inhabited by a negro man and woman, and set in a garden wherein the weeds have all but choked the few ornamental plants and bushes which once graced the scene.

Upon returning to town I learned that in truth the prince lived in that house only a short time, though his widow, who survived him twenty years, made it her home. His true home in this country had been upon his plantation, a few miles from the capital. Poor man! his fame even in Tallahassee has degenerated into a recollection of his eccentricities, and he is remembered to have eaten crow, and to have tried to eat buzzard. It is also recalled that he once discovered a dye, and dyed all his wife's gowns before she reached home one day; also that he, for some reason, induced his slaves to eat cherry-tree sawdust, and was nearly the death of them all.

He deserves a far more dignified echo of his existence, for in his portrait on the walls of the town library he is seen to have been a man of intellectual and forceful mien, and in his book, or rather a collection of his letters made into a book, he writes himself down as a very observant and clear-headed man, reflective and broad, proud of citizenship in this country, and able to speak of himself seldom, and only with modesty. Writing in 1830-32, in the course of some remarks upon Washington, he includes a short study of the American girl of the period, one that will not now be considered far amiss. He notes that "parents seldom oppose their daughters in the choice of a husband; . . . moreover, the interference of parents is looked upon as an act of indiscretion in these matters. Nothing can be more happy than the lot of a young American lady from the age of fifteen to twenty-five, particularly if she possesses the attraction of beauty (which they generally do). She becomes the idol and admiration of all; her life is passed amid festivities and pleasure; she knows no contradiction to mar her inclinations, much less refusals. She has only to select from a hundred worshippers the one whom she considers will contribute to her future happiness in life—for here all marry, and, with of course some exceptions, all are happy."

Another note of even wider interest the prince makes in these words: "It is only a few years since that waltzing was proscribed in society, and only Scotch reels and quadrilles were danced. From the moment of its introduction, the waltz was looked upon as most indelicate, and, in fact, an outrage on female delicacy. Even preachers denounced in public the circumstance of a man who was neither lover nor husband encircling the waist and whirling the lady about in his arms, as a heinous sin and an abomination."

165

" Nobody can forget," writes the prince, " the arrival of the ballet corps in New York from Paris. I happened to be at the first representation. The appearance of dancers in short petticoats created an indescribable astonishment; but at the first 'pirouette,' when these appendages, charged with lead at the extremities, whirled round, taking a horizontal position, such a noise was created in the theatre that I question whether even the uproar at one of Musard's carnival 'bals infernals' at Paris could equal it. The ladies screamed out for very shame and left the theatre, and the gentlemen for the most part remained, crying and laughing at the very fun of the thing, while *they* only remarked its ridiculousness. They had yet to learn and admire and appreciate the gracefulness and voluptuous ease of a Taglioni, Cerito, and a Fanny Elssler."

The time I spent in Tallahassee I never shall regret. It is a pure and typical Southern capital, with very many landmarks and mementos of a proud past in full preservation. It is not like any other part of Florida, for, in fact, it is a great piece of Georgia soil and landscape, high, wholesome, picturesque, hospitable, and quaintly old-fashioned. The climate is as warm as any, except that of the southern end of the State, and yet the face of nature is more like what we in the North are accustomed to and consider beautiful.

The route from Tallahassee to Jacksonville is by way of pine-barrens and cypress swamps, and even in winter was found to be exceedingly hot and dusty, as all railway travel in the State is apt to be. So far as concerns whatever of settlement and civilization is seen, it is a country with the dry-rot. Everything that is in use seems patched up; the rest is tumbling to pieces. The fences are tinkered and gaping; the unpainted cabins are dilapidated, and patched with whatever was hand-

ON A HOTEL PORCH, TALLAHASSEE

iest when they needed repairing; the horses or mules
and oxen are hitched to weather-beaten ploughs with
bits of rope and chain. In a word, the people are lazy,
and, as they best express it in the South, "shiftless."

At Jacksonville, with the stopping of the train, we
were flung into the watering-place life of the dog-days

in the North. It was not merely the summer maiden that we found there—though her sort was abundant—but she moved amid nearly all her Northern concomitants and surroundings. Jacksonville might easily have been mistaken for Long Branch in July, with its great hotels illuminated from top to basement, its sounds of dance music in all the great parlors, and its array of long porches crowded with ease-taking men and women in flannels and tennis caps and russet slippers and gossamer gowns. We stopped at the well-managed Windsor Hotel, but it might have passed for the West End or the Howland, except that there were no sounds of a near-by heaving sea. The Jacksonville house exhibited the same bevy of young girls clustered before the clerk's desk — for all the world like those we saw at Asbury Park and Long Branch in midsummer—the same long, light-carpeted parlor, the apparently identical semicircle of scraping musicians half enclosing a piano, the same old ladies and plain girls in the glare of light on the porches, while the prettiest girls were all in the darker corners and places. There were the same laughter and chatter, and rollicking semi-grown children; the same aimless but happy couples keeping slow-measured tread on the pavements; the frames of staring photographs, the nickel-in-the-slot machines, the shops full of gimcrack souvenirs made in Germany and New York, the peanuts and soda-water, the odor of perfumery, the rustle of silks, the peeping slippers—the very same; all the same.

And in the morning the chief attraction of Florida made itself felt as it had not done before. It was the heat of summer in Lent, the warm sun which blazed in the bedroom windows and roused at least one sleeper with that close, confined, sticky feeling that we all know too well in July. It was too cool on the piazzas, for that tropical condition obtains there which produces a breeze that may not be felt in the sun, and yet is almost chilly in the shade. In that warmth, wholly apart from any attractions of scene or sport, is the secret of the peopling of Florida by Northerners in the winter months, of the transformation of one of the United States into a pleasure-park and loafing-place during three months of each year. The official records show that during those months the mean temperature varies, in the different parts of the State, between 56° and 70° Fahrenheit. There is not, I am assured, any part of the State which is absolutely exempt from frost, but it is an unfamiliar visitor, and with the general warmth comes a royal proportion of clear days — a general average of twenty-four fine days in each month between December and May in all parts of the State. In March the average is about twenty-seven days, and in April twenty-six. I held the common impression that the State was resorted to as a sanitarium; but when, after several days in Tallahassee and Jacksonville, I had seen but few persons who had the appearance of being victims of any lung disease, I altered my opinion. It was the resort of invalids for many years. it seems, but those who spent their winters there now go to the so-called piny-woods and mountain resorts of Georgia and the Carolinas.

Florida has become a resting-place for those who can afford to loaf at the busiest time in the year—the men who have "made their piles," or organized their business to run automatically. As a rule, they are beyond the middle age and of comfortable figures. It is within the mark to say that each of these men brings two women with him—his wife and a daughter, or a sister or a niece. I frequently counted the persons around me at the hotels in the larger resorts, and never once found as many men as women; there were more often three than two women to a man. Of young men who should be at work, and boys and girls who should be at school, there were few to be seen. In some places, as in the big hotels at St. Augustine, it struck me that the young women must find it rather dull where young men were so few.

If what is said of the present frequenters of Florida creates the impression that it is only the rich who form the winter colony, it is necessary to add that this is not the case. In all the large towns there are many hotels in which board can be had for two dollars a day, and in almost all the towns there are hotels and boarding-houses that are frequented by those who pay only eight or ten dollars a week. An unexpected peculiarity of the great watering - place is that it is growing to be more and more the custom for the winter visitors to spend a large part of their time in travelling. Few miss the great Alameda group of palatial hotels in the quaint old village of St. Augustine; many cross the State to the very promising port of Tampa, with its superb hotel; others travel the erratic and the scenic rivers, visit the phosphate district, the tarpon grounds, the almost tropical section at Lake Worth, and as many as they care to of the four or five score settlements and resorts of more or less note that lie along these routes. This is the thing to do in Florida, although my experience in buying railway tickets in that State led me to regard it as a practice calculated to humble the rich more speedily than any anarchist plan of which I had ever heard.

Jacksonville is the busiest place in Florida, and the starting - point for most tours. Nearly all comers by rail or ship from the North pay toll to it. From the porch of the Windsor they see the first orange - trees: in the streets they hear a whole choir of caged mocking-

"WHILE THE PRETTIEST GIRLS WERE ALL IN THE DARKER
CORNERS"

birds; palmettoes, bananas, and a wealth of flowers em-
bellish many of the views about town; and the lazy,
luxurious holiday life at the almost always crowded
hotels sounds the key-note of the general spirit of the
winter population. The main street is fit to be called
Alligator Avenue, because of the myriad ways in which
that animal is offered as a sacrifice to the curiosity and
thoughtlessness of the crowds. I did not happen to see
any alligators served on toast there, but I saw them
stuffed and skinned, turned into bags, or kept in tanks
and boxes and cages; their babies made into ornaments
or on sale as toys; their claws used as purses, their teeth
as jewelry, their eggs as curios. Figures of them were
carved on canes, moulded on souvenir spoons, painted on
china, and sold in the forms of photographs, water-color
studies, breastpins, and carvings. I could not, for the
life of me, help thinking of the fate of the buffalo every
time I walked that street.

The true Southern negro abounds in the city, and is
a never-ceasing source of amusement and interest.
Among them all not any are more peculiar than the
hackmen, who drive slowly up and down before the
hotels, calling out to the boarders. "I'd just as lieve
drive you as Vanderbilt," said one. "Dere ain't no
bars put up agin any one what can pay de price."
Then the next one halts his team and says, in a general
public address directed to no one in particular: "Lend
me a dime, an' I'll pay you back or sing you a song. I
know lots of songs, and when I open my mouth you'll
think I either got music or delirium tremens." The
market also is very interesting. It slightly suggests a
corner in some old French city. The display of fish,
vegetables, and fruit is both gorgeous and appetizing.
On the market wharf the tourist may see a policeman
in a New York uniform, a ferry-boat from New York

crossing the river, and a New York river boat lying at a neighboring pier.

In a glance at the principal tours of the winter visitors to Florida the short one to St. Augustine must be considered first. The great Capitol at Washington, the State Capitol at Albany, and the Equitable Building in New York are the most costly houses in America. These were the subjects of a far greater outlay than the Flagler group of St. Augustine hotels, but their cost is not uppermost in the minds of those who spend much time in them. I know of no place, public or private, where the power of wealth so impresses itself upon the mind as at this group of Florida hotels. It is not because the owner's constant presence brings millions to the mind, or that he is known to have made his own way, and is said to have brought his dinner to his office with him every day until he was worth a million. It is the spot itself—the finding of a group of palaces in such strong contrast with all the rest in Florida. It is the change from a field where the other charms are all natural to a mass of beauties that are made by hand. To live in the Ponce de Leon is as if we had been invited to stop at a royal palace. It is as if a modern Haroun-al-Raschid, in order the better to study his people, had turned his royal residence into a hotel. And, after all, that would be but little more unexpected than that a many-millionaire should use his means in this way. It is said of the proprietor (than whom there is no more unassuming boarder in the building) that the reading which most impressed him in his youth was tales of Spanish affluence and history and adventure. When the day came that he could build a great structure, the Spanish types were the only ones that were in his mind. Upon the first crude idea of constructing something that should celebrate the beauties of Spanish

173

architecture grew the plan for a hotel. The after-thought became the prime impulse, and was allowed its way.

It is said that a famous writer remarked that he had not the ability to describe the Ponce de Leon and its out-look upon the luxurious court and park, and opposing Cordova and Alcazar hotels. I see here no excuse for trying a hand upon it at this late day. It is its general effect, rather than its details, that charms the beholder, and that effect can be expressed in a sentence—it is a melody or a poem in gray and red and green. The pearl-gray walls of shell-stone lift their cool sides be-tween billows of foliage and masses of bright red tiling. The graceful towers, quaint dormer-windows, airy log-gias, and jewel-like settings of stained glass, like the palms and the fountains and galleries, all melt, unnoted, into the main effect. It is all too fine for some persons, too dear for others, too artificial for others, and for an-other class not sufficiently restful. Many find the life there too closely like what they left behind in New York, or they see there the same club and business friends from whom they wish to get away. Al-Raschid could not please every one if he gave away his wealth and sceptre, and even his clothes. I was so perfectly content and thoroughly fascinated in the week I lived there that the place seemed all-sufficient. Yet when I went to another resort, and saw a green and white coun-try hotel in a shady grove beside a cool river, and ob-served the men and women in the refreshing undress of flannels and soft hats, I confess that my heart went out to the old, old joy of country rest and quiet and uncon-cern.

But, for a time, it was pleasant to elbow the rich and watch the fashionable, to see the gowns and turnouts, to hear the small talk, and now and then to have a *tête-à-*

ON THE PIAZZA OF THE WINDSOR HOTEL, JACKSONVILLE

tête with a dressy woman, and to find that she could re-peat the pretty prattlings of her babe recorded in the last of a grandma's letters; or to sit with a very wealthy man, as I did, and hear him exclaim : "Don't lay any stress on wealth; there's nothing in it. I have it, and I tell you I would rather have a college education and enough to live in plain comfort than to hold on to my millions. I only give away my surplus. All the world seems banded to get it away from me, and it does me little good. Give your boys an education; you will be kinder than if you gave them riches."

This was an unlooked-for note to be sounded in a house where a woman and her lady friend and maid were pay-ing $39 a day for rooms and meals; where an Astor and his bride had paid the same sum per day during a week of their honey-moon ; where one lady took a room solely for her trunks at $10 a day; and where an eco-nomical young woman told me that she was filling her mother's closets and her own with dresses, while the mother put her things on the chairs. " Mamma has had her day, you know," said the maiden, "and she doesn't care."

There was one little party that occupied three bed-rooms, a bath-room, and a parlor, taking up a whole corner of the house on the ground-floor, whose bill at the hotel might easily have been $75 a day. And in all these instances the extras are lost sight of—the $5 to the head waiter, the $2 or $3 a week to the waiter at table, the fees to the bell-boys and the ice-water boy and bootblack. I noted, though, that these minor expenses are variously met. In modest Jacksonville I saw a man meet them cheaply, and yet with a flourish. He was leaving. " How many boys are there here ?" he asked. " Nine, sir." " Then call them all up—all of them," said the man, and he handed to each one a dime. It was done so that it seemed as if he might be giving double eagles instead of dimes. I doubt whether the High Chief Almoner of England hands out shillings in the Queen's name to poor old women with more of an air. Then, again, I was in one hotel in Florida where a rich man brought his own wines, and actually sent his own coffee into the kitchen to be brewed. And in yet another hotel I was asked to swell a purse that was being raised for the cook. But, despite all this, a modest and contented man may live in Florida, and even hobnob with millionaires at the Ponce de Leon, upon $5 per diem.

Out in the fairylike court of that most beautiful hotel, where the lights in the windows met the lights littered on the ground beneath the greenery, I heard a gentleman and maiden approach and meet and actually solve the problem of the perpetual summer girl's existence.

"We came down to Old Point Comfort after leaving Newport," said she, "and then we went to Asheville. Then we were at New Orleans on *mardi gras*."

"And when do you ever go home?" the man inquired.

"Oh," said the girl, in surprise, "why, we always spend Christmas at home."

There was also a rich mother who, talking in the presence of her daughter, said to me that she held very old-fashioned notions about young girls. "I still believe in love," said she. "I think a girl should marry only for love, and that she had better choose an ambitious, promising young man with success ahead of him than mere wealth with an elderly man or a brainless money-bag. Such marriages are the most unhappy ones. Ah, me! I am sure if I were a young girl I could be happy in a tiny house in a village if I were with the choice of my heart."

The daughter listened stiffly at first. Then her face beamed, and a ripple of laughter escaped her.

"Mamma," said she, "your love-in-a-cottage ideas are out of style. I am thoroughly modern—up to date—*fin de siècle.* Your notions are pretty, but *they don't go.*"

Then the maiden turned to me, as being one who could sympathize with her, she thought, and said: "I want to live in one of the world's capitals, where they have grand opera, and miles of swell carriages, and a distinguished society, and—and—where something happens every night. I am dreadfully miserable when there's nothing going on. Mamma, do you remember the night in Vienna last winter when we neither of us knew what on earth to do?"

To sum up the impression St. Augustine made upon me, it seems that nearly every taste may be gratified there. The quaint old city, with some streets that are too narrow for pavements, and a score of ancient houses that would be notable anywhere else, is in itself a joy. The fishing is good; the sailing on the almost constantly sunlit, ever-breezy river is better. The driving and horseback rides are pleasant; there are country walks and orange groves. The old fort is never less than picturesque, and it is prized by lovers almost above a certain leafy terrace at West Point. There are tennis and bathing and shopping. Concerts and dances and exhibitions are frequent. All these and more are for the active. For the indolent and idle there are the loggias and the lobbies of the big hotels, with music every evening, and a grand panorama of life all the time.

Whoever likes all this can have it over again, with some new conditions, at Tampa, where Mr. H. B. Plant, the express and steamship operator, maintains another grand and enormous hotel — Moorish in design in this instance. Its beautiful and often historic furniture, fine pictures, gay crowds, very notable table, excellent music, and Gulf-side views make it easily the second of the

LAKE WORTH

leading resorts of Florida. Here, too, nature is adorned by artistic gardening, and the hours may be spent in riding, dancing, fishing, boating, and loafing. "The Inn," above the water, on a grand pier that is at once the terminus of a railway and steamship line, is not too far distant to be easily reached, and visitors there enjoy fine fishing, good fare, music, and delightful air and views. The town of Tampa, across the river from the great hotel, should be visited, not only because it is a historic spot and the seat of a notable cigar industry, but because it is predicted that it will become a great port for the shipment of the future phosphate yield and of those other products of the State which seem promising.

A very pleasant journey which no Florida tourist should miss is that up the St. Johns River by boat from Jacksonville to Sanford. The steamer *City of Jacksonville* and her capain, William A. Shaw, are among the very best of their kinds, and whosoever accompanies them will find by the time the pretty part of the river is reached, above Palatka, the passengers will have been brought together into something like a family circle, on good terms with one another, and with the captain as the recognized head and well-spring of constant entertainment. He is a salt-water sailor, and has often taken his frail-looking but really stanch boat to New York and back upon the ocean. The recollection of these venturesome deep-water journeys lingers upon the steamboat in the uniform of the master, the ringing of a ship's bell to note the passing hours, and in the maintenance of a captain's table in the dining-hall, whereat the prettiest ladies and the most distinguished men find places. Far from carrying a trumpet through which to bellow his orders, Captain Shaw adopts what I may call a confidential course with his subordinates.

The two black pilots, working together at the wheel like double song-and-dance men, leave the windows of their house open to catch his softest tones, and soft tones are all they ever get, even when he swears at them. "Stop port," he says, lightly, over his shoulder. "Back port. Start both engines. Hook her up. Stop both." It is the perfect way of managing a business, and one gathers the thought that if his boat were in a hurricane at sea, the passengers would never hear any other tone in the captain's voice than that in which he asks the nearest lady to him at his table whether she will not help herself to the celery.

The one apparent purpose of all who journey by boat to Florida is to see alligators, and to keep account of the number they have seen, as desperate Indians in yellow-covered books tote up the sum of the scalps they have lifted. At first the St. Johns River is of the broad type of Floridian streams—a wide expanse of fretted blue walled in tamely with banks of low vegetation. There are only two types, that and the tortuous narrow sort, running like leafy lanes in cramped ribbons, hedged close by trees. It is when the St. Johns is compressed and squeezed until it wriggles like a landed eel that the search for 'gators begins. I had never seen a wild alligator at large when I made the voyage, and, to tell the truth, I had seen so many others like me, and such signs of a general slaughter of the saurians, their babies, and even their eggs, that I fancied I might leave Florida with the luck of one who goes to Dakota to get a shot at a buffalo. But I was wrong. Not all the alligators are killed yet, though that consummation is not far off in the older parts of Florida. When we came to the narrow end of the river we saw plenty of the amphibians, and discovered also that they are apparently the only things that induce the captain

181

to raise his voice and to betray an inward excitement.

"Alligator on the left bank! Quick!" he shouted to all the passengers. "Alligator—big one—on the left bank, close ahead!"

Sure enough, there was the huge lizard-like animal upon the low bank, between the water and the trees, where he had been basking until the approach of the boat aroused him. Already, with a snakish motion, he was moving towards the river, his head sweeping in one direction, and his thick strong tail in the other. There was time to see that he was ten feet long, and to wonder how the captain detected a thing so nearly the color of the earth it rested upon, when, with a graceful giant wriggle, the beast slipped into the river and showed us only a black snout and two bumplike eyes rippling the surface of the stream.

There were some persons among the passengers who all but raved with delight over the beauty of the scenery in the narrow part of the river. Pretty it is, but not extremely beautiful, and the extravagant expressions of those who find extreme beauty where others see only tameness, or, at the utmost, mere prettiness, inspire compassion for all who live where nature is ill-favored or tedious, as on the plains, for instance. The St. Johns was here a pretty winding stream, curving amid more or less dense growths of oak, cypress, and palmetto. Spanish-moss hung its greenish-gray tails upon many of the trees, and augmented the strangeness of the scenery; for strange it would seem to any American from beyond the few States that border the Gulf of Mexico. It got its prettiness from the fresh new green that nature was lavishing upon the trees and the undergrowth. So narrow was the stream that the boat was seen to push the water ahead of it, and to suck a great billow

PRESIDENT CLEVELAND RECEIVING

DANCE AT THE PONCE DE LEON

along behind it — a billow that crashed upon the low banks and hurried the cows ashore, the buzzards to flight, and the turtles and alligators off their resting-places. The experience suggested steamboating on some crooked narrow route like Pearl Street in New York ; but sometimes the loops in the stream were so sharp that steamers making the same course appeared to be, and were, going in opposite directions. The turtles were amusing. Sometimes half a dozen would drop from a projecting log to fall upon their backs and scramble wildly into correct positions. Lazy and beautiful cranes were seen at times, and the boat passed many buzzard roosts, where the great ugly birds were seen stalking awkwardly on the earth, or roosting like turkeys on the tree limbs. I saw eleven alligators, many of them very large. One favored me with an exhibition of his pedestrianism by turning into the woods instead of the water. It was worth seeing. He lifted his head and six-sevenths of his tail above the ground upon ungainly legs that stood out from his body almost like a spider's limbs. Then he walked as if he had not learned how. The customary man with a gun, and with a general and all-embracing ambition to murder something, had come upon the boat to kill an alligator. This he was forbidden to do, and I think I am right in saying that from no steamboat running in Florida is shooting now permitted. The captain explained why this was when he said, "If passengers were allowed to shoot, they would be apt to alarm or anger the people ashore, and some of the crackers would be sure to turn and send a fusillade of buckshot into the boat." Those who have followed my experiences in other parts of the South will be interested in this further proof of the fact that steamboating there is not unlike managing a travelling target for buckshot.

184

I have spoken elsewhere of the black laborers on the Southern boats, and have put stress upon the fact that I never saw white men work as hard as these negroes do, urged constantly as they are by the white mates of the vessels. But the labor I saw performed on the Mississippi and on the bayous in Louisiana was feeble beside that which was obtained from the crew on this St. Johns River steamboat. The negroes on this boat were very much superior to the dull-eyed, shambling, and stolid hands of the other Southern States. These were comparatively fine fellows, full of ambition and energy, with intelligence quickening in their faces, well clad, and, I think, less given to demoralizing holiday habits than the others. I never saw any men work so hard. They moved the freight on those heavy small-wheeled trucks that are in use at all railway stations, and they literally flung these vehicles and themselves up and down the steep gang-planks at each landing. They never walked. They ran, whether they were going loaded or returning light. They slid down the gang-planks like men on an ice slide, and they bounced up the sharp incline with such force that it seemed a miracle that saved the heavy trucks from breaking apart. The hollow iron hull of the steamer roared like a drum as these men raced their loads over the deck, not merely for a few minutes, but sometimes for an hour, or for hours, at a time. Perspiration shot from the men's faces, and their half-bared breasts shone with moisture. Their pride in their strength and quickness was manifest; with grinning faces and sparkling eyes they kept up the tension of their utmost effort. To be sure, trunks flew about like cannon-balls now and then, men fell down, and trucks were let fly like battering-rams, but the double line of racing, straining laborers, coming and going at full speed, was never broken while there was freight to move. If there are white men of the laboring kind who can be hired to work as these negroes do, I can only say that I shall not believe it until I see them. In the truer Southern States (for the motive spirit in Florida is imported from the North) I digested the axiom that "a negro and a mule work better than a white man and a horse if they are pushed," but in Florida I improved the saying by leaving out the mule, and entering this note in my book: "The negro laborer is at least as good as a white man if managed wisely." I suspect that if I were to spend another season in the South I would recommend that all the present steamboat mates be discharged, and that gentler men be put in their places. The very qualities that cause them to be chosen to superintend black labor appear to me to be the ones that limit the result of that labor. I am wrong, in all probability, because the South knows the negro, and, in his place, admires him. He in turn loves the South and his relation to it. Nevertheless, in Florida I saw the best work done, and there the typical mate and his methods were replaced by plain business principles reared upon a basis of kindliness.

The return trip on the St. Johns brings the tourist through some pleasing parts of the river at night; but not all of its beauties are lost, for the boat carries a powerful electric search-light, whose glare is often thrown upon the shores. One becomes familiar with these powerful lights after a little travelling on the Southern rivers, but it is difficult to conceive that any one ever could tire of their weird and splendid effect upon nature. Now it is an orange grove of softly rounded trees that is thrown before the vision as on a stage canvas; now a pretty villa is materialized out of the darkness, a green and white cottage, upon whose porch men and women are surprised as they woo the

IN THE GARDENS FACING THE PONCE DE LEON

cooling, calm night; anon a dense and tangled cypress swamp, whose tree limbs bear startled turkeys instead of vegetable fruit, leaps into the cold white light; and at another time a village wharf is thrown upon the black curtain of the night. The knots of men and women, the yellow lights, the sentimental pairs in nooks that had been shaded from the lamp-lights, the drowsy negroes prone upon the boards, the white sheds, and the leafy background of the village trees — all flash into sharp definition, such as daylight could not augment. As illustrating the companionship which grows up between the captain and the passengers, I made a note of this bit of dialogue, that sounded upon the darkness aboard the boat while the captain was flashing the search-light here and there for our edification:

"Now," said he, "we are hugging the other shore quite close. I'll light it up and show you."

"Oh, captain!" said a lady, "don't — if it's being hugged."

But the most instructive result of unconscious eavesdropping on that voyage was a snatch of conversation between a woman and her husband earlier in the day:

"I wish we could go ashore at Palatka," said the wife, "to get some cakes or pie, and figs and dates."

"Why! The meals are good on the boat."

"Oh, I hate steamboat eating; it's worse than hotel food. I'm getting really sick. Just cakes or pie 'll do me now."

"It's curious," said the husband, as if announcing the result of much reflection. "When folks has been away from home about so long, their stummicks gets out of order, and nothing 'll do 'em but plain home cooking. That's the way it is with me, anyhow. I want to go home soon as I kin—don't you? They must be a bak-
188

ery at some of these here towns. Let's get off and see what we kin git."

The Ocklawaha trip is, next to a stop in St. Augustine, the chief sensational feature of a tour of Florida, if one may rate the attractions of the region according as one hears them talked about by those who are " doing " the State. The Ocklawaha is oftenest spoken of as the crookedest river in the State, but it is in reality merely the narrowest of the many very crooked rivers upon which one may travel by steamboat. Crooked rivers twisting between scalloped banks of verdure are far too numerous for it to be lightly said which bears off the palm for this sort of eccentricity, and these streams are so nearly alike that whoever makes a trip upon one or two of them may properly flatter himself that he knows about them all. However, the Ocklawaha experience is by far the most peculiar, because on that stream the little steamers are actually raked by the branches of the trees, because the part of the journey made in the night-time is illuminated in an old-fashioned way by bonfire-light, and because the trip begins (or ends) at Silver Spring, with a view of a mysterious and beautiful freak of nature in the form of a full-fledged river bursting out of the earth.

The tourist attends the perpetual birth of a river of crystal-clear water, coming no one knows whence, and purged in the journey. Some persons have thrown old cans and bits of tin into the translucent depths of this strange fountain, and these glisten and gleam and take on the appearance of silver and of mother-of-pearl as one looks down upon them from above. If it is true that here De Soto fancied he had found the fabled fountain of youth, it will remain a matter of eternal regret that he did not see those old cans and bits of tin, for they not only emphasize the clearness of the water, but are the chief objects of interest and observation in the locality. The water has a bluish tinge, as pale as the tone of a Montana sapphire, and in its depths the tourists see its denizens pursuing their daily task of running away from the boats that affright them. Turtles and gar - fish, trout, and other swimmers are thus observed as one seldom has a chance to see them outside of an aquarium.

The Ocklawaha is met at the end of a nine-mile run through this avenue of liquid sapphire, and since I could not by any effort describe its attractions so well as I heard them set forth by a rustic Western man on the Windsor hotel porch in Jacksonville, I will repeat what he said : "It's a leetle the derndest river I ever saw," he began. "It winds and twists and curves and turns like nothing else in the world, and when you've been all over it, from Palatky to Silver Springs, and have been travelling a daytime and a night-time, you take the cars and go back to where you started from with a ride of fifty mile. The fare is seven dollars one way and five dollars to come back, but there ain't no way of taking the five - dollar ride first, and then skipping the rest. They give you good eating — strawberries and short-cake—oh, my! it ain't bad, I tell you. You get three meals on the trip. There's only room for thirty passengers, so you better start at Palatky, and be sure and get a berth, else mebbe you won't get no place to sleep. But the boats ain't so dern little neither. They're big enough to choke up the river, I'm a-tellin' you. Many's the time the boat rubs up agin the bank, and the branches of the trees come slatting along the sides, and a-breaking the windows, and a-littering the whole concern with broken branches. If you are lookin' out, you won't see no place for the boat to go, the curves is so sudden.

"Well, I'll tell you just how she twists. The two

190

A BIT OF THE COURT-YARD OF THE PONCE DE LEON

boats meets at about seven o'clock. Well, seven o'clock come, an' there we was; so the capt'n begin to toot his whistle for the other boat. By that time we was lighting our way with a big iron vessel full of blazing pine knots atop of the pilot-house, which has an iron roof, so's not to catch fire. But, between you and me, you'd think she was afire, and that the whole forest was afire also, or going to be every minute—that there pitch-pine does make such a dernation blaze. And it's ghostlike, too; sending the light fur an' wide, and blazing up the whole surroundings light as day, with black shadows a-dancin' wherever you set your eyes. It's worth seein', now, I'm a-tellin' you. Well, the capt'n he was a-tootin' his whistle, and there was the woods just howlin' with the ache-o of the noise. Pretty soon we heard the other boat whistle, and we just had to hunt a hole lively for to let her pass. You see the river ain't more than twenty-five feet wide some places — 'tain't wider than one boat — leastwise, it only spares six inches at one spot. Well, we found a dent in the woods, and we tucked in an' tied up to a tree and waited. Pretty soon I seen the other boat a-sloshin' up to us. I could see her through the trees, and I'll swear she warn't more'n two or three rod off by land. Well, sir, she must have been that many mile off by water, for it was a good sixteen minutes before she come splashin' by us. I never see nothing like it in my life."

The most extended vibration of the restless mass of winter travellers in Florida is up and down the Indian River. The starting-point for this journey is Ormond, on the Halifax, and in all Florida I saw nothing more picturesque or alluring than the hotel and its surroundings at that place. Going from St. Augustine, the major part of the short journey is through the usual hot, dusty, and monotonous pine-barrens, which make travelling by train in Florida almost unendurable. A few notable orange groves displaying fruit and flower side by side, and weighting the atmosphere with a heavy but delicious odor, give a quarter of an hour's relief at the outset. But ten minutes before Ormond is reached the scenery changes with startling suddenness, and the piny woods end and the palmetto groves begin, as if nature had drawn an invisible and narrow line between the temperate and the tropic zones at right angles across the railroad track. Strange rather than beautiful is the sight of these unfamiliar trees; and the traveller, as he looks out upon them, is apt to think again, as he so often has occasion to do in the Floral State, that beyond its chief charm of unapt warm weather the allurements of the State to the average visitor from the rest of the Union consist in the novelty of his surroundings far more than in any other charms it possesses. These palmettoes scarcely can be said to grace any view, but they render many a vista interesting by their peculiarity. They save themselves from utter tediousness by having some of their trunks bent into serpentine curves, while others remain thatched with the pretty patterning made by the joints of former and lower branches. The trees themselves are ugly because they are ill-fashioned. Their tops are too small for their trunks, and make them look like exaggerated mops—or as a broomstick would look with a woman's bonnet on top of it. Artists often greatly improve upon nature in their pictures of palmettoes by drawing them with noble umbrageous tops, such as the finer varieties of the palm, not seen in our country, possess.

The crackers call the remnants of old branches of former years "boot-jacks," and have a still more surprising name for the palmettoes themselves. When I was at the Ormond I heard a Floridian praising the artistic work of a remarkable New England woman who was the house-keeper of the hotel, and who freshly decorated the public rooms and porches of the great house every morning. "She puts a cabbage-leaf on the ceiling, or sprays of fern on the sash curtains, or a cabbage-leaf on a wall — and the effect is splendid," said he. I innocently ventured the remark that I had never considered a cabbage as a decorative subject; and the cracker replied, with a laugh: "Ah! I forgot; you don't understand. 'Cabbage' is what we call the palmetto down here."

But to return. Suddenly the pine-barrens end, and the tourist sees regiments of palmettoes, or thickly massed platoons of them, guarding swampy hammocks of cypress and oak bearded with moss. Then just as unexpectedly the landscape breaks and the Halifax River appears — a wide blue arm of the sea, at whose edges the advancing forests have halted. A white bridge spans the noble sheet of water, and at its farther end is seen the Ormond, whose flags and towers and galleries peep out above and between the thick foliage that forms its shady and picturesque retreat. It is well worth a visit, not only because it is well kept, and continually filled with a lively and select company, but because it is the seat of a New England colony in the heart of Florida. One of the proprietors, nearly all the employés, and many of the boarders are of those who regard Boston as the seat of learning and the hub of progress. The waiter-girls in the dining-room support an air which begets the suspicion that after the tables are cleared they retire to their chambers to enjoy an hour with Browning, or, at least, to catch up with their Chautauquan obligations. The possibility that any of them were among the shadowy couples I met on the moonlit road to the sea-beach back of the hotel is a thought of which I was ashamed when it occurred. Those couples! What a sanctuary for Cupid's victims is that white sand road to the ocean at Ormond! Ahead of me that night I saw a swaying line of bodies, each of which appeared like one absurdly thick personage. When my footfall sounded near one of these forms it would slowly separate into two distinct objects, between whose shapes the night light shone broadly; and then, if I turned and looked back (guiltily), I saw a pair of arms appear, contrariwise, and cross and draw together, and the two figures melted into one again, as if in anticipation of that composite blending of individualities which nature's law ordains in a certain blissful state. But there was scant time on that dim road to pursue even so pretty a thought. In another hundred yards I came upon another composite, and turned it into two—though still with but the single thought that I could not hurry by too quickly to please them.

It was quite appropriate in a typical New England colony to find some such novelty as a perpetually heated urn of hot water in the hotel office for the use of those with whom what one of the guests called "the hot-water craze" is not yet grown cool. It was not due to New England influence, though, that the resources of the hotel were strained in providing sufficient men to take part in two sets of the Lancers. The feat would not be attempted in many Floridian resorts. When I took my first meal at the Ormond I counted fifty-one women and sixteen men around me at the tables—rather an undue proportion of males, I thought. The fishing is profitable there, and weak-fish, sheepshead, channel-bass, cavaillé, and other fishes are plentiful, the weak-fish being of a temper to take either fly or minnow bait, and the sport remaining active by night as well as day. Much of the region around Ormond was once cut up into great plantations, but the Seminole war caused their abandonment, and one of these great sugar farms now serves as a show-place—not as a model farm, but as a jungle of dense and apparently primeval luxuriance. All over where the fields were, over the canals and ditches, the forgotten slave quarters, and the still apparent ruins of the work buildings, grows a rank and lush verdure curious to see, and so thick that the road through it has the character of a tunnel, whose round farther end lets in a circle of daylight as the barrel of a telescope would do.

The place is known as "the Hammock," a term which is necessarily in very common use in Florida, since it describes a constantly recurring feature of nearly every district in that country. The word does not signify what we mean either by the term hammock or by the word hummock. Hammock, as it is used in Florida, serves to characterize fertile soil, not by reference to the dirt itself, but to what grows in it, the custom in Florida being to look up at the trees on a bit of land, instead of down at the earth, in order to determine the quality of the soil. Wherever there is a dense forest, swamp, or jungle growth, the place is called a hammock, and the term is variously qualified to suit differing conditions by such prefixes as high, low, gray, shell, marl, mulatto, hickory, live-oak, and cabbage.

The Indian River is by far the longest one of a series of inland salt-water courses which lie along the east coast close to the ocean. Six miles of marsh and three of dry land are the only obstacles now in the way of an inland boat journey from St. Augustine to the end of the series below Lake Worth, almost at the southern end of Florida. From Ormond, on the Halifax, to Port Orange, eleven miles, the way is broad and comparatively uninteresting; but below Port Orange the course is choked with islands covered by black mangrove-trees. Here is fine pasturage for myriads of bees, and the apiaries that are seen there show honey-gathering to be a leading industry. Here it is that we trace to its source the proverb that "oysters grow on trees in Florida," for it is to the half-uncovered roots of the mangroves that

AN OLD BIT OF ST. AUGUSTINE

the bivalves cling like barnacles on a derelict hulk at sea. The mangrove is the island-maker of the region. A reef forms, débris catches upon it, the mangrove springs up, its roots form a crib, more flotsam catches in and around them, and as the tree grows it keeps lifting up the material around it, until an island results. The

197

Hillsborough River, as this second link is called, is merely a channel winding among these queer islands, and broadening now and again into pools that are no flatter than the country around them. By the Haulover Canal, at a point where the Indians found a "carry" or portage, access is had to the Indian River in the neighborhood that gave the first fame to Florida oranges. This great inlet, banded to the sea, and also fed by rivers from the mainland, holds a straight course of 142 miles to Jupiter Inlet, and being wide everywhere except at the long reach called the Narrows, attains a breadth of more than three miles in places.

The trip through the Narrows is the most enjoyable part of the voyage to very many persons. But over all the journey the flocks of unfamiliar birds, the slowly changing character of the vegetation as it takes on more and more of a tropical nature, the flashing phosphorescence of the water, the occasional sight of a steamer's rigging across the reef that parts the river and ocean, and, more than all, the clear skies and unusually golden, sunny weather, are all charming novelties to the tourist. At Jupiter Inlet is found Captain Vail's floating hotel— an old steamboat that serves well as a boarding-house, and that entertains not only fishermen, but many ladies who come with them. Beyond, the termination of the tour at Lake Worth is made by what is called the "celestial railway system," so called because it starts at Jupiter and passes stations called Juno and Mars. The numerous country houses of winter residents at and near the lake-side prove it to be as charming a resort as it appears to the eye. Here the cocoa-palm flourishes, and every landscape is far more tropic in appearance than those of northern Florida. It is on Pitt's Island, at the head of the lake, that one may see the possibilities of that climate, not only because Mrs. Pitts came to Florida expecting to die, and yet remains a comely and vigorous factor in the world, but because she and her husband cultivate almost every semi-tropical fruit that will grow there. Mr. and Mrs. Pitts, unlike the average agriculturist, who despoils nature ruthlessly wherever he calls upon it to support him, have religiously left the most beautiful nooks and bowers that they found for the pleasure not only of their boarders, but of the excursionists who freely and frequently visit the island. This island was once a pelican roost, and owes its wondrous fertility to that fact. I have heard it spoken of by travellers as "the most picturesque spot in Florida," though one must have seen all the others to say that fairly. There is excellent fishing for very many kinds of fish at the inlets and in the lake, and the country around offers good sport with the gun. In addition to the private residences, there are hotels at Lake Worth and at Palm Beach. I should have said in its place that there are many pleasant stopping-places along the route from Ormond to Lake Worth, such as Daytona, Titusville, Rock Ledge, and others.

Lake Worth is east of the Everglades, and southeast of the great lake Okeechobee—a fact that suggests a mention of the stupendous task that Mr. Hamilton Diston, the well-known Philadelphian, has undertaken in a region reaching far to the north and west of the lake. A study of the character of the southern centre of Florida and of its lakes and watercourses led him to believe that by a series of canals a great territory could be drained and made useful agriculturally. Starting with the great lakes near Kissimmee City, he has dredged out canals that connect them with one another and with Lake Kissimmee, which in turn sends its waters into Okeechobee by way of the Kissimmee River. By another canal he connects Okeechobee with the Caloosahatchee River, emptying into the Gulf of Mexico. This work has so far progressed that the northerly lakes have already been lowered eight feet and seven feet, in separate instances, and an appreciable diminution of water in Okeechobee has been brought about. This drainage from the lakes implies the reclamation of a great area of neighboring land, on some of which the confident conqueror of nature has already established rice and sugar plantations, with a refinery of the first rank in connection with the last-named industry. The land that has been recovered is described as exceedingly rich, being covered with a heavy deposit of decayed vegetable matter.

Between Okeechobee and Jupiter Inlet, and thence deep into the Everglades, are found such of the Seminole Indians as remain. Their number is variously estimated at from 250 to 1200 souls, and I fancy that the latter figures are more nearly correct. They are described as fine men and women physically. They pole about the waterways in dugouts, and for a living fish, hunt, grow sugar-cane, a few cereals and vegetables, and collect the skins of the otter, deer, and bear. Some of them read and write, and many of them have rescued white men who have become lost in the interminable mazes of the grassy and island-cluttered Everglades. West of Okeechobee on the Gulf coast is the famous Charlotte Harbor, the seat of the sport of tarpon-fishing. This huge and gamy fish, the capture of which is the supreme delight and ambition of all salt-water fishermen, is sought mainly at this point, or, to be more accurate, from Punta Gorda to Punta Rassa, and some distance up the Caloosahatchee River, but it is generally held that the great fish is found all over the Gulf, even on the Louisiana and Texas coasts.

The commercial situation in Florida is not so agree-

A STREET IN ST. AUGUSTINE—THE OLD CHURCH IN THE DISTANCE.

able a subject as its holiday side. To put the case bluntly, as it was put to me by one of the shrewdest and most famous of the self-made millionaires of our country, who has an intimate knowledge of his subject, "Florida has been a great sink for Northern and Western capital, and not a dollar of profit on any single line of investments has ever been taken out of the State." The State has a completely serviceable system of railroads, but their opportunities for money-making have been mainly limited to three winter months in the year. The hotels, taken as a whole, have not paid, for the same reason, and one of the shrewdest men in that business complained to me that the invasion of rich men and land companies into the business, with their magnificent buildings and indifference to profit or loss, will not better the outlook in that avenue for investment. Orange culture has returned the interest on the sum invested only in one year out of every four, and cocoanut culture and the other industries, with the exception of sugar-making, have not yet proved profitable.

The state of the orange trade, which is associated with Florida first in every American mind, is peculiar. The trade in that fruit is at a disadvantage in one respect, especially when the crop is heavy and fine. It is so because the oranges can only be distributed by ventilated cars among the large towns and railroad centres, and are not—at present, certainly—in use as a general and popular article of food, but rather as ornaments on the tables of the well-to-do. But the main trouble is apart from this. It is that when what is known as "the boom" in Florida was in progress, in 1873 to 1876, the bulk of the land that was for sale was in the form of land grants to railways, land company tracts, and the sections taken upon homestead rights by persons who came to Florida simply to get land for nothing, and

who afterwards wanted less of it, and some cash for
what they could sell. The land thus at hand to meet
the "boom" was nearly all pine land. All Florida was
interested in saying that this pine land was the best
orange land in the world. It is a fact that oranges can
be forced to grow on that land, though this is often
done only at a great cost, and when the object is at-
tained the fruit brings prices that, to say the least,
leave no profit for the planter. Thus it came about
that ninety-nine one-hundredths of the groves in Florida
were established where they would not produce returns
on the first investment; in all probability the majority
will not pay the second owners. They are not on orange land. On the other hand, a few shrewder invest-
ors came to Florida, and went about the State studying
the characteristics and peculiarities of the business.
They noted what sort of land and locations promised
success, observing that the lands which produced the
best fruit were confined to certain sorts, and that the
best protection against frost was water to the northward or northwestward. These deliberate and observing men find no fault with their investments. They have
not only produced what are rated as the best oranges
in the world, but they have obtained extra and even
fancy prices for their yields, and have made handsome
profits. Halifax and Indian river fruit, for instance,
usually grown on high shell hammock land or heavy
marl hammock land, is quoted regularly at a dollar
above the market. This account of the history of the
trade, concurred in by the shrewdest planters I met,
explains why Florida oranges differ as they do in quality. The perfect Florida orange is thin-coated, heavy,
full of sugar, and yet with sufficient sub-acid to give it
sprightliness—like something richer than a rich lemon-
ade. The groves that produce this fruit will remain

and continue to make profits. Many of the other sort must be abandoned, and many of intermediate value must be sold for little money to new owners.

Shrewd business men who know the State and its resources assert that the finding of the phosphate beds in the region west of the centre of the peninsula is one of the greatest of recent American discoveries. The phosphate beds are heaviest on what may be called the divide or high ground from which the waters flow in contrary directions. As is almost always the case, the district contains countless lakes and much spongy soil. Here are found potash and vegetable ammonia, but their commercial fitness remains to be determined. The thick beds of rock phosphate are along either side of the Withlacoochee River, in Hernando and Pasco counties, and to a lesser extent in other counties as far north as Gainesville. All the phosphate land is from 200 to 400 feet higher than the sea-level, and it is popularly believed that it was an island when the major part of the peninsula was under water. Possibly it may have been a bird roost, like the guano islands of Peru. It is being mined in several places, and cargoes containing eighty to eighty-five per cent. of phosphate have been shipped. A cargo of seventy-seven per cent. phosphate showed only one per cent. of iron.

There has been a boom in this product, and with the usual unhappy consequences. Men were induced to put money into something like 200 organized companies. As was the case in the oil region, and in the history of so many other speculative enterprises, the first holders are being sacrificed. That rock which contains eighty per cent. or more of phosphate is marketable at a profit, but the difficulty in most cases is that to get out a ton of this it is necessary to move five tons of phosphate of an inferior grade. When men learn how to separate

the impurity from the valuable product in the inferior
grades, and when means of transportation and moderate
freight rates are obtained, the value of the mines to the
then holders will be very great. The supply appears to
be inexhaustible, and it would seem that our entire
South must use it, and that (if it is marketed at prices
that will popularize it) it must cause the abandonment
of other mines elsewhere, and find a market abroad.
In Hillsborough, Polk, Manatee, and De Soto counties
are deposits of pebble phosphates which are being
heavily worked, particularly along the Peace River.
This is being shipped in large quantities.

VI

THE INDUSTRIAL REGION OF NORTHERN ALABAMA, TENNESSEE, AND GEORGIA

ONE of the most remarkable curios in Uncle Sam's cabinet is Lookout Mountain, at Chattanooga, Tennessee. The traveller expects such occasional combinations of mountain and plain on the edges of the Rockies, the Selkirks, and other great mountain chains, and yet it is doubtful whether any other as beautiful is to be found. For it has seldom happened that a tall mountain rises abruptly to interrupt and dominate a view so majestic and of such varied features. Glistening water, smiling farm-land, forest, city, hill, and island, all lie upon the gorgeous and gigantic canvas of the Master Painter, who there invites mankind to his studio to enjoy such views as we had fancied only the stupid denizens of the air are privileged to dully scan.

To surfeit one's self with the wondrous, changing, widening beauty of that splendid scene one does not have to consider the martial records that brave men wrote with their blood all over the foreground of the prospect. But when it happens that the spectator is an American whose soul has been stirred by the poor printed annals of Chickamauga and Mission Ridge, the feast spread before Lookout Mountain ministers to the understanding the while it ravishes the eye.

In nothing is this wonder-spot more wonderful than in its accessibility. It is even more convenient to the tourist than Niagara Falls—almost the solitary great natural curiosity in our country for which one does not have to travel far and labor hard. In this case the grand view is one of the sights of Chattanooga, "the Little Pittsburg" of the South. The city enjoys it as a householder does his garden, by merely travelling to a back window, as it were, for the historic mountain is at the end of a five-cent trolley line. During half the year the tourist is even better served, for the railroads haul the "sleepers" up the mountain-side in summer, and discharge the passengers on the very edge that divides *terra firma* and eagle's vision. I took the trolley line during what the Southern folk are pleased to call winter-time. The way led to just such a looking railway as one finds at Niagara Falls going down to the water's edge, though this one darts up the two-thousand-foot-high mountain-side, and is famed among professional engineers as a remarkable creation. It was planned and built by Colonel W. R. King, U.S.A. It is 4500 feet in length, with an elevation of 1400 feet, and a grade of nearly one foot in three at the steepest place.

The terminus is the Lookout Point Hotel, which appears to stand upon a bowlder suspended over the remainder of creation, as if a mountain rising out of a plain had thrust out a finger and men had put up a building on the finger-nail. The biblical word-picture which tells of our Saviour being taken up on a high mountain and shown the kingdoms of the earth conveys the idea that the view from this point suggests. One can but have an idea of it, and it can only be expressed or described with a figure of speech. To be told that it commands 500 miles of the earth's surface, and that the most distant objects are parts of seven different States, is too much for the mind to master.

What the eye takes in is a checker-board made up of
farms, roads, villages, woods, ridges, and mountain
ranges, all in miniature. The Tennessee River glad-
dens the scene. Though it is 1400 feet wide, it looks
like a ribbon, and, like a ribbon thrown carelessly from
the mountain-top, it lies in many curves and convolu-
tions, a dull green band everywhere fringed with a thin
line of trees that wall in the farmers' fields. You may
count ten of its curves, and three of them, immediately
below the mountain, form the exact shape of an Indian
moccasin, around the toe of which a toy freight-train
crawls lazily with a muffled gasping out of all proportion
to its size. A brown and white mound of smoke and
steam beyond the nearest farms is pointed out as Chattanooga, and a rolling wooded region on the right is
spoken of as the bloodiest field of the rebellion—fearful
Chickamauga. The low dark green mound in the immediate foreground is Mission Ridge, and between that
and the curtain of smoke that hides the busy city a
tiny bit of yellow road is seen to disappear at a microscopic white gate, which is the portal of a cemetery
wherein thirteen full regiments of Northern heroes lie
—the blue who have turned to gray in the long embrace of death—five thousand of them not remembered
by name.

The rapid run by narrow-gauge road to Sunset Rock
suggests a panorama in which the swiftly changing
scene stands steady and the spectator whirls beside it.
Coloradan views are strongly called to mind, but the
memory of them is at a disadvantage, since here all
nature is green and fertile instead of dead and burned.
Here the land is peopled, and there it is deserted. And
yet the mountain-side is precisely the same as if we
were back in the Rockies, piled up with great gray
rocks in mounds and giant fret-work. Sunset Rock

itself is another finger or knuckle of the mountain,
clinging to its side, yet seeming to hang in mid-air over
the ravishing landscape far below. There are several
minor battle-fields within the view from it, but at the
first vantage-point the splendors of nature crowd the
memories of the war out of the chief place in the mind.
The charm that has made this rock the favorite rendezvous of the scores of thousands who journey to the
mountain every year comes with the views at sunset
when Phœbus's fires burn many-colored, and tint and
tinge and illumine every distant object, from the lowly
fields to the highest heavens, with slowly changing
brilliant hues. I did not see it, and will not attempt a
description of what I am assured is one of the most extravagant and splendid, almost daily, triumphs of nature.
Let the reader imagine it, or go and be ravished by it.
The stage-setting includes three ranges of hills, which

even as I saw them in the early afternoon were rosy, green, and darkest blue, and behind the farthest of these the fire-god shifts his colored slides and throws his gorgeous lights from earth to sky.

Bridegrooms and beaux, and brides and *fiancées* — in a word, all lovers—make quite another use of Sunset Rock. There is a photographer there, and his exhibit of pictures shows him to be a modern Cupid, ever attendant upon Love. All around his show-room are photographs of the smitten, a pair at a time invariably, taken in the very act of being in love, seated side by side upon the gray insensate rock that juts above the diminished lands below. Each new couple that drifts along sees the portraits of all the others, and negotiations with the photographer follow close upon quick glances, hushed whispers, and coy giggling. Then out go the lovers to the rock, and out comes Cupid with his camera. He is a wag, this Cupid, for he says of his clients, "We git 'em in all stages of the disease." His collection easily divides the lovers into two classes—the self-conscious and the ecstatic. The self-conscious ones sit bolt-upright, a trifle apart, with glances fixed sternly upon nothing. The ecstatic lovers cling together, and look with sheep's eyes at one another or at Cupid. Sometimes the classes mix, and one sees an ecstatic bride leaning all her weight of love and charms upon a self-conscious groom, who frowns and pulls away. There are such pictures in the collection as would serve in a divorce court without a word of testimony on either side; but, thank Heaven, the ecstatics supply photographs that need only to be kept framed at home in order to banish discord as long as the wedded pair have sight to see how happy they had planned to be and were. Mingled discordantly with these trophies of the court of love are reminders of that class of idiots who would manage to desecrate a junk-shop if they were admitted to it. They have themselves pictured as flinging themselves off the dizzy rock; one has actually got his comrade to hold him by one too-servile trousers leg while he dangles head downwards over the precipice. That is a touch of nature that does not make the whole world kin.

There are too many other points of interest on the mountain for mention here — curious freaks of nature and charming spots in abundance. It is several days' work to see them, but there are plenty of hotels and villa settlements there for those who have the time to enjoy the place in its entireness. Lookout Inn, a hotel that will accommodate three hundred boarders, is on the tip-top of the mountain, and has the reputation of being one of the very best hotels in the South. It is owned and controlled by a land and improvement company, and the principal stockholders are New-Englanders. The railways carry cars to its doors, and it is to be kept open all the year round. At the end of such a visit as I made the visitor simply tumbles back to the commonplace earth on the inclined railway. The car is built in the form of an inclined plane, like the gallery in a playhouse, with one side open towards the nether wall of rocks, and the other side glazed to command the marvellous view which seems to rise as the car descends, just as fairy views come up out of the stage in a transformation scene at the end of a Christmas pantomime. Then, suddenly, the car tumbles into a forest, and the only view is of the preposterous alley down which the vehicle is rolling like a ball sent back to the players in a bowling-alley.

My task here is to tell of something that lies under and in that mountain view of parts of seven Southern States, of something the eye cannot see except as a hint

211

of it is thrown up in the clouds of smoke and steam that hang over Chattanooga. That something is the industrial awakening of the South, or more particularly of that part of that section where since the war the coal and iron buried in the rocks and soil now meet their resurrection in an activity that has connected Georgia with Pennsylvania.

A very sage writer upon the industrial history of the South has shown that early in the century it promised to lead the other sections of the country, but slavery exerted the effect of humbling the artisan beneath the planter and the professional man in the general estimation. A wonderful agricultural prosperity was developed, and mechanical pursuits languished. Up to the time of the late war the South did not enthrone cotton. The South then grew its own meat and meal and flour. But after the war, when the most frightful poverty oppressed the region, the people turned to the exclusive cultivation of cotton, because that was the only staple that could be mortgaged in advance of the crop to give the planters the means of living until it could be harvested. The poverty of the planters, their dependence on the negro, and the shiftlessness of the negro, which led him to favor cotton as the easiest crop to handle on shares and to borrow money upon, were the causes of cotton's enthronement. Carpet-bag rule and the demoralization of the peculiar labor of the South added ten years to the period of Southern prostration, and it was not until 1880 that the present great industrial development of that section began. It is therefore a growth of a dozen years — a wonderful growth for so short a time.

Before the war there were a few small furnaces in this now busy district overlooked by Chattanooga's mountain, and formed of parts of Tennessee, Alabama,

212

CHATTANOOGA AND MOCCASIN BEND, FROM LOOKOUT MOUNTAIN

and Georgia. These furnaces were mainly on the Tennessee River and in eastern Tennessee, and the smelting was done with charcoal. The first coke furnace was established at Rockwood in 1868 with Northern capital on Southern credit. The industry thus begun has continued to be the enterprise of Southern men, for such are the majority of the persons engaged in the business —men of the wide-awake commercial class. The Chattanooga district, so called, is in the centre of a region of coking coals and iron ores, embracing a circle of 150 miles in diameter, and covering parts of Tennessee, northern Alabama, and northern Georgia. It takes in one medium-sized furnace in northern Georgia and some smaller ones, which number nineteen, where there were none at all before the war. Its Alabama section—where there was no iron industry when the war closed, except at a few little furnaces built by the Confederates to cast their cannon—now boasts fifty-three large plants. In a word, the development has grown from the smelting of 150,000 tons of charcoal and coke irons in 1870 to the making of no less than 1,800,000 tons of pig-iron in 1889, '90, and '91. The steel industry is prospective. The name of the town of Bessemer is misleading. Basic steel has been made in the district from the ordinary foundry ore, and has been tested by the government, and declared to be admirable. A mine of Bessemer ore has been worked at Johnson City, North Carolina, but the capital for a steel-works to compete with those of the North has not at this time been obtained.

Eighty per cent. of the Tennessee iron is sold in the East, North, and Northwest — in Cleveland, Chicago, St. Louis, New York, and Philadelphia. It competes with the best foundry iron for stove plates and all sorts of foundry-work. It ranks with the best Lehigh product, and is the favorite iron with the pipe, plough,

and stove makers of the East and North. Considerable
foundry-work is done in the Chattanooga district.
There are several stove-works there and some machine-
shops that turn out both heavy and light castings.
There are two large pipe-works (in Chattanooga and in
Bridgeport), both owned by one corporation, and there

THE TENNESSEE RIVER AT CHATTANOOGA

is also in the district a very large establishment for the
manufacture of railway-brake shoes and other goods.

The region in which the Chattanooga district is situated is a reach of bituminous coal and red hematite iron
ore of limitless abundance that extends from Roanoke,
Virginia, to Birmingham, Alabama. The coal crops out
in West Virginia, crosses eastern Kentucky, where it is
worked as pure cannel, semi-anthracite, and bituminous; crosses Tennessee through the Tennessee Valley
to northern Alabama. It is a belt containing 26,000

square miles in three States, and everywhere the coal and iron accompany each other at pistol range. As an illustration, at Red Mountain, near Birmingham, the Tennessee Coal, Iron, and Railway Company gets coal on one side of a valley and iron on the other side. This great company has several plants, and made more than 400,000 tons of pig-iron in 1891. It has the largest coal plant in the Chattanooga district—one that has put out 600,000 tons of high-grade coking coal in a year. Its leading men are Southerners, and its capital is from the Northern States and England.

The labor in this great industrial section is mainly black, of course. The negroes dig all the iron ore and do all the rough work at the furnaces. The coal is mainly dug by white men. The very great quantities of limestone that are quarried for smelting-flux and for building-work are taken out by negroes. It is found that with what is called "thorough foremanizing" the negro is satisfactory at these occupations. He needs strict and even sharp "bossing" to keep him at his work, and it has been found that to invest one of his own race with the authority of an overseer is to produce the strictest, even the savagest, kind of a boss.

The whole coal and iron region suffered severely after the Baring failure in London. During three years the price of iron fell from $12, $14 50, and $15 a ton down to $8 50 and $7 75, by reason of excessive over-production. Only the few companies that relied upon convict labor were able to make both ends meet at those prices, and it became painfully apparent that there is no decent profit in iron-making at a lower price than $10 a ton. The Southern industry suffered more severely than it should have done because not enough of the iron product was utilized in home manufactures. The transition from an agricultural to an iron-making district had been brought about too suddenly, and was allowed to go to an extreme point. The time was one of money-making in the iron industry, and the people were led to "booming" their new industry, so that nearly every one went into the manufacture of pig - iron, and too few into the conversion of it into manufactured goods. This will be fully understood when it is known that not a pound of hardware and not a pound of steel boiler plate is made in the South. Where there is room for many large stove factories there are yet but a few small ones. But, as has been shown, the manufactures are started. Such changes are brought about by one thing at a time, and already in addition to the works that have been mentioned there are large works in Chattanooga and in Atlanta for the making of ploughs and cane - mills, which contribute to a trade that already reaches into South America, the East Indies, and Australia.

The *Tradesman*, of Chattanooga, Tennessee, the leading authority upon Southern industrial affairs, published for its chief article in its "Annual" for 1893 a paper by I. D. Imboden, of Damascus, Virginia, which makes very bold and confident prophecies for the iron and steel industries of the South, and fortifies them with expert and official government reports. This is interesting and valuable, at least as showing how the leaders of opinion in the South feel upon the subject. He says that from his knowledge he forms a conclusion as strong as if it were mathematical that "the period is near when, as a group, the States of Virginia, North Carolina, Tennessee, Georgia, Alabama, and Kentucky will become the largest and most successful iron and steel producing district of like area in the world." He adds that "contemporaneously or ultimately all the related industries will spring up and flourish at every exceptionally favorable locality in these States, such as

Richmond, Lynchburg, and Roanoke, Va.; Chattanooga, Nashville, Knoxville, and Memphis, Tenn.; Atlanta, Ga.; Greensboro, Wilmington, and Charlotte, N. C.; Birmingham, Anniston, and Decatur, Ala.; Louisville and Covington, Ky.; Wheeling, Charleston, and Huntington, W. Va.; and at many other points." He predicts an eventual overflow of material for iron and steel ship-building in the Atlantic and Gulf seaports, thus extending to the cotton, rice, and tobacco States an incidental participation in the inland mineral wealth, creating diversified industries and a larger home market

CHATTANOOGA, FROM THE RIVER

for their crops. He answers "yes" to the important question whether the Southern mineral region can compete with the Northern mineral region in the supply of coal and iron. The mineral belt that underlies 25,000 square miles of the Virginias extends into and across North Carolina and Tennessee, carrying equally rich and exhaustless stores of iron; "and even beyond the southern boundaries of these States, in Georgia and Alabama, there are supplies of these ores so great that exhaustion will not probably take place while the human race exists." Kentucky he includes as an ore-producing State of high rank. He asserts that in recent years the South has produced a richer and better coke than the famous Connellsville product, which is equalled nowhere else in the North. The New River, West Virginia, coke was six years ago proved to be better than the Connellsville article; but farther southwest, in Virginia and in the same coalfield, a still richer coal is found underlying Wise and Dickenson counties and extending far into Kentucky. "Taking the New River field in West Virginia, the Pocahontas and Big Stone Gap and intermediate basins in Virginia, and their unbroken extension into several counties in Kentucky (and in the Cahaba basin in Alabama), we have an aggregation of several thousand square miles of coking coals superior" (to that of Connellsville), "and so distributed as to make a comparatively short haul from some one or other of these districts to one of our ore districts." This writer believes that the average haul—an important consideration— will be shorter in the South than that by which the coal and iron of the North have been brought together. He says that six of the seven States he has named possess an abundance of bituminous coal, such as is largely used for a lower but useful grade of coke. Southern coal is much more easily and cheaply mined than that in the North, and of the Southern iron ores the greater part is mined, not at the bottom of deep shafts, but from the hill and mountain sides in the full light of the sun. He thinks that the continued presence of negro labor in such great force in the Southern States is "providential." The negro's brawn and muscle, his cheap labor, and his acquaintance and characteristic contentment with his surroundings are considered as a large element in the early prospective growth of Southern coal and iron industries.

The last census bulletin upon the iron and steel industry of the South shows that in the ten years between 1880 and 1890 there has been a remarkable growth of these businesses, and that they have begun to follow a course of concentration, with the result that the capital invested in blast-furnaces has increased from sixteen millions to thirty-three millions of dollars, while the money put into rolling-mills and steel-works has grown from eleven millions to seventeen millions. The output has increased enormously, and the quality of the product has greatly improved. In the amount of capital invested Alabama is now "far in the lead," Virginia is second, and West Virginia is third; but West Virginia is close to Alabama in the value of her iron products, because a larger proportion of her iron and steel is worked into valuable grades of finished products. In 1880 the South produced nine per cent. of the pig-iron yield of the whole country, but in 1890 she produced nineteen per cent. Alabama shows the greatest increase in the blast-furnace industry during the decade, and Jefferson County—that in which Birmingham is situated—is now the most important iron-making district in the South. In 1880 there were but two establishments there, with a capital of one million; now there are ten such establishments, with a capital of almost nine millions of dollars. Steel-making has made but little progress, the government report says, because the Southern ores are generally unsuitable for use in the established processes of steel-manufacture. It is insisted, however, that good steel has been made in the South, though whether it can be made in competition with the North is certainly an open question yet.

Tennessee has more resources that can be utilized in manufactures than any other one of the Southern States, and already she leads in the possession of the greater number of manufacturing towns. She is the largest grain - producer among the Southern States, and the output of her flour and grist mills is so great as to amount to one-fifth of the total of her manufactured products. Cotton and woollen manufacturing grows there so rapidly that one mill now turns out more than the whole State produced ten years ago. Three millions of dollars are invested in twenty cotton-mills, and the woollen industry is sufficient to produce $1,250,000 worth of goods, or half as much as the manufactured cotton product of the State. Of tobacco and cotton-seed oil production there is a great deal, and the iron industry near Chattanooga has an importance that is dwelt upon elsewhere. The State is famous for its manufacture of wagons, which brought in $2,395,000 in 1892. Its cotton goods fetched a little more. No less than $4,617,000 was brought by its cotton-seed oil and other cotton-seed products. Its distilling and brewing, its furniture-making, and its slaughtering and packing, each was worth $2,000,000 in 1892. One mill-

POINT LOOKOUT, LOOKOUT
MOUNTAIN

ion or more represents the value in that year of the following industries: tin-ware, manufactured tobacco and cigars, woollen goods, brick and tile, marble, clothing, saddlery and harness-making, printing and publishing, and blacksmithing and wheelwright work. The value of other leading industries was as follows: lumber, $10,000,000; flour and grist-mill products, $17,000,000; foundry and machine-shop work, $6,000,000; iron and steel, $5,000,000; and leather, $3,000,000.

Is this dull reading? Stop a bit and consider whether such detailed accounts of the new industrial activity in the South do not show that times have changed since that section deserved to be ridiculed and pitied for a stupid and slavelike reliance upon one product of the soil. And yet in greater or less degree I show the same facts about nearly all the Southern States. There are parts of our West of which it can truly be said that nearly the entire reliance of the people is upon silver ore or upon wheat; but the old indictment against the South will not stand anywhere, except it be in purely agricultural Mississippi; and there, as I shall show, the fruit-grower and truck-farmer are treading on the emaciated toes of old King Cotton.

Chattanooga (under its veil of steam and smoke, and backed against a towering hill suggestive of the wealth of which it is one capital) is a city in which a man of cosmopolitan training could live without shock or sacrifice. It and its close suburbs shelter nearly 50,000 persons. It is the third city in Tennessee, though it is more truly to be considered in its relation to the industrial district around it. It is an imposing, clean, tidy, modern, wide-awake town. The mixture that forms its population has prevented the formation of Southern types in architecture, dress, or any other detail, and left it what an artist would call commonplace, though it is

SMELTING-WORKS, CHATTANOOGA

in reality such a city as would be creditable to California, Minnesota, Ohio, or Pennsylvania. It is notable among all the smaller cities of the country for its well-paved and orderly streets. Its principal thoroughfare is floored with asphalt, but so many other streets are paved with fire-brick, made near by, that it may be said to be almost completely a brick city—brick below as well as above. All its improvements, like its industries and most of its people, have come since the war, and it is most peculiar in possessing a people so largely from the North and West that natives are very scarce indeed. It typifies the industrial region around it by its varied industries. Its manufactures embrace ploughs, wood-working factories, lead and slate pencil making, boiler-works, electrical apparatus manufacture, stove-building, large iron-pipe works, and a great malleable

223

iron works that turns out car-couplings and railway-brake shoes. It has several flour-mills, a brewery, a clothing-manufactory, an engine and machine works, several foundries, an extensive cotton compress, a tobacco-warehouse, and the beginning of a cigar and tobacco manufacturing industry that must grow in unison with the new practice of tobacco-raising by the farmers of the neighboring country.

Chattanooga is a very pretty city, climbing two or three hills and abounding in view points that take in very beautiful land and water scenery, and city vistas that are parklike. Of course it has electric cars, and floods of electric light at night—for these new Southern towns are built by the same spirits that dominate the new West. It is typically American also in the fact that every family in it inhabits a separate house with a garden attached. It is distinguished, like Brooklyn, by its churches. All the considerable denominations have meeting-houses there, and even the Swedenborgians and Christian Scientists are in the list. Some of these edifices are very handsome. The Opera-house and the home of the Mountain City Club are deserving of equal praise, and all alike speak volumes for the taste and refinement of the dominant element of the population. Its people, its progressive government, and its proud educational system are deserving of extended mention, but the limits of each subject in a chapter that aims to cover so busy and wide a territory are too narrow to make this possible.

Students of the progress of the State of Alabama show that it has made greater industrial advance in the twelve months of 1892-93 than in any preceding twenty years of its history. This is true alike of her manufactures, agriculture, commerce, and railroads. In the utilization of her mineral resources she has accomplished, relatively, greater progress than any State in the Union. Her iron productions constitute a third of her output, and have led to the establishment of her rolling-mills, machine-shops, pipe-foundries, and the rest, though it is still true that the State sends out far too much of her iron for manufacture elsewhere into goods whose home man-

ENTRANCE TO A COAL MINE

ufacture would, and will yet, greatly swell her revenues. But, apart from her mineral resources, she has trebled her cotton-mill output, multiplied her cotton-seed produce by eight, and gone largely into the manufacture of lumber and wooden articles, agricultural implements, boots and shoes, wagons, furniture, flour and meal, and naval stores. The State stands fourth in the South in the manufacture of cotton goods. In two years previous to January 1, 1893, she added nearly 2000 looms and more than 100,000 spindles to her milling facilities. In 1880 she had invested $3,300,000 in her iron industries, but in 1890 this sum had been swelled to $19,000,000. In 1892 she furnished more than 5,000,000 tons of coal, or more than one-fifth of the entire Southern coal product, and led all her sister States except West Virginia. She is the fifth coal-producing State in the Union. Of coke her production in 1891 was about 1,300,000 short tons.

The census shows that the increase of population in the last decade was a little less than 20 per cent., but the assessed valuation of real estate in Alabama increased 60.40 per cent., and the enrolment of children in the public schools increased 61.53 per cent. Northern Alabama has felt the first tide of immigration to the South more strongly than any other section of equal extent. Birmingham is said to have been a farm at the close of the rebellion, and busy Anniston was a group of timbered hills very much later than that. There is a truly Western flavor to the history of a land company in one of these cities. It divided more than $5,500,000 with its stockholders in a little more than five years, upon an investment of $100,000.

The new city of Birmingham in 1880 had 60 establishments and 27 industries, and in 1890 its establishments numbered 417 and its industries 48, while the capital invested had swelled from two millions to seven millions of dollars. Its leading workshops are carriage and wagon factories, foundries, and machine-shops, three iron and steel working plants, planing-mills, and printing and publishing works. In what is known as the

IN THE BLUE RIDGE RANGE

Birmingham district there are 25 iron-furnaces, with a capacity for 2600 tons of pig-iron daily. All are within twenty miles of the town. Consolidations of large companies have recently strengthened this remarkable iron centre, adding to the economy with which its products are obtained, and fitting it to meet a dull market better than before. Experts have declared that several of the works at this place stand as models in judicious construction and economical results to the whole country and to Europe also. Some are so favorably located near ore and coal that it has been proved that nowhere in this country, and scarcely anywhere in Europe, can iron be made as cheaply as they can make it. These facts are of interest as showing the permanency and value of the industry which has revolutionized northern Alabama. It has not only come to stay, but it has come to grow. During the summer of 1892 the furnace men there were put to a severe test. They had to make iron at a minimum or shut up their works. They did make it, and only the smaller furnaces shut down for a time; the larger ones ran on steadily, and without losing money. Their owners assert that this experience proved that Alabama can make iron cheaper than it can be made in Pennsylvania.

Wherever coal, limestone, and iron are found close together the situation is favorable for the economical production of pig-iron; and as that condition distinguishes a large part of northern Alabama, the extension of the industrial activity of the Birmingham district is confidently looked for. On this account the capital of some shrewd Northern men has been invested in a promising new town — midway between Birmingham and Chattanooga — called Wyeth City. It is on the Tennessee River, which is 600 yards in width at that point, and offers uninterrupted navigation to the Ohio

MARKET STREET, CHATTANOOGA

and Mississippi and their tributaries. The railroad from Brunswick, Georgia, makes Wyeth City the nearest to the Atlantic coast of any point upon the tremendous inland water system of the Mississippi and its connections. The railway facilities at Wyeth City are also excellent. The Nashville and Chattanooga Railroad, one of the best-equipped and most progressive roads in the South, has built into the new city, and work is being pushed upon two local railroads—all of which place the new city on the direct route from Brunswick, on the Atlantic coast, to Nashville, St. Louis, and the Northwest, and from New Orleans and Mobile to Cincinnati and the North and East. The Louisville and Nashville system is soon to meet the Nashville and Chattanooga at this point.

I never want to miss a chance to combat the idea that the waste lands of the South are sterile, and the worked lands are played out. This theory has taken a deep hold upon a large part of the popular mind, and is kept alive by able men who command influential avenues to the public ear, though why they do so I do not understand. I have found that the most prosperous farmers in the South, and perhaps in the United States, are operating on the tide-water lands of North Carolina, and that trucking and fruit-growing in the sandy soil of the Piny Woods land of Louisiana and Mississippi are accompanied by the very brightest prospects. I have no other master to serve than the truth, and the plain truth is that the reason I cannot declare the major part of that country gladdened by prosperous farming is that the South has not tried to attract poor immigrants, that her enemies and critics have kept them from going there unbidden, that the swarms of semi-idle and parasitic negroes stand in the way of better brawn and muscle, and that the total new or foreign-born part of the population of nineteen million souls in those States is less than three per cent.—is almost *nil* in some of the States.

And yet there are examples of what can be done there—strawlike in dimensions though they be. Let me condense the facts given by Mr. Thurston II. Allen in a recent issue of the *Manufacturers' Record* respect-

COURT-HOUSE, CHATTANOOGA

ing an instance in Alabama. In 1878, he says, the Rev. Father IIuser, a German Catholic priest, bought a tract of two thousand acres of worn-out land known as the Wilson Plantation, in St. Florian, Lauderdale County, Alabama. It had grown cotton exclusively till at last it was abandoned to broom-sedge and briars, and pronounced worthless. The priest got it for four dollars an acre.

"Dr. Huser built a church and a school-house, and in 1878 divided the plantation into tracts of from ten to fifty acres each, and placed thereon some forty-five families, all German Catholics, from Pennsylvania, Ohio, Illinois, New York, and other States, to whom he sold these lands at from $8 to $15 per acre, according to location and improvements. These colonists had experienced the rigors of the Northern and Western climates with the certainty of cold and drought.

"They were all poor; their industry elsewhere had not hitherto availed them to any great extent. It had taken all the fruits of their labor to sustain them up to this time, so that most, if not all of them, were forced to go in debt for their land. Some of those who are now the most prosperous and independent commenced with mortgages upon their lands, and with but one mule or steer with which to break and cultivate the soil."

To add to their troubles, there was a defalcation which compelled them to pay twice for part of their holdings. They nursed the dead land back to life, and built houses,

FIRST BAPTIST CHURCH, CHATTANOOGA

fences, and improvements; but wood was cheap, the winters were mild, they could work all the year round,

232

POST-OFFICE, BIRMINGHAM

and they needed to spend little for clothing. The long summers brought them two crops instead of one.

"Vineyards and orchards were planted, and it was not long before a general improvement began to be apparent not only in the lands, but in the condition of the colonists themselves. As they gradually became more independent they built better houses and larger barns, adopted improved machinery and raised better stock, until to-day I am informed that there is not a family among them that is in debt. They raise almost everything they need upon their own land, and always have something to sell. They pay cash for what they buy and ask credit of no man. Their houses are comfortable, their barns and barnyards in good order, their fences substantial, their horses, mules, and cattle fat and sleek; their lands bring them every year abundant crops of wheat at the rate of twenty bushels to the acre without the use of commercial fertilizers), corn, Irish potatoes, clover, millet, vegetables of all kinds, while their vineyards afford enormous yields of grapes, much of which is made into wine of a good quality, for which there is ready sale."

In 1878 the played-out land brought four dollars an

acre, and many a laugh and shrug of the neighborhood
shoulders. To-day it is rated at fifty dollars an acre.
One may say that there was as much in the patience
and industry and thrift of those settlers as there was in
the soil, and, indeed, those are wonder-breeding qualities; but they will not enable a man to raise double
crops in the summer even in the rich Red River Valley
of Minnesota. They won't enable a man to work out-
of-doors most of the year, not even in Ohio.

The palace-car in which I rode from Chattanooga to
Atlanta represented something more than a mere vehicle to me, and so does every palace-car to every constant
or frequent traveller. If there are forty-four States in
the Union, the palace-car stands for a forty-fifth. True,
it is all-pervasive and common to all, like the atmosphere or the national flag, the Derby hat and the re-
volver, but it is still a creation by itself, which, taken
largely, constitutes a very great area of space and a distinctive condition and routine of daily life separate and
apart from that in the other States. It has its own distinctive population, its own peculiar etiquette; its conventions, its three classes of citizens (conductor, porter,
and passengers), even the food that its inhabitants live
upon, all differ from those in the rest of the States of
the republic. I have called the palace-car commonwealth all-pervasive, like an atmosphere, and yet it even
has an atmosphere of its own—a hot African air that is
seldom changed or freshened, and that is gotten ingeniously either out of the sun or out of a stove, according
to the season of the year in the outer world, by a unan-
imous army of negroes, who insist, with a loyalty that
pales enthusiasm, upon carrying the climate of the Congo
wherever they may go.

Persons of microscopic intellect would remind the
writer that there are two sorts of palace-cars — the

PEACHTREE STREET, ATLANTA

Wagner and the Pullman; but since they differ only in the buttons and cap plates of the servants, and in the presence of a fish-net stretched across the bunks that is found in one sort and not in the other, it is not worth while to make the mistake of dividing this new State of the Union into a North Palace and a South Palace, as was done with even less reason with the Territory of Dakota when that was taken into the Union. No; the Palace-car State is one commonwealth, indivisible and alike in all its parts. I will admit that it is viewed differently in different parts of the country. Even the constant traveller who has lived enough of his life in it to be able to vote there, if the right of suffrage were extended to its people, regards it with varying moods in differing localities. Between New York or Boston and Chicago he looks out of its windows at the splendid homes and hotels of New York, Ohio, and Illinois with regret that he is hurrying by them, and that, when the time comes, he must eat in the car, taking chicken *à la Marengo* or baked pork and beans this time, because he chose the mutton stew, the only other hot dish, for his last meal. But I know one resident of the Palace-car State who has deliberately left a mining town in Montana on Christmas to clamber joyously into a palace-car solely in order to breathe its familiar Congo air, to wag between the velvet cushions of his Lower Six and the similar cushions of the smoking compartment, to eat the chicken *à la Marengo* with an added pint of claret, solely because of a sentimental yearning for the same sort of a Christmas, poor fellow, that others were having at home in the East.

As the porter drew the customary pillows out of the walls of the car and scattered them about, and knelt and brushed the carpet around the passengers' feet, and as the conductor leaned over the settee that held the

usual solitary woman passenger and grinned and chatted
with her, the sentimental journeyer thought how strange
it was that in every part of the land the palace-car held
to its population, selecting it everywhere from the varying masses of the people. He need not have thought
about it; he had only to look out of the windows and
witness the process of selection at each station. The
soft hats went into the other cars; the beavers and
Derbys came into the palace-car. The hoods and shawls
went elsewhere, but the French bonnets and seal-skins
and modish gowns all swept into the palace-car. Not a
pair of boots was there on any platform but was sure to
lead its owner to the ordinary coaches; and so it was

MARIETTA STREET, ATLANTA

with the Indians, the negroes, the flat-faced Swedish
laborers, and the poor toiling women with the tagging
children. All went into the other coaches, and left the
sentimental journeyer surrounded by a people that

never can be better described than when they are called the inhabitants of the Palace-car State; the same in looks, manners, dress, and tastes, whether they board the palace-car in Montana or New Jersey—the conventional folks — the men who smoke cigars and wear gloves, and the women who wear furs and read the magazines.

They are perfectly at home, as persons of one region are apt to be when they are where they belong. They greet the conductor with "Well, it's as hot as usual here," and they say to the porter, "You need not bring the bill of fare; I know it by heart." At night they catch the white eye of the Afric-American, and remark, "Feet towards the engine, you know." When they converse with one another they tell how tired they used to become on the first day out, but that now they could ride a year without minding it. They add that at first they made it a rule to get out and walk at each divisional terminus where the engines were changed, but that they soon found that all depot sheds were disagreeable alike, and as for the exercise — well, a bottle of Apollinaris in the morning or a Seidlitz-powder answers instead. But the people of the forty-fifth State of the Union are not given to making one another's acquaintance. Their situation is not so novel and unfamiliar as to break the bonds of custom, like that of persons aboard an ocean liner. The one object of the inhabitants of the Palace-car State is to achieve a lethargic, semi-comatose condition, and loll the length of the railway, minding nobody's affairs, resenting all outside efforts to mind theirs, and capable of rousing to a normal activity and interest in life only when the train passes the débris of a collision-wreck, or rushes through a prairie fire, or a fire in an autumn forest.

In many respects the Palace-car State is the best feat-

238

THE CAPITOL, ATLANTA

ure of Southern travel; indeed, nothing else enables one to enjoy the beauties of that section and ignore its blemishes so well as does the palace-car. This is because the main blemishes of the South are its bad hotels. Until very lately the few "best hotels" in the South—such as the Charleston, the Ballard Exchange, the Royale, and the St. Charles—were all as old as the Astor House, and had the added and general defect of serving only fried food. There are new hotels just now at Savannah, Atlanta, St. Augustine, New Orleans, and one or two other places; otherwise the South still stands in need of a general reform.

In the Palace-car State of the Union there are perhaps twenty counties that possess little smoking-car libraries, containing the earlier works of Messrs. Howells, Stockton, Harte, Clemens, and Hale, but the great majority of rolling villages, towns, and counties offer but one book for the distraction of the mind and the elevation thereof. That is the Hotel Directory. Having nothing half so good to do, after the lamps were lit and the shades were drawn down, during this journey from Chattanooga to Atlanta, I took this directory on my lap and counted the hotels at which I had stopped— one time or many—in the other forty-four States of the Union. I found that the inn to which I was going in Atlanta would become the two hundred and eighty-fourth hostelry on my list. What a volume of reminiscence that discovery suggested! A genius, an inspired instrument of kindly fate, whispered that there was a new hotel in Atlanta. To it I went, and entered a blaze of electric light that shone upon resplendent plate-glass and gilding and marble. Then to my room to find it better than I would have ordered it had I the fairy gift of making my way by wishing. It was a symphony of white lace curtains, creamy Wilton carpet, carved-oak furniture of the sort that proclaims Grand Rapids, Michigan, the mother of art and comfort, a great snow-white bed, and hovering about, with a touch of a feather-duster

THE GRADY MONUMENT, ATLANTA

here and a touch of it there, a *white* chambermaid in a mob-cap—the only white chambermaid I ever saw in the South. There were well-chosen etchings on the warmly tinted walls. There was a reading-lamp at the head of the immaculate bed. The battery of toilet ware upon the pretty wash-stand was pretty enough to stop all the women in the streets had it been exposed in a shop-window. It did not seem possible. It was like a trick of the mind—a dream taken standing.

Then the dining-room! If I had been obliged to describe it while the full effect of its first burst of splendor was upon me, the reader would suspect either my veracity or my brain, for remember I had lived upon corn pone and bacon and bacon and corn pone, with occasional interruptions of fried chicken, for nearly a month.

The ample, brilliant room, the swift, silent waiters, the white damask, the crystal, the plate, the broad hospitable chairs, the fashion-plate ladies with shining evening faces, each face between great shoulder-puffs of silks— these were the surprises that rushed upon my vision. And then the bill of fare! Blue Points led the elegant minuet, and consommé with marrow balls was the first fair partner. Then came smelts with tartare sauce, but without any final e on the name of the sauce, that having been lost in the long journey from France. Among the several sets that took their places in this gastronomic function were many such familiar cosmopolitans as young turkey and calf's head with brown sauce, and mushrooms and olives, banana ice-cream, six sorts of cheeses, every approved wine, nuts and raisins and candy with the pastry. Having eaten many times but never dined, I fear I misbehaved, and at the last I scattered silver like a Russian roué, giving a quarter to the waiter, another to the wine-boy, one to the head waiter, ten cents to the sable reminder of the court of Louis XV. who handed round the hats, and barely succeeded in holding back a dime from the portly man who asked if I had dined well, and who lost the money by explaining that he was the manager of the hotel. In this age of introspective analysis and psychologic literature it is as well to put on record the sensations of an impressionable traveller upon encountering a good hotel.

The old soldier who, in revisiting each spot where he served under fire, fights his battles over again before his younger friends, will be puzzled how to play his rôle in Atlanta. What was a village when General Sherman destroyed it now spreads over a city's area. For Atlanta is truly a fine, substantial, genuine, bustling city. It is the busy, throbbing heart of a revolutionized region that includes the best parts of several States. It does not grow upon — it bursts upon the visitor. He alights from the cars in a noisy, crowded, smoke-grimed depot, and sees that his is but one of many trains—to New York, to New Orleans, to the West, and to smaller places nearer by. Leaving the depot, he finds himself in a solid, imposing, genuine city, built of brick, paved with stone, thick with towering buildings. It is Western, rather than Northern or Eastern, and the first impression is that it is Chicagoesque; but it is so only in the older parts. The newer districts are much more suggestive of Denver—clean and tasteful and artistic. However, that is not borne in upon the visitor's faculties until he has entered the newest office buildings and the newest hotels and theatres, and seen how rich and yet how chaste and well controlled is the use of costly material and the distribution of ornament. The Aragon, the Equitable Building, the Opera-house, and more than one of the bank buildings might all have been built for Denver, the parlor or Pullman city of America.

Atlanta is the commercial distributing centre for the southeastern part of our country. It is both old and new. It was first settled in 1839, and presently was christened Terminus. Then it became Marthasville, and in 1847 it took the name Atlanta. It was destroyed in 1864 — an occurrence that no more hinders the growth of American cities than heavy showers disturb so many ducks. New York and Boston have been all but burned up, and Chicago and Atlanta quite so, yet such trifles soon turn to memories, and then to mere sentences in the local histories. I take it that the most interesting thing about Atlanta is that — even to a greater extent than this has been true of Chicago during many years—it is a city wherein every man works for his living. The bustle in the wholesale and the retail business streets, and the eternal whiz-ziz-ziz of the

electric cars that run upon seventy-four miles of streets,
typify and emphasize this feature that seems so peculiar
to us of the older cities.   Nine steam railway lines
meet in the black, iron-mouthed railway depot, which is
in the precise centre of a circular area of buildings and
streets—a circle nearly four miles in diameter.   Within
this area is all that should complete a city, and more
besides, for the imposing State Capitol is one of the institutions it contains, and besides there is a notable collection of educational foundations, including several
private medical colleges, a dental college, a law-school,
several seminaries for girls, and two collegiate schools
for boys, six institutions for the tuition of negroes, two
libraries, and the State Technological School of Georgia.
Of church buildings there are no less than ninety-eight.
The piety of the masses of the Southern people is sufficiently remarkable to be worthy a chapter by itself, and
it is thus reflected in this work-a-day capital.   Grant

THE LAKE, GRANT PARK, ATLANTA

Park, the popular pleasure-ground, is, I suspect, the most ambitious city play-ground in the South, and will hold its rank if the people have their will with it.

But it is as a commercial and manufacturing city that Atlanta must get the most praise and excite the greatest wonder. According to the most reliable figures I could obtain the city contains 225 wholesale mercantile houses, which transact an annual business of $95,000,000. The city also operates six hundred and forty-odd manufactories that are capitalized at about $20,000,000. It is close to coal and iron, workable clays, and soft and hard wood forests, and these materials enter most largely into the local manufactures. All these are growing, and the annual investments in new buildings reach deep into the millions.

Very like so many Western folks—that is to say, very American—are the business men of the city. Nowhere else in the South do the methods of the merchants and manufacturers carry so many reminders of what, when we see it elsewhere, we call the "hustling" spirit. As an illustration, I have at hand an appeal to the Atlanta City Council for an appropriation of $10,000 for the Manufacturers' Association, which claims to represent about $10,000,000 in factories and other property. Its members say they want to spend the appropriation and twice as much of their own raising to " put Atlanta-made goods in every retail store in Georgia, and induce our people to patronize home industries and keep Georgia money in Georgia." They promised to keep at home millions of dollars a month that were then spent in purchasing elsewhere goods that are made and could be bought at home, and they add that they "can duplicate any order in the world" (the Western hustlers never stop short of "the world" in their similes) "for the same money. We can do it, we are

THE ZOOLOGICAL GARDEN AT GRANT PARK, ATLANTA

doing it, and we want to teach that fact to the consumers." In one respect Atlanta will disappoint the idle traveller; it is not typically Southern. The strongest proof it offers to the eye of being in the South is in the multitude of negroes in the streets, and, of course, in its mild winter climate. The climate reaches neither extreme of heat or cold, and although the city is upon a considerable elevation above the sea, it has had winters without snow, though a little which melts almost as it falls is expected there each year. Its negroes are fewer than one would expect to find, and though there are other such cities, it is the only place where my attention has been called to the fact that white and black men work together—not merely in mixed gangs of unskilled men sweeping the streets and digging the cellars, but just such parti-colored bands of skilled workmen also, for Atlanta has both black and white masons, bricklayers, carpenters, and artisans of other sorts.

In the years between 1880 and 1890 the manufactures of Georgia were exactly doubled in value. The articles which return millions of revenue each are brick and tile, carpentering, road vehicles, cars, cotton goods, fertilizers, flour and meal, foundry and machine-shop work, iron and steel, liquors, lumber, cotton-seed products, rice-cleaning, tar, turpentine, and naval stores. Agricultural implements, leather, and printing and publishing, each brings nearly a million a year.

Improved methods of farming have greatly raised the yield of cotton, and the general agricultural prosperity is indicated by the fact that forty-two per cent. of the farmers own their farms, all but four per cent. of this number having them free and clear of encumbrance. The fifty-eight per cent. of non-owners are, of course, the negroes, who rent or farm on shares. There are less than 1,000,000 whites in Georgia and 858,000 negroes, but neither there nor anywhere else in the South are the negroes multiplying as rapidly as the whites. It was in Georgia that the movement to bring the cotton and the mill side by side had its first trial before the war. After the war the mills multiplied and grew, and considerable mill towns were developed. The State has been pushed down in the scale in this respect, rather in the number of its mills, however, than in the quality of its manufactures, which is still very high. Its iron industry is in what is part of the Chattanooga-Alabama district, but it has profited exceptionally from this minor resource by utilizing the iron in home manufactures to a greater extent than at least one of the neighboring States has done.

VII

CHARLESTON AND THE CAROLINAS

AFTER one good look around Charleston, South Carolina, the thing which most amazed me was that no one had ever happened to prepare me for finding a city so unlike our others that it actually may be said to be "built sidewise," as if all its houses were at odds with the streets. Strange also it seemed that no one had warned me that I should find it a water-color city of reds and pinks and soft yellows and white set against abundant greenery, and with horse-cars of still stronger colors flaming through the streets in the sunshine. Its own lovers, down there, like to speak of it as "old and mellow," but that expresses only a little bit of what it is.

First, it is very beautiful; next, it is dignified and proud; third, it is the cleanest city (or was when I was there) that I have yet seen in America; and, last of all, it is a creation by itself—a city unlike any other that I know of. It is built on a spit of land with water on three sides, like New York, and this gives its people that constant and enduring delight which continual views of moving water never fail to provide. Part of its early history is that of a planters' summer resort, and something of that forgotten holiday air still clings to it. If it suggests any city that I have ever seen, it is New Orleans—perhaps because of an indefinable Latin trace that is seen in the stuccoed houses and walled gardens, and again, because of the important part the gardens play there, and the profusion of flowers that results from them.

The most peculiar feature of Charleston is the arrangement of its houses, which, as a rule, are built with the side of each dwelling towards the pavement. This has been done to provide for either a southern or western prospect from the galleries, or "piazzas," as they call them, with which each house is prettily and invitingly adorned. Because of this method of building, the entrances, which, without knowing better, we would take to be the front doors, in reality admit the members of each household either to the end of the lower porch or into the garden. The true front doors open on the inner gardens or courts. Full enjoyment of the gardens is thus combined with privacy; and though one may get only glimpses of these little preserves from the streets, strong hints of their prettinesses are often carried up to the lofty balconies in the forms of vines and potted plants, like extensions of the gardens, the which whoever runs may enjoy. How very pretty and how very peculiar Charleston has thus become only a visit can disclose. Wherever one sees a fine garden, the palmetto, which gave the State its popular nickname, is chief among its treasures; but the trees have all been transplanted, for they do not naturally grow there, but on the islands and low shores of the coast. In the public grounds about the Capitol at Columbia, in the interior of the State, there is a majestic palmetto, but it is made of iron, the triumph of an ingenious metal-worker.

I quite boldly referred to the French appearance of the city during my visit, and though there were those who upheld me in my opinion, one very prominent gentleman, himself of Huguenot descent, insisted that I

was mistaken. He thought it more than likely— almost
positive—that the courtly manners and formal politeness
that distinguished the leaders of Charleston's best society in the city's palmiest days, and that have by no

THE IRON PALMETTO-TREE AT COLUMBIA

means yet departed, were a direct inheritance from the
French. But for the rest he insisted that, such was
the strength of the English domination, Charleston was

always and is to-day pure English at all important points. In 1793 nearly five hundred French refugees from San Domingo made Charleston their refuge, and one thoughtful citizen argued, without insistence, that possibly that mere essence which made the place seem French to me was due to the San Domingans. However, the discussion was and will be futile, and for myself I can only say that much in the style of many of the houses suggests the same adaptation from the French that we see in and around New Orleans, and in the decorations and ornaments that continually confront a visitor the French style is pure and indubitable.

Mr. Yates Snowden has gathered in a published paper some notes of the various immigrations of the French to Charleston, and if they were not influential in the life and accessories of the people, it will at least be admitted that they were numerous and important. He shows that after the various large immigrations of the Huguenots there came to South Carolina fully twelve hundred Acadian refugees in 1755–57, and thirty-six years later the five hundred French came from San Domingo and settled in Charleston. The contrast between the results of these immigrations and those which have caused New Orleans to be still a partially French city is so great as to make the points of comparison few and weak. The San Domingans made a very small impression upon Charleston. Whether they had been weakened by an indolent life in the tropics, they certainly were not a forceful people. They clung to their French customs and language, it is said, and yet they were swallowed up to such an extent that traces of them were few even fifty years ago. The Huguenots, on the other hand, coming as humble folk, disowning France and warmly adopting our country as their own, made a very great impression even upon the aristocracy and the history

251

of the State. To return to Mr. Snowden's paper, he mentions the fact that one of the active philanthropic societies of Charleston is of French origin. "The South Carolina Society," he says, "founded in 1736 as the French Club, afterwards known as the Two Bit Club, and called the Carolina Society when the Huguenots more thoroughly identified themselves with their new home, is probably, with one exception, the oldest organization in active operation in the South."

But from whatever its peculiar foreignness may be derived, Charleston is old and finished and complete— a small, inviting, pretty — a dignified, almost splendid little city.

While I was in Charleston preparations were making for the celebration of the coming of age of a notable fashionable dancing circle in New York. Twenty-one years is indeed a long time for a coterie of purely fashionable pleasure - seekers to hold together, and that age, perhaps, represents with some fairness the period during which the great fortunes made since the war have both aided and incited our own wealthy people to display their good - fortune with more ostentation and in circles more conspicuous by numbers than used to be either the rule or the possibility in earlier times. And yet at that very time I read the following notice in a fresh copy of the *News and Courier*, the great and dignified daily journal of Charleston :

MEETINGS.

ST. CECILIA SOCIETY.—The One Hundred and Thirty-first Anniversary Meeting will be held at the South Carolina Hall on Wednesday, Nov. 22, at 8 P.M.   WILMOT D. PORCHER,
Secretary and Treasurer.

That notice concerned the members of what I suppose must be the oldest social fashionable organization in

AN OLD RESIDENCE, CHARLESTON

America. If it is no longer wealthy, it will nevertheless be conceded that no such circle is more exclusive than it is, or than it has been for a longer time than our government has existed. Its name indicates its original purpose. That name, which is said to have been adopted by more musical societies than bear any other title, all over Christendom, was chosen in Charleston to distinguish a musical coterie formed from among the leading people. Next, the St. Cecilias, as they are called, added dancing to music, and finally their sole purpose became that of giving three grand balls every winter. Two hundred men form the membership, but they issue about four hundred invitations to ladies, the number of persons who are thus entitled to attend the dance being between five hundred and six hundred. The invitation list is the élite directory of the town, so to speak. Once the name of a lady is entered upon it, that name is never taken off, unless the lady dies or marries out of the membership.

The eligibles are declared to be "any person in whose family there has been a member, as well as all men in Charleston who are credited with possessing the manners and instincts of gentlemen, without regard to birth or worldly condition." A great many men of wealth in Charleston could not be admitted if they desired to, and for some who have made the attempt there have been heart-burnings, as must always be the case where a society attempts to keep its membership wholly and thoroughly congenial. On the other hand, young men who boast neither wealth nor pedigree are admitted annually when their course of life and traits of character have won them the support of the others. As a rule, whoever has the entrée of the houses of the members has little or nothing to fear if he applies for membership; then he needs only the support of four-fifths of those who attend the meeting at which his application is considered. The society is managed by a president, vice-president, secretary, and treasurer, and twelve managers, chosen annually.

Intensely proud among themselves, the members eschew display and notoriety so far as the society is concerned, and the rule that nothing concerning its annual dances shall be printed or given out for publication is believed never to have been broken. The only publications concerning the society that are ever made are the notices of its annual meetings and of the days on which the balls are given. Josiah Quincy, in his memoirs, mentions having attended a meeting of the society prior to the war of the Revolution, and speaks of the care then taken to make it private. Amid all the old things in Charleston (and it is a veritable museum, with its ancient churches, its pre-revolutionary post-office building, its library of colonial origin, and its old Chamber of Commerce) the fashionable society is it-

OLD IRON GATE, CHARLESTON
255

self largely composed of men and women rather younger than those of similar societies in other cities. The beautiful Battery—situated like that in New York—is so dependent upon nature that it is forever young and gay, and is the promenade for the St. Cecilias and the rest. It faces the beautiful harbor, with the sea and Fort Sumter (looking very small for anything with so big a history) in the distance across the broad blue bay. Facing the Battery, in turn, is a curving row of residences, almost as fine and as beautiful as any in America. The especial beauty of the show they make is due to the fact that they, also, keep up a process of rejuvenation, by the addition of new houses of the latest fashion. The result is a number of noble old-time mansions lording it over ample semi-tropical gardens, with their shady, breeze-inviting piazzas commanding the water and the promenade, side by side with dainty modern dwellings of what we would call suburban villa types, that give Charleston's old Battery a distinct air of youth and vigor. The men who enjoy these luxuries of the promenade and the fine houses of the showy parts of town are mainly those who maintain the Charleston Club, in which so many New-Yorkers have been so well entertained, and the Carolina Yacht Club, with its notable fleet and its fine sailing courses, both in the harbor and at sea.

Somewhat more popular in its scope is the Queen City Club, also a fine organization. Society, it is explained, is in the hands of the young because their elders have not the means to entertain as they would prefer to do; but however that may be, it seems to me an admirable society, in which mere money cuts as slight a figure as it is possible to conceive. But it is wonderful—and doubtless sad from the former point of view—to note how the wealthy class has changed since the days

CAROLINA HALL, CHARLESTON

when the planter was king. On the Battery, once a row of planters' mansions, only one house is that of a planter. Now the homes there are those of retired factors, prosperous lawyers, bankers, real-estate operators, and men who have accumulated their means elsewhere and returned to the charming old city.

The custom these people maintain of eating dinner at three or four o'clock in the afternoon will strike a stranger from the North as peculiar. In some degree it obtains all through the South—at least, after one leaves North Carolina. Another thing—a trifle, but equally odd—is the habit the shopkeepers have of hanging cards in their doors to show the legend "Shut" or "Open." To a fevered New-Yorker it is lovely to think that perhaps this indicates that when trade is slow or the shopkeeper desires to attend a wedding, he can close his shop, and that the customers who come will exclaim, "Bother! It's shut. I must come again to-morrow," as they used to do under the same circumstances in New York not so very long ago.

A very notable charity, distinguished further by being the only one of its kind in the South, is the "Home for the Mothers, Widows, and Daughters of Confederate Soldiers." It was founded by women and is managed by women, solely for women and girls. The chief spirit among the founders was Mrs. M. E. Snowden, who has seen the noble work flourish for a quarter of a century, who has mourned the loss of many who were associated with her at the outset, and yet who remains active and at the head of the foundation. The undertaking has been completely successful. The women own the home building, and have a handsome bank account besides. They have given relief to as many as 2000 persons, and an education to hundreds who could not otherwise have obtained it. The home now shelters about thirty women and something like fifty girls, who must have been under fourteen years of age when entered there. The school-girls spend ten months in each year in the building. They are the offspring of the families of the upper grade, as a rule, though the only requirement is that they shall be white. The women are not all of the same social standing.

The Home is in a historic building. Where now is the school-room the sessions of the United States court were held, and at one sensational session in 1860 one of the Federal judges threw off his robe, saying, "The time for action has come." Tossing his robe on the floor, he left the room, and thus summarily ended the Federal jurisdiction in South Carolina. However, it is a dove-cote now, and breathes an atmosphere of grace, mercy, and peace, whose genius is felt amid such surroundings that the glimpse I got of the garden, with its cool piazzas, its banana-trees, and its happy tenants, seemed altogether idyllic.

In nothing is Charleston more admirable and interesting than in its church buildings. Better yet, the people know this—which is not always the case in such matters —and are as proud of them as they should be. The two old English churches of St. Michael's and St. Philip's are to the city what superb statues are to a park. They are beautiful ornaments—monuments to a wealth of pride and taste which may exist there, but will not be easily excelled in any modern memorials. But the Huguenot Church, the only one in America, is equally beautiful in its history. Its pastor, the Rev. Dr. Charles S. Vedder, has written this concise statement of its claims upon those who venerate the cause of religion, and especially that of these liberty-loving exiles of old. These are his words:

"Established by French Protestants, Refugees from

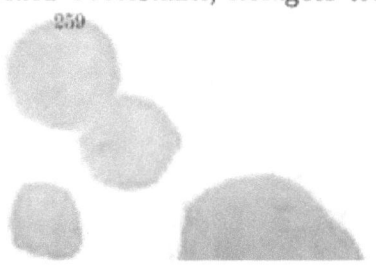

France on account of Religious persecution. Their Descendants, venerating that steadfastness to principle so conspicuous in their Ancestors, continue to worship To-Day with the same liturgy (translated) published at Neuf-

CHARLESTON CLUB HOUSE

chatel in 1737 and 1772, in this, the Only Huguenot Church in America."

In a paper which Dr. Vedder read before the Huguenot Society of America a few years ago he declared that the first Protestant settlement on this continent was made in South Carolina by Huguenots. Admiral de Coligny, seeking a place of refuge for the unhappy French Protestants, fitted out an unlucky expedition, which made an abortive effort to form a settlement in Brazil. Then he despatched another expedition, under Jean Ribaut, which formed a settlement at or near the site of

Port Royal, South Carolina, in 1562, which, as the Doctor says, was forty-five years earlier than the English colonization of Virginia, fifty-two years before the Dutch settlement of New York, and fifty-eight years before the foundation of the Plymouth colony. And yet more than a hundred years were to pass before the Huguenots became important factors in the making of South Carolina. Fire destroyed this first fort of the Protestants; distress fell upon them; and while Ribaut was away attempting to bring them re-enforcements, they built a ship, and after fearful hardships and losses of life a few survivors reached England. In 1680 the second Charles of England sent over fifty families to raise wine, oil, and silk, the English colony being then ten years old; and after the revocation of the edict of Nantes in 1685 there was "a constant stream of Huguenot immigration to South Carolina." Four settlements were founded, and one historian, who saw the French there in 1700, says that, being temperate and industrious, they "have outstripped our English who brought with them large fortunes." But the colonial government was English, and the Huguenots were made to suffer great discomfort on account of their religion, even the right to vote being denied to them. At last the three rural congregations merged their churches into the Established (Episcopal) Church, translating the English liturgy into the French tongue for their own use. This was not done in Charleston, but after 1728 the services were held in English. The church itself was established there in 1681-82, and in the interval between that time and this the Marions, the Laurenses, the Manigaults, and many, many others have distinguished the Huguenot race, and their own State as well.

The two Episcopal churches of St. Philip's and St. Michael's are, as I have intimated, the most beautiful church edifices in the Carolinas. They ennoble almost every view of Charleston that one gets. St. Philip's has the third building in which the congregation has worshipped, but it copies the second one, destroyed in 1835, of which Edmund Burke said that it was "executed in a very handsome taste, exceeding everything of that kind which we have in America." The dramatic poem, still recited wherever English is spoken, which tells of the daring of a slave-boy who climbed a steeple to put out the fire that threatened its destruction, wherefore his master set him free, tells the true story of an incident in the history of St. Philip's. The poem credits the incident to St. Michael's, but that is a mistake. Both these churches are of the general style of our old St. Paul's in New York, but both are very much handsomer. St. Michael's is said to be very like St. Martin's-in-the-Fields in London, so familiar to most Americans who have visited that city. The steeple is made up of a series of graduated chambers, so well proportioned that each new study of them is a fresh delight. It is no wonder that the Charlestonians like to mention that it has always been a tradition that Sir Christopher Wren was the designer of the building, though there is better reason to believe that it was Gibbs, the architect of the London church which it so greatly resembles. In the steeple hang the bells which are Charleston's most beloved possession. Not only were they imported from England in 1764, but when the British retired from the city at the close of the Revolution they were seized as a military perquisite and sent to London. There a Mr. Ryhiner, who had been a merchant in Charleston, bought them and sent them back to Charleston. In 1861 they were sent to Columbia for safety, and when that city was burned by the Federal troops they were ruined by the flames. In 1866 they were sent back to

England to be recast by the descendants of the original founders, and in another twelve months they were back again, practically the same eight bells, but held by the government for the payment of $2200 duty. That was paid, and the money has since been refunded by especial act of Congress.

Two old institutions carry a strong suggestion of Yankee influence, or, at least, of Yankee kinship. One is the Charleston New England Society, a century old, which observes Forefathers' day with regularity; an-

THE CUSTOM-HOUSE, CHARLESTON

other is an influential old Congregational church, now worshipping in a fourth and very fine modern edifice; and—I had almost forgotten it—there is actually a Unitarian church, which one day split off from the

263

Congregational church quite as it might have done in Boston.

Nothing in Charleston seemed more peculiar to me than the colony of buzzards which the citizens have developed by taming and protection, and which spends a part of each day around the market in the very heart of the city. There one may almost stumble over these huge black birds, which are elsewhere scarcely seen, except at great heights, circling and sailing like creatures of another world. I one day counted thirty-eight buzzards on the cobble-stones of the street upon only one side of the market. They are quite as large as eagles, and as black and lustrous as crows, but have white legs, and bare wrinkled brown necks that make them look like caricatures of old-fashioned parsons in high "chokers." They are extremely ungainly, stiff-legged, and awkward when they walk, and when they begin that flight which they are able to master so that they appear even more at ease in the air than are fishes in the sea, they start out with a supremely ridiculous upward movement, during which their long legs hang down straight, and their heads and tails flap almost together on either side of their feet. They then look as if they were being lifted by a string around each one's middle, and were struggling to get free. I do not think they are the common buzzards, without which no view in the Southern country is complete, but I could not find in book or acquaintance any enlightenment on the subject further than the jocular statement that they are called "the Charleston canaries."

They are splendid scavengers. They roost on the low gutters around the market, and wait until the butchers begin business. Then, as customers come and the men of the cleaver and knife begin to cut off and discard the fag ends and worthless bits of the meat and toss them into the street, the great birds drop down, one by one, and begin eating the waste. I said I almost stumbled over them; I certainly could have walked upon and over them for all the heed they gave me.

"Well," said I to a negro man who was priding himself on having found the sunniest loafing-place in the neighborhood, "these are mighty independent buzzards."

"Yaas," said he, "dey is in'pendent, an' dey is proud.

ST. MICHAEL'S CHURCH, CHARLESTON

265

Dey's gittin' so tame, now, dey hangs round de city all de while. When de butchers done leave, de buzzards done leave. Then de buzzards light out to de pen where de meat am slaughtered. Oh, dey knows what's goin' on; doan't need no one to tell 'em.

" Dese yer buzzards use ter sleep 'crost de ribber in de woods. Over dat away dey isn't king, like dey is here. Over dere de raid-haid raven is king, an' dese yer big birds ain't nuffin like so in'pendent an' proud like you see 'em here, 'cause dey ain't king. De raid-haid raven is a bigger bird, an' he bosses de whole roos'. If carrion lay daid a day or two days, dese yer buzzards dassent tech it; no 'deed dey dassent. Dey doan't meddle wid nuffin tell de raid-haid raven comes. Pretty soon, when he just gits ready, he comes 'long, more proud an' in-'pendent dan de king lion hisself, an' he picks out de eye ob de carrion. After dat dese yer birds is 'lowed to pitch in an' eat all dey want to. Dese yer buzzards doan't know dat carrion is sure enough daid till de raid-haid raven comes an' teks de eye."

Queer people are the darkies, and a queer thing about them is that they believe there is always a king over every bird and beast and creeping thing around them.

It is a statutory offence to molest these "Charleston canaries," and as the law is enforced, they revel there as if they owned the market.

Long ago Charleston grew tired of "fighting the war over again," and left it to the Northern politicians to do. Business and activity is what they talk of now, not as of things they possess in sufficiency, but as of essentials which they cry for. The city has been left in an eddy. Its local railways are but links of a great line which makes Charleston an incident and at times a side issue. The hope and prayer of the people is that their city may become the terminus of some great system—

the Louisville and Nashville, perhaps. The relation of the city to the North, the West, and the Southwest, and to Europe, could easily become very important, for her position would seem to guarantee it as an eventual certainty. The deepening of the entrance to the harbor is a necessary preliminary, and this is being accomplished by the Federal government. The harbor itself is suffi-

INTERIOR OF ST. MICHAEL'S

ciently deep, but there were only sixteen feet over the bar. This is being increased to a depth sufficient to admit modern ocean vessels.

In the old days the cotton of South Carolina and northern Georgia was all handled and shipped at

Charleston. A very great number of persons shared the profits. The factors who bought and shipped the cotton made their profits; the men who mended the bales, those who pressed them, the stevedores—all lived upon the business. Now the cotton is shipped directly from every point where a thousand bales are collected, and it is even sent to Europe from mere railroad stations which may not have importance from any other cause. If it had not been for the phosphate industry Charleston could not have supported 25,000 souls.

The phosphates are found to the northward of Charleston, mainly on the Ashley and Stono rivers, and in less extent and of inferior quality between the Ashley and Cooper rivers. The best phosphates, and those that are "most workable," are along the west bank of the Ashley. Then, again, in Colleton County, between the Edisto and Ashepoo rivers, there are deposits, but they are more expensive to handle because they are not as handy to navigable water as those which lie near the Ashley River. These are all land phosphates, and the title to them lies in the land. The river phosphates are in the Stono and the Edisto rivers, though the greatest and best deposits are in the waters around Beaufort and Port Royal, the best being in the Coosaw River, on the bottom beneath the water. The phosphates have to be washed and ground, and then treated with sulphuric acid, which frees the phosphoric acid from the lime, and gives free phosphoric acid of the kind generally used in the manufacture of fertilizers. Charleston has fifteen factories, situated along both the rivers that flow past the city, and making 200,000 tons a year. There are two factories near Beaufort, and there are others elsewhere in the State. That phosphate which is treated in these factories is used for what may be called home consumption in both Caro-

linas, Alabama, Georgia, and, to less extent, in Mississippi. A great deal of land phosphate, washed, but
not ground, is shipped to Baltimore, Atlanta, Charlotte,
Columbia, and many interior towns in the neighboring States. The greater part of the water phosphates

A BIT OF CHARLESTON FROM ST. MICHAEL'S CHURCH

has been shipped direct to Europe, though some has
been used at home when the price has been lower
than that of the land rock. The State owns the water
phosphate, and charges the companies that work it
one dollar a ton royalty. This tax netted $234,000 to
the State in one recent year. But Florida phosphates

ST. PHILIP'S CHURCH

of equal grade are being marketed quite as cheaply, and the South Carolina trade is menaced. The remedy must be a reduction of the State tax. That this relief will be granted, perhaps before this is published, I have very little doubt.

Taking South Carolina as a whole, we find it singularly attractive to immigration, and yet singularly avoided by it. It is one of the richest of our States in the possibilities of its soil, which are very varied indeed. Yet it has only about one-third of its acreage under cultivation by a population more largely black than white, and so little infused with the foreign elements which have literally populated and enriched great parts of our domain that its Governor truly says of it: "The people of South Carolina are homogeneous. Most of the whites have common origin." But the majority of the people

BUZZARDS NEAR THE MARKET

are negroes, who, being under little stimulus towards social improvement, or any ambition except that of being able to live from day to day, deprive the State of that reservoir of latent strength and potential wealth which an industrious and ambitious multitude of the not-at-all-to-be-despised foreign immigrants would bring to it.

We find stern competition in Florida threatening the revenue from the phosphates, and still more injurious competition in Louisiana injuring the returns from the Carolina rice, and yet the prospect for the State is not gloomy. The diversification of its farm industries and the remarkable growth of the cotton-milling business make it otherwise. Within the last six months (this was written at the opening of 1894) no less than three millions of dollars have been expended in the building of new mills in the Carolinas, and the people of those States and of Georgia are not unreasonable in insisting, as they do, that in time the mills generally must come to the cotton, and that the bulk of the manufacture of cotton must be done in the South. Governor Tillman did well in calling attention (in his paper prepared for the Convention of Southern Governors in Richmond in 1893) to the abundance and cheapness of the water-power in his State. He wrote: " Mr. Swaim, the special agent of the census of 1880, made a careful estimate of the water-power of our streams as reaching a million horse-power. If developed, these would give employment to six millions of operatives in cotton-mills," and allow for a corresponding increase of population. He says that " owing to want of capital in the State, these powers can be bought cheaply now, and they would prove capital investments. The winters are so mild that there is comparatively no trouble from freezing. The benignity of the climate makes living cheaper, and this adds to the advantages offered to manufacturers by our water-powers."

The use of fertilizers has pushed the cultivation of cotton to the very feet of the mountains in the western part of the State, and though it has been overdone, as it has everywhere else in the South, there has been no need to caution the planters, for with the consequent decline of the price of their staple they have learned wisdom—bitterly as it so often comes—and are beginning to diversify

A NEGRO FUNERAL

their crops, at least sufficiently to provide themselves
with meat and bread, as well as, in some parts of the
State, to raise fruits and vegetables for market. In the
mean time the starting of cotton-mills has gone on, until
from a possession of twelve mills in 1870 the State had
forty-four in 1892, representing a capital of $12,000,000,
and employing thousands of operatives — nearly all
white.

Turning to North Carolina, we find this particular industry much more extensive. The latest statistics I
have been able to procure—the truly excellent hand-
book prepared for the Columbian Exposition by the
North Carolina Board of Agriculture—include the facts
and figures concerning one hundred and forty cotton-
mills, and a statement that six other mills were then under construction. To these should be added thirteen
woollen mills, one of which manufactures both cotton
and wool. The strangest thing about this woollen industry is that though the State is admirably calculated to
rank high as a wool-producing one, and though the industry would be highly profitable, the fact remains that
many of the principal mills buy their wool elsewhere,
because the ravages of the dogs make sheep-raising prof-
itless, and because the people of the State will not en-
force or permit the enforcement of the laws for the protection of the sheep.

But the manufacture of tobacco has brought more
prosperity to this truly enterprising State than any other industry. It has not only awakened, enriched, and
increased many towns, but it has built up several new
ones, like Durham and Winston and others. The business is enormous. The State contains no less than one
hundred and ten factories where plug tobacco is made,
nine smoking-tobacco factories, and three cigarette-fac-
tories. Several of these are world-famous and truly

PLANTING RICE ON A CAROLINA PLANTATION

enormous. The plug-tobacco-making town of Winston sold eleven millions of pounds of manufactured tobacco and paid more than $660,000 revenue tax in 1891. Durham paid $616,000.

It has been said that the activity in cotton-manufacturing has stimulated the many other manufacturing activities that we find keeping the Old North State astir. To my mind the fact is that the character of her people, her most admirable climate, and the opportunities afforded by her extraordinarily varied resources are at the bottom of it all, the cotton manufacture as well as the rest; at all events we certainly find the activity reaching out in many new industries, notably the manufacture of buggies and wagons; of furniture; of paper, in several mills; of cotton hosiery and other knitted goods, in ten places; of canning, in twenty-eight establishments, exclusive of several oyster-canneries; of cotton-seed-oil manufacture, by nine mills; of fertilizers, extensively, in very many places. And, finally, among something like two dozen establishments for the making and working of iron, there has been newly founded a million-dollar steel and iron plant at Greensboro.

The Capitol of North Carolina, at Raleigh, is a materialized echo of the past, in and about which there is no note of the transformation of the State and its people. Built sixty years ago by a slave-holding people, it has remained unchanged through the calamities of war and the brilliant evolution of the new spirit of enlightened industry. There it stands, classic, dignified, aged, but well preserved, as if it typified all that was good and enduring in the courtly, generous, but feudal masters whose rule has passed away forever in the Old North State. The beautifully proportioned old palace stands embowered among trees at least as old and majestic as itself in a rather modern-looking little park. The build-

THE CAPITOL AT RALEIGH

ing is of granite quarried near by. The last glimpse and the first, like all the views one gets of its interior, suggest just such a strange blending of age and careful keeping as one notes in the ancient trinkets which now

ENTRANCE TO ASSEMBLY CHAMBER

and then some wrinkled old spinster brings out to exhibit as the choicest, tenderest relics of a distant generation of her people.

The walls and floor are clean and fresh, for instance, but on the doorway to the Assembly Chamber is the strange legend, "Commons Hall." An aged but diligent servitor who guides you wastes no time over the great portrait of Washington on one wall, but dwells

278

feelingly upon the fact that in the cruel, tyrannical days
of "carpet-bag rule" the negroes, who were then the
legislators, broke two of the precious old hard-wood
chairs which were the especial treasures in that chamber.
He takes you across the hall—carrying with his spare,
bent form a strong suggestion of a past as extensive as
that of the capital itself—and there you are stirred by
the sight of the prim but noble mahogany provided for
the statesmen of the luxurious past to rest and to write
upon. The old man stirs you in quite another way by
the remark that a Northern firm has offered to exchange
modern furniture for all that is in the old room. A
bust of John C. Calhoun is the chief ornament in the

A NICHE IN THE CAPITOL.

Senate Chamber, though the neatness and reverential
order that rule there strike you as better than any ornament could be.

You carry with you to the executive offices down-
stairs a mind wholly given up to reflections upon the
past, and, lo! the officials in those ancient rooms all but

RAILWAY STATION AT RALEIGH

stun you with the zeal and zest with which they press
you to consider the present needs of the State, its bustling progress, and its wealth of unworked resources.
You'd hardly find a quicker spirit in Ohio or Rhode Isl-
and. Moreover, there is little buncombe about it. If
they tell you, as they will, that no State in all our Union has such varied capabilities, or that its climate embraces nearly the full extremes that are represented in
our minds by Maine and Florida, they make their words
good by showing you photographs of the snow-silvered
spruce forests of the western mountains, and palm-lit-
tered, all but tropical views taken along the sunny coast.

They boast a little, as good Americans always do, and
if some of the things they say show a trifle of jealousy,
or if some of the topics they choose seem somewhat un-
sentimental, you must remind yourself that the jealousy
springs from a pride that has been wounded, and that

the best elements of wealth are not apt to be of a poetic nature. Thus they tell you that the excellent peanuts which North Carolina raises in abundance have failed to bring her the credit she deserves, and that the golden, beautiful tobacco which for generations has been known as "bright Virginia leaf," so much admired for use in pipes and cigarettes, was and is largely grown in North Carolina. The way in which the Yankee-like old State came to be robbed of the credit for its peanuts was this: For years the farmers of eastern North Carolina have been raising the nuts and shipping them in crude condition to Norfolk. There they have been cleaned and bagged and sold as Virginia produce. This is yet the case, although the eastern North Carolina nuts are unexcelled by any others that are grown in the world. But the wedge of justice has been inserted in this case. The work of separating and cleaning the nuts has been begun in a small way by the North Carolina farmers, and the world at large will soon learn that though Virginia and Tennessee grow good peanuts, they never pro-

GOVERNOR'S MANSION, RALEIGH

duce finer ones than are grown in North Carolina. As for the "goobers" that gave Georgia its nickname of "the Goober State," they are small and poor by comparison.

It is different with the splendid tobacco of the State. At last North Carolina is establishing a reputation for its own excellent "weed that cheers." Buyers now come to the North Carolina market-towns, and the best bright leaf is coming to be classed under its true name. The town of Durham, so famous among men who smoke, is the capital of the golden-tobacco belt, which embraces ten or twelve counties in the middle of the State. The "mahogany," or plug-tobacco leaf, is grown in the western part, and Winston, which maintains forty plug factories, is its industrial capital.

From the Northern evergreen to the perennial Southern palm is the measure of the State's fertility, and her people do not hesitate to say that all that should bridge the two extremes is also theirs. That they can and do grow whatever is grown elsewhere in the United States is true, with a few marked exceptions that distinguish the extreme South. It is the boast of the people that at Chicago's great exposition no State displayed such a great variety of the products of the soil.

Under such circumstances the most practical student of the commonwealth cannot be altogether prosaic in listing its products. If I have the good fortune to possess the eye of that friend whom the novelist always addresses as "fair reader," let me also turn directly to her and ask what she thinks of whole farms given up to tuberoses! Such, it seems, are among the triumphs of North Carolinian husbandry. Some farms devote as many as twenty-five acres, "in a patch," to the cultivation of tuberoses. During the first year the tuberose bulb multiplies, and does not flower. It is during its

282

A TOBACCO MARKET IN NORTH CAROLINA

STATE PRISON, RALEIGH

second year that it spreads its delicate, waxen, and aromatic blossoms, and a great industry in this State is the development of the bulbs in the earth for the first year, and then the shipment of them to the North in barrels, to be sold by the florists, and set out to blossom. North Carolina is chosen for this graceful branch of farming because of the properties of the soil, and because the bulbs can be kept out in it all winter. It is true that in fancy I see the pink and white nose of my fair reader lift a little at the disclosure that the suggested fields of aromatic flowers prove only to be furrows of raw earth hiding bulbs, but only think how many of the flowers are not sent away, but mingle their beauty and sweetness with the vast bouquet that blossoms all over such a region. And only think, when next you see a tuberose in bloom, that it was in the Old North State that it started on its fragrant, and, alas! too often pathetic, mission.

It will be equally interesting to all my readers—for I fear I have not been altogether successful with my special address to the fair ones alone—to know that in Raleigh thousands and tens of thousands of rose-cuttings are planted in the gardens and fields for the Northern market. The Northern florists send the cuttings down to be planted and kept a year in order that they may grow roots, and that each may become a plant, a baby rose bush. Then they are shipped back in the spring to be sold as young plants. It is too expensive to do this under glass, as it would have to be done in the North, but it costs a mere trifle, by comparison, to assist nature at the task down there in Raleigh; for in that clement

STOCKADE AT THE STATE PRISON, RALEIGH

city the people actually keep tulips, hyacinths, and such plants out in their door-yards all winter. Thus does North Carolina so cheapen the flowers with which we deck ourselves and our homes, and which we have so long mistaken for Northerners, like ourselves. She may be said almost to hand them to us—in the profusion in which we have them, at least—as a charming sister brightens the chamber of a gallant knight.

With the flowers go the fruits, as they naturally should. The growing of berries and of garden-truck is an industry that has developed truly magnificent proportions in North Carolina. It is mainly confined to the sea-coast section, but it is rapidly covering the whole of the front of the State. This particular phase of the industrial revolution in the South, which we shall have to mention again and again as different sections are treated, may not be as revolutionary as the appearance of the cotton-manufacturers in such great force in three of the States, but it is, nevertheless, very remarkable. Along the Atlantic edge of Virginia, the Carolinas, Georgia, and Florida the planters in the *ante-bellum* time grew little else than cotton, and depended wholly on the money it brought for the purchase of everything else, even to the goods that were made of the cotton. If vegetables and small fruits were seen to grow on this land in those days the fact made no impression, and the insignificant produce got only contempt. But cotton fell in value; it proved itself a monarch in which too many persons had trusted blindly. There ensued an era of distress and gloom. It was in southeastern Virginia, close to the borders of North Carolina, that the warm climate, the humid atmosphere, and the rich soil were found to offer the essentials for maturing small fruits and vegetables in advance of those for which the Northern people waited yearly with impatience. Here truck-farming grew from an experiment to a successful industry. Then came the travel to Florida as a winter resort, and then the almost wild scramble for land in that State for orange orchards—a scramble in which, as I have shown, the land that grew no oranges and that which grew poor oranges went with the rest. The natural shortening of the journey between Florida and the North was rapidly brought about by railroad combinations and

PREPARING TUBEROSE BULBS FOR THE NORTHERN MARKET

enterprise, and by the perfection and increase of steamship facilities. Thus easy access to the Northern market was afforded all the coast-line between Florida and

A WILMINGTON RESIDENCE

Norfolk, the first market-town of the new trade in garden-truck. As each State grasped the new opportunity the arrival of spring and summer produce was hastened in the North, and Georgia came to be first with her treasures, then South Carolina, next North Carolina, and then Virginia, last where she had been first, but still in demand to lengthen the link between summer and summer, and to shorten the period of winter deprivation in the North. As early as 1884 Charleston alone was shipping half a million quarts of strawberries, a tenth as many barrels of potatoes, and 62,333 packages of vegetables in a season.

To-day the Commissioner of Agriculture announces truck-farming to be "among the foremost occupations in North Carolina as a money resource." The best dis-

trict is around New-Berne, where there are 8000 acres
planted in strawberries, asparagus, green pease, cabbages, beans, kale, beets, turnips, Irish potatoes, tomatoes, cucumbers, egg-plants, radishes, etc. During the
shipping season the railroad has run from one to three
trains a day from this district, and two steamers have
made five trips a week laden with the produce. It is
said, as a result of careful calculation, that this New-
Berne section realized $750,000 from its produce in the
season of 1891, and the farmers netted half a million of
dollars. Wilmington, Elizabeth City, Goldsboro, are
other large shipping-points for other districts, but there
are many others that are marked by mere railway side-
tracks, where many cars are loaded daily in the season.
There is a good deal of very enlightened farming down
there, and, in consequence, there are farmers whose profits at the end of a single year are what the mass of men

A CAROLINA MANSION

would call fortunes. On one—the farm most wisely managed, perhaps—we find 170 head of cattle, 66 horses, 139 hogs, a dairy, a saw-mill for the needs of the box-factory, and a fertilizer-making plant. On this farm 600 acres were put into truck last year, and 300 were sown with oats and grass. When one considers how short a time it is since the farmers there were exclusively plant-ers of cotton, and what a precarious living their meth-ods brought, this seems indeed a long stride ahead.

And this is not true merely of the truck region of the coast. "The low price of cotton and the high price of everything else," as one State official put it, "have led the farmers, in great numbers, to diversify their industry and to raise what they consume at home." More meat was killed in North Carolina last year than ever before. Hogs, cattle, horses, milk, butter, fruit, vegetables, and corn are products that are increasing very rapidly. Sheep also are multiplying, though sheep-raising calls for so much outlay in guarding the stock against dogs that only men with capital make a business of it. Ra-leigh is now supplied with all the milk and butter it uses, though not sufficient dairying is yet done to make the products articles of export. The result of all this, as might have been expected, has been a remarkable re-moval of mortgages all over the State within the past few years. And this prosperity reflects upon the State itself, so that her debt is trifling, and at least one issue of bonds by the commonwealth rates almost as high as the bonds of the Federal government.

The revolution is also reflected in the cities. Wil-mington is a bustling, wide-awake town, with a solid and very active business quarter, and all the superficial signs of a prosperous and ambitious population. Char-lotte, the richest city in the State, has invested so heav-ily in cotton-mills and other ventures in various other

FERRY AND NAVAL STORES, WILMINGTON

towns and sections that it is said she would have a population of 60,000 were her industries all at home. It is doubtful whether the place would then be as inviting as it is now, for though it is busy, it is also beautiful.

COURT-HOUSE AND CITY HALL, WILMINGTON

Raleigh, the capital, which is so well shaded that a bird's-eye view of it discloses little else than trees, is at once neat and substantial, and rather more Northern than Southern looking, except for the (typically Southern) great width of its main streets. And yet these are paved and well cared for, besides being busy. The city is credited with 17,000 inhabitants, and maintains three cotton-mills, several machine-shops, two fertilizer-factories, an oil-mill, a car-works, and several candy-factories, one of which is celebrated far beyond Raleigh. It is also a trading centre, and has large commercial establishments. All these businesses are supplied with local capital, and it is important to add that this is generally the case in both the Carolinas.

Raleigh has several fine educational foundations, but one that interested me very much indeed was the College of Agricultural and Mechanic Arts. The other Southern States possess more or less similar institutions, maintained with Federal aid, and if they are in any great degree as well and even proudly managed as this of North Carolina, it is a grand thing, particularly where men have been too prone to think it undignified to work for themselves. Here we find an expensively

AGRICULTURAL SCHOOL AND
DORMITORIES, RALEIGH

housed and well-equipped institution, which, although only four years old, has already graduated one class, two-thirds of whose members obtained situations at once. Both teachers and pupils were alike enthusiastic when I went through the buildings. I found there a fine smithy, a forge-room, a machine-shop (in which stood a steam-engine made by the graduates); a wood-turning department and joiner-work class-room; a very fine chemical laboratory presided over by an ambitious Cornell man; a model barn, a dairy building, a large experimental farm, and an agricultural experiment and State weather station. The young men are here fitted to become intelligent, educated, and practical farmers, horticulturists, cattle and stock raisers, dairymen, as well as machinists, carpenters, architects, draughtsmen, manufacturers, and contractors. I do not mean to claim too much in saying this; what I do mean is that they learn the rudiments of these occupations, as well as to use their brains and their hands. A full mathematical course is part of the curriculum, and a much more important source of strength to each pupil is the association with the ambitious young fellows of the State, and the daily intercourse with the able and accomplished members of the faculty. Here were some boys from very humble homes, and yet so intent upon becoming masters, instead of dependents, as to be found waiting on the others at the dining-table in order to earn their living while they studied. A certain number of pupils are admitted free, subject to an examination in rudimentary studies. They pay $8 a month for board and extras. The others pay $20 a year for tuition in addition to the same charge for board and extras.

But the good work of the institution does not stop there. The officers reply to all requests for information by the farmers of the State, and hold farmers' meetings wherever requested for the discussion of subjects connected with practical farming. Dr. H. B. Battle, as head of the experiment station, also issues frequent and very valuable bulletins, sent free to thousands of farmers, telling them how to guard against insect pests, warning them against inferior or fraudulent fertilizers, discussing methods of farming, explaining how waste can be prevented, how they can determine the best things to grow, and, in a sentence, scattering the most practical and most needed advice, in thick pamphlets as well as mere fly-sheets, among the agriculturists of the State. Further yet, the station is pushing an almost unique plan of spreading information by sending

PHOSPHATE MINES NEAR WILMINGTON

out stereotyped-plate matter free to the newspapers of the State. Alexander Q. Halladay, Esq., is the president of the college and its allied farm and stations.

Leaving agriculture out of further consideration, we will observe that, for variety, the resources of the State do not depend upon that industry, though it is, of course, mainly and primarily a farming State. But its turpentine stills are a source of revenue, its forests are of great extent and value, its fisheries employ about 6000 persons, gold-mining is carried on in several counties, and the quarrying of marble, granite, sandstone, and of Belgian blocks for the paving of city streets is done in many parts of the State. The story of the traveller who, on being shown a beautiful piece of mahogany furniture, replied, " Yes, where I live they make fence rails of mahogany," could be paralleled by many citizens of western North Carolina if any were called upon to admire a granite building, for they might truly say that in their parts of the State there are towns where all the fence posts are made of granite. Coal-mining is a new industry in North Carolina, but it is carried on with all the rest. There are two coal belts there. A company of Northern capitalists is working a rich field of good bituminous coal at Egypt, and another Northern company owns some mines of what is called semi-anthracite a little southwest of that place. At Kings Mountain a company has been formed to develop a tin-bearing region, which it is thought they can mine profitably.

The exporting of grapes and even the manufacture of wine have been a source of revenue to North Carolina during a quarter of a century. A new and quickened interest in these businesses is shown in the gradual multiplication of vineyards, and in the profits and growth of certain of the older ones, and, since wild grapes are said to have grown naturally all over the State, these may yet become important industries. Mineral springs of more or less celebrity are numerous ; and of popular resorts for tourists and invalids, led by the thriving and beautiful town of Asheville, there are many, as well as sites for ten times as many more, in the healthful and picturesque mountain districts. The population of the State is no greater than that of New York city, but, unlike South Carolina, the whites are nearly twice as numerous as the negroes, the difference (according to the last census) being that there were 1,055,382 whites and 562,565 colored persons. One would argue from this fact that North Carolina would attract immigrants in greater number than almost any of the more southerly

NEGRO CEMETERY AT WILMINGTON

States, and yet in 1890 there were only 3742 foreign-born persons in the State. John Robinson, Esq., the Commissioner of Agriculture, says, upon this subject : "The immigration into North Carolina is largely from the New England, Middle, and some of the Northwestern States, and gives many and much-desired and much-valued accessions to sources of material development."

It seems, then, to whatever small extent this increase comes, the Old North State is enjoying what the most influential men in all the Southern States desire and demand. The South wants men with capital, and not men with mere hands and energy and willingness to work. It wants men who will buy and cultivate plantations, who will establish mills, and who will organize corporations for the development of its resources.

The Charleston *News and Courier* of November 22, 1893, says, " Those who would not make desirable citizens *should not be encouraged* to seek homes in the South." After arguing that those farmers in New England and parts of the West whose farms are poor would do well to leave them and go South, it generously asserts that there is room for such new-comers "as the Germans, Scandinavians, Swiss, Scotch, and Yankees" —an intentional compliment, for he adds, " *none but the best are good enough for South Carolina.*"

VIII

WHERE TIME HAS SLUMBERED

" MEBBY Mrs. Cap'n will have one," or, " You'd better go and see Mrs. Cap'n," or, " If there's any sich thing around, mebbe Mrs. Cap'n 'll have it." These things were so often said to the hunter from New York, who was down in West Virginia partly for deer, and largely for relics of a by-gone era, that he determined to see " Mrs. Cap'n," and to know more about her. There seemed to be little to know, and that was told readily in answer to his questions, for it was evident that she was the most conspicuous woman on the mountain on which she lived. All the mountain folk knew her or knew about her, but at the same time it became clear to the stranger from New York that there was some little mystery—something kept back. It was said of her that she was " more forehanded " than most women, that she was very industrious, that she was proud, and " kep' her head well up," and that she had been a widow through the best part of her life—a widow so stricken by her bereavement that no man had since been able to make any impression upon her affections, though the best men in that section had tried. That in itself was peculiar enough to make her conspicuous.

Freely as this was told, it was often accompanied by a manner that led the stranger to fancy there was more to learn. His failure to break through this reserve whetted his curiosity, and one day he went straight to the woman herself in her cabin. The cabin, externally, was very like all the rest—a little log house with a stone chimney projecting from one end, with a roof made of those large shingles that they call "clapboards" down there, with a row of three small window-panes set in the end opposite the chimney for an extra window, in addition to the real window that was beside the door-way, and that was also like a window in the daytime, and was usually left open to serve as such. Over and in front of the door was a rude, ramshackle porch. It was made of a few boards held up at the outer ends by a beam laid across two posts. It was apparently maintained to protect a flooring of rough logs sunk in the ground, but it could shelter them only from such rare rains as fell straight down from overhead, so that perhaps its best service was to accommodate several bunches of dried or drying "yarbs." They hung at just the right height beneath the porch to hit a visitor's hat, and cause him to glance quickly around for the assailant who had made a target of his head-gear. The house or cabin stood in a little clearing of much trampled and furrowed dirt, with its chimney end towards the road, and its door and porch facing the rest of "Mrs. Cap'n's" buildings—a corn and tobacco house, a stable, and a pig-sty—properties not altogether uncommon in those mountains, and yet not so common but that they reflected proudly upon the family as one that was pretty well-to-do as things go in that country. The corn-house and pigsty were commonplace, but the stable was one to arrest a stranger's attention. It was built on the plan of a canary-cage, with its sides almost as open as if you were expected to hand in hay by the half-bale to the horse through the space between the boards, or to pass him in a pail of water whenever he was thirsty, without bothering with the door. And even that kind of stable

300

INTERIOR OF A MOUNTAIN CABIN

is commonplace in West Virginia, for that is the kind they build there, either because the climate is never severe, or possibly because a great storm would blow right through the building without carrying it away, as the winds pass through a net-work banner in the streets. But that is a mere ignorant conjecture, such as a stranger might make, since West Virginia is one of the few of our commonwealths that are free from really big American weather, with all that the term implies.

"Can I come in?" said the hunter from New York, pausing in the open doorway.

"Yaas; come in and hev a warm," said a man who sat before some blazing logs in the deep tall recess in the Dutch chimney. "Draw up a cheer by the fire and hev a warm."

"Is this Mrs. Captain's?"

"Yaas," said the man; "Mrs. Cap'n is my sister. She's up above. That's her a-shakin' things with her loom—makin' a little rag kyarpet fer Killis Kyar's folks. Sence Killis Kyar's moved into his new house on the valley road his gals is mighty ticky. And yit" (thoughtfully) "they ain't nothin' like's ticky as some. When I see the young folks that's so awful nice about hevin' kyarpets on the floor an' curtings on the winders and that-all, I often say to 'em, 'Ef you-all could see how yer fathers lived without none of them things, you-all wouldn't be so ticky.'"

"But you've got a carpet here—and curtains," said the stranger.

"Oh, *we* hev," said the man. "That's Mrs. Cap'n—she's different."

It was evident that she and much besides were different, as the old man said. We shall see that most mountain cabins are bare (floor, ceiling, walls, and all), but here was a floor-covering of rag-carpet, and the window had a small section of a yellow lace curtain drawn across it, and the ceiling was clean, instead of being grimy with smoke like most others. And there were several tintypes grouped together not inartistically on one wall, and some gay lithographs, such as one gets at a country grocery, on the opposite wall. Two long mountain rifles, made pretty by brass-work inlaid in the stocks, ornamented two rafters, and some powder-horns and pouches and a dog-horn—the very sort of curios the hunter was seeking—hung upon other rafters. But the marvel of marvels in the cabin was one of the beds. It was a century-old "four-poster," standing so high above the floor that no man could reach the tops of the solid fluted posts, and no man would care to meet with such a mishap as to fall from the bedding to the floor. As the stranger looked about him the old man followed his eyes, and commented upon whatever they took in.

"Yaas," said he; "Mrs. Cap'n is different, you know. That's hern, that big bed. Me and young Cap'n, when he's to home, sleeps on that low bed thar" (nodding at an ordinary bed made up in a sort of low open box that sat on the floor without legs beneath it). "Them guns and things she takes fer the kyarpets and jeans she weaves, and sells 'em to strangers like you-all fer ten times what they're wuth. Them picters is hern too."

"Everybody speaks highly of her; she must be a remarkable woman," said the stranger.

"Waal, 'tain't *that*, so much," said the old man, pausing, and puffing at his pipe, and reflecting rather dreamily as he began to talk. "I reckon it's the hard times she's had, an' the way she's bore up through it. Her husband bein' killed so quick, an' her mournin' for him so stiddy. I reckon that's it."

"How was he killed?"

"The Cap'n? He was shot takin' some deserters into

camp; ambushed not more'n a mile away from here. I reckon that's why folks is so set towards her. He on'y was here a short time, but he stuck to her 'bout all the time he could spare. Our house was his quarters till the General give orders to forward the hull of the army on further west. I was away, 'listed on the Confed'rit side; but I'm Union now—because the Cap'n was Union. Anyhow, 'most nine in ten 'round here was always Union. My sister was Union soon as she seen the Cap'n, tho' she hadn't been before. That's near thirty year ago, and she's been mournin' and takin' on ever since. They were jist surely cut out for one another, and were agreed to be married, an' everything was arranged—and then he was ambushed by some friends of the men he was arrestin'."

"What was his name?"

"Thar, now," said the old man, "she kin tell you that. I never could just rightly remember it. Her bein' called 'Mrs. Cap'n' by they-all just drove his name outer my head. He was from Ohier—I know *that* —and had a name you couldn't take hold of easy, endin' in 'berger,' or—no, maybe it wasn't just 'berger' neither."

At this point a cessation of the regular thud-thud of the loom overhead gave notice that Mrs. Cap'n was resting. A moment later her voice sounded down through the square hole at the top of the ladder that served for the stairs to the second story.

"Pole!" the voice said; "what does he want, Pole?"

"Well, I declare; that's so," said the old man; "what did you want—anything 'sides a warm? I reckon maybe you'd like a cold slice."

"No," said the stranger; "I came to see if I could buy an old gun, like one of those I see you have there. I heard your sister had one or two."

304

THE OLD TAVERN IN THE VALLEY

"Reckon you'd better come down, Tish," said the old man. "He wants one o' your rifles, maybe."

With much deliberation and extraordinary disturbance of mind over her skirts, which were as contumacious as they might be expected to be when forced through a two-foot hole and down a ladder nailed against a wall, Mrs. Letitia Cap'n (for Tish is the diminutive of Letitia in those mountains) came down into the main room. Except that she was not as shy as most mountain women in the presence of a strange man, she was very like the rest —a spare, angular woman of middle age, in a dress that was as simple as a woman's dress could be, and that consisted of a plain waist of pink calico, and a plain skirt of the same stuff that no more than reached to her shoe-tops. She differed from the other women whom the stranger had seen thereabouts in that she wore a white apron—a superfluity trifling in itself, and yet impressive in the effect of neatness and self-respect that it produced. Perhaps, too, she was more comely than her neighbors in the sight of the mountain men. They could make closer comparisons than a stranger might. To this stranger who now regarded her she had, in common with the rest, the colorless lips, the pinched features, and the lack-lustre eyes of all the typical, badly nourished, over-worked, dyspeptic mountain folk. At the suggestion of an offer of his right hand by the stranger, she put both her long bony hands behind her back—not rudely, but from a blending of awkwardness and shyness. The bartering for the gun being over, the stranger remarked that he and her brother had been speaking of "the Captain." Something very like a spark of life lighted up the woman's eyes when the subject was introduced, and she stepped to the wall and took down two pictures — both tintypes.

"This is Cap'n's picture," said she, handling one tenderly, and offering it with a little enthusiasm, as something certain to be admired, though it was a wretchedly bad piece of workmanship. It was a photograph of a soldier in uniform.

"And hain't this one like him?" she asked, putting the other card in the stranger's hand. He saw no resemblance to one in the other; but understanding that even a bad picture may convey a perfect portraiture to the mind of one who knows the face that is hinted at, he avoided her question, and asked whose was the second portrait.

"It's young Cap'n's—my son's," said she, very proudly; "and I can see the Cap'n growing up in him all over again when I look at him. To me it's just like the Cap'n had come back, fer they're both the same age. Young Cap'n is about twenty-nine, and so was his father when he was killed."

The stranger looked at the tintypes more closely. To him the face of the soldier appeared that of a vain and weak man. The low brow, the immense mustachios curled up at the ends, the small eyes, and the abnormal breadth of the face at the cheek-bones suggested something that quite startled him—the possibility that the Captain had been such a man as might, had he lived, have broken the heart of the woman who now held his memory so sacred.

"Young Cap'n's on the railroad — telegraph operatin'," said she. "When he comes home I see him and his father together. You hain't from Ohier, be yer? No! 'Cause there wuz a man from Ohier 'bout ten year ago—I just can't happen to think out his name— and he told 'round that the Cap'n was married a'ready when he 'listed fer the war. Pole here—my brother— might 'a' found out what the man knew, if he'd a-been more keerful. I was sorry fer what you done, Pole, and you know it—gittin' down your ole rifle and huntin' the man outen the country, the way you done."

"I'd like to 'a' raised my ole gyurl rifle on that critter till his head darkened the sight," said the old hunter. "That's all me and my ole gyurl wanted that time, Tish. Reckon I was too keerful with Bird Jiney, too, mebbe."

"I don't say you was, Pole," Mrs. Captain replied, "fer Bird Jiney was ornery."

She then explained to the stranger that a neighbor of the name of Jiney—a man so contemptible that even his folks were "mean" (a hard thing to say of any one) —had "dar'd" to speak slightingly of her and her widowhood, and that, after giving him fair warning to leave the country, her brother had met him on a mountain road, and jerking him from the back of his horse, had dropped him over the edge of a cliff. Mrs. Captain added that Jiney had not been killed, but, after his broken bones had healed, had gone away "to some of them cities in old Virginia" to start life over again. After an interval of several years he had sent her the bed on which she had slept ever since—the huge semi-royal four-poster close by—far and away the most impressive, pretentious, and costly article of household furniture in the county. Mrs. Captain had accepted the gift as a peace-offering, she being a very thrifty woman, and the bed being a thing that could not be sent back without great expense. After that she had expected Bird Jiney to limp back into the neighborhood among his friends and family, but he had never been heard from again.

It was evident that brother Pole's energy in protecting his sister was enough to account for the brake on the gossiping tendencies of the neighbors. He made it "unhealthy," as they say out West, to talk too much

THE CIRCUIT-RIDER

about Mrs. Cap'n, even though no one had anything but praise to speak of her.

"They-all round here says I'm proud, mebbe," Mrs. Captain continued; "but I'm only proud fer my husband. If he'd 'a' lived I'd 'a' been better off than any of they-all, and since he died I'm bound to work and save money, and live's near as I kin to the way he'd have had me. If I'm puttin' on, I'm on'y puttin' on fer Cap'n—hain't I, Pole? Mebbe he's where he kin see me and the kyarpet like he told me he had in Ohier, and the curting and—and the bed—and kin see me workin' and doing my best."

"She don't keer fer herself," said the old man; "she on'y thinks of him and young Cap'n. I never see anything like it."

"And I don't keer if you're fom Ohier er not," she went on; "fer, tell the truth, your voice did naturally remind me of Ohier, somehow. I don't·keer if Cap'n *was* married 'fore he 'listed in the war."

"Tish!" said the brother, warningly.

"No, Pole; mebbe it don't sound fittin'—and it ain't fittin'—fer any one to say that; and we know he *couldn't* 'a' been married; but yit if Cap'n had a wife in Ohier I pity her with all my heart. He might have had her, Pole, *but I just certainly had his love.*"

The stranger who told me of that adventure, as we sat before a log fire in a West Virginia tavern, told it to illustrate something of the peculiarity of the mountain people—not so much by the woman's history, for that was peculiar even there, but by the setting and accessories of the tale. After that I looked in many a cabin in the hope that I might see the great bed, which stood transfigured in my mind as a sort of altar, but I never saw it or the woman, who, without acknowledg-

ing or even realizing her fault, retrieved it so completely afterwards.

The mountain districts of West Virginia are as strange
in their primitive population as in their tossed and
tumbled surface. The cities and larger towns and many
of the cultivated valleys compare favorably with those
of other States, and it is not of them that I am writing.
But the greater part of the State is made up of mountains, and it is there that we see how unique are her
people and their ways. New Mexico, with its glare of
sands and its half-Mexican population, is more foreign,
but it is not so picturesque nor nearly so peculiar as
this abiding-place of a genuine and pure American population, whose civilization has stood still for more than
a century. We go to Europe to seek what is less
strange; indeed, it is a far journey to such another
anachronism as West Virginia. Those reformers who
fancy that legislation is a short-cut to virtue, and that
nature can be altered by a change of statutes, might almost find their dreams realized in West Virginia; for
when that State was cut off from Old Virginia, leaving the old Mother of Presidents with her original
boundaries on the West, the progress of two centuries
and a half seemed also to have been cut off. And West
Virginia began, thirty years ago, where old Virginia
did, with a civilization that is to-day what might be expected of thirty years of settlement in a rough country.

It is not strange that travellers should find the scenery and flora of the Alleghanies so similar from Pennsylvania to Georgia that a blindfolded man taken to
any part of them and uncovered could never tell in
which State he stood. The mountain altitudes regu-
late the climate, and that makes all the rest nearly uniform. But it is strange to find the people so much
alike from end to end of the great chain of mountains

311

—to find them all so backward and simple, all so tall and spare and angular, all speaking so nearly the same dialect, all living in cabins of nearly one pattern, and copying one another even in such little details as lead them to use one sort of broad-strap harness that one sees put upon no other horses than theirs. To be sure, the valleys run parallel up and down the ranges, but there are passes from east to west, and through some of these are run latter-day railroads, with Pullman coaches, "diners," and the accompaniments of telephone and telegraph. And there are old railroads, too, which long ago broke through the fastnesses, and carried the nineteenth century in their wake. Yet the old life turned not aside. It still follows the trend of the valleys. And the new life hurries through as if it was conveyed "in bond," as we send goods through Canada to Chicago. At any point on the frontier or in the heart of West Virginia you step from your Pullman to the wagon that awaits you, and the length of a morning's "constitutional" finds you in the dominion of a belated century. The time is right by your watch, but your pocket-calendar is a hundred years too far ahead. It is true that the present era jars the past in places. The Chesapeake and Ohio Railroad, which bisects the State, is modern even to elegance, but thousands of the people near its steel threads have never ridden over a mile of it. That very modern statesman W. L. Wilson hails from there; but the life in the mountains is so ancient that George Washington, were he back on earth, would say, after a tour of the whole country, "At last, here I find a part of the world as I left it."

I went into West Virginia over the Pennsylvania border last summer, and put up at a mountain-spring resort. There was a clashing of two centuries there. The arch city maiden in white flannel was there trim-

ming her hat with butterflies, sticking a hat-pin into
them at twenty places, "so as to find their hearts and
kill them without hurting them too much," and at
night she banged out Sousa's last two-step in a way
that filled the old woods with the breath of a Michigan
Avenue boarding-house. But in the early morning,
when her flannel suit hung over a chair, and her "white
sailor" sat the top of the bedroom pitcher with a
rakish cant to one side, the squirrels and the locusts and
katydids had the forests to themselves, and the early
stirrers on the mountain roads were the old-time West-
Virginians, as simple and genuine as fresh air.

Observing that the strangers at the Springs came
from unthought-of distances to drink the sulphur water
that bubbled up in the meadow by the hotel, they too
paid the tardy century the compliment of drinking its
catholicon. But with never-failing shyness they always

came at sunup, without noise or bustle, though in strong
force, to fill their pails and cans and blickeys and carry
the liquid away. They and the nineteenth - century
boarders were impressed and cozened by the same fact:
the water smelled so bad and tasted so nasty that it
must certainly be good medicine. I never will forget
how the mountaineers interested me. The women came
sidewise, bobbing lightly up and down on the horses,
with both feet side by side on the animal's ribs. The
capes of their calico hoods waved prettily in the breeze.
The teamsters knew better than to sit on the jolting
wagons that pounded over the rocks in the roads, so
each saddled the left-hand horse of his team and rode at
ease, while the horses tugged up the hills with a force
that had to be met and eased by means of the harness
of broad straps which is the horse-gear of the entire
Appalachian world. The little boys brought trousers
that did not know their shoes, never having met them,
and jackets that mimicked the trousers by being too
short — in the sleeves as well as the body. The little
girls were bare at both top and toe, as befitted creatures
that did not have to go into the thorn and bramble
thickets, as the boys had to do in order to be boys. But
their tubular cotton drawers desired to see as much of
life as possible, and therefore reached below their little
dresses. All alike were simple, honest, unobtrusive, and
shy. Nothing but a "bush-meeting" seemed powerful
enough to bring them out in force, but at that they
opened their shells like clams at high-water—for everywhere, from one end of the mountains to the other,
they are deeply religious. They are "Baptis'" and
"Methodys" wherever I saw them. Mr. Remington
and I met one in the Potts Creek Valley, over near
the old Virginia line, who had been out to Oregon,
and was doing well there, but came back to Potts

Creek "because they didn't respect the Sabbath out West."

There are church buildings in the villages, but the villages are few and far apart, and in this particular place the custom was for some preacher to spring as it were out of nowhere and to announce a bush-meeting by means of a written placard nailed to a tree by the spring. It was to be held at two o'clock in a certain patch of woods, so commonly and frequently the scene of such meetings that the rude benches made of planks nailed to tree stumps were always there, and kept in good order, apparently by a devout mountaineer who lived in the nearest cabin. The meeting lasted less than an hour, but the people made it the affair of a day. They came from as far as the news of the meeting had been carried by the equestrians and wagoners who had reined up at sight of the placard and halted "to see what's a-goin' on." Some, therefore, had been obliged to set out soon after breakfast — and that would not make a long journey where six miles of road may loop over the top of a tremendous mountain, up which the horses crawl, and the more humane men lead instead of riding them. Before noon the wagons began to come in. Bars were let down at various points near the camp-ground, and the teams were tethered to the trees in half a dozen scattered parts of the woods. The wagons were such as one sees all over the land, made in Racine, Wisconsin, or South Bend, Indiana, or Cortland, New York. Out of them came men and women, girls and boys, and even babies. By noon nearly all the worshippers were on hand — strolling from hitching-place to hitching-place to see who had come, and to gossip with friends and acquaintances. It is wonderful how far and wide men are known to one another in these mountains. The people are sociable in the extreme. We would call them "shiftless" as a race, for it is a fact that they have inherited the discouragement of their ancestors, who must have early given up the effort to wrest more than a bare living out of agriculture in a territory that is rich only where it is mined for coal and iron and stone.

Wherever nature refuses a living in return for fair effort, humanity becomes stagnant or demoralized, and in West Virginia, still the great game-preserve for the Middle and Atlantic States, the rod and gun were early found to be more profitable companions than the plough and shovel, so that a race of hunters developed there —hunters with the patience and philosophy that the Indian emphasizes, and that lead all such men, white, red, or black, to snub Dame Fortune if she comes with that heavy tax of care and responsibility which we call civilization, and which the woodsman sees through as if it were plate-glass, and regards as bringing very little at a very great cost.

Therefore these mountain folk take a great deal of time and pains to know one another, and having this wide acquaintance, they solder it to their lives with incessant gatherings like this bush-meeting. They hold "log-rollings" and "corn-shuckings" and dances and shooting-matches and "gander-pulls," and one thing or another, to make up a circle of gatherings that reaches around the whole year, and closes around every life in each district. I paid a visit one day at the tip-top of a mountain and at the end of a trail that hadn't one other cabin by its side. To me the cabin seemed a mere accentuation of a solitude I had scarcely believed possible. I remarked to the woman of the cabin that I should have thought she would be very lonely. Lonely? That showed my ignorance. Why, there never passed a day on which some of the "neighbors" did not drop in, and

MOUNTAIN WOMEN

at least once or twice a week she would "git to go 'round 'mong the neighborhood women." Then there was "allers some of the neighborhood chillun and her chillun passin' to and fro; an' on'y night before last there was a corn-shuckin' and a dance here; on'y it wasn't so big but what the beds was left standin', 'stid of bein' sot out, same as when we hev a big dance; an' my man's got some corn to shuck yit."

To return to the out-door church service, the interchange of visits was followed by a return of each party to its wagon for a picnic dinner upon whatever had been brought along—cold corn pone principally. When all the worshippers gathered at the bush-meeting it was seen not to be very different from a Northern camp-meeting, such as one sees in New Jersey particularly. The men wore soft felt hats and long beards, and seemed never to have combed their hair. The women had on broad-brimmed black straw hats, such as I was told a mountain woman is able to keep and use for "Sunday best" for a quarter of a century. The boys looked boldly at the girls, and the girls looked slyly at the boys out of the tails of their eyes. The sudden rattling of a wagon among the trees, followed by a loud "Whoa there!" occasionally sounded above the prayer and song. Some of the men who came without women stood away from the worshippers, smoking, and talking as country-men converse, in broken sentences wide apart, with the fractures filled up by vigorous tobacco-chewing. The preacher was a woman—a "Mrs. Lawson of Kentucky, the celebrated evangelist." She brought a young man with her to "open with prayer," and to pass around his hat, and after his prayer she delivered an address, which, if it were right to pass judgment upon it, I should declare to be the most noisy and the least thoughtful sermon or talk that I ever heard. There was singing before and after her address, and it was noticeable that though the young man had to sing nearly the whole first verse entirely alone, the people afterwards sang the remaining verses, though there was not a book or printed copy of the hymn in the forest.

In the eastern part of the State, nearer to Virginia, I found that the circuit-rider still ministers to the religious welfare of the mountain folks. There are neat little white and green church buildings in the valleys, but they are opened only once a month. About as often as that, and in some cases regularly, the circuit-rider sends word of his coming to the elders or deacons, or puts the notice in the country paper if one is published near the meeting-house, and on the given day he appears on horseback, with a few extra belongings and his Bible and song-book rolled up behind him on his saddle. Wherever he preaches he has a large meeting, and he "boards 'round" with the religious families in the old time-honored way. But to end the glimpse I got of the State in the summer requires a mention of the mountaineer laundress at "the Springs." Her name was "Miss" Sony Bowyer—"Miss" meaning Mistress, and "Sony" being the abbreviation of the not uncommon name of Lasonia. She was down at the spring with her pitcher for the day's drinking water.

"I'd like to send up my washing to you this afternoon," said I.

"I'd rather you wouldn't, not to-day," said "Miss" Bowyer. "It would just certainly muddle me. You see how it is: I'm ironin' the Adamses now, and I hate ter mix the families up. I'm so afraid there'll be some mistake, so I wash and iron each family separate. To-day I'm ironin' the Adamses, and in the morning I'll wash the Browns. In the afternoon I'll iron the Browns, and by Wednesday I'll take up— What's your name? Ralph? Yes, by Wednesday I'll be able to wash the Ralphs."

Virginia, according to the historians, was settled in 1607; and West Virginia, the territory west of the mountains, was invaded by settlers nearly a century and a half later—in 1750. "Many a young man," as I read somewhere, "married the girl of his choice, and, with axe in belt and rifle on shoulder, accompanied by his bride, started out to locate on a purchase of land he had made in the wild but beautiful new country." Beautiful it is to-day, and very largely wild. The picturesque young pioneer felled trees, made logs, and put up a cabin, raising a chimney of rough stones at the end of the shanty against the arrival of the winter, if not to provide for immediate culinary needs. He hung his rifle and pouch and powder-horn on the rafters, and his wife got a spinning-wheel and loom somehow from old Virginia. As schools did not follow him into the woods he grew up with a mind as placid as a mill-pond, unruffled by any of those dreams and doubts which in other minds elsewhere became the fathers and mothers of progress. All that, says the historian, was in and after 1750, and yet it is very little different now in by far the greater part of West Virginia. The cabins are precisely the same as the first pioneer would have built when he let go his faithful bride's hand and began to swing his axe. The flintlock rifle, nearly seven feet long, that he first shouldered, he ordered cut down, and cut down again, in Richmond and Baltimore, as his carelessness allowed the saltpetre to corrode the pan; and at one time or another he allowed the gunsmith to tear off the flintlock and make his piece a "cushion" gun—that being what he calls a rifle that fires by means of a percussion-cap. Even the Winchester is creeping into the cabins now. The young bride, reproduced in

320

THE UNITED STATES MAIL IN THE MOUNTAINS

her progeny, is slowly giving up the use of her spinning-
wheel and loom, because there is no profit in the wondrous jean she makes, at less than a dollar a yard, and
yet factory jean brings only a few cents. Nevertheless,
there is still some call for her art to-day. Plenty of
mountain folk are wearing homespun stuff from their
bodies outward, and I saw two spinning-wheels and two

looms at work in one small valley, besides hearing of at least one other pair of these last-century machines in a cabin I did not visit.

The greatest difference between the present time and the long ago is seen in the presence of numerous free schools all over the mountains, and already they are awakening the people.

I made notes of the primitive out-door and in-door scenes in the parts of West Virginia where I wandered, and perhaps nothing that I could do would serve the purpose better than to smoothly transcribe them without their losing the freshness of the views they reflect. The scenery is the same from the middle of Pennsylvania to Georgia—the same rounded, wooded mountains; the same green, often fertile valleys, checkerboarded with farms; the same stone-strewn watercourses brawling down the hill-sides; the same frequent, almost general, forests; the same few roads and many trails; the same log cabins; the same clearings. Everywhere the same deep blue hangs overhead, and the mountains turn from near-by green to distant purple. The wood fires everywhere send up thin blue veils of smoke above the cabins, and the scenes in which humanity figures are played by characters that are everywhere very much alike. Perhaps in the North there are more covered bridges, but the rule, over the entire mountain system, is for the horses and wagons to cross the streams by means of fords over "branches" and creeks that are floored with great thicknesses of shaly, flat, smooth stones. The pedestrians get over the streams by means of foot-bridges, some of which are mere tree trunks resting on cross-bucks, and some of which are quite ornamental though simple suspension-bridges, with certainly one hand-rail, if not two, beside the planking.

It's a horseback country. There are main roads and

there are wagons to use upon them, but they are both "valley improvements," the products of the greater fertility of the lowlands, where the "quality" lived as planters before the war and worked large tracts with slaves, or where the small farms of the poor whites begat a prosperous middle class between the quality folk and the mountaineers. But a great population lives on the mountain-sides and mountain-tops, along bridle-paths that are mere trails, and these are not at all fit for wagoneering.

It has never occurred to any one to clear most of these trails. They run up and down the steepest inclines that a horse can climb, and they wind through forests and jungles of low growth so dense that I had to buy canvas "chaps" or leggings to ward off the thorns. Nevertheless I met men, and even women, on these trails who were dressed just as they would be at home, and who got through without tatters—how, I don't know. Often the vegetation was so thick that if my companions or I halted for even less than a minute, those who kept on were totally lost to view. This wildness is on the steep hill-sides. Wherever there is a bench or a plateau one comes upon a clearing here and there, with fields sown in oats, potatoes, and buckwheat, and perhaps a little tobacco, to be rolled into twists for home consumption and for barter with the "neighborhood men."

It is on the wagon roads that one meets the greater number of people, but the roads are not exactly Parisian boulevards. Those roads that cross the mountains have a queer way of going into partnership with the streams. Sometimes they run up the streams, so that at high-water a farmer fording his way looks like a human Neptune floating in his wagon, while his horses, up to their bellies in the crystal water, show neither legs nor flippers. Sometimes the stream abandons its bed and takes to the roadway for a piece, each such interchange by the one or the other being made to get a clear right of way through the tree-cluttered, bowlder-strewn region. Down in the valleys the roads are latticed in by the very tallest fences that are anywhere used by farmers. They are called stake-and-ridered fences, and are made of from seven to eleven rails laid zigzag, one pile of bars set this way and the next pile set the other way, with at least one " rider," and sometimes two, perched on tall crossed poles above the rest. Thus does West Virginia pay generous tribute to the agility of her mountain-bred cattle, poor and thin to look at or get milk or beef from, yet able to bound about like self-propelling rubber balls.

Between these towering gridiron fences one meets the people. Ah! those generous, hospitable, manly, frank, and narrow-minded people! Now it is two women that one meets—a mother and daughter, both on one horse, the mother on the saddle and the daughter behind her on an old shawl. They sit as if the horse was a chair, with their four shoes in a row, and their big hoods bobbing in unison. Next comes a farmer astride his steed, with a sack of meal in front of him, the wind blowing the front of his soft hat up against the crown, and the horse's sides working his trouser-legs up so as to show his blue and white home-knit woollen stockings. All along the sides of the road are pigs—the Africans of the brute creation—grunting contentedly, and eating, and clinging to the places where the sun is hottest. Deer-hounds skulk along wherever there are houses—the instruments of a short-sighted people for the ruin of the game which brings them not merely food, but the generous patronage of holiday huntsmen from all over the North and East.

A PRIVATE HUNTER

And here comes a wagon with its driver a-horseback, driving two of the four horses that are hitched by a net-work of broad black leather bands to a rumbling green box-wagon, loaded either with lumber, stone, or corn, you may be sure. The district doctor, certain to be the only "citified" man in a rude district, comes lolloping along on a better horse than his neighbors own, with his medicines in a leather roll on the back of his saddle, under his coat-tails.

"What sort of cases make up your practice, doctor?"

"Dyspepsia and child-birth—that is about all," he says, speaking the good English he learned at home in old Virginia and in college.

"And gunshot wounds?"

"Only accidental ones, and those very rarely," he replies.

"What of the morals of the people back in the mountains, doctor?"

"They have their own code, sir; one that differs slightly from that of more polished folk, but it is honest. They do not regard it as criminal to make moonshine whiskey. They make it because that is the only way they can get it. Marriages which you would say might better have been hurried are not uncommon, but here they preserve good names unharmed. There is little or no laxness beyond that. There is very little vagabondage of any sort. We have no tramps, no thieves, except a few who filch corn and meat rather than beg for it. Ambushing has not been practised for a long time, and only one murder has been committed in many years in the very large district in which I practise. Dog-poisoning by private hunters is the worst crime that is rampant. By-the-way, here comes a private hunter now."

It was Daniel Boone come back, in woollen clothes

instead of buck-skin,
and in a soft felt hat
instead of a 'coon-skin
cap. His tall lithe fig-
ure came rapidly, for
his strides were long
and light—a natural
man who thought
nothing of striding
like that from sunrise
until long after dark.
Over his shoulder he
carried a long old-
fashioned rifle, and
slung from his neck
by a strap and leather
thong were his pow-
der-horn, and his shot-
pouch, (with its deer-

OLD MOUNTAIN TYPE

horn "charger" for measuring the powder, and its bent-
wire hook crowded with cotton, "patches" to wrap
around the bullets). He had moccasins on his feet, and
his trousers were tied tight around the ankles with
brown twine. He was called a "private hunter" because
he hunted by and for himself, without the dogs that
are unleashed for strangers by men who hunt for pay.
Pretty nearly every mountain man is a "private hunter."

"You private hunters hate the dogs, and drop poi-
soned meat about to kill them." I so spoke.

"Ya-a-s," said the private hunter. "Reckon some of
'em does."

"Why?"

"'Cause the dogs is driving the game away. Every
season we has to go further and further away, and the
deer gits sca'cer and sca'cer."

327

"I'll tell you what you do," said I, "poison all the dogs you can. I am sorry to give you that advice, because the dogs are better than the men who use them—in fact, a good dog is better than any man. But keep on poisoning them."

The private hunter went off marvelling, for he knew that the jolly doctor by my side had the best dogs in the country. So did I.

"Strange advice to give," said the doctor, looking after the hunter, "for we've been saying that the dog - poisoner is the meanest varmint in the woods. I hunt with dogs myself, but I reckon you're right."

"Why do you do it? You surely know better."

"Oh, merely because everybody else does. It's got so that we cannot get deer without the dogs; and even then we have to go ten miles farther from the railroad."

"'Eve tempted me and I ate,'" said I. "Well, soon you will go without eating—venison, at any rate."

We rode on, and presently the doctor met a patient. The meeting was peculiar, since it took place when both men were in the middle of a rushing stream, whose waters brawled over their stony course and sent up little tongues that licked the knees of the horses. The patient wore a big soft hat and overcoat, and carried a pail in what should have been his free hand.

"Doctor," said he, "I've got a misery. They-all say you kin cure me. Kin you cure me, doctor?"

"Well, what's the matter with you?"

"I've got a smotherin' feelin', doctor," said the man, making up a face expressive of great distress. "'Pears like water washing 'round in my stummick." Here he made a rotary movement covering his whole trunk, from his chin to his legs, to show what he appeared to regard as his stomach. "Old Charley Jones says you kin knock 'em out. Kin you do it, doc? They're smotherin' spells. I've been takin' pills. Dun'no' what they are, but they're right black; only they don't go for the misery. Kin you cure me, doc?"

"Oh, I think so," said the doctor.

"Well, if you kin git to go up to my place and bring some better pills, I'll be right glad, doctor."

To describe the in-door life of the people we will begin with their picturesque little cabins. They are nearly all log cabins, often of one room, occasionally of two, and never of three. Each has a heavy chimney on one end, built of the stones picked off the ground near by. The chimneys are all alike—broad at the base to allow for the fireplace, and either daubed with mud inside and out, or left in the rough on the outside. The fireplace is made of slabs of stone, and usually two large stones project into the room to keep the fire from the flooring. The thrifty folk maintain little door-yards, in which a few simple old-fashioned flowers grow without order or arrangement. Each place, whether it be a mere clearing or a tidy yard, maintains the man's dogs—a starving, snarling, barking breed of mongrel hounds, made up of ribs, spine, and an open mouth. Show me the dogs, and I can give you the commercial rating of a people. I have never yet seen dogs so mean and so numerous as those of the Swampy Cree Indians of Canada, therefore I know that those people are poorer than even the negro farmers along the Mississippi.

But let us step into a few West Virginia cabins. The door is the principal source of daylight, but some have daylight streaming in through many uncared-for cracks or chinks between the log walls. The draughts are such that one would think the bedclothes had to be nailed down to keep them on the beds in such cabins. Some cabins have regular windows, and others revel in a few

329

panes of glass let into one wall. The lofts over the main room of each cabin are reached in different ways, but I did not see one that had a pair of stairs. There is not room for stairs, or talent enough to build a pair. Sometimes a ladder outside the house serves the purpose, and often as I reined up before a cottage I saw the women and girls—all as shy as deer—scamper out and up the ladder. If their curiosity was strong they came down again by-and-by, in their best but very cheap gowns, and it was delightful to see in them the same femininity that is observable on Madison Avenue, displayed in the way they smoothed down their dresses, disciplined their hair with their fingers, and tiptoed to glance into a cracked bit of mirror over one another's shoulders.

The rule is to reach the loft by a ladder inside, at the foot of the bed, but there are cabins so primitive that when the woman takes you up to show you her loom she calls to her eldest girl child, "Nance, git the pegs and set 'em in fer we-all to go up." Then the girl finds a number of rough-whittled wooden pins twice the size of clothes-pins, and fits them into the line of holes in the logs under the loft-hole. Such cabins are seldom found except in the true wilderness parts of West Virginia, the parts farthest from the railroads. In those parts we see truly preserved the mode of life of the picturesque pioneer of 1750, whom the historian describes as stalking into West Virginia with his gun, his axe, and his bride. In such cabins one finds beds made in the hollow trunks of trees, which have pegs set in the corners for legs to raise them up. It is said that the under-bedding is often nothing more than a mass of autumn leaves. The women in these most primitive homes make the corn-pone bread in dug-out troughs skilfully bitten out of a cucumber or poplar log with the husband's axe, and I have been told that travellers have frequently seen the youngest baby seated in one end of such a trough while the mother kneaded the dough in the other end.

To return to the average typical house, the routine of life is pursued in the one room. In one corner is the dining-table, in another is the closet or bureau, and in the others are the beds. The dreadful absence of privacy, or, to put it better, the incessant publicity, which shocks us so when we read of tenement-house

A NATIVE SPORTSMAN
331

life in New York, obtains in all the mountaineer homes, where land is abundant to a greater degree than it is scarce and hard to acquire in the metropolis. In these cottages other phases of life are as peculiar. A pail, a wash-bowl, and a dipper set out-of-doors serve for the requirements of the toilet. I am told that the people never wash their bodies, and I judge that the men rarely comb their hair. The women "slick" theirs over with water and a comb. The children simply "grow up" in a long juvenile fight against heavy odds of dirt and tangles.

Over the yawning fireplace in each cabin one sees the beginning of the high colonial mantel which we so eagerly borrow for our houses — a tall narrow shelf bearing a line of bottles and cans. There or on a closet or bureau one is certain to see a cheap Connecticut clock, and under the tall old-fashioned principal bed is apt to be seen the most important article in a mountain household—the cradle. Never thought of till the last minute, and there being no money to buy a thing that can be made at home, the cradle is usually a heavy pine box on a pair of eccentric rockers, so that it is apt to rock as a snake travels—one end at a time. In very tidy cabins the walls are covered with newspaper to keep out the draught; the wife has a little cupboard for her cups and dishes, her pepper, sugar, and salt, and a bureau for her clothing. Several times I saw some fresh flowers in a broken cup on the bureau, and a few noisy-looking chromos, usually presenting scenes of courtship, or pictures of women in gorgeous attire, stuck about on the walls. A lamp is a rare thing in a mountain cabin. Living there is simpler than the rule of three. When daylight fails, the people go to bed. If they sit up, they do so in the light of the logs in the fireplace. If they need to find anything which that light does not disclose, they pick out a blazing pine knot

332

from the fire and carry it about as we would carry a lantern or a lamp. The pine knots smoke so prodigiously that the ceilings of these cabins are as black as ebony: not a bad effect from an artistic point of view, for the dead black is soft and rich, and shows off everything against and beneath it, particularly the brass-trimmed gun that is certain to hang on a rafter just in front of the door.

The mountain folk are often "squatters" on the land. A man plants two or three acres—rarely as much as ten acres—in corn, and if he has two apple-trees that bear fruit he is very lucky. He has the corn ground into meal by paying a tithe of it to the miller, and takes it home sitting on it on his horse. His wife makes it into big rocklike "dodgers" or pone-cakes with salt and water and "no rising." It gives out towards February, as a rule, and then come the annual hard times. Then the woman collects "sang" and herbs, and packs up bark for those who ship it to the distant tanners. "Sang" is a staple source of income in the mountains. It is so called as a nickname for ginseng, a root that is becoming more and more rare, and fetches $2 50 a pound now, whereas it used to fetch only fifty cents. It looks a little like ginger, and the authorities disagree as to whether it is the real ginseng of China, or, indeed, whether it is at all related to it. If it is not, it is used in China as a cheap substitute for that mysterious, most expensive drug, which the Chinese believe to be able to prolong life, and even to restore virility to the aged.

These should be the most ruggedly healthy of all us Americans. Their mountain air, sweetened by the breath of the pine forests, is only excelled in purity by the water they drink. They live simply and without haste or worry, as we know it would be better for us all to do. They are not an immoral or dissipated people. And yet they never know a day of health or bodily content. Dyspepsia is a raging lion among them all. This is because of the bad, the monstrously bad, cooking their food gets. That demon combination of the darkey and the frying-pan which rules the entire South produces a mild and delectable form of cookery compared to the kind that gnaws the vitals of the West-Virginians. Smoking-hot, half-cooked corn-dodger is their main reliance, and it is always helped down with a great deal of still hotter and very bad coffee. Those who get meat at all get salt meat.

Let us drop in upon a mountaineer's home—one of the tidy sort, where they have apple-trees, and the woman has made a few pots of dark and lumpy apple-butter. The logs are blazing on the simple black and-irons, and the kettle is sputtering as it swings on the pot-hook over the flames. As a preliminary to the meal the man takes down the bottle of "bitters" from the mantel-piece and helps himself to a goodly draught. He makes the bitters himself of new proof moonshine whiskey, tinctured with cucumber fruit, burdock or sarsaparilla root.

"I wuz down to the Springs," says the man, "an' I heard one o' them loud-talkin' city women fussin' a great deal 'bout the evils of drink. I wouldn't 'a' minded her ef she'd a-leaved me 'lone, but she kep' talkin' at me. After a bit I just let her have what was bilin' in me. 'I allers 'low,' says I, 'that whiskey is a good thing. A little whiskey and sarsaparil' of a mornin' fer me and the ole woman,' says I, 'an' a little whiskey an' burdock every mornin' fer the chillen—why, it's a pervision of natur' fer turnin' chillen inter men an' women, and then keepin' 'em men an' women after you've turned 'em that way.' Gosh! she didn't like me—that woman didn't."

The wife, as a first step, takes a tin can and goes out

to milk the cow. A tomato-can serves for the milking
of the average mountain cow, and the women hold the
can with one hand and milk with the other. The appearance of the cow and the size of the can suggest the
idea that it might be better to milk the wild deer, if one
could catch them. Milking over, the woman comes in
to cook the meal. Any one can tell what meal she is
preparing by the time of day; there is no other way,
as all three meals of the day are precisely alike. She
puts a handful of coffee-beans into a skillet, and holds
them over the fire until they are coaled on the outside
like charcoal. She empties the skillet into a coffee-
grinder on the wall, and holds the coffee-pot under the

grinder while she grinds the beans. She puts some corn meal into a box-trough or a dug-out trough, throws in a little water and salt, and works the dough with her fingers until it feels of the right consistency, when she takes it out in handfuls patted into cakes that are ornamented with her finger-marks. These she puts into a little iron oven shoved up close to the fire. She pours cold water into the coffee-pot, and presses that into the embers and close to the burning logs. Then she slices some bacon, and puts it into a long-handled frying-pan, where it is soon burned without being cooked. As soon as the coffee boils the work is done, and she says, " Your bite is ready ; sit by." Earthen-ware plates, steel knives, two-pronged forks, cups and saucers, and a dish of apple-butter are already on the table, with the milk-can, and another can which holds the sugar. A storekeeper in that region once tried to introduce forks with three prongs, but the people were not ready for such a revolution. "We want a fork that 'll straddle a bone," they said.

I wish there was room for descriptions of their dances, their old-fashioned shooting-matches and log-rollings, and of that queerest of all sports, the gander-pull, the fun of which consists in hanging a gander by the legs or in a bag from a tree limb or a gallows, and then greasing his neck, and offering him as a prize to whoever can grip his head and pull it off while riding beneath him at full speed. The old houses of the "quality folk" and their formal lives and warm hospitality shine like gems in this rough setting. The stealthy activity of the "moonshiners," who have the moral as well as the financial support of the people, would form a good part of still another chapter. But these subjects are not so new as the broader view of the simple habits and surroundings of these backward people who live as did the founders of our republic.

IX

OUR NATIONAL CAPITAL

WASHINGTON is already the most beautiful city in our country. Planned by man, instead of being the outgrowth of circumstance, it greets the beholder as a work of art—a gem among cities, a place of parks and palaces. It has all the dignity that power and place reflect, and all the beauty that should go with the social rulership it is developing.

It is the capital of authority and pleasure. The confidence of the one and the restfulness of the other are in its soft and mainly languorous atmosphere. Take the Congressional Limited train from New York of a morning, so as to land on Pennsylvania Avenue in the afternoon. There are no crowds. Only on the 4th of March, when 200,000 sight-seers line one street, can there be crowds in those magnificent boulevards. But the avenue is alive with people. They are different from the people of our other cities. They are American. That is to say, they are persons from all the States and Territories, who are well enough established in citizenship to be of the government, of fashionable society, or of a population which has not manufactures or commerce to attract foreigners or new citizens.

The people on the avenue are well-dressed, self respecting, a little proud, and confident. As much freedom and equality as you will find reflected in the manners of any multitude on earth are visible in that

Y
337

assembly. They walk as no other cityful walks in this country—always with a parade step. There is no bolting along as in New York, or slouching along as in the South. There are no strained faces of men who plunge ahead muttering to themselves as in Chicago. The paraders of Washington all wear their best clothes, and move in stately measure—right foot, 1, 2, 3; left foot, 1, 2, 3; right foot—from the Capitol to the Treasury, and back again, keeping to the right as the law directs.

Nobody works hard there except the present President. More than 70,000 persons live on assured incomes from the government, with ease of mind, and little need to lay a penny by. In turn 75,000 negroes live upon them, with greater ease of mind, and a constitutional objection to guarding against a rainy day. That accounts for close to 150,000 out of the less than 230,000 souls in the placid city. The rest are keeping stores, keeping great and nearly always white hotels, keeping boarding - houses, keeping saloons and livery - stables. Many are maintaining great mansions for the giving of balls and routs and receptions. Then there are the white servants and clerks and assistants of all these. And somewhere in the swarm (but I never saw a sign of them in all my intimacy with Washington) are the folks who have made Washington a manufacturing city.

The Hon. Henry Cabot Lodge has said that "it is a government city and nothing else. It has practically no manufactures and no commerce, and its population is made up of persons engaged in the government service and of those who supply their wants, together with a constantly increasing class of people who come to dwell there because it is a pleasant place to live." And Mrs. Frances Hodgson Burnett, who also has lived there, finds the city unlike all others in the main, and particularly because it has no manufactories. That is the way it has

EASY-GOING NEGROES IN THE MARKET-SPACE

struck me, and yet Special Bulletin 158 of the last census declares it to be the eighteenth city in the value of its manufactures. As the fact jars upon the very spirit of the Washington its admirers know, the reader and I may be pardoned for pausing to examine this disturbing document. The parade on Pennsylvania Avenue will not mind halting. It would do as much for a half-dozen singing negroes with Salvation Army ribbons on their hats. It has all the time in the world, and would rather halt than not.

Lo! the twenty-five principal subjects of labor are bottling, brick and tile making, carpentering, carriages and wagons, candy, engraving, flour and grist milling, architectural and ornamental iron-working, furniture, liquors, lithographing, sash, door, and blind making, marble and stone work and masonry, painting and paper-hanging, plastering, paving, plumbing and gas-fitting, printing and publishing, saddlery and harness, tinware, tobacco, watch and clock and jewelry repairing. In other words, the city is building up very fast, and the work is mainly in support of that extension and in the maintenance of life and comfort there.

Pennsylvania Avenue's paraders pass the finest shops that any city of the size in the country can muster. They are not all so large as they are elegant. They reflect the prosperity and polish of the population. The windows form a beautiful exposition, one that interests and pleases the visitors from the biggest cities. The display is led by the jewellers, picture, art, and bric-à-brac dealers, photographers, furnishers, and fancy-goods dealers. A great book-store, such as few of our cities can show, is the rendezvous of the scholarly and literary folk, who love Washington best of all, I think.

It is interesting to watch the people in the parade before the windows. In the quieter residence avenues of

340

the northwestern section one may see the rich to better
advantage, in far separated couples or in carriages, and
one may see the mansions and gardens, and the nurses,
and those toddlers who are the luckiest children in the
Union; for of all places Washington is the most heaven-
like for children. But in the mixed throng on Pennsylvania Avenue there is a chance to see the people of a
city so distinctively American as to contain only 18,000
foreign-born men and women. The Southerners attract
the eye first. Their soft hats and Prince Albert coats
betray them. The lawyer, the leader in the South, has
set the fashion for all his people. So it comes that all
Southern men dress like lawyers—in sober black with
long coat-tails. In their carriage one sees a strange
conflict of pride and slovenliness—pride in the pose of
the head, and indolence in their gait. Their women,
petted to the spoiling-point when they are young, are
the life of the avenue, and of all Washington. To be
typical they must be blondes, and we see hundreds of
pure blondes in the parade. And they must be merry
and much in evidence, having never been restrained.
They are absolutely queens at home, and hesitate at
nothing. Literature, art, wit, vocalization, dramatic entertainment, reform, equestrianism, leadership of fashion,
social activity—there is nothing into which they do not
plunge; and they and their peculiarities are all intensi-
fied in Washington. Their husbands and brothers look
on in blind idolatry. For themselves the Southern men
ask only to be considered orators; and that they all are.
What should we do but for the Southerners in Washington—but for their spirited and pretty women especially?
But there is no need to discuss doing without this leaven
in the great lump. And it is fitting that they should be
most conspicuous there, for Washington is a Southern
city geographically. True, George Washington and his

341

testy engineer, L'Enfant, planned to have it grow to the eastward of the Capitol, on the high plateau that was best suited for a city's site. And they intended the White House to be a semi-country-seat, apart from the town. The Southerners were in control then, and where they thought the city would come they laid out avenues for their beloved States — Virginia and Georgia and North and South Carolina avenues. Alas for their hopes! the greedy land-owners and speculators held that land too high, and we built the city so that to-day the elegant streets are the ones that bear the names of the down-East Yankee States.

Next in order of notability in the parade are the Western folk—great in numbers, as befits the representatives of nearly two-thirds of the Union. There is no mistaking them, either. Their men are bearded, hot-eyed, intense beings, self-concentrated, as you can see in their every action and movement and conversation. Their women include many of the leaders of the official and the social sets, and yet, taking them by and large, as the sailor phrase goes, the Western women are the ones that come oftenest raw and ill at ease in the formal, ultra-conventional routine of the public and social life, where power and place are graded in one set, and etiquette and eating rule the other. The darkies are very conspicuous by reason of their peculiarities and their numbers. They divide themselves into two bodies. The elegant and ambitious form one, and the lazy, happy, easy-going work-folk and vagrants form the other. But the darky mob is most picturesque, with its red-waisted nurse-girls, its huge bandanna-crowned "mammies," its white-bearded, rheumatic old "uncles" in the whitewashing line, its ragtag and bobtail loafers, out at elbow, toggle-jointed, loose all over, and content whenever the sun shines on them.

THE STEPS OF THE CAPITOL

That which we have called the parade is no parade at all. It is so spoken of because of the slow-measured pace and holiday air of the people on the main avenue, but it is the whole body of the population we have been describing, and not any fraction of them, except as we have particularized. There is no promenade in Washington, though there is a big Fifth Avenue following that wishes for one. These fashionables and official leaders have been for a long time endeavoring to establish a carriage parade like Rotten Row, for they have not even that. Back of the White House, where used to be "the Flats," is a vast meadow set with clumps of trees here and there, and cut by a great circular drive. It is called the White Lot, and lies between the Monument on the east and the Van Ness mansion on the west. Another ring of road encircles the adjoining Monument lot. Mrs. Harrison and Mrs. Morton lent the highest sanction to the plan for holding a carriage meet there once a week, but it did not succeed. Again, as I write this, at Easter-time in 1894, the diversion has been revived, and with more success, since the assemblies have shown barons and counts and generals and millionairesses rolling in an endless circle, and bowing and lounging back upon upholstered seats quite in the way that has been wished for. The use of these two rather naked lots makes the plan somewhat too arbitrary, though it may succeed. But when the greatest of Washington improvements is accomplished we shall see a grand field for such a weekly meet—one that will resound with the heavy rumble of elegant landaus and drags on every fine day in the season. I refer to that time when the entire south side of Pennsylvania Avenue, from the Capitol to the Monument, shall be made a park. On that side of the avenue (excepting the buildings on the avenue itself) there is now a series of narrow parks all the way. It is

344

broken only by the Pennsylvania Railway crossing; but between that greenery and the avenue the buildings form what is called "the Division"—the disreputable quarter of the city. It is an eyesore physically as well as morally. Legislation looking towards the razing of these buildings and the establishment of a noble park where they stand has been sought for in more than one bill that has failed of passage. But it is to be done as surely as anything mundane can be promised.

The park area of Washington is only 538 acres, but at every circle where the avenues cross one another is a little park. Every view along the avenues ends at a cloud of foliage, with an equestrian statue in the heart of it. Every avenue is doubly fringed with trees, and when one looks down on the city from an eminence the whole place—excepting the wide canal cut by Pennsylvania Avenue—is hid under foliage. A dome or two, the Monument, and a few steeples rise above the leaves, as if to suggest the presence of a city that has been abandoned and swallowed up by a forest. The planting of trees has been an official mania, and the faster they have multiplied the faster the malaria, that once ruled the place, has dwindled out of consideration.

The basis of the unique plan of the city is a mathematical, checker-board arrangement of squares made by streets running north and south and streets running east and west. One set is numbered, and the other set is known by letters, so that a child can easily master the system. But L'Enfant planned the city when the horrors of the French Revolution were fresh in mind, and in order that it should never be barricaded, and that troops could be swiftly moved to any point of it, he devised a double system of wheel spokes laid across the whole city—one set of spokes having the Capitol for its hub, and the other set meeting at the White House.

The spokes that cut up the sub-system so peculiarly are the great avenues that bear the names of the States. The streets are from 80 to 120 feet wide, and the avenues are from 120 to 160 feet wide. Not only are many of the streets all but roofed over by trees, and not alone are there the numerous tree-filled squares of which I have spoken, but where the avenues cross the streets and cut off corners and leave little wedges of land cut off from the blocks, there also are flower-beds and shady little park bits. There are 235 miles of thoroughfares in the city, and of these 163 miles are paved, 90 miles being asphalt. The city is kept beautifully clean, and the loudest imitation of a city's roar that is heard in the bowery, begardened residential districts is the melodious click-a-tick made by the hoofs of the horses—a constant chorus peculiar to Washington.

There are many delightful country drives in the suburbs of Washington, and nearly all the suburbs are very beautiful. The city is in a basin, in the bottom of a pass, with a rim of hills all around it. The Virginia hills are on one side, and those of Maryland are on the other. The prime drive is along Rock Creek. For two or three miles along it the government has laid out a zoological park, which one great traveller characterizes as the most beautiful natural park in the world. On the hottest days this charming drive is shaded during the afternoons. It has a continuation called the Pierce's Mill Road, which starts from a picturesque old mill and leads to the Tenallytown (pronounced "Tenlytown") Road near Red Top, the President's first suburban home. Another drive in this pretty region leads behind Grasslands and ends in Georgetown, now a part of Washington, and one of the most substantial and interesting of our Southern cities. In the opposite end of town—in South Washington—is the St. Elizabeth Drive,

IN THE ROTUNDA OF THE CAPITOL

which offers at least one view as fine as any in the rich gallery of Washington's natural scenes. The Bladensburg Road, and the drive to Arlington and on to Alexandria, are excellent, and there are many others almost as fine. The drive to Cabin John Bridge is perhaps the most famous, though no longer fashionable; the most popular is the one to and in the grounds of the Soldiers' Home. There are twenty miles of carriage roads within these superb grounds, and adjoining them is the new Roman Catholic university, which occupies one of the finest sites that can well be imagined for the effective display of noble buildings and for the enjoyment of a beautiful outlook.

There is not space to describe the grand houses of what is already called " old " Washington, or the palaces of those who seek to make the city a social capital. Perhaps it would be fairer to say, " the men and women who are seeking Washington and its society because it is the social capital." New Washington must be seen to be appreciated. Its houses are of as many designs as their owners have minds and tastes. They stand free and clear amid gardens. They are big and tall and roomy. Some are grand and many are pretty, and all are comfortable.

" Society in Washington," said one of the men who lead it, " is the only cosmopolitan society in America. That in New York is very narrow and provincial, controlled by a limited set of people of one origin. Here in Washington it is made up of high-bred people from all over Christendom, and it entertains all the people of distinction who come to this country, as well as all who are of the country and come to Washington."

" It is not pretentious," he said at another time. " In spite of the men of mere wealth who have come into it, one may entertain here with tea and ices at times when an elaborate dinner costing thousands would be the thing in New York."

The different social sets and their values and relations are as hard for a stranger to understand as the horns that are treated of in Revelation. The problem may be simplified by dividing society into two sets—the official and the fashionable. The official society appeals tremendously to persons from small towns. The wife who comes to Washington with the member from Podunk, or with the Senator's private secretary from Lonely City, gets her first shock when, at the hotel where she is stopping, she attends a reception by a woman from her own section, and sees other women in low-necked dresses for the first time. She has always associated *décolleté* and disrepute together. Sometimes she withdraws into her little shell, and has a dreary stay in Washington with a few chosen spirits of like narrowness. Sometimes she broadens and meets the conditions around her. In numberless instances the husband broadens and leaves the wife at home; in many the wife takes up society and the husband takes to his shell.

The beginnings of official experience are peculiar. First the new-comers meet the persons from their locality. Then they make the acquaintance of the wives of Congressmen—other Congressmen if they are Congressional. They attend a reception at the National Hotel, perhaps, and meet the other Congressional new-comers, many clerks and their wives, Mrs. and Mrs. Third Assistant Comptroller So-and-so, Fish-Commissioner Thus, and Superintendent This. Then is the time the unsophisticated man and woman first see the *décolleté* dresses and have their future determined. They will have established themselves in a hotel, and will breakfast, sup, and dine at a table set apart for the men and women of the Congress delegation of the State from which they hail. There they will anchor if they are of the kind that sing "provincial I was born and provincial I will die." But very many develop and widen, and quickly choose their own friends and resorts from among all the people and houses of Washington. They are aided to choose from a larger or a lesser field by their own merits, their personalities and brains, and ability to take part and place, high or low, as the case may be.

The Congressional people and their alphabetical friends at the hotel table, where all meet at first — I call them alphabetical because they are designated by counties and districts of one State—these people meet fragments of all circles at the President's receptions and the receptions of members of the cabinet, and at the houses of great politicians who have gone heavily into society. They go with crude ideas and crude sensations at first. They especially like to meet the members of the diplomatic corps. They are curious about the diplomats, and enjoy seeing them, as the people of the courts of Europe like to see the Shah and his retinue. Barons and Señors, Dons and Counts, are novelties to them. They have all read about them in novels, and they consider them romantic. They like to write home that their wives and daughters have danced with these novelties. But at the same time—and in the course of business in Congress—they are getting their chances for *entrée* into whatever circles they admire and are fitted for.

Curiously enough, there is another body of persons that seek the diplomatic corps, and not for novelty, but to feel flattered by being known to its members. These are purely society people, and are mainly from the North and East. They always come with an exagger-

IN THE WHISPERING GALLERY OF THE CAPITOL

ated estimate of the diplomatic corps, and with a determination to court its members. The truth is that there are nice diplomats, as there are nice missionaries or nice Congressmen, but many who do not know the facts will be astonished to hear that we send a better grade of men abroad than the foreign rulers send to us. Often our ministers stand head and shoulders above theirs when measured from the standpoints of manhood, ability, presentableness, and sometimes family distinction. The men who come to us may excel in polish, but often that is nearly all they have to recommend them. An exception must be made in the case of the British ministers, who, since the Sackville-West episode, have been and will be men of ability. The actual fact in Washington is that the senatorial circle views the diplomatic circle from a slight eminence, good-humoredly, with indifference. And the senatorial circle is not by itself a high circle outside of official society. That is where the author of a recent novel that has had great vogue shows a lack of knowledge of the real springs of Washington life as seen from the inside. He makes diplomatic recognition the "open sesame" to the best society. The truth is that there may be, once in a while, a society woman from another city who aspires to enter Washington society from abroad rather than by the home doorway, but such a person is apt to have doubts about her own social position.

The set that counts in Washington—the cream—is made up of the few who combine high official position with high social standing. They are so broad as to have established the only elegant society in this country to which a man of brains, without wealth, can rise. I am in doubt whether mere wealth gives *entrée* to it; in doubt because good authorities deny that it is so, while others point to men and women within the circle who

THE WHITE HOUSE ENTRANCE

seem to them to have nothing but millions. Apart
from wealth, it is certain that no public position carries
the key with it. A cabinet position does not. It happens that there are and have been cabinet members who
attend only purely official and formal receptions and
levees. Some cabinet men have asked no more than to
"keep solid" with the delegations from their own States.

In the round of a winter's festivities in this leading

social circle you see how cosmopolitan it is; you get bits of experience such as the cream of London society offers, and that of New York never does. You pay homage to explorers, army and navy heroes, historians, artists, scientists, and the lights that illumine the whole world of genius. In this society are people of Murray Hill and Beacon Street who never could force the geniuses of politics and statecraft and art and letters on their little circles at home, and yet they do so in Washington, and therefore enjoy the capital best.

This set has outgrown the stage at which it may have felt that a titled foreigner conferred distinction upon it. If James Bryce and the Duke of Westminster came simultaneously to Washington, the Duke would receive the attention his letters called for, but the historian would be sought and honored for his worth. Such, at least, is what the best-known men in that circle assure me. Any person of note who comes to America must bring letters to some one in this circle in order to enter it—another distinct stride in advance of some circles elsewhere that boast of exclusiveness.

This best Washington circle makes much of certain public men who are not in a position to entertain. There is a *quid pro quo* that it asks of all who enjoy its houses and dinners and assemblies, and that is that they must be entertaining; they must contribute their share towards the general enjoyment wherever they go. I am assured that the standard of morality is what one would expect in a circle made up of men and women from all parts of our young country. The case of a talented foreigner who brought a mistress to Washington with him is still remembered. As he lived in Washington he could have lived in almost any Old World capital, but in Washington he was invited nowhere. He had to go home to be happy.

IN THE TOP OF THE WASHINGTON MONUMENT

Despite what I have written of exclusive society, democracy is more evident at the seat of our government than anywhere else in America. Washington is a great leveller. Had the capital been set up in New York, or any great commercial or manufacturing city, the result would surely have been very different. The people or the officials would have drawn a line between the two classes. But as it is, Washington is nothing else than official, and the men who hold place become ordinary by mere force of numbers. Heart pangs come to new Congressmen, who find themselves counting for no more than ordinary citizens outside their council-chamber. Indeed, only the members of the Upper House have been able, by reason of their fewness and long tenure of office, to create an artificial dignity for themselves wholly within one wing of the Capitol. In the hotel lobbies and in the streets no one points out a Senator as a Senator, though especial gifts and strong personality, or great wealth or eccentricity, may cause a few to be whispered about as they pass in the crowds.

And how can this help but be the case where even the President walks about the streets on fine afternoons, is met in the shops, goes on foot to and from church, and rides about the country roads in a carriage not different from those of his genteel neighbors? President Arthur's fine figure was a common feature of out-of-door life in Washington. General Garfield had been long known, by sight, to all Washington before he was President. Neither Grant nor Hayes nor Harrison ever secluded himself; and if President Cleveland does so it is because he is a poor pedestrian and an ill-advised worker, attending to even the routine duties which other Presidents have shouldered upon subordinates. The custom of tri-weekly receptions to the public which Mr. Cleveland made a feature of Washington life during his first term, which Benjamin Harrison kept up, and which many Presidents have observed, had great levelling effect. The Member from Podunk could not give himself airs if his humblest constituent had shaken hands with the Executive that day, and meant to do so again day after to-morrow. The custom must have made many a foreigner marvel. It was ultra-American—the best thing for the people, and the most disagreeable for their chief servant of any phase of the relationship of the office-holder to the masses in our government. The man whose personality made him seem to fill the place more fully and majestically—to the eye, at any rate—than any man since Washington, used to hold such receptions wherever he went, and any man could shake his hand. I have seen him receive the people of a pastoral region in the parlor of a

356

country hotel, and put new pride into the Americanism of thousands.

It must be a singular strain upon a man to be President. Three of our Presidents have told me that the pains and penalties of that greatness were all but beyond endurance, and that they looked forward with grand impatience to a release from the cares of government. "I am hunted like a jack-rabbit," is the way one put it. "Everywhere I put up my head the office-seekers jump on me." Yet two of these felt a melancholy they could not hide when they left the White House, and all three worked hard to be re-elected.

Washington is the capital of good dining. It is true, as one leading entertainer said to me, that there is no really first-class restaurant there, but the truth of the assertion depends upon the standard one sets and the point from which one views the question. Washington society is the most cosmopolitan in this country, but its dishes, like the body of its population, are American. It is fitting that this should be so. Not long ago one of our Presidents sent for Mr. John F. Chamberlin, the heartiest celebrator of Americanism in dining in this country. "I am in trouble," said he. "I have no cook and no wines, but I am to give a dinner to a royal personage. Will you attend to it for me? There are to be thirty-three at table." Mr. Chamberlin "saved the nation." He sent to the White House his best cook and his best waiters, and they prepared and served a dinner in which a few edible Americanisms so delighted royalty that it sent its plate away for second servings of more than one course. It was a peculiar dinner. It began with oysters roasted in their shells. Then came celery, for which Washington is celebrated and envied, and canvas-back ducks cut in two with a cleaver, and cooked so that one half was on the fire when the other was being eaten. Cakes of hominy came with it, of course. A rich and heavy dessert was followed by coffee and cheese and biscuit toasted. Champagne was served with the oysters, and burgundy with the duck.

The test of the quality of that dinner would be to ask any American now in Paris how he would like to sit down to just such another to-night. It is safe to say that the White House guests would rather have had that dinner than such a one as they would be entertained with to-day—since there is now a French cook, at $150 a month, installed in the kitchen of that grand and beautiful old mansion.

Understanding, then, that the food, the cooks, and the methods of cooking are all American, and that oysters, game-birds, terrapin, and fish are the monarchs of all the *menus* that are fit to discuss, the lover of good eating can decide for himself whether the facts are to his taste or not. In the mean time I will reproduce what a great gourmet told me of the *pièces de résistance* of the Washington markets. First came the Lynnhaven Bay oysters, whose supremacy was never disputed until fraud entered their field and began to call any and every cheaper sort of oyster by that name. The real ones still are plenty in Washington, and when broiled by a darky cook, or served with curry dressing by a white cook, are the most delicious bivalves in the world.

From the near-by waters of the Potomac and Chesapeake Bay come the rock-fish, which tastes like bass, but is so big as to weigh between six and twenty pounds; the hog-fish, which is a most delicious pan-fish; the Potomac perch, so extraordinarily sweet and melting that Roscoe Conkling ate one every morning in its season every year; the black bass of the Potomac; and the Chesapeake hard crabs, which come nearly the whole year

EXCITING SCENE IN THE HOUSE OF REPRESENTATIVES

around, and in Washington are eaten deviled after the
most elaborate preparation. First the meat is scooped
out until the shell is as clean as a whistle. Then the
meat is chopped—but not as fine as French cooks chop
it—and deviled, and put in the shells and cooked. From
the same waters and the near-by land come many birds.
In Washington the men who believe with Carlyle that
this is "the age of the belly," and is worth enduring on
that account, all insist that the game-birds from the
Chesapeake, like the oysters and fish from there, are not
approached in excellence by the same creatures caught
or shot anywhere else in America. The best canvas-
back ducks, for instance, are the Chesapeake birds, and
if they are beyond the diner's purse, he will find that
the Chesapeake yields mallard, teal, black-head, butter-
ball, and red-head ducks, which are superior to any of
their more northerly or southerly congeners. So true
is this, at least of the famous canvas-backs of the Chesapeake, that during the past two years ducks have been
sent up from the North Carolina marshes to dealers on
the Chesapeake shores to be shipped as Chesapeake
birds. All the game-ducks are abundant in Washington at the very season when their presence is most op-
portune.

Quail, woodcock, and partridges from Maryland are
also cheap and plenty there; and far from last or least
is the abundant sora, delicious consort of the hog-fish in
what the Washingtonians love and call their "hog-fish
and sora dinners." These repasts are a feature in the
life of those who live to eat. We have said that the
hog-fish is the greatest delicacy that the frying-pan produces. There are very few frying-pan delicacies, and
most of those are deadly, but not so the hog-fish. It is
caught in northern Virginia, in the Fortress Monroe
neighborhood, in autumn, and the supply lasts a little

longer than the birds abound. For about a month the fish and bird flock together—in the markets. The sora-birds are a species of rail, a third larger than the reed-bird. They come in September, and they stay a month or two. They are so plentiful in Virginia that men have killed them with clubs.

A Chesapeake terrapin is worth four times what any other terrapin fetches in the market. It is Chesapeake terrapin that the Washingtonians think they eat; but, alas! very few of them, or of us, have tasted terrapin of late. It is so expensive, so rare, that real diamond-back fetches $80 the dozen, and only the rich and the people of Baltimore really get it. Chicken, veal, and mud-turtle are made to do duty for terrapin now. It is easy to deceive the diner with these substitutes, because the principal taste of the dish, as it is generally cooked, is that of the seasoning of the sauce. True Baltimoreans alone are not to be deceived in terrapin, because they serve the meat in thick slices on top of the sauce, and have very little sauce, and none of the sherry in it which would serve to hide counterfeit terrapin in other cities.

The subject of good living recalls the fact that at Hancock's, one of the oldest resorts, where old-time dishes are prepared by an old-time Virginia cook, the *habitués* like to tell of the days when men of great renown made it a practice to stop there every day for a cobbler, a julep, or a toddy. That, in turn, suggests the good news that drinking is no longer done in public by men of national fame, and heavy drinking has no longer the privilege to mention many honored names among its votaries.

It is astonishing how many persons at Washington are in the city and not of it, how many live there and enjoy life there without any certainty as to the tenure of their stay. Of all the vast body of the government's employés only those who come under the civil service rules regard the city as their permanent abiding-place. The rest are "long-termers" or "short-termers"—like those who go to prison—if so odious an illustration is permissible in explaining so delightful a condition. I have no doubt at all that this fact adds to the gayety of the place, enhances the holiday, pleasure-loving spirit of the populace, and is a great factor in the making of the delights of the beautiful city. To the rest of those who have merely camped there must be added the newspaper correspondents—a large and important body. The leading correspondents, heads of the bureaus of the great newspapers, are the flower of the flock of journalism. They are picked and trusted men. Their work is seldom and little edited. They are the guardians of the policies of their papers, like the editors themselves. Indeed, in the present deluge of news that has followed the abundance and cheapness of the facilities for distributing it, these gentlemen have become news-brokers and editors as well as correspondents. A swarm of unplaced men and women search the capital for items, and bring them to the bureaus. The special correspondents now command corps of reporters as well, and buy and order the news of fashion, dress, society, the courts, hotel arrivals, and all the rest. Interviews, descriptive articles, and even editorials are now arranged for by some of them. The rest follows—that they are talented, well known, prosperous, and influential. In Washington no bar is set against such inclinations of any of them as are reasonable in men of their means and duties. (I speak solely of the leaders, the heads of bureaus.) To such extent as their personalities, methods, and journals are respected they have access to the better clubs, their wives entertain, and their homes are the resorts of diplomats and statesmen.

FEMALE LOBBYISTS

Their contribution to the joyous life of Washington takes the form of the Gridiron Club, now the leading organization of its peculiar kind in this country. A party of Washington correspondents were dining at Chamberlin's with Judge Crowell on January 11, 1885, when it was suggested that such a dining-club be formed. On January 24, 1885, at a meeting at Welcker's, a constitution and by-laws were submitted for a club that was then spoken of as the "Terrapin Club." A week later it was formally named the Gridiron Club. The first president was Ben: Perley Poore, and from the first dinner it grew steadily in fame and importance.

The club was at first planned upon the lines of the well-known Clover Club of Philadelphia, but has since developed characteristics of its own. At the Gridiron dinners the absurd and indefensible habit of interrupting and "guying" those who speak to the gatherings is not made an annoying characteristic. If a speaker at a Gridiron dinner is a bore or becomes offensive, he receives such sharp interruption that he is glad to sit down as quickly as he can. Then, again, a rigid rule of the Gridiron Club is that nothing shall be spoken that should not be said in the presence of women. No matter what their importance, or what the "news quality" of such addresses may be, it is a rule that what is said at these dinners is always spoken "under the rose." So thoroughly is this understood that at the annual dinner of 1892 ex-President Harrison spoke with as much ease as he would have talked in his own parlor, and with a frankness that rendered his speech an important contribution to the history of the day. Nearly every member of his cabinet sat at the table on that occasion. The Gridiron Club is one of the most interesting developments of the mania for after-dinner oratory which is epidemic in our country, and which is by no means always attended by such admirable, useful, or dignified consequences as at the symposiums of this famous club.

Of clubs that are notable, but not peculiar, the exclusive Metropolitan Club is at the head. The Cosmos and the University clubs are not far behind it. There are several others.

Washington is the Afro-American's earthly paradise, and there are 75,000 there to enjoy it. It is the only place in this country (except, possibly, in so far as a small circle in New Orleans is concerned) where these people have a genteel society of their own, and it is the place where they have the best standing and treatment. To explain the position of the negro, North and South, let me tell a true story. In one of the great Southern States there is a fine cotton plantation that descended to an eccentric white man. He never married, but his negro house-keeper bore him two sons. The man was fond of them. They were as white to the eye as he was. He treated them as any well-to-do and kindly father would treat his boys. He sent them to a New England college, and before and after that they benefited by his guidance, his learning, and his fine library and genteel surroundings. In time he died, and left them the plantation and manor-house and what money he had. In worldly means they were the equals of any planters in that region. In polish and breeding and knowledge they were the superiors of very many.

Their credit at the banks of the nearest city was first-class, and they came to be known as scrupulously honest. When they went to town the bankers enjoyed conversing with them. They often talked of their hard lot, their pariahlike existence—of the curse that came with their color. The best men of the country-side bowed to them, even conversed with them, in passing on the roads, but no white man ever visited their beautiful, well-appointed home. They knew not a single white woman even to bow to. One of the brothers, perhaps a little finer in mettle than the other, rebelled against the unnatural, false, and heartless attitude of his neighbors, and sold out his interest in the plantation to his brother. He went West with his money to one of the new cities of the Pacific coast. He invested shrewdly, principally in street-car stocks. He made his dollars multiply. Perhaps there is a dark line down the spine of a man who has African blood in him, as some say: perhaps there is an uncommon whiteness in the eyes of such a man, a telltale pinkness of the finger-nails. But no one suspected that this handsome capitalist was a mulatto. He was tall, with Caucasian features and long black hair, and he carried himself proudly. He had his desire. He lived on terms of more than equality—great popularity, in fact—with the white men and women of his city.

The curse took the shape of Cupid. He fell in love with a charming woman, and she told him she returned his fond regard. A happy courtship was carried on, and at the end he, being honest, told her that African blood ran in his veins. She said he had insulted her, and she ordered him out of her house. He went, and blew his brains out.

All this has happened in our present day. The brother on the plantation said a few months ago that he was likely at any moment to follow the example of the suicide. In all his forty years of life only one white man had ever visited him. That was the Episcopal bishop of the diocese, who not only called upon but dined with him—a very brave thing for even a bishop to do in the South. He died soon afterwards—last win-

ter—and passed to God's judgment before many white men knew of his daring. The lonely brother is a married man. Years ago he went into the Southwest and married a woman of tainted blood, as white as himself. They have children who are as white as themselves. The blacks of the neighborhood hate and revile the entire family, and will have nothing to do with them. There is only one place in this country where they may hold up their heads and move in a society fitted for persons of their pride and intelligence—that is Washington. It would be an Afro-American society which

367

they would enter, but one modelled closely upon the lines of white society, and living in amity with that body.

Of the 75,000 negroes in Washington, 3000 are in government employ. Negroes own eight millions of dollars' worth of real estate in the District of Columbia. They have their editors, teachers, professors, doctors, dentists, druggists, dancing-masters, their clubs, their saloons, their newspapers, churches, schools, and halls. Whites and blacks work together as mechanics and laborers, and the typographical union contains black printers, just as the barbers' union includes white barbers. Alas! the mortality among the blacks is very much larger than among the whites, and so is the percentage of illegitimacy—but this latter evil is the product of the swarm of ignorant "trash" that hive around the city and touch the regenerated colored folk at no point except as servants and laborers.

To estimate the apparent progress of the negroes in Washington, one must go to their fashionable churches. They have scores of churches, but the three leading ones are on Fifteenth Street, just back of the Monument, and in a line with it. The nearest to the heart of the city is the finest—the Fifteenth Street Presbyterian Church—but all three are among the notable "sights" of the capital. The Presbyterian church is known as the religious rendezvous of the educated set, and is necessarily small. The Rev. F. J. Grimke, a negro and a Princeton graduate, is the pastor. His flock is composed of school-teachers, doctors, lawyers, dentists, and those colored folk from all over America who come to Washington when they have money to get the worth of it. You see nothing to laugh at, no darky peculiarities, in that edifice. The people dress, look, and behave precisely like nice white people, only some are

368

black, and others are shaded off from white. You see women with lorgnettes, and men with pointed beards and button-hole bouquets. Polite ushers move softly to and fro, flowers deck the altar at the proper times, a melodious choir enchants the ear, and young men dressed like the best-dressed men on Fifth Avenue wait on the sidewalk for sweethearts or drive up in fine carriages for mothers and sisters.

The next fine church is St. Augustine's Roman Catholic house of worship, farther down the street. It is a large pile of brick and stone. On last Palm-Sunday it was crowded. Of all things unexpected, Irish servant-girls were there worshipping beside the blacks. A portly and fashionable-looking white woman sat just within one door, in the vestibule, with an ivory and gold prayer-book open on her black satin lap. A white priest was assisted by black altar-boys. So great is the blockade when the women issue from that church that the police come to keep the street clear.

St. Luke's Episcopal Church, of stone, with a beautiful stained-glass window behind the chancel, is the last of these "swell" colored churches. A white-haired, white-bearded colored man is the rector, and on Palm-Sunday he preached to a congregation that included at least fifteen white women of the neighborhood, who came because it was convenient to do so. In this church ten days earlier the servant of a cultivated foreigner living in Washington was married to an Afro-American belle. The foreigner and many friends of his, whites of both sexes, and persons moving in high society, attended the wedding. They say they had expected to see something peculiar, but everything was ordered as at a white folks' wedding, and at the end the men handed their dark-toned women into the carriages and banged the doors and rode away quite as if they were accustomed to elaborate weddings and the comforts of the rich.

As you ride the length of Fifteenth Street you see the small houses and even the shanties of negroes close to the great mansions of the wealthy white people. The Hon. Levi P. Morton's great house is not more than a block from many negro tenements. I am told that the case is the same all over the edges of the newer and better parts of Washington. In that fact you see one reason for the wealth of so many families of colored persons. "Before 1870," says one historian, writing of the now elegant and populous northwestern section of the town, "it was dreary and unhealthy, abounding in swamps, and mainly occupied by the tumble - down shanties of negro squatters. But the Board of Public Works, under the leadership of Governor Shepherd, began an extensive system of public improvement; the swamps were drained, streets were laid out, and now the quarter is noted for the beauty of its highways and the elegance of its buildings." For the making of this beauty and elegance the property-holders were assessed. Many negroes surrendered their lots, but many others paid the assessments, held on, and were made wealthy when fashion led the rich to buy up the land and build upon it. Thus the provident colored folk who had worked and saved were able to become capitalists. Some other fortunes were made in trade, and by cooks, restaurateurs, and men who practise the professions among the people of their own race. One popular professional man of the ebon race is said to be son of a man who mixed cocktails for forty years in a saloon on Pennsylvania Avenue—but, hoity, toity! why should our white brothers in high fashionable circles look down on the man for that?

I have spoken of the musical click-a-tick of the horses'

hoofs on the miles of asphalt pavement. But there is a part of the year when it is not heard. That is the long summer-time, when Washington is hot, and when, instead of regarding the capital as a majestic monument to the Father of his Country, those who are forced to live there speak of the place as the sub-basement of Hades. Oh, how hot it is then! The asphalt becomes hot lava. The horses' hoofs sink into it. The carriage wheels make ruts in it—ruts that quickly close up again as marks made in molasses will do. Detectives, equally hot upon the heels of a criminal, can trace the fugitive by his footprints where he has crossed a street. The beautiful city of gardens and palaces and power and pleasure becomes like a capital of the Congo country.

There are plenty of people there at that time. Sometimes Congress is sitting even in midsummer. But if it is not, still plenty are there—clerks, heads of departments, the whole of bureaucracy and trade and dependent labor, led by the members of the well-to-do who must direct the machinery. What a queer experience they have! After dark they venture out for breath and gentle exercise, and the enjoyment of a respite from the terrors of the day; to prepare for the terrors of the night in the bedrooms. At nine o'clock at night all is dark. Heavy shadows and light shadows cover everything. All is silent as if it were a city on the Mozambique coast. Shadowy forms are seen on the porches of the dwellings, on the high stoops and the galleries over the bay-windows. They are the women. They have learned a trick from their negress servants and from the fixed tropical conditions. It regards their dress, which is such that they would not tell how little they have on. Though it is a trifle, it is not to be told. Upon the porches and the balconies, out of reach, they can and do dress like Sandwich Islanders. If a pedes-

371

trian turns towards a house, these feminine shadows rise and disappear in-doors.

In time the pedestrian turns in at his own gate and into his own bed. Exhausted, he sleeps, but it is fitful sleeping, and every now and then he wakes to find his pillow drenched. On some nights—and there are ten such in every summer—the oxygen leaves the air, and it becomes dead and motionless. When day breaks and the city bustles and the sun rises high, one sees the air shimmer in front of the Treasury Building as if that gray pile were a furnace. Then the people pray for rain. If it comes, it presents itself with tropical severity, in slanting sheets. It may do good, and probably does, but never enough to satisfy the populace. After it is over, the streets remind the beholder of pictures of the earth at the time of the coal formation—a hot, hissing, steaming mass.

During the entire hot season the people have time and inclination to reflect upon the disadvantages of having two extremes of climate in one year, and upon the impossibility of building a city to meet both extremes. Having to choose between the two, Washington necessarily elected to become a winter city. It is a Northern city on a Southern site. The winter is the time for business; it is the period of one session of each Congress, and it is when the people of the North resort there to enjoy what we may call social Washington. And yet it was not necessary to build the town of red brick and white asphalt. That was a sad mistake—a combination ingeniously contrived for turning the place into a cook-stove in summer.

X

THE PLANTATION NEGRO

No Northern man ever journeys far into the South without hearing that his people do not understand the negro. Every Southern man and woman says so. We do not know how to make the negro work, they say; we do not know how few his wants are, and how eccentric they are; we do not know how to make him happy, how to treat him so that he will love us. I never understood why this is so insisted upon. But I never went South without being impressed by the fact that no Northern man who has not been South can even faintly appreciate the relation there between the whites and the colored people. We make fair treatment of the negro voter a political battle-cry. Our sense of justice compels this. But until all Northern men in politics have seen the South—have seen a certain black parish in Louisiana, for instance, where there are 400 whites and 3600 blacks—it will not be easy for them to exercise patience, discrimination, and justice in the battle for fair play.

However, that is on the edge of politics, which have no place in this chapter. I am setting out only to narrate some anecdotes, and to describe some scenes which have the colored folks prominent in them. Once, when I was in a Massachusetts town, I saw the people in the newspaper office run to the windows to look at a negro. He lived a few miles away, and was the only man of his color in the neighborhood, so that he was looked upon as a curiosity. Not many years afterwards I found myself in the town of Newcastle, Delaware. I saw colored people by the hundred. They stood in knots in the streets, they lay in the roadways basking in the sun, they filled rows and rows of dwellings. Putting the two experiences together, I supposed I had seen the two extremes of the relation between the whites and the blacks. I know now that I had seen neither, for I have since been all through "the Black Belt," where even the mechanics are often colored men, and I have been where there are no negroes, as well as where negroes are seldom seen, and are admitted to a perfect equality with whites of the humbler class, even in the matter of wedlock. That, of course, was in Europe.

Such a condition as the latter is hard to understand, yet it can exist. A waitress in a quaint old temperance hotel in Liverpool, at which I once stopped, was indignant at the conduct and language of a Kentucky gentleman who found himself at the same dining-table with a black missionary. She could not understand his feelings. She said she had supposed America "was where all men were equals." It transpired that she was engaged to marry the colored preacher, and wore a ring that marked her engagement to him. He seemed a very nice and kindly man, she said, and she expected to endure three years of hard living in Liberia, "in order to come back to New York with him and be made a lady." It was a disagreeable task to tell her how far from happy or respected she would be if she did come to New York as the white wife of a black man, but the truth caused the ending of the match.

Last spring, on a Mississippi packet, I told that story to the Republican postmistress of a Mississippi riverside village. She was amazed. "The colored people all love me where I live," said she. "Some would almost give their right hands to help me if I asked them. But I would starve to death before I would eat a crust of bread at the same table with one; and rather than see my daughter at school with a colored child—as I have heard white children and black are schooled together in the North—I would see her grow up in ignorance. I am kindness itself to the negroes. I am the best friend and chief support of many of them; but I want them to keep their place, as I mean to keep my own."

There are the two extremes indeed.

It is a curious fact—or it seems so until the reasons are studied—that one must go North to find the sharpest and most unreasoning prejudice against the blacks. In a journey I once took, through a majority of the Southern States, I did not see a single instance of brutality towards the blacks by the whites; but in Indiana, not long ago, I found a whole county where the people boasted that no negro was ever permitted to stay overnight. There was not a colored family or individual in that county, which was the seat of the White Cap terrorism of a few years ago. And it was in Asbury Park, New Jersey, within fifty miles of New York (where the anti-negro riots once took place), that the people protested against the presence of colored persons on the "Boardwalk" or sea-side promenade of the village. Of course, there is a great difference between the colored people of the Black Belt and those in the North. Down South they are and always have been the laborers. Up North they are sometimes lawyers, teachers, tradesmen, and persons of means. It was in North Dakota that the wife of an editor boasted to me that she had an excellent colored kitchen-girl. "But," said she, "if I called her a servant, she would be very angry. We have to address her as 'Miss Reynolds' in order to keep her with us."

To me the colored folks form the most interesting spectacle in the South. They are so abundant everywhere you travel; they are so eternally happy, even against fate; they are so picturesque and funny in dress and looks and speech; their faults are so open and so very human, and their virtues are so human and admirable. As I think of them, a dozen familiar scenes arise that are commonplace there, yet to a Northerner are most interesting. I think of their fondness for fishing. Somebody has called fishing "idle time not idly spent," and that must be how the Southern colored people regard it, for they seem to be eternally at it wherever they and any piece of water, no matter how small, are thrown together. One would scarcely expect to find the New Orleans darkies given to fishing, yet it is a constant delight to them. They do not merely dangle their legs over the sides of the luggers and steamers to sit in meditative repose above a line thrown into the yellow Mississippi, but they fish in the canals and open sewers in the streets that lie just beyond the heart of the city. It is delightful to see them. Those open waterways flowing between grassy banks out towards the west end might seem offensive otherwise, but when at every few hundred feet a calm and placid negro man, or a "mammy" with a brood of moon-faced pickaninnies sprawling beside her, is seen bent over the edges, pole in hand, the scenery becomes picturesque, and the sewers turn poetical. After one has seen a few darkies putting their whole souls into fishing it is painful to see a white man with a rod and line. The white man always looks like an imitation and a fraud.

From St. Louis to New Orleans, and all the way through the Gulf States, negroes and fish-poles were for-

"IDLE TIME NOT IDLY SPENT".

ever together, like the happiest subjects of wedlock. At least one darky fishing dotted the water view. Along the lower Mississippi many colored men now own little farms of a few acres, with a log cabin, a rifle, a mule, a plough, some chickens and children, a wife, and a fishing-rod. When I passed by, the corn was planted, the spring-time sun was pleasantly warm, and these ebon monarchs were seated in their dugouts and skiffs watching their lines. Some hypercritical white men were apt to call attention to a gaping rent in the cabin roof, or to the fact that a day's toil at remunerative labor would bring the means to put in panes of glass where the window holes were stuffed with old trousers and hats. But that is according to how one looks at life. If happiness is its main aim, and the old hats and trousers keep the weather out, the fishermen have the best of the argument. The Indians on the plains believe that the more a man is civilized, the more care and responsibility he has, and the darky planters who take nature into partnership on a three-acre claim know that the Indians are right. Down in Florida, where the St. John's River is narrow and very tortuous, the passengers on the regular boat one day last spring were occasionally startled by stentorian yells. "Hi, dar! what you doin'? Can't yer see what yer about? Don't you come a-nigh me." The reason was evident. A colored man here and there had fallen asleep over his fishing-rod, and the great muddy wave which the steamer sucked along behind her had engulfed his little boat, and startled the fisherman out of half his senses.

In every view of the country outside the cities one gets an idea of how greatly the negroes are in the majority. At the plantation landings on the river-sides one sees the planter's house standing alone, while near by there is always a huddle of negro cabins, or perhaps a double row of them forming a little street, or a great scattering of them over the fields. Sometimes they are neat and in good repair, but neatness is far from being a characteristic of field life in the Southern States. As a rule, the cabins are dilapidated, their yards are littered, the fences are in ruins, and even the harness on the horses and mules is made up of tatters of leather, rope, and chains. It is a mystery how the average field hand keeps his or her garments from falling off in pieces, for they hang on in pieces almost like the scales on a fish.

Wherever a boat lands or a train stops, one is sure to find half a dozen, or even two dozen, negroes to each white person in the crowd that gathers on the levee or at the station. At one boat-landing in Florida I saw the colored "dominie," or preacher, followed down to the levee by a knot of his female parishioners. It was a burlesque on a burlesque, for it parodied Bunthorne in the comic opera of "Patience." He was a very stout and comfortable parson, not without a double shine upon his broadcloth, partly of wear and partly of grease. Like Bunthorne, he rather lorded it over the women, paying very little attention to them, and standing apart like a superior being. I wondered that he did not give his carpet-bag to one of them to carry. They stood in twos and threes, snickering and giggling, with little rolly-poly babies clinging to the skirts of some. Each woman had some red about her; if not a red dress, it was a red shawl or a red waist or red hood. And they chewed tobacco. These are two common inclinations of the female sex among the negroes—a love of red and of tobacco. The dominie had a Napoleonic face and great gravity, but I am sorry to say that the latter quality was seriously disturbed when he took his departure on our boat. The gang-plank had to be put almost straight up and down to connect the boat with the river-bank, and the unfortunate dominie slipped on the top of it, threw his carpet-bag in the air, and went down the plank like a barrel, to land in a heap on the steamboat deck. To the cries of " Did yer hurt yer?" by his disciples he volunteered no reply; but later, when he had brushed the flour and dirt off his coat and was calm again, he was graciously pleased to remark, " You may tell der congergation I will be wid dem in de spirit, and will soon return if de Lord spares me."

On the same trip I heard a pathetic bit of a dialogue between two colored women who were waiting for a train.

" Hello, Lize!" one said. " Dat's a nice dress you got on."

The other replied that it was, and ought to be, as it cost seven dollars. " But," said she, " der seams are all made so coa'se and clumsy, I's a'most ashame to be seen."

" Well, don't you know why dat is?" the other replied. " It's 'cause you're colored. White folks gits what dey want; colored folks takes what dey gits—and dey gits de wors' ebery time."

But to return to their numbers. At every landing on the rivers the banks were lined by idle colored people from the fields and villages, and the white men were always very few; the white women seldom seen at all. It always seemed to me that these idlers enjoyed seeing the roustabout boat crews do their heavy work—and very heavy work it is that these negro deck hands perform. They use no barrows or trucks, but " tote " nearly everything on their heads and shoulders. For this purpose merchandise is put up in suitable packages in the South and West, the sugar and flour and meal being put in sacks, and the other staples being divided into small boxes, packages, and barrels. All day long, and often all night as well, the roustabouts put on and take off the freight at the frequent stations, not merely dumping it on a wharf—for there are no wharves—but carrying it up the banks and into the sheds and storehouses at each place.

One boat on which I travelled carried fifty of these tireless human pack-horses; the smallest crew I saw was half that size. They slept as best they could—in their clothing—on the main-deck near the boilers, and they were dressed as fortune had favored them—which is to say, mainly in rags. They worked in processions, like ants, one line moving one way loaded, and the other returning empty-handed. Their common gait was a trot, for this primitive mode of moving a cargo is slow at best, and the loads would never be put on or off if the men walked. So they went at a dog-trot, hitching up their trousers, rolling like sailors, scraping their feet, and slouching along, and all the while chanting or muttering some singsong phrases. They livened up every little village they came to, making such a noise and bustle that it was rather a wonder that everybody, white and black, did not turn out to share the excitement than that the idle darkies were the only lookers-on. The Mississippi River hands got a dollar a day for their almost superhuman work—the very hardest I ever saw performed anywhere or by anybody. They were a dull and almost barbaric-looking crew, and I was told that they drank up all their earnings at Natchez and New Orleans, where the boat lines terminate, and that they carried knives and razors, and were scarred all over their bodies as the result of their frequent fights and quarrels. Of course that was one-sided testimony, but I learned long ago that there are two sorts of colored folks in the South—the rude dull field hands and the spruce.

polite, and far more intelligent and ambitious house-servants—both originating in and descending from similar classes in the time of slavery.

In New Orleans I was shown the quarter in which the roustabouts throw away their earnings, and it is safe to say that there is not in any other of the capitals of Christendom such a spectacle of low and almost absent morality. The dance-house, which is the headquarters of the district, suggested a place in the heart of Africa at a savage merrymaking. The place was small, not much higher than the people's heads, dark, smoky, and intensely hot. The women were in one long line, and the men in another, facing them, as in a Virginia reel. The dancing was primitive, the only figures being a jig by both lines preparatory to a general swinging of partners. The place was curiously called "the coonje dance-house."

Once, when Mr. Smedley and I were taking a steamboat trip on a Louisiana bayou, we reclined on a pile of sacks of freight the better to enjoy comfort and the scenery at once. We attracted the attention and interest of the roustabouts. We heard them talk to one another about us as they passed bowed under backbending loads.

"H'm!" said one. "Guess dem gemmen been steamboatin' befo'. Never seen white folks lay around on de freight that way. Seen niggers do it, though."

Almost always what they said was interesting, either in itself or because of the rich-toned voices and peculiar dialect they used. Sometimes what they were heard to say was extremely laughable. On this steamer the poor fellows had a night of almost incessant work on the heels of a day of frequent landings. They were tired; indeed, I never will be able to understand how they performed the tasks that were set them, though, on

382

the other hand, their all day of work was preceded and followed by days of idleness. This is how we heard them discuss the situation.

"I don't work on dis yer boat no mo'," said one.

"Work on dis yer boat?" another exclaimed. "I wouldn't work agin on dis boat ef she was loaded wid griddle-cakes, an' de molasses was drippin' ober de sides."

"I," said the first speaker—"I wouldn't work agin on dis yer boat ef she was loaded wid rabbits, and dey was all jumpin' off."

With that word-picture of a boat's cargo that was able to unload itself the roustabout threw a sack of grain upon his shoulders and slouched up the gangplank, apparently unconscious that he had said anything at all humorous or uncommon.

In Tallahassee we had a coach-driver who kindly showed us the town, including "the Colored Af'can Church." There is a street or road there which has upon it a cemetery and a seminary. The two words confused our guide. "Some says cemetery and some says seminary," said he. "I can't rightly judge which is de mos' correct."

We visited several cabins of the field hands on different plantations, and for my part I was astonished at the disorder and uncleanness they displayed. I never saw worse habitations, except the tepees of wild Indians. In the North it is noticeable that colored women keep their rooms tidy, and their children are particularly well cared for, as compared with the children of white persons in similar circumstances; but in these field cabins the conditions were reversed. Thus again we saw the line drawn between the mere laborers and the upper servants, for the maids and men at work in the planters' houses were usually smart in appearance and orderly in their work. The manner of treating the two classes was just as different. I had no opportunity to see any work performed in the fields, but the laborers on the boats and in the freight depots were "bossed" by mates of severe aspect and terrific voices, who distributed themselves where they could watch every "hand" at his work, and could spur them incessantly by shouts, and often by profanity. I heard a great deal about violence by these mates, but saw none exercised, and cannot say that their manner was unkindly in spirit. They simply acted on each crew as a pair of spurs are used on an unwilling horse.

In the cases of the house-servants there was a diametric change. Every born Southerner who was spoken to on the subject seemed to have in his employ some old and faithful servant, and all had enjoyed the care of some "mammy," either dead and tenderly remembered, or alive and gently cared for. Stories of one-time slaves who had never left their former owners are still plenty, and reveal the attachment these better-class servants developed for their homes and masters. A brave general of the Confederacy told me a sample story of the pleasant side of the relations between the masters and slaves, as typical to-day as in slavery times. His body-servant had married just before leaving for the seat of war. Years passed, and one day the general said to the servant : "Tom, an officer is about to start for the neighborhood of our home. You have not seen your wife for a long while, and if you go with this officer you will have a chance to visit or even to remain with her."

"Pshaw!" said the servant. "Tink I do dat? How on earth could you git along widout me? You must tink I goin' crazy."

And here is a story of to-day. It is about another general, who is fond of his cups. One day his body-servant, seeing that he was tipsy, took his watch and money for safe-keeping.

"See here," said the general, "you are taking a great deal of liberty with me. I'd like to know who is boss."

"Well, Marse ——," said the servant, "I reckon when you's sober, you's de boss; but when you's drunk, tings is different."

There is a very curious side to the relationship between the house-servants and the employers which has no counterpart among white persons of differing circumstances. An artist, looking about New Orleans for characteristic costumes to be used by models for his paintings, discovered that there are few second-hand clothing shops in that city, and that those which are there offer only the most ragged cast-off raiment of the negroes. The reason is that the white men and women give their clothing to the colored people—to servants or dependents—when it is no longer serviceable for them. Of course I cannot speak too generally or positively, but it seems to me that every man and woman is accustomed to make this use of his or her discarded goods, and that every white family has at least one colored family in charge in this way. The servants look upon this descent of clothing and finery as a right, and the dependents take it for granted that what remains shall be theirs. Everywhere I went I heard stories illustrative of this queer relation between the races. In a conversation about the reason for the common assertion that "all darkies will steal," a planter thus expressed himself:

"It is true that they all 'take things'," said he; "but they make a difference between stealing and taking. For instance, they will not steal money if you leave it on every mantel-piece and bureau in a house. It is the same with jewelry. They condemn such a theft as severely as we do. But they pilfer provisions and clothing with easy consciences. Servants are apt to have poor relatives or friends, to whom a never-ceasing stream of tea, sugar, flour, bacon, and other necessaries finds its way from your kitchen door. That is not stealing, in their opinion, nor is it stealing to clothe themselves with your apparel if they need clothes, or if they imagine you have more than you require."

I heard two stories to illustrate this. In one case a servant was detected with a heavy basket going out of the garden gate. Asked what she was carrying away, she replied, "Nothing." Pressed to be more specific, she lifted the lid of the basket and exhibited a generous and miscellaneous load of selections from the larder. "Dey's nothing 'cept 'fluities," she said, meaning "superfluities." In another instance a man-servant boldly appeared in his master's trousers. "I was 'shamed to see you hab 'em any longer," said he; "you done wore dem pants at leas' five year, an' I need 'em."

They cannot resist the temptation to take medicine. It is almost an absolute rule in the South that every negro will say he or she is "poorly" or "not very well dis mawnin', sah," if their health is asked after, even with the stereotyped salutation, "How are you?" Perhaps they are not well and never feel so. At all events, I am told that the house servants constantly take doses of whatever medicine their employers leave about, and if a bottle of physic is thrown away it is pretty certain to be taken "all at once" by whatever darky finds it.

It is apparent that we in the North do not treat the colored people as our white brethren of the South do; but whether we know how to treat them is as difficult to decide as it is to discover what rules govern their treatment in the South. There the common laborers are ruled almost as severely as old-time sailors on a wooden packet, while the house-servants are permitted liberties and familiarities repugnant to our sense of what is fit between employer and "help."

I have not sought to discuss the merits of the political situation, or the probabilities of the negro's future in the South. They seem happy there, in the main, and many who have emigrated to the West during recent "crazes" have toiled back again, singing of their love for "Dixie's land." Many Northern men established in business in the South declare that white men can never fill the place the colored man occupies as a general laborer there. The most serious question is that of the free ballot, but there are two sides to that. If we lived with our wives and children in a lonely planter's house in a region where a far ruder people outnumbered us ten to one, it is possible that we would get a glimpse of a side not visible from any Northern standpoint. But even then we might not see why the education of the colored man, the presence and example of newly imported European labor, the steady influx of new peoples and Northern capital should not some day alter the conditions there, and remove the complaints. Time is needed, and with it patience.

XI

THE NEW GROWTH OF ST. LOUIS

POPULATION and wealth are classified by the same standards. In both cases a million is the utmost figure that is popularly comprehended. A million of citizens or of dollars suggests the ripening of success in both fields. It is true that London has five millions of citizens and the Astors have thirty times as many dollars; but London is simply one of the world's capitals, and the Astors are but millionaires in the general thought and speech. In America we are growing familiar with big figures, and now it seems logically likely that another town will soon increase our acquaintance with them. It startled the English-speaking world to learn that Chicago had reached the million mark, but to-day we foresee that in a few years—perhaps the next census will record it— St. Louis is to share the honor with her. No other Western city has such a start in the race. It is true, if the signs are to be trusted, that the Twin Cities—Minneapolis and St. Paul—may then have a joint population of a million, but St. Louis is the commercial rival of all three of her great Northern neighbors, and is drawing trade which they were seeking, while the Twins are separate cities. The only millionaire towns, so to speak. will be Chicago and St. Louis.

St. Louis is already the fifth in size among the cities of the land, and would be fourth if Brooklyn were rated what she is in fact—a bedchamber of New York. But it is the new growth of St. Louis, her re-start in life, that is most significant and interesting ; it began so recently, and is gathering momentum so fast. And we shall see that never was city's growth more firmly rooted or genuine. What is accomplished there is performed without trumpeting or bluster, by natural causes, and with the advantages of conservatism and great wealth. More remarkable yet, and still more admirable, the new growth of the city is superimposed upon an old foundation. It is an age, as this world goes, since this proud city could be called new and crude. The greater St. Louis of the near future will be a fine, dignified, solid city, with a firmly established and polished society, cultivated tastes, and the monuments, ornaments, and atmosphere of an old capital.

I have had occasion once or twice in the course of my studies of the development of our West to speak of what may be called the "booming organizations" which father the commercial interests of the more ambitious cities, and in some instances of the newer States. These should have had more prominence, and should have been mentioned more frequently. Though they have nothing to do with the governments of the cities, they are, like the governments, the instruments of the united will of the people, working for the general good ; and when they and the governments conflict, the will of "the boomers" often rises supreme above the local laws. For instance, it was announced in one city that the excise laws would be ignored, in order that the place might prove more attractive to a convention of politicians while they were the city's guests. There are good reasons for such supremacy of these powerful and active unions. Their leading spirits are always the most energetic and enterprising men in the cities, and their interest in their schemes for the general advantage is more enthusiastic than that which is felt in the government.

The phrase "booming organizations" is applied to these institutions for the benefit of Northern and transatlantic readers. It is not altogether satisfactory to the persons to whom it is applied, because, in parts of the South and West, booming is a word that is coupled with unwarranted and disastrous inflation, as when a new town is made the field of adventure for town-site and corner-lot gamblers. I use the phrase as we did when we succeeded in getting General Horace Porter to "boom" the completion of the Grant monument in Riverside Park. To "boom," then, is to put a plan generally and favorably before the people, to put a scheme in motion with *éclat*, to vaunt the merits of an undertaking. And that is what is done with and for the interest and merits of the newer cities by these organizations, which are there variously known as Boards of Trade, Chambers of Commerce, and Commercial Clubs. They are in essence what our Chambers of Commerce in Eastern seaports are, but in some cities they work apart from the Chamber of Commerce and on separate lines, while in others they do some of the same work and a great deal else that is very different. They are in some cities what an engine is to a machine-shop or a locomotive is to a railway train. Whoever visits a city that is well equipped in this respect feels the pulsations and is conscious of the power and influence of its Board of Trade, as we note the presence of the dynamo in a boat that is lighted by electricity.

These unions consider the needs of their cities, and set to work to supply them. They raise the money for a fine hotel, if one is lacking; and in at least one city of which I know they turn what trade they can over to the hotel after it is built, even going to the extreme of

390

giving a grand annual banquet there, and paying a purely fancy price per plate to the lessee of the house, in order that he may get a good profit out of it. They raise the means to build street railroads; they organize companies for the erection and maintenance of a first-class theatre in such a city, for the holding of an annual fair or carnival parade, for the construction of a great hall, to which they afterwards invite conventions. These ventures are not all expected to be profitable by any means, particularly in the smaller cities; but they are "attractions," they swell the local pride, they promote that civicism which is such a truly marvellous factor in the even more marvellous progress of our Western cities. But these local unions go farther. They obtain the passage of laws exempting certain manufactures from license fees and taxes on the buildings in which they are carried on, and then they induce manufacturers to establish their workshops in those cities, giving them bonuses in the form of exemption from taxes, in the form of a gift of land, or even of a gift of a building designed and constructed as the recipients desire to have it. To give one illustration out of ten thousand, the little town of Rapid City, South Dakota, gave a noble storehouse of brick and stone to a wholesale grocery firm for coming there to do business. To give another view of the subject, the editor of an influential newspaper in one of the ambitious smaller cities of the West resigned his membership in the local Board of Trade because he said it contained so many wealthy men, and they so frequently subscribed large sums of money for public improvements, that he was uncomfortable at the meetings, and preferred to do his share of the work outside "until he had made his pile" and could "chip in with the rest."

These commercial circles send committees to Congress,

to the heads of great societies, to the capitalists of the East and of the Old World, to urge their needs and merits, for especial ends. They cause the building of railroads and railroad spurs; they print books, pamphlets, and "folders" to scatter praise of their cities wherever English is read. They stop at nothing which will tend towards the advancement of their local interests. They are unions of business men, land-owners, and capitalists; but, as in all things, one man is the dominant spirit and the most fertile in expedients. This is usually the secretary, who is a salaried officer. Men with an especial genius for the work drift into such positions, and when they prove especially and signally capable officials, such as those are who are in St. Paul, Spokane, and St. Louis, other cities try to secure them.

St. Louis has one of the most progressive and influential of these bodies in its Merchants' Exchange. It is by no means a mere exchange. It does very much of the work towards the public and general good of which I have spoken; indeed, it may be said that the entire Southwest, and the immense territory drained by the Mississippi, find in it the ablest and most active champion of their needs. It is to the central West and the Southwest what our Chamber of Commerce is to New York and the commercial interests of the Atlantic coast.

But with the sudden assumption of a new youthfulness, in old St. Louis there has sprung up an auxiliary, or, at all events, another organization for the exploitation and advancement of local interests. It is called "The Autumnal Festivities Association," and is one of the most remarkable of the mediums through which American enterprise works.

The story of its inception and organization, with the incidents I gathered concerning the firelike rush of the movement among all classes of St. Louis citizens, presents a peculiarly clear reflection of the character of the new life that now dominates that city.

When St. Louis failed to secure the World's Fair, instead of sinking back discouraged, its leading men concluded that one fault with the city must be that its merits were not as widely or as clearly understood as was necessary. Therefore, in the spring of 1891, a meeting was called at the Exposition Building to discuss the advisability of forming an organization which, for three years at least, should devote itself to celebrating the achievements and adding to the attractions of the city. From the stage the crude plan of the campaign was announced, and suggestions from the audience were asked for. As my informants put it, " the first 'suggestion' was a subscription of $10,000 from a dry-goods firm; the second was a similar gift from a rich tobacconist. Then came two subscriptions of $7500 each, and others of amounts between $5000 and $1000. Mr. John S. Moffitt, a leading merchant, as chairman of the Finance Committee, promised to undertake the raising of one million dollars within three years, and received promises of sums amounting to $100,000 on that first evening. The sense of the meeting was that this large amount should be expended in attracting visitors to the city, and in interesting and caring for them after they came.

A sum of money was set aside as a bonus for any persons who should build a one million dollar fire-proof hotel in the city, on a site to be approved by the executive committee. It was resolved to appropriate as much as would be needed to illuminate the city with between 20,000 and 100,000 gas and electric lights on especial evenings during each year's autumnal festivities, and committees were appointed to look after illuminations, transportation, and whatever. It was also arranged that one-third of the full amount raised should be expended under the supervision of a branch of the organization to be called the Bureau of Information, and to be headed by Mr. Goodman King as chairman. Mr. James Cox, who had been the managing editor of one of the daily newspapers, became the secretary of this bureau. It has offices in St. Louis, and it arranged to open others in London and other cities in pursuit of a systematic effort to advertise the commercial, social, and sanitary advantages which St. Louis possesses.

Without waiting for the raising of the prescribed amount of money, the association fell to work at once, and the illuminations and festivities of the autumn of 1891 attracted hundreds of thousands of persons to the city, and were characterized as the finest displays of their kind that had up to that time been made in the country. In the mean time the Finance Committee began its task of raising a million of dollars. It adopted a shrewdly devised plan. Every trade was appealed to with a request that a committee be appointed and a canvass be made within its own field. Within a week 200 such sub-committees were at work. Each vied with the other in an effort to secure the largest sum, and subscriptions, in sums that ranged between three dollars and $5000, poured in. Those who did not subscribe promised to do so at a later time. In answer to about 4000 applications by these committees, it is said that there were only five refusals to join the popular movement.

It had not occurred to the leaders, even in this general sifting of the population, to ask the police for any subscriptions, the feeling being that the money was to be expended for purposes that would greatly increase their work; but, after waiting for months to be asked to join the movement, the police force applied for a thousand subscription cards, appointed their own collectors, and sent the money to the association headquarters in silver dollars carried in sacks. The citizens who were not directly appealed to — the lawyers and doctors and all the rest—sent in their checks, and five months after the organization was effected the finance committee reported the receipt of two-thirds of the total amount that was to have been raised in three years, or $600,000.

It will be seen that this association was formed after the city failed to secure the World's Fair, and that its term of duration covers the period of preparation for and the holding of the exposition. It was not antagonistic to the fair, however, but was simply due to the determination of St. Louis not to be lost sight of, and not to hide its light under a bushel, while the country was filled with visitors to Chicago.

It may cause a smile to read that Chairman King and Secretary Cox report, in a circular now before me, what work the Bureau of Information has done " to correct any false impressions which have been created by the *too great modesty* of St. Louisans in the past." But they are right, for, as compared with its rivals, St. Louis possessed that defect, and the frank admission of such a hated fault shows how far removed and reformed from retarding bashfulness that city has since become. The bureau reports that it is causing the publication of half-page advertisements of St. Louis, precisely as if it were a business or a patent-medicine, in sixty-two papers, circulating more than a million copies; that it has obtained reading notices in all those dailies; that "articles on St. Louis as a manufacturing and commercial metropolis and as a carnival city" are sent out every day; that arrangements are making for a weekly mail letter to 500 Southern and Western journals; and that once or twice a week news items are sent to the principal dailies of the whole country. It was found that St. Louis was not fairly treated in the weekly trade reports published generally throughout the country, and this source of complaint has been removed. Invading the camp of the arch-enemy — Chicago — the bureau has caused a handsome "guide to Chicago" to add to its title the words "and St. Louis, the carnival city of America." It has also got up a rich and notable book, called *St. Louis through a Camera*, for circulation among all English-speaking peoples. The local service for the press telegraphic agencies has been greatly improved, "and the efforts of the bureau to increase the number and extent of the notices of St. Louis in the daily papers throughout the United States have continued to prove successful," so that "instead of St. Louis being ignored or referred to in a very casual manner, it is now recognized as fully as any other large city in America."

I have described the operations of this association and its most active bureau at some length, because they exhibit the farthest extreme yet reached in the development of the most extraordinary phase of that which we call Western enterprise, though it has long since crept far into the South. There we see a city managed by its people as a wide-awake modern merchant looks after his business. It is advertised and "written up" and pushed upon the attention of the world, with all its good features clearly and proudly set forth. There is boasting in the process, but it is always based upon actual merit, for St. Louis is an old and proud city; and there is no begging at all. The methods are distinctly legitimate, and the work accomplished is hard work, paid for by hard cash. It is considered a shrewd investment of energy and capital, and not a speculation. If we in the Northern cities, who are said to be "fossilized," are not inclined to imitate such a remarkable example of enterprise, we cannot help admiring the concord and the hearty local pride from which it springs.

St. Louis is the one large city of the South and West (for it belongs to both sections) in which a man from our Northern cities would feel at once at home. It seems to require no more explanation than Boston would to a New Yorker, or Baltimore to a Bostonian. It speaks for itself in a familiar language of street scenes, architecture, and the faces and manners of the people. In saying this I make no comparison that is unfavorable to other cities, for it is not unfriendly to say that their most striking characteristic is their newness, or that this is lacking in St. Louis. And yet to-day St. Louis is new-born, and her appearance of age and of similarity to the older cities of the Northeast belies her. She is not in the least what she looks. Ten or a dozen years ago there began the operation of influences which were to rejuvenate her, to fill her old veins with new blood, to give her the momentum of the most vigorous Western enterprise. Six or seven years ago these began to bear fruit, and the new metropolitan spirit commenced to throb in the veins of the old city. The change is not like the awakening of Rip Van Winkle, for the city never slept; it is rather a repetition of the case of that boy god of mythology whose slender form grew sturdy when his brother was born. It was the new life around the old that spurred it to sudden growth.

There is much striving and straining to fix upon a reason for the growth of St. Louis, and in my conversations with a great number of citizens of all sorts between the City Hall and the Merchants' Exchange, I heard it ascribed to the cheapness of coal, iron, and wood; to river improvement, reconstructed streets, manufactures, and even to politics. All these are parts of the reason, the whole of which carries us back to the late war. In the war-time the streets of St. Louis were green with grass because the tributary country was cut off. After the war, and until a dozen years ago, the tide of immigration was composed of the hardy races of Northern Europe, who were seeking their own old climate in the New World. Chicago was the great gainer among the cities. That tide from Northern Europe not only built up Chicago, but it poured into the now well-settled region around it, where are found such cities as St. Paul, Minneapolis, Duluth, Milwaukee, Omaha, and a hundred considerable places of lesser size. It was a consequence of climatic and, to a less extent, of political and social conditions, and it caused St. Louis to stand still. But for the past twelve or more years the tide of immigration has been running into the Southwest, into Missouri, and the country south and southwest of it.

St. Louis is commonly spoken of as the capital of the Mississippi Valley, but her field is larger. It is true that there is no other large city between her and New Orleans—a distance of 800 miles—but there is no other on the way to Kansas City, 283 miles; or to Chicago, 280 miles; or for a long way east or southwest. Her tributary territory is every State and city south of her; east of her, to the distance of 150 miles; north, for a distance of 250 miles; and in the West and Southwest as far as the Rocky Mountains.

Between 1880 and 1890 the State of Missouri gained more than half a million of inhabitants; Arkansas gained 326,000; Colorado, 300,000; Kansas, 430,000; Kentucky, 200,000; Nebraska, 600,000; Texas, 640,000; Utah, 64,000; New Mexico, Arizona, and Oklahoma,

114,000. Here, then, was a gain of 3,174,000 in population in St. Louis's tributary country, and this has not only been greatly added to in the last two and a half years, but it leaves out of account the growth in population of the States of Illinois, Iowa, Indiana, Mississippi, and Louisiana. St. Louis had 350,518 souls in 1880; now she calls herself a city of half a million inhabitants. Her most envious critics grant that she has 470,000 souls. In 1891 permits were granted for 4435 new buildings, to cost $13,259,370, only eleven hundred thousand dollars of the sum being for wooden houses.

The city now has 347½ miles of paved streets, and they are no longer the streets of crumbling limestone, which once almost rendered the place an abomination. They now are as fine thoroughfares as any city possesses, 272 miles being of macadam, 41 of granite blocks, and the rest being mainly of wooden blocks, asphaltum, and other modern materials. A system of boulevards, of great extent and beauty, is planned and begun. New waterworks are being constructed beyond the present ones at a cost of four millions of dollars, but with the result that a daily supply of one hundred millions of gallons will be insured. The principal districts of the city are now electrically lighted. A new million-dollar hotel is promised.

The old city, with its stereotyped forms of dwellings and stores, is being rapidly rebuilt, and individual tastes, which search the world for types, are dominating the new growth. The new residence quarters, where the city is reaching far from the river in the vicinage of the great parks, are very pretty and open, and are embellished with a great number of splendid mansions. In the heart of the city are many high, modern office buildings. They are not towering steeples, as in Chicago, nor are they massed together. They are scattered over the unusually extended business district, and in their company is an uncommon number of very large and substantial warehouses, which would scarcely attract the eye of a New Yorker, because they form one of the striking resemblances St. Louis, both new and old, bears to the metropolis. The most conspicuous of the office buildings are distinguished for their massive walls and general strength. Beside some of the Chicago and Minneapolis buildings of the same sort they appear dark and crowded, and are rather more like our own office piles, where room is very high-priced. But they are little worlds, like their kind in all the enterprising towns, having fly-away elevators, laundry offices, drug shops, type-writers' headquarters, barber shops, gentlemen's furnishing shops, bootblacks' stands, and so on.

But in praising the new orders of architecture in St. Louis I do not mean to condemn all of the old. The public and semi-public edifices of its former eras should be, in my opinion, the pride of her people. That cultivated taste which led to the revival of the pure and the classic in architecture, especially in the capitals of the Southern States, found full expression in St. Louis, and it commands praise from whoever sees such examples of it as the Court-house, the old Cathedral, and several other notable buildings. What was ugly in old St. Louis was that cut-and-dried uniformity in storehouses and dwellings which once made New York tiresome and Philadelphia hideous.

But to return to the size and growth of the city. It reaches along the river front nineteen miles. It extends six and sixty-two one-hundredth miles inland, and it contains 40,000 acres, or 61.37 square miles. This immense territory is well served by a great and thoroughly modern system of surface street railways, having more than 214 miles of tracks, and run almost entirely by electric and cable power. Some of the newer cars in use on the electric roads are as large again as our New York street cars, and almost half as large as steam railway coaches. Their rapid movements, their flashing head - lights at night, and the cling-clang of the cracked-sounding gongs in the streets seem to epitomize the rush and force of American enterprise. There is an element of sorcery in both of them—in modern progress and in the electric cars. Was it not Dr. Holmes who likened those cars to witches flying along with their broomsticks sweeping the air?

If Chicago was not the first, it was at least a very early railway centre in the West, and her citizens are right in ascribing to that fact much of her prosperity. To-day St. Louis has become remarkable as a centring-place of railways. The city is like a hub to these spokes of steel that reach out in a circle, which, unlike that of most other towns of prominence, is nowhere broken by lake, sea, or mountain chain. Nine very important rail-roads and a dozen lesser ones meet there. The mileage of the roads thus centring at the city is 25,678, or nearly 11,000 more than in 1880, while the mileage of roads that are tributary to the city has grown from 35,000 to more than 57,000. These railways span the continent from New York to San Francisco. They reach from New Orleans to Chicago, and from the Northwestern States to Florida. Through Pullman cars are now run from St. Louis to San Francisco, to the city of Mexico, and to St. Augustine and Tampa in the season. New lines that have the city as their objective point are pro-jected, old lines that have not gone there are preparing to build connecting branches, and several of the largest systems that reach there are just now greatly increasing their terminal facilities in the city with notable works and at immense cost. The new railway bridge across the river is yet a novelty, but it has been followed by a union depot, which is said to be the most commodious passenger station in the world. It embraces all the latest and most admirable concomitants of a first-class station, and is substantial and costly, following an architectural design which renders it a public ornament.

But St. Louis is something besides the focal point of 57,000 miles of railways. She is the chief port in 18,000 miles of inland waterways. She is superior to the nickname she often gets as the mere "capital of the Mississippi Valley," but her leading men have never been blind to the value of that mightiest of American waterways as a medium for the transportation of non-perishable and coarse freights, and as a guarantor of moderate freight rates. The Merchants' Exchange of St. Louis has for twenty years been pressing the Government to expend upon the improvement of this highway such sums as will render it navigable at a profit at all times. The Government has greatly bettered the condition of the river, but it will require a large expenditure and long-continued work to insure a fair depth all along the channel at low water. What is wanted is a ten-foot channel. Now it drops to five feet and a half, and even less where there are obstructions in the form of shoals and bars. It is argued that the improvement asked for would so reduce the cost of freighting on the river as to bring to the residents of the valleys of the river and its tributaries a gain that would be greater than the cost of the work. In the language of a resolution offered in Congress by Mr. Cruise, of Kansas, "it would reclaim an area of lands equal to some of the great States, and so improve the property of the people and increase their trade relations with other sections of the United States, and improve the condition of our foreign trade, as to benefit every interest and every part of the whole country."

Recently the Exchange and the city government, with the leading industrial bodies of the city, sent a memorial to Congress which they called "a plea in favor of isolating the Mississippi River, and making it the subject of an annual appropriation of $8,000,000 until it shall be permanently improved for safe and useful navigation." They said that the removal of a snag or rock anywhere between Cairo and New Orleans extends relief to Pittsburg, Little Rock, Nashville, and Kansas City. This is because the stream runs past and through ten States, and (with its tributaries) waters and drains, wholly or in part, more than one-half the States and Territories of the Union.

After proving that 28,000,000 persons inhabit the region directly interested in the improvement of the river, the memorialists proceed to show that the railroads in 1890 carried freight at .941 cents per ton per mile, and that this amounted to $11 29 for 1200 miles, the distance between Boston or New Orleans and St. Louis, whereas the river rate for that distance was $2 20 a ton. They show that whereas it cost 42½ cents to send a bushel of wheat by rail from Chicago to New York in 1868, the rate had decreased in 1891 to .941 of a cent. This saving to the people was not brought about solely by competition among the railroads; the competition of the water lines with the railroads also influenced the reduction. Upon the basis of an estimate that fifty millions of dollars must be spent upon the river, they offer other reasons for believing that the money will be well spent. They assert that before the jetties deepened the mouth of the river, only half a million bushels of wheat were annually exported to Europe from New Orleans. Now eighteen millions of bushels are shipped thus, and

403

the amount is increasing. Had that wheat not gone by that route at the rate of 14⅓ cents a bushel from St. Louis to Liverpool, it must have been sent by rail to New York at 21⅓ cents a bushel—a difference of seven cents a bushel in favor of the river route, or a saving of $1,260,000 on the annual shipment of wheat alone. The census figures of 1890 show that the amount of freight carried on the river and its tributaries in 1889 was 31,-000,000 tons. It is impossible to here follow the arguments and pleas that are embodied in the memorial, but it is well to know that they are not the outcome of the interests and ambition of St. Louis alone, but of the entire region which makes use of the now erratic, destructive, and uncertain river. What St. Louis asks is what New Orleans wants, and this is what Memphis, Vicksburg, Cairo, and the masses of the people in several large and populous States believe should be granted for their relief and gain.

The demand of the people of all this great region is that the river, from the Falls of St. Anthony to the jetties, be permanently improved under the direction of the Secretary of War and the chief engineers of the army; that $8,000,000 be appropriated for said improvement, and that a similar sum be annually expended under the direction of the Secretary of War until the river is permanently improved for safe and useful navigation.

The coal supply, which has had so much to do with the development of the new St. Louis as a manufacturing centre, comes from Illinois, the bulk of it being obtained within from ten to twenty miles of the city. St. Louis is itself built over a coal bed, and the fuel was once mined in Forest Park, though not profitably. The Illinois soft coal is found to be the most economical for making steam. It is sold in the city for from $1 15 to $1 50 a ton. The Merchants' Exchange has it hauled

404

to its furnaces in wagons for $1 56 a ton, but Mr. Morgan, the secretary—to whom I am greatly indebted for many facts respecting the commerce of the city—says that those manufacturers who buy the same coal by the car-load get it cheaper. All southern Illinois, across the Mississippi, is covered with coal. Fifty or sixty miles farther south in that State a higher grade of bituminous coal is found, and marketed in St. Louis for household use. It is cleaner and burns with less waste, but it costs between 25 and 30 per cent. more.

The Exposition and Music Hall Building was the subject of what was perhaps the first great expression of the renewed youth of the city. It is a monument to the St. Louis of to-day. It is said to be the largest structure used for "exposition" purposes in this country since the Centennial World's Fair at Philadelphia. It is 506 feet long, 332 feet wide, and encloses 280,000 feet of space. The history of its construction is one of those stories of popular co-operation and swift execution of which St. Louis seems likely to offer the world a volume. A fund of three-quarters of a million was raised by popular subscription about ten years ago, and the building was finished within twelve months of the birth of the project. It is built of brick, stone, and terracotta, has a main hall so large that a national political convention took up only one nave in it, contains the largest music hall in the country, with a seating capacity for 4000 persons, and a smaller entertainment hall to accommodate 1500 persons. The famous pageants and illuminations which mark the carnival in that city are coincident with the opening of the exhibitions. Six of these fairs have been held in this building, each continuing forty days, and showing the manufactured products of the whole country, but principally of the Mississippi Valley. The merchants and manufacturers of St.

Louis naturally make a very important contribution to the display.

I say "naturally," because this busy capital of the centre of the country, and of its main internal water system, has an imposing position as one of the greatest workshops and trading-points of the nation. In the making of boots and shoes no Western city outstrips St. Louis, and her jobbing trade in these lines is enormous, and rapidly increasing. Boston, the shoe-distributing centre of the country, sent 310,500 cases of goods to St. Louis in 1891, as against 288,000 to Chicago, and 284,000 to New York. The gain in the manufactured product of St. Louis was 17 per cent. in 1891, and in the jobbing trade it was more than 40 per cent. *The Shoe and Leather Gazette* of that city makes the confident prediction that, "at this rate of progress, in five years St. Louis will lead the world in the number of shoes manufactured and in the aggregate distribution of the same."

She has an enormous flour-milling interest, having sold in 1891 no less than 4,932,465 barrels of flour. Her 14 mills in the city have a capacity of 11,850 barrels a day, and her 16 mills close around the city, and run by St. Louis men and capital, grind 9850 barrels a day. The city turned out 1,748,190 barrels, and the suburbs 1,542,416 barrels, in 1891. In the neck-and-neck race in flour-milling between St. Louis and Milwaukee, St. Louis has recently suffered through the loss of a large mill by fire. The figures for the two cities were, St. Louis, 1,748,190 barrels; Milwaukee, 1,827,284 barrels. It is seen that our reciprocal treaties with the Central and South American countries and the islands off our coast will open up a large and lucrative trade in flour, as well as in many other commodities. While I was preparing this chapter, in 1892, a large shipment of flour had been made to Cuba, where the duty on that staple had been reduced from nearly five dollars to one dollar a barrel. The city exported 344,506 barrels to Europe, and sold more than two millions of barrels to supply the Southern States.

Cotton is received in St. Louis from Missouri, Oklahoma, Kansas, Arkansas, Texas, and Indian Territory. It seeks that way to the East, and as much passes on as is stopped in St. Louis. It is used to a slight extent in manufactures there. A wooden-ware company in the city sells fully one-half of all that ware that is marketed in the country, and manufactures, or controls the manufacture, in many places. The largest hardware company in the country which does not make, but carries on a jobbing trade in those goods, is a St. Louis institution. The saddlery and harness makers do a business of three millions; the clothing-makers have a trade of six millions; the new and growing trade in the manufacture of electrical supplies reached a value of five millions last year; four millions in wagons and carriages was an item of the city's manufactures; the making of lumber, boxes, sashes, doors, and blinds amounted to five millions; of paints, to three millions, and of printing, publishing, and the periodical press, to eight and a quarter millions. The businesses of the manufacture of iron and iron supplies, brass goods, and drugs and chemicals are all very large.

Within ten years the furniture - making industry has doubled, and there are now about sixty furniture factories, employing four thousand men, and making $5,500,000 worth of goods. The territory of distribution includes Mexico and the Central American States. The fact that the city is a great hard - wood lumber market, coupled with her cheap coal, accounts for this growth.

The cattle business is another line in which St. Louis,

407

among the larger cattle depots, made a unique progress. She handled more than three-quarters of a million of cattle, nearly half a million of sheep, 1,380,000 hogs, and 55,975 horses and mules. The only falling off was in the horse and mule trade, and that was due to the supremacy of electric and cable power over horse-power on street railroads. St. Louis is still the great mule market of the country.

The city caters to human weakness by an enormous output of beer and tobacco. Of each of these luxuries she makes fourteen millions of dollars' worth annually. Here is the largest lager-beer brewery in the country, if not in the world, and the city is third in the list of brewing towns. The business excited the interest of English capital, and a syndicate bought up a great number of the breweries, but the two largest remain the property of the original companies. Twenty millions of dollars are invested in this trade, which is carried from St. Louis into every State, into Canada and Mexico, and even into Australia and Europe.

St. Louis is our biggest market for manufactured tobacco. Thus the principal depots of the trade compare with one another:

	Pounds.
Total sales of chewing and smoking tobacco in the United States	243,505,848
St. Louis	52,214,862
Fifth New Jersey District	22,000,000
Cincinnati	21,000,000
Petersburg, Virginia	18,000,000

Of plug tobacco, 44,503,098 pounds were taxed as the city's product in 1891; of smoking tobacco, about 5,682,000 pounds; and of fine-cut chewing tobacco, 314,702 pounds. The cigars made there numbered fifty-three and a quarter millions.

St. Louis had twenty-three national and State banks

and four trust companies in 1892, with a joint banking capital of $29,661,075. The city of St. Louis is one of the two second-class national banking depositories, New York being the other, and Washington (the United States Treasury) being the one of the first-class.

It is a comfortable and a dignified city, with every sign of wealth in its commercial and residence districts, and with a shopping district whose windows form a perpetual world's fair.

The knowledge of the value of tasteful and attractive shop-window displays always accompanies push and prosperity in a city, and in this respect none in America excels this one. Yet it offers a chance to compare modern customs in this respect with the shabby inert ways of the traders of the past.

To see the contrast it is only necessary to leave the centre of Broadway and walk to where that street passes the French Market. Here is the cramped, careless untidiness of half a century ago; but the place has a distinct interest for a New Yorker, because it is his Eighth Ward transplanted. The same low brick houses, the same dormer-windows, the same cheap signs, and the stalls and stands and tiny shops that are found near Spring Street market are all repeated.

But it is easy to change one's point of view of the city, and declare it to be one of the most open, clean, and clear of settlements. This can be accomplished by going out to Grand Avenue and beyond, and riding through the dwelling districts. There one sees broad tree-lined streets, costly houses, and many beautiful, semi-private, courtlike streets that are the seats of pretty homes. In this neighborhood are the parks which are the crown and glory of the city. Some, like

Forest Park, boast nature's beauties merely tidied and treasured up; but others show the blending of human taste with natural greenery and blossom adorned by statuary and fountains. But St. Louis is rich otherwise in those possessions which have elsewhere been described —her fine theatres, her clubs and churches, her great fire-proof hotel, her schools, and her old and cultivated society.

The levee along the river-side is worth a visit. It is diametrically different in itself and its atmosphere from the city that lies back of it, and that seems so familiar to a New-Yorker. It is a wide and imposing incline of stone paving, perhaps 250 feet broad. It is not Western; it is Southern. Hides, wool, cotton, and tobacco are heaped about on the wharf-boats, which seem to cling to the levee with gangways that are like the antennæ of an insect. There is a line of huge old-time river packets, looking as open and frail as bird-cages, but with towering black funnels from which jet smoke curls lazily up. Beyond is the turgid, hurrying river. The street along the top of the levee is a single line of warehouses and shops. The latter recall those of our own water-side in New York. In place of our bronzed and bearded salt-water men, here are shiftless white laborers and negro roustabouts. But the same petty traders are among them, keeping drinking-places and stands for the sale of brass watches and rings, dirks, brass-knuckles, pistols, cartridges. Cheap gin, cheaper clothing, and still cheaper jewelry are the prime articles all along the thoroughfare, precisely as in New York or Liverpool or Havre.

The water supply of the city is drawn from the Mississippi, as is the case in New Orleans, and the cities between there and St. Louis. It is mud-colored, and seems thick and soupy, whether it is or no. I was assured that it was second in high sanitary qualities to the Nile water, which is still muddier.

It used to be said that the sum of the collective ambition of St. Louis was represented by a pretty woman with jewels in her ears and mounted on a thoroughbred horse. Women, horses, and diamonds, in other words, were the things dearest to its heart in the by-gone days. I do not know whether this taste has changed with the inrush of new inhabitants. They certainly have the fine horses in plenty, and St. Louis is likely long to maintain her fame as a seat of womanly beauty. Having observed several very large and splendid jeweller's shops that are a notable feature of the showy business streets, I went into one of the finest and inquired of the manager whether the city still is true to its old love, the diamond. Behold his answer:

"There is no one of moderate means in St. Louis who does not own and wear diamonds," said he; "however, they are not worn as large as formerly. Two and a half carats is the size of the largest stones now worn by men or women. The ladies who possess ear-rings still wear them, but few are now bought. There is no nonsensical law, such as obtains in London and Paris, making it bad form to wear diamonds in the daytime. Those who have them wear them when they please."

The Chief of Police, Mr. Lawrence Harrigan, assured me that there is no fixed gaming-place in St. Louis—not one regular "game," even of poker. The people did not want it, and the police did not want it, so it was stopped, he said. The men play at their homes, in clubs, and in the hotels, but I saw no sign of any indulgence in cards anywhere in this which was once the greatest gambling-town, next to New Orleans, in the country

I do not mean to say that the city is a moral one, for its people are distinctly human, and the imperfections of

411

their lives are apparent and, in some respects, lively. The theatres are open seven nights in the week, and, while Friday is the play-going night for the fashionables, Sunday is the night for the people.

They have an American Sunday in St. Louis. It is the same as what we in the North call a European Sunday. But it becomes apparent to whoever travels far in the United States that the only Sunday which deserves a distinct title is that of England, New England, and the Atlantic coast. The Sunday of Chicago, San Francisco, Cincinnati, New Orleans, St. Louis, and most of the larger cities of the major part of our land is European, if you please; but it is also American. In St. Louis the theatres, groggeries, dives, "melodeons," cigar stores, candy stores, and refreshment places of every kind are all kept wide open. The street cars carry on their heaviest trade, and the streets are crowded then as on no other day of the week. On the other days the city keeps up, in great part, the measure of its old riverside hospitality, a survival of the merry era of the steamboats. The numerous night resorts—the variety and music halls, the dance-houses and the beer-gardens, blaze out with a prominence nothing gets by day.

To conclude, in the language of the editor of one of the several thoroughly equipped newspapers of the city: "St. Louis prefers to do business according to safe and creditable doctrines, and to win success by honestly deserving it. Her experience has vindicated her policy. She has never taken a step backward. She does her business with her own money. She has multiplied her mercantile and manufacturing establishments, her blocks of magnificent buildings, and her facilities of trade in every direction out of her legitimate profits. As she has been in the past, so she will be in the future—the country's best example of a truly thrifty city."

THE END

ILLUSTRATED BOOKS OF TRAVEL AND DESCRIPTION

CATHEDRALS AND ABBEYS IN GREAT BRITAIN AND IRELAND. With Descriptive Letter-press by the Rev. RICHARD WHEATLEY, D.D. Illustrated. Folio, Illuminated Cloth, $10 00. (*In a Box.*)

MENTONE, CAIRO, AND CORFU. By CONSTANCE FENIMORE WOOLSON. Illustrated. Post 8vo, Cloth, Ornamental. (*About Ready.*)

THE BORDERLAND OF CZAR AND KAISER. By POULTNEY BIGELOW. Illustrated. Post 8vo, Cloth, Ornamental, $2 00.

A HOUSE-HUNTER IN EUROPE. By WILLIAM HENRY BISHOP. With Plans and an Illustration. Post 8vo, Cloth, Ornamental, $1 50.

LITERARY LANDMARKS OF LONDON. By LAURENCE HUTTON. With Many Portraits. Post 8vo, Cloth, Ornamental, $1 75.

LITERARY LANDMARKS OF EDINBURGH. By LAURENCE HUTTON. Illustrated. Post 8vo, Cloth, Ornamental, $1 00.

LITERARY LANDMARKS OF JERUSALEM. By LAURENCE HUTTON. Illustrated. Post 8vo, Cloth, Ornamental, 75 cents.

OUR ITALY. (Southern California.) By CHARLES DUDLEY WARNER. Illustrated. Square 8vo, Cloth, Ornamental, Uncut Edges and Gilt Top, $2 50.

THEIR PILGRIMAGE. By CHARLES DUDLEY WARNER. Illustrated. Post 8vo, Half Leather, Ornamental, Uncut Edges and Gilt Top, $2 00.

ON CANADA'S FRONTIER. Sketches of History, Sport, and Adventure; and of the Indians, Missionaries, Fur-traders, and Newer Settlers of Western Canada. By JULIAN RALPH. Illustrated. 8vo, Cloth, Ornamental, $2 50.

OUR GREAT WEST. A Study of the Present Conditions and Future Possibilities of the New Commonwealths and Capitals of the United States. By JULIAN RALPH. Illustrated. 8vo, Cloth, Ornamental, $2 50.

THE ARMIES OF TO-DAY. By Brigadier-general WESLEY MERRITT, U.S.A., VISCOUNT WOLSELEY, and Others. Profusely Illustrated. 8vo, Cloth, Ornamental, Uncut Edges and Gilt Top, $3 50.

SPANISH-AMERICAN REPUBLICS. By THEODORE CHILD. Profusely Illustrated by T. DE THULSTRUP, FREDERIC REMINGTON, and Others. 8vo, Cloth, Ornamental, $3 50.

WINTERS IN ALGERIA. Written and Illustrated by FREDERICK ARTHUR BRIDGMAN. Square 8vo, Cloth, Ornamental, $2 50.

THE TSAR AND HIS PEOPLE. By THEODORE CHILD. 8vo, Cloth, Ornamental, Uncut Edges and Gilt Top, $3 00.

PUBLISHED BY HARPER & BROTHERS, NEW YORK

☞ *The above works are for sale by all booksellers, or will be mailed by the publishers, postage prepaid, on receipt of the price.*